Mike O'Neill is a former Executive Vice-President of a Fortune 500 company in the field of Health Sciences. Throughout his career he got to know many of the world's leading scientists and Nobel laureates.

His academic background is in science and engineering and during his tenure he directed the development of instrumentation in the field of DNA and Protein research. When he left the company he was in charge of World-Wide Operations with responsibility for several thousand employees.

For ten years Mike served on the Dean's Advisory Board at the College of Medicine at the University of California, Irvine. He also served for seven years on the Advisory Board of the Susan Samueli Center for Integrative Medicine.

For eleven years Mike served on the Board of Directors of Newport Corporation, a publicly traded company as well as six years as a Member of the American College of Corporate Directors.

Mike was also a very early member of the Innovation Society at Oxford University and served for a period of five years.

A lifelong runner, completing several marathons and over fifty half-marathons, Mike splits his time between England and the United States.

Dedication

For my children, Lisa O'Neill Hill, Craig and Chris who
are so different in many ways, and have such unique
and individual talents.
Each have made me proud and brought me great joy.

Mike O'Neill

THE RESURRECTION

CHRIST HAS DIED,
CHRIST IS RISEN

CHRIST WILL COME AGAIN

(TRADITIONAL CHRISTIAN
LITURGY)

AUSTIN MACAULEY PUBLISHERS™
LONDON • CAMBRIDGE • NEW YORK • SHARJAH

A CIP catalogue record for this title is available from the British Library.

ISBN 9781788233613 (Paperback)
ISBN 9781788233620 (E-Book)
www.austinmacauley.com

First Published (2018)
Austin Macauley Publishers Ltd™
25 Canada Square
Canary Wharf
London
E14 5LQ

Acknowledgments

There are many people I wish to thank for their feedback and encouragement during the writing of this book. I am very grateful to my daughter, Lisa O'Neill Hill, a writer extraordinaire, who worked with me in the early stages editing and re-editing chapter after chapter. I would like to acknowledge the initial team of reviewers who provided such valuable feedback and suggestions. In addition to Lisa, it included Bob Gamez, Cal McLaughlin, Kevin Morton and John Siracuse. I particularly want to thank Professor Cal McLaughlin who suggested that I change the original working title to the Resurrection.

Version one of the completed manuscript was edited by Steve Finbow who also advised on restructuring and repositioning many of the chapters and I am grateful for his professional expertise.

During the extensive research of the religious and scientific content of the novel, I have drawn on the work of a lot of different writers but there are two books in particular from which I gained a lot of insight about the Shroud of Turin. I would specifically like to acknowledge Ian Wilson's book, The Blood and the Shroud, 1999 and Baigent, Leigh and Lincoln's book, The Holy Blood and the Holy Grail, 1996.

The cover design and artwork was created by Tracey Millier Radnall, an international award winning graphic artist, to whom I would like to offer a special thanks.

I would also like to thank the many friends and family members who reviewed and provided feedback of the pre-publication manuscript.

FRANCIS CRICK'S BRAG IN
THE EAGLE, THE PUB WHERE WE HABITUALLY
ATE LUNCH, THAT WE HAD INDEED DISCOVERED
THE SECRET OF LIFE, STRUCK ME AS SOMEWHAT
IMMODEST, ESPECIALLY IN ENGLAND,
WHERE UNDERSTATEMENT
IS A WAY OF LIFE

JAMES WATSON.

Prologue

Lirey, France

In the fourteenth century, sometime between 1345 and 1350, the Holy Shroud came into the possession of French knight, Geoffrey de Charny ("A true and perfect knight") who acquired the Shroud perhaps as a dowry through marriage. He, and others at the time, believed it to be the original cloth that covered Christ's body after the crucifixion. Rumored to have changed hands many times and traveled thousands of miles between Jerusalem, Edessa, Constantinople, Athens, Cyprus, Marseilles, Paris and other cities, the Shroud had survived fires, floods and plagues, dozens of wars and the hands and mouths of the thousands of people who touched and kissed the relic during public expositions.

By the time de Charny acquired the Shroud, its edges were ragged and tears ran toward the image in the center of the cloth. De Charny showed the Shroud to several of the elite clergy in the area, including Henri de Poitiers, Bishop of Troyes, and told them of his intention to build a chapel for the Shroud in the small town of Lirey. However, in December 1349, before he could begin work on the project, the English captured de Charny for the second time and imprisoned him in Goodrich Castle, Herefordshire.

For three summers during de Charny's teenage years, his family recruited Walter de Thaxted, a Cambridge scholar, to teach him mathematics and divinity. The two became close friends and thereafter wrote to each other at least once a year. In the spring of 1351, de Thaxted, concerned that he had not heard from his friend in more than eighteen months, contacted the de Charny family in Lirey who informed the scholar that Edward III had captured Geoffrey and was holding him prisoner.

Appointed to the Great Council (a prototype for parliament) after sixteen years tenure as Master of Clare College, de Thaxted had direct access to the Bishop of Winchester, the King's Treasurer. On July 31, 1351, after months of negotiations – and for a sizeable ransom of 12,000 gold crowns, paid by King John II of France – de Thaxted secured the release of de Charny.

Now, free to complete the chapel, de Charny started work on the Shroud's restoration and preservation. In appreciation for securing his release from prison, de Charny invited de Thaxted to Lirey to view the relic. As others had done before him, when he saw Christ's image on the cloth, de Thaxted sank to his knees in prayer.

Pointing to the wear and tear on the cloth, de Charny expressed concern that further public showings might damage the Shroud forever and asked de Thaxted if he had any suggestions on how to preserve and restore the relic before he displayed it again. De Thaxted suggested he contact Paolo Aquinas - a Benedictine alchemist and the grandnephew of Thomas Aquinas - at Mont-Saint-Michel. After six months and dozens of experiments, Aquinas came up with an innovative yet risky solution to the Shroud problem. De Charny agreed to take the risk.

Upon successful completion of Aquinas' final experiment, de Charny sent a letter by messenger to Pope Clement VI, who immediately sent word back summoning them to the papal residence in Avignon.

The French knight ordered his servants to prepare two of his best horses. He ran up the front steps, raced across the Great

Hall past the magnificent tapestries and holy paintings his family had accumulated over the centuries, bounded up the staircase two steps at a time, entered his dressing room, discarded his work clothes and quickly adorned his knight's garments, finally donning his red mantle emboldened with three escutcheons argent – the coat of arms of the de Charny family.

In the preservation room, Aquinas carefully folded the Shroud and its mirror image and placed them into separate caskets. In the courtyard, he waited by the two horses for de Charny while the servants fastened a casket to each horse.

De Charny grabbed his helmet and sword and ran down the stairs to the outside. From the third step, he leapt onto his horse as if heading into battle, gesturing to Aquinas to get on the other horse, and shouted, "*Allez! Allez!*" Aquinas mounted the steed and the two men galloped off into the distance. They would reach Avignon before dusk the next day.

Each carrying a casket, they entered the pope's private chambers and carefully unrolled the two pieces of linen across the marble floor. Pope Clement VI stared at the two cloths and said, "What kind of miracle is this I see before my very own eyes?" Aquinas tried to describe the process to the pope but Clement VI preferred a more divine explanation.

The Pope accepted De Charny's offer to hand over the original Shroud for safekeeping and they agreed that no one else but the three of them should be privy to the 'Secret of the Shroud'. Pope Clement V1 instructed Aquinas to record the process on a parchment, which all three signed and dated. He then attached his own letter instructing all future popes on how to protect this most holy of relics, put the two documents in a pouch, closed it with the papal seal, placed the pouch on top of the original Shroud, returned it to the casket and sealed it. After more than thirteen hundred years, the original Shroud was now the property of the Catholic Church.

Pope Clement VI died in December 1352 and the 'Secret of the Shroud' passed to the new pope, Innocent VI. Only three people knew the 'Secret of the Shroud'. Two years later, Aquinas died leaving only two people knowing the truth.

Between 1353 and 1354, de Charny completed the construction of the Chapel of Lirey. In 1355, with great fanfare, the new Shroud went on display for the first time. Pilgrims came from all over Europe to see this venerated relic. One of them was the Bishop of Troyes, Henri de Poitiers, who six years earlier had seen the original Shroud. He immediately called for a stop to the exposition, adamant that this Shroud was a forgery, the new cloth not showing the tattered edges he had observed before.

In September 1356, during a ferocious encounter while protecting King John II of France at the battle of Poitiers, the English killed de Charny. In less than four years, all of the original three who knew the 'Secret of the Shroud' were dead. Since that day, only one man on Earth has known this secret: the sitting pope.

Historical Timeline

33	The Crucifixion of Jesus Christ; Joseph of Arimathea wraps Christ's body in a burial cloth
590	Discovery of the Shroud in the city walls of Edessa
1066	William of Normandy conquers England
1209	Fleeing staff and students from Oxford establish Cambridge University
1348	The Shroud comes into possession of French knight, Geoffrey de Charny
1532	The Shroud is almost destroyed by a fire at Sainte Chapelle, Chambéry
1534	The Poor Clare nuns of Chambéry repair the Shroud with thirty patches of cloth
1578	The Shroud is transferred to the Royal Chapel of Turin Cathedral
1866	A Czech monk, Gregor Mendel, experiments with peas and demonstrates heredity – genes
1898	Secondo Pia, an Italian lawyer, takes the first known photograph of the Shroud of Turin
1953	Watson and Crick discover the molecular structure of DNA – The Double Helix
1962	Watson and Crick are awarded the Nobel Prize in Physiology or Medicine
2003	Completion of the Human Genome Project and the confirmation of less than 30,000 genes

Scientific Team

Sir Francis MacLeod, PhD, FRS
World renowned scientist, Nobel laureate in
Physiology/Medicine.
Managing Director of Genon, PLC.

Kathleen Murphy, PhD
Biochemistry, Trinity College, Oxford.
Geneticist and former graduate of Trinity College, Dublin, born
in Dundalk, Ireland

Ian Walton, PhD
Biochemistry, Cambridge, Geneticist and formerly from Alpha
Genetics.
Born in Oundle, Northamptonshire, England

V. J. Gupta, PhD
Math and Engineering, MIT, Software Engineer, formerly from
Microsoft.
Head of IT at Genon, PLC. Born in Hyderabad, India

Rob Elliott, PhD
Molecular Biology, Newcastle University, an expert in Stem
Cell research,
Born in Newcastle, England

Darren Richards, PhD
Biochemistry, UCI, California and a US citizen, born in
Encinitas, California

Chapter 1

They seemed an odd couple: he, a world-famous Nobel laureate, and a quintessential English aristocrat; she, a redhead with a mischievous personality and fiery Irish temper. And now they were planning to get married.

The day before, the fastidious Sir Francis MacLeod had actually gone down on one knee and proposed. Brimming with pride, she had never been so happy. He seemed calm and steady, except for one minor annoyance. As the last rays of the setting sun shone through the windscreen glistening on her new engagement ring Kathleen playfully maneuvered the reflection into Francis' eyes, who, driving in his careful, lawful and precise manner, squinted and smiled at her affectionately.

"Stop shining that ring in my eyes. Put it away or I'll take it back. I'm trying to stay on the road, for heaven's sake. Or would you prefer we end up in a ditch?"

They were heading southwest to Cambridge and the sun was slipping over the horizon. She put her right hand over the diamond and emerald cluster, smiled, and said nothing.

He mischievously grabbed her knee and squeezed tightly. "Kitchen, put it away!"

"I have." A closed smile slowly appeared across Kathleen's face as she recalled the first time Francis had used that term of endearment.

"Kitchen, I *mean* it, now. Can't see a thing with that glare." He was straining to one side, and then she understood. Someone had turned on their headlights, no doubt warning the overly cautious driver they were about to pass. It happened so often that Kathleen hardly noticed any more.

MacLeod slowed down the Jaguar to let the other car pass. They were in no hurry.

As the large Mercedes approached, the driver began steering to the left as if about to overtake them on the inside. He mounted the narrow grassy verge, scraping the tree branches and bushes as he pulled level. Then, in a split second he accelerated, steering the Mercedes across the front of the Jaguar, clipping the front passenger side and sending it into a tailspin.

"Shit!" MacLeod shouted, as he steered into the spin. The airbags inflated as the Jaguar careened across the opposite lane, stopping as the front end slammed into a horse chestnut tree. The Mercedes sped off in a shower of dirt and gravel.

Steam, hissing like a geyser from the radiator, broke the silence of the after-impact. Fingers crept slowly from one body to the other; hands clasped momentarily, before they dared look at each other. On all fours, MacLeod and Kathleen crawled out of the car, stood and then embraced.

"A few bruises and minor scratches," MacLeod remarked. "Luck of the Irish."

"What in the hell was that all about?" Kathleen shrieked. "Jesus, Mary and Joseph, we could have been killed and your work would have gone to the grave with us."

"I think that was the intention," MacLeod said, having recognized the driver.

"What?" Kathleen stuttered.

"Let's not worry about that right now, we can talk about it later. We need to get the car towed into Mildenhall and then arrange a ride back to Cambridge."

Kathleen fumed, "In the name of Jesus Christ, for heaven's sake, we almost got killed and you are shrugging it off without telling me what's going on. What in the h---"

"I really don't want to talk about it right now."

Kathleen pulled off her new engagement ring and threw it at him. "Damn you, Francis, if we don't have trust starting out, we don't have anything." She stormed off in the direction of Mildenhall.

MacLeod ran after her but stopped when he saw her awkwardly hobbling down the country lane, the heel of her left shoe lying by the roadside. He shook his head wondering what he'd got himself into and grinned as she angrily removed her shoes and threw them over a hedge.

"Irish as they come." He phoned for help.

Kathleen had almost reached the town by the time the tow truck passed her. MacLeod wound down the passenger window, smiled and waved, then closed it without saying a word.

She stopped in her tracks and shouted profanities at him, her eyes filling with tears.

"How could such a wonderful weekend go downhill so quickly?" She wished she could talk to JP.

Chapter 2

Wednesday, April 19, 2028, Cambridge, England

Sitting at his favorite table in the Eagle pub, near what was once a fireplace, MacLeod finished off his third gin and tonic. He rarely drank at lunch and almost never before an important presentation. Brenda, his personal assistant, raised her eyebrows at Ian Walton, a heavy-set rugby-player-type with a full beard and a key member of MacLeod's research team.

"Well, Ian, the 'Day of Judgement' has arrived," MacLeod said, slurring his words slightly.

"I'll order him some coffee," Brenda said to Ian.

MacLeod drank two cups, and then paid the bill. As the three of them strolled out of the pub and up Free School Lane toward the university, MacLeod stumbled on the cobble stones and fell tearing his trousers at the kneecap. "Damn," he said.

Brenda and Ian wanted to laugh until they saw the blood oozing from MacLeod's leg. Ian helped him to his feet while Brenda took a tissue out of her purse and pressed it against MacLeod's knee.

"What am I going to do about the tear in my trousers?"

"Wait here," Brenda said, as she hurriedly back-tracked and went into a local store. Returning with adhesive tape, she patched the torn cloth.

"Good as new. And nobody will notice anyway," she added, grabbing his arm so he wouldn't fall again.

MacLeod limped into the lecture hall to instant applause. Straightening his shoulders, he strode to the front of the room as best he could. Brenda and Ian followed and took their reserved seats in the second row next to Kathleen and two other colleagues. Kathleen had not spoken to MacLeod since Sunday.

There was standing room only and those who had not arrived early were lining the walls of the auditorium two and three deep.

MacLeod removed his blazer and neatly placed it over the back of a chair, then adjusted his tie as he took a deep breath and turned to face his audience. He tapped the microphone three times, took a drink of water, cleared his throat and addressed the dignitaries sitting in the front row. "Lord and Lady Blundell, Sir Charles and Lady Palmer, my fellow scientists, ladies and gentlemen," MacLeod began. "To say that this is indeed a great honor for me would be understatement of the first order, so let me just say thank you to everyone."

He picked up the remote and clicked to the title slide of his talk.

Perfect DNA

Whispers spread throughout the audience. No one except MacLeod and his closest colleagues knew the contents of his address but rumors had been circulating in the scientific community for months that he was going to make a startling revelation.

"What I am about to reveal to you is an extraordinary hypothesis based on eight years of our genon research." He glanced toward the back of the room, cheeks draining of color. He stared at a familiar face and then his eyes drew away from it and focused on another man. The stranger had a tight hold of the familiar man's left forearm. In his other hand, the stranger gripped a white stick. MacLeod blinked and paused. When he continued, his voice quivered. Several people in the front row observed the scientist starting to perspire and exchanged puzzled expressions.

MacLeod's hands trembled, small beads of sweat appeared on his forehead, dampened his shirt underneath the armpits. He stared into space as the words 'highest integrity' and 'unblemished scientific reputation,' raced through his head. He tried to continue as if nothing were out of the ordinary.

Fidgeting with the gold locket around his neck, he glanced again quickly at the back of the room. The blind man appeared to be staring back at him.

MacLeod reached into his trouser pocket for something, then took a sip of water before continuing. He clicked through several more slides then hesitated before clicking onto the next one. Those close to the front heard a slight "phssh" sound.

MacLeod's body shook and he collapsed behind the podium. Kathleen screamed and rushed onto the platform.

"A doctor, quickly!" she yelled into the microphone.

Several of the audience jumped up and rushed to help. A doctor who got there first pressed his emergency GPS then began CPR. "He's had a heart attack," he said. "An ambulance is on the way."

"Francis, Francis can you hear me?" Kathleen shrieked, cradling his head in her arms, tears streaming down her cheeks.

Members of the audience stood, pushing forward and straining their necks to see what was happening.

The blind man turned to his companion. "What's going on?"

The guide steered the man toward the exit, whispering, "I'll tell you when we get in the car."

Chapter 3

Kathleen, the palms of her hands covering her nose and mouth, knelt back on her heels and rocked gently. Ian stared helplessly at MacLeod, not knowing what to do.

The doctor shouted at the crowd who were shoving their way to the front, "Stand back and give the poor man room to breathe."

The ambulance arrived within minutes. The emergency medical technicians scrambled to put an oxygen mask over MacLeod's face and attach an IV line to his arm before putting him on a gurney and loading him into the ambulance. Once inside the vehicle, the medics connected him to a heart monitor. The display showed only the occasional peak, then several seconds of a flat green line.

Shaking, Kathleen climbed into the back of the ambulance, Ian following.

MacLeod's face seemed frozen in fear. Kathleen grabbed his right hand and held it tightly as the ambulance sped down Regent Street on its way to Addenbrooke's Hospital.

As the ambulance screeched to a halt and the doors opened, two nurses cleared the way and the technicians hurriedly transferred MacLeod to the Emergency Assessment Unit.

One of the nurses looked up at the consultant cardiologist as they passed by him just inside the entrance. The nurse knew Professor Richard Simpson and MacLeod were colleagues. She tightened her lips, raised her eyebrows and shook her head.

Simpson studied MacLeod as he ran alongside the gurney.

Kathleen and Ian, quiet as they entered the bright beige and blue waiting room, took two seats closest to the critical-care section.

"He's going to be fine," Ian said, as much for his own reassurance as for Kathleen's. "I just think that the pressure has been building up for weeks. It's not too surprising, given what he was about to reveal. Let me go and get us both a cup of tea. One spoon?"

Kathleen nodded.

When Ian returned, Kathleen was wiping her eyes with an embroidered lace handkerchief Francis had given her last Christmas. She accepted the hot tea and took a few sips.

"You know, Ian, I was just thinking that you never know what is around the corner in life," she said. "And who would ever have thought that a man as fit as Francis was likely to have a heart attack? He'll only be fifty-nine on Sunday, for God's sake!"

Ian put his arm around her. "I am sure he is going to be fine," he whispered.

"You know Francis used to teach here."

"I know. He was on the faculty."

"He told me he loved it, toying with the students and 'getting inside their heads', as he put it. In fact, I think he still has a lab and office here."

At that moment, Professor Simpson emerged from the EAU. A few seconds passed before he looked directly at Kathleen.

She stood and felt dizzy. Sat down again.

"Sir Francis has not had a heart attack, but I am sorry to have to tell you that he is in a coma."

"Oh, Jesus," she stammered as she made a sign of the cross. "A coma . . . what . . . how?"

Simpson touched her shoulder. "We don't have any answers yet. We need to complete our testing. We'll know more by morning and I'll call you as soon as I know something."

"May I see him?" Kathleen asked.

"I think it's better if you come back tomorrow, Ms. Murphy."

Kathleen pushed him aside. "I can't leave him here all alone. We're engaged." She glanced at her bare ring finger and winced.

Simpson held her arm. "Please wait for ten minutes while he's moved to a private room. I'll send a nurse to get you and you can see him through the viewing window. I'm afraid that's the best I can do today."

Simpson waited until the nurses left then turned the heart monitor to the back wall obscuring it from anyone's view. He told one of the nurses to fetch Kathleen.

Kathleen pressed her face against the window, straining to see her fiancé.

"Is that him?" It could have been anyone. Moving from side to side, she tried to get a better view. It didn't help. The form on the bed might as well have been a lifeless body with no more than a nose and mouth visible between the pillow and sheet. She reluctantly returned to the waiting room and shook her head as she approached Ian. He put his arm around her and slowly led her out to the front entrance where he phoned for a taxi.

Kathleen, gasping for air, almost hyperventilated as she and Ian climbed into the taxi and headed back to the lab.

While Ian explained to the team that MacLeod was in a coma, Kathleen, still weeping, stepped out into the hallway. She desperately needed to talk to JP. She keyed in his number.

Hesitated. Pressed 'end call' after the first ring.

* * * * *

23

Professor Simpson sat by his friend's bedside, staring at the heart monitor.

"What is going on, Francis?" he said.

He closed his eyes in a moment of reflection. He felt the vibration and instinctively cocked his wrist to look at the number. He didn't recognize it.

Ten minutes later, someone called again from the same number. Simpson again ignored the call.

When his phone rang a third time, Simpson walked out of MacLeod's room. "Who *is* this?" he asked firmly.

"Professor Simpson, thanks for taking my call. Is Sir Francis still alive?"

"Who wants to know?" Simpson said, raising his voice. "Yes, Sir Francis is alive, but who is this and why are you calling me?"

"Thank goodness," the caller let out a deep sigh. "My name is Stephen Hatton, Sir Francis' solicitor. I need to see you on a matter of the greatest urgency."

Chapter 4

Thursday, April 20, 2028

On Thursday morning, Professor Simpson called Parkside Police Station and left a message for the chief superintendent.

Built in the 1950s, the police station on the east side of Parker's Piece, is an ugly and dirty-looking glass and cement structure, a stark contrast to the medieval architecture of the city center. In a drab grey office within the building's greyer walls, Detective Chief Superintendent Graham Duncan, a burly Scotsman in his fifties with a fluffy moustache and a wry smile slanting toward the upper-right corner of his mouth, called back forty-five minutes later. Duncan and Simpson had met before at a number of cocktail parties.

"How are you, Richard?" Duncan asked.

"I'm fine, thanks," Simpson replied. "Thanks for getting back to me, Graham. I wanted to let you know that I have completed my preliminary tests on Sir Francis."

"And?"

"There is a little problem. It originally appeared that Sir Francis had a heart attack but that is not the case. However, his situation is odd, one I haven't come across before. I was wondering if you could come by here this afternoon so that I can show you something."

"So, he didn't have a heart attack, but I heard he's in a coma, right? Why do I need to be there?" Duncan said impatiently, his other phone ringing continuously. "Damn it, excuse me a moment." It was DCI Butterfield. Duncan told him he would talk to him later. "Sorry, you were saying, Richard."

"Given it is Sir Francis MacLeod and given that he was very fit and had no health problems, I cannot rule out that the coma was possibly induced in some way."

"Bugger me," Duncan said. He was suddenly interested. "Induced? What the hell does that mean? Are you suggesting foul play?"

"I am not suggesting anything other than that you see for yourself," Simpson answered.

"Okay, okay, what time?"

"Say around two p.m."

"I'll be there." Duncan hung up the phone, clasped his hands behind his head and leaned back in his brown leather chair. A thin smile appeared as he looked up toward the ceiling, puzzled.

After lunch at precisely two o'clock, Duncan walked into Simpson's office. Simpson was sipping a cup of hot tea. He offered Duncan a cup.

Duncan took the tea and sat down. "Know him personally, did you?" Duncan inquired.

"Yes, very well. Not only were we colleagues at the university, he has been one of my patients for the last ten years."

"He had heart problems?" Duncan asked, making a likely connection between the cardiologist and MacLeod.

Simpson continued, "No, on the contrary. He was extremely fit. However, like most of us, once he turned forty, he had a full physical every two years with his local doctor who referred him to me to supervise his stress-testing. And the last time I tested him was about ten months ago."

"And he was in good shape?" the superintendent asked, sucking in his belly an inch or two.

"Let me put it this way, Graham, if any physician looked at Sir Francis' charts without knowing the patient's age, he would assume the results were that of a twenty-five to thirty-year-old athlete. He was that fit!"

"Interesting," Duncan responded, nodding his head. "So what's this little problem?"

Simpson pointed to a wall monitor. A vivid image of MacLeod's heart appeared. "As you can see, his heart is perfectly normal in every way, it's an unusually healthy organ. And the same is true for the rest of his cardiovascular system. His brain scan is also perfectly normal. There is absolutely no evidence of a heart attack or stroke."

Simpson took a sip of tea, then put the cup down on his desk and got up. "If you follow me I'll take you to see him."

Once inside MacLeod's room, Simpson pointed to the heart monitor. "Look, his heart rhythm is perfectly symmetrical, and there is no evidence of any irregularity, but look at his heart rate, it is only twelve beats per minute. He shouldn't be alive."

"So, what you're saying is, that there's a chance he might not live long?" Duncan asked.

"Extremely fit athletes often have a heart rate under forty and there have been reported cases of some super-fit cyclists recording heart rates below thirty, but we're talking about an average of twelve here, it's an unheard-of phenomenon. I thought you'd better be aware of this, just in case."

"And you have no idea what might have caused this phenomenon, as you call it?"

"Not really, except that there is one other thing I want to show you." Simpson clicked on a remote to bring up an image of MacLeod's torso on the overhead monitor. "See here? He has biochip implants in his upper right thigh and left shoulder."

"So what? These days, most people have biochip implants, it's not unusual."

"Yes, that's true, but he has two for some reason. Also, they're custom-made and have a lot more features than normal, similar to the type used by the Prime Minister and other high-profile people. I just thought you might like to take a look before we extract them and send them to the lab for evaluation."

"Fine, anything else?" Duncan seemed anxious to leave.

"We don't have a toxicity report back yet, but will probably have it by tomorrow."

"Okay, Richard, if that's it, I'll be off, but keep me posted."

Back in his office, the chief superintendent threw his jacket across a chair and summoned his assistant. "Tell Butterfield to get his arse in here. Now."

A hardworking and dedicated murder detective, DCI Tom Butterfield, blond, blue-eyed and in his early forties, was one of Cambridgeshire Constabulary's rising stars. Charming, ruthless, ambitious, and a likely successor to Duncan, Butterfield knocked on Duncan's door. "Need something?" he asked.

"Aye, as a matter of fact I do. Have a seat. I want you to open up a new case file."

"Sure. Anyone interesting?"

"Sir Francis MacLeod."

"MacLeod?" Butterfield said. "Bloody hell, isn't he in the ICU after having a heart attack yesterday? Did he die?"

Duncan fiddled with his moustache. "Aye, he *is* in the ICU, but *no,* he didn't have a heart attack, and *no,* he didn't die, at least not yet. He's in a deep coma, but by all accounts he should be dead. Although he didn't come out and say it, Simpson, his cardiologist, seems to suspect foul play, so this could soon turn into a high-profile murder investigation."

"So, where do you want me to start?" Butterfield asked.

"First, I want you to go over to the hall where he collapsed and close it off and get a couple of lab nerds over there to do their thing."

The phone rang. After the third ring, Duncan barked to no one in particular, "Somebody answer the damned phone." He stood up, clearly irritated by the interruption. "Then talk to some of the people who were closest to the podium. Also, it probably wouldn't hurt if you did a little background checking. How much do you know about him and his company, Genon?"

"I know of him. Who doesn't in this city? I mean, his picture has been in plenty of newspapers and magazines. In fact, there was a big article in the *Times Online* last weekend about him being the keynote speaker at this week's conference. I think I have heard of Genon and that MacLeod is involved in some way. A handsome bugger from the photos I've seen in the media. And a bit of a ladies' man, from what I hear."

"Why does that not surprise me?" Duncan said with a cynical smile. "Maybe you should start digging there first. You never know, you might find someone that he's pissed off."

Chapter 5

Eight years earlier, Stockholm City Hall, Sweden

As the lights in the Blue Hall gradually dimmed to near darkness, the loud chatter subsided to a whisper. Then, with precision, two long lines of meticulously dressed waiters and waitresses descended the spiral stairway, carefully carrying their trays aloft, holding the renowned Baked Alaska.

MacLeod turned to the elegant woman sitting next to him.

"Impressive," he whispered. Princess Madeleine, seventh in line to the Swedish throne and one hundred and eighty-ninth in line to the British throne, nodded politely. The waiters and waitresses took up their positions beside the long banquet tables, their flaming desserts illuminating the room like lights on a runway. The audience of twelve hundred applauded, then gradually settled back in their seats to enjoy the dessert and resume their conversations.

After coffee, Princess Madeleine's husband took his wife's hand. He steered her into the royal procession heading toward the Grand Ballroom where they would lead off the dancing for the evening.

MacLeod excused himself from his fellow dinner guests and took the five-minute taxi ride to the Grand Hotel. Once in his room, he called Brenda. She answered her phone on the fifth ring sounding a little out of breath,

"Sorry, Sir Francis, my phone was upstairs in the bedroom. How was the banquet?"

"First class all the way, just as you would expect. Anyway, the reason I am calling is I want you to do something for me first thing in the morning."

"Of course," Brenda replied. "Anything."

"Call 'the group' and tell them we'll be meeting in Cambridge next Wednesday. Make reservations for them at the University Arms." He hesitated before continuing. "After you talk to them, contact Anne Benton and ask her to come to Cambridge around five and I will talk to her between the meeting and dinner. Reserve a room for her at the Hilton."

Brenda told him she would get on it first thing in the morning.

"Thanks. I'd better get back to the banquet," he continued. "Bye."

After he hung up, MacLeod opened the mini-bar and poured himself a gin and tonic. As he took his first sip, he glanced at his reflection in the full-length mirror. He mused to himself how much more handsome and sophisticated he appeared to be in his full evening suit, complete with tails. It was true of most men: the less exposed, the better they looked. Now, women on the other hand--- he took another sip of his drink. He kicked off his shoes and lay back on the king-size bed with his G and T, deep in thought. He had bought his evening suit in early summer at Anderson & Sheppard of 30 Savile Row, London – one of the district's oldest and most reputable tailors – for another very special occasion, his investiture in July at Buckingham Palace when he received his knighthood. Before that, whenever he needed to look like a penguin he had hired a suit from Oscar de la Rental.

And here he was now, in Stockholm, the sole winner of the 2020 Nobel Prize in Physiology and Medicine. None of his current colleagues could claim to be both a Nobel laureate and a Knight of the Realm.

How proud his mother would be if she were still alive. It was because of her he studied biochemistry in the first place. She had died eighteen months ago at the age of eighty-three. In 1962, she had been a post-doc at Cambridge, one of the few female scientists studying DNA at the Cavendish Labs when Watson and Crick won their Nobel Prize in Chemistry. He was born seven years later and given their names, Francis and James. Being of Scottish heritage, it would have been more usual to have James as his first name, but Watson was an American. This time, he had to take second place to Crick, the Englishman. MacLeod had never known father's identity, and his mother had always refused to discuss the matter. Now, almost sixty years later, he had joined Watson and Crick as a Nobel laureate and had become a member of one of the most exclusive clubs in the world. The prestige of his two titles provided him with more power and influence. Certainly, the members of the group would find it difficult to turn down his invitation to a meeting in Cambridge next week.

He finished off the drink, placed the empty glass on the bedside table, put on his shoes and stood up straight to look in the mirror. Not bad, not too bad, he thought. He was fifty-one years old with a full head of brown hair, a little graying at the sides. It gave him a rather distinguished look. At six feet one and in good physical shape – thanks to a weekly regime of jogging and squash – he felt young and fit enough should the right woman come along.

He hadn't always been single, but his first marriage had not turned out the way he had hoped. He and Mary Lou divorced after four years, waiting two years longer – they agreed later – than they should have. Born in San Francisco in 1970, Mary Lou was a love-child of the 1969 Woodstock West Festival and, like MacLeod, never knew her father. Having just graduated from Cambridge and been suddenly thrust into the culture of Northern California, MacLeod was smitten from the moment he met Mary Lou, a breath of fresh air, and so different from the girls he knew at Cambridge. Mary Lou taught him about sex and free love but otherwise they were culturally incompatible; apart from sex, the only thing they had in common was their dedication to DNA research.

They had met at Stanford University in 1999 when they were both post-docs in genetics; they married a year later amid the euphoria of the Human Genome Project. Their lives at the time were so intertwined that they thought of each other as the perfect match, but they soon found out it took more than a passion for DNA to make a marriage work. They gradually drifted apart. The final straw came in the summer of 2003 when MacLeod found out Mary Lou was having an affair with a business manager of an East Coast pharmaceutical company. It would be years later before he found out the man's name.

MacLeod glanced at his watch. He had been gone twenty minutes longer than he had intended. He straightened his bow tie, then with his right forefinger nail removed a small piece of dirt from under his left thumbnail before hurrying out to catch a taxi back to the banquet.

MacLeod returned from the banquet and started undressing for bed and glanced at the time, after all of the excitement of the evening he wasn't tired; after he had removed his evening suit, he put on some casual clothes and took the elevator down to the first floor. As he approached the Cadier bar, he noticed a woman sitting alone at the other end. He sat down and signaled to the barman. "A gin and tonic with a slice of lemon and ask the lady if she would like a drink on me."

An attractive brunette in her mid-thirties, the woman smiled across the bar at MacLeod and told the barman she would only accept the drink if MacLeod joined her. Twenty seconds later, he was sitting next to her. When he told her why he was in

Stockholm, she was fascinated to hear there was such a thing as a Nobel Prize.

"I don't think I've met a Nobleman before," she said with apparent innocence.

They both chuckled then he moved in closer and clasped her hand.

"That's not all, young lady. I am also a Knight of the Realm."

"Really, is it true what they say?"

"Is what true?"

She giggled. "That once a king, always a king, but once a night---"

He squeezed her hand tightly. "Well let's find out."

He wrote down his room number on a piece of paper, took a five hundred Krona bill from his wallet, placed it on the bar, and nonchalantly strolled toward the elevator. It had not occurred to him to ask what such a well-dressed woman from New York was doing sitting alone late at night in a Swedish hotel bar.

By the time she knocked on the door a few minutes later, MacLeod had already taken a bottle of white wine from the mini-bar and poured two glasses. He handed her a glass as he took her other hand and led her to the bed and kissed her on the forehead.

"Make yourself comfortable while I freshen up."

He stood in front of the bathroom sink in his royal-blue silk pajamas with FJM embroidered on the pocket and squeezed paste onto his toothbrush. He looked at himself in the mirror and smiled.

The woman was sitting on the end of the bed with her legs crossed when MacLeod came out of the bathroom and sat down beside her.

"You are very beautiful," he said.

"And you are very rich," she said. "Now let's talk about the price."

"Price? And I thought you were here because of my good looks and quick wit." MacLeod sat up and spun around to face her.

"I have never paid for that in my life, and in good conscience I don't intend to start now."

"And I don't intend to leave here empty-handed, so pay up, Knight, or I will call security and Britain's newest Nobel Prize winner will be on the front page of the tabloids this weekend."

MacLeod grimaced and reached for his wallet. He took out a thousand Krona bill. She raised two fingers. He handed her another thousand then took her gently by the hand and steered her to the door.

She stepped across the threshold, turned and said, "I guess I got the answer to my question. You might be a Knight, but you're not a man!"

The battle between conscience and ego waged on for a microsecond. Ego synapses five, Conscience synapses nil. MacLeod pulled her back into the room and shut the door.

"We'll see about that. Besides, I've already paid for the ticket, I may as well enjoy the ride."

After she had left, he lay in bed thinking that he had behaved like an old fool and should have known better, after all this *was* Stockholm. He laughed and thought, 'What the hell, it was fun while it lasted!' He changed his thoughts to past relationships – there had been plenty – but none of them had lasted very long and some had ended in bitterness. He wondered whether he would ever marry again and suddenly became restless as he thought about his first marriage to Mary Lou and the fact that it had ended when he discovered she was having an affair.

MacLeod got out of bed, took a small bottle of cognac from the mini-bar and poured it into a glass. Propping up the pillows, he lay back against the headboard. Thoughts of Mary Lou's past lover agitated him. Their marriage had been on the rocks at the time and was about to end. Why was he hanging onto a grudge all this time? Maybe it was a character flaw and he couldn't stand competition in his life. It had been a long time ago, but he wanted revenge. As if it would bring some sort of closure. He sat on the bed slowly sipping the cognac and grinning at the thought of humiliating his wife's ex-lover.

The next morning, Brenda made her first call

Hans Meier's private secretary answered the phone.

"Good morning Anna. It's Brenda here. How are you?"

"Very fine, Brenda. How are you with all of the excitement of Sir Francis' Nobel Prize?"

"Very well, thank you, and thrilled as you would imagine. Anna, I am calling to let you know that Sir Francis is arranging a meeting in Cambridge next Wednesday afternoon and needs Herr Meier to attend. Can you arrange that?"

"It should not be a problem. He has a couple of meetings scheduled but I am sure we can rearrange those. Let me talk to him and get back to you this afternoon."

"Thanks, I'll reserve a hotel room for him," Brenda replied. "Talk to you later. Bye."

Meier had held his current position as Chief Executive of Tronavis, Switzerland's largest pharmaceutical company, for the past five years, having worked his way through the ranks from the time he graduated from the University of Geneva. Unlike most conservative Swiss businessmen, Meier seized any opportunities that fast-forwarded his ambitions. He and MacLeod started working together in the field of gene therapy a few years after Meier had become CEO.

Brenda followed up with calls to Fisona in France and SKG in the UK. Later in the day, she called Prezfi and SMB in the US. The executive assistant of SMB's chairman and CEO, Harry Sawyer, said her boss had been expecting the call, but he himself would not be attending the meeting, someone else would take his place. She told Brenda to ask MacLeod to call Sawyer. Brenda called the Grand Hotel to pass on the message to Macleod and left him a voicemail. She then called the University Arms to provisionally book four rooms for the following Wednesday night. She knew Sir Charles Palmer, SKG's chairman, would probably not stay overnight. As usual, his chauffeur would drive him back to London. She called MacLeod's hotel again to advise MacLeod that the hotel rooms had been booked.

MacLeod had the morning free, so he started off with a jog before breakfast around the spectacular waterfront and old town with views of the Royal Palace and mid-morning he indulged himself with a classic Swedish massage. After lunch he and other Nobel Prize winners were given a VIP tour of Drottningholm Palace, the official home of the Swedish Royal Family, located seven miles west of the city. Dinner in the evening was at one of the oldest restaurants in Stockholm, the Operakälleren. After dinner Macleod strolled back to the hotel with two of his fellow recipients.

Once in his room MacLeod checked his messages, both were from Brenda, he looked at the time - ten fifteen. Early evening on the East Coast. Shaking his head, he decided to postpone the call to Sawyer until the following afternoon after he got back to Cambridge.

He knew that Sir Charles Palmer would still be up, so he called his home.

"Hello, Charles. It's Francis."

"Francis, old chap, so I guess it is official: you are a Nobel laureate. How does it feel?"

"It's a great honor, of course, and I would be less than honest if I didn't say that I'm very proud that my work has been recognized this way."

"Well done, old chap, what can I do for you?"

"I think I might have a bit of a problem with SMB. Harry has asked me to call him and I think I know why. He's retiring in a few months and I think he wants to send Henry Anderson in his place. There's no way I want to be around that son-of-a-bitch, so I would prefer that we replace Anderson with Anne Benton. What do you think?"

"It's your project, Francis, although Harry has supported you well over the years. But I'm really surprised that he is giving that asshole Anderson the top job in a few months," Palmer said. "Anne would be a much better choice, but how are you going to force Henry out?"

"I think the way I'm setting it up, he will not be able to commit to the funding in a timely manner," MacLeod replied.

"Really, how much are we talking about here?"

"Five million pounds a year for ten years. Henry will not be able to commit to that."

"Why not? That's peanuts to all of us."

"I'm going to ask everybody to sign an agreement on Wednesday committing to the fifty million upfront. Henry doesn't have the authority to do that at SMB because of that financial scandal they had last year. Henry's limit is around ten million. Everything above that has to go before the Corporate Governance and Audit committees and then be signed off by the chairman, and that will take weeks."

"You are a sly old fox, Francis," Palmer said with a chuckle.

"You have to be these days. Anyway, if you can get there in time for lunch I would be happy to share our most recent research with you. Say twelve o'clock at my office."

"I'll do my best. Have my secretary work it out with Brenda. Good night, Francis."

"Good night, Charles, and thanks again."

The following afternoon, MacLeod called Harry Sawyer who confirmed his suspicions and told him that Henry Anderson, the future chairman and CEO of SMB would be attending the meeting.

Chapter 6

A week after the Nobel Prize Awards in Stockholm, MacLeod was in the Biffen Lecture Theatre. It was jammed with academics, students and reporters from top scientific journals and leading newspapers, all eager to hear what he had to say.

MacLeod stood at the podium in front of a large screen.

"Good afternoon, ladies and gentlemen, last week was a very special week for me and it is a great honor to be the recipient of the Nobel Prize. However, this would not have been possible without the great scientific work that preceded my own. I would like to take a couple of minutes to remind you of what has been accomplished in the last seventy years and then give you a glimpse into the future."

An image appeared on the screen showing the famous black and white picture of Watson and Crick in front of their model of the molecular structure of DNA (Deoxyribonucleic acid) taken at Cambridge University in 1953.

MacLeod continued, "I think it is fair to say that Watson and Crick's discovery of the double helix deserves most of the credit for just about every advance in genetics these past sixty to seventy years and certainly if it had not been for Watson's passion and persistence, I doubt whether the Human Genome Project would have ever gotten off the ground. So we owe a debt of gratitude to these Cambridge scholars, and although Crick's boast that they had discovered the secret of life may have been somewhat premature, it may well be that when future generations do figure this out they will look at Watson and Crick as having provided the first part of the genetic road map."

The audience stood and applauded.

MacLeod explained that when the Human Genome Project was published in 2003, most molecular biologists throughout the world were surprised to learn that there were less than thirty thousand genes, meaning that over ninety-nine percent of DNA is junk.

"I don't believe for one minute," he told the audience, "that there is such a thing as junk DNA. No, in my opinion, all DNA has a purpose and function. It's just that no one has yet figured it out." He went on to say that his genon research convinced him that what had previously been described as junk DNA were just sections of inactive DNA or genes that had been mutated in one way or another because their genons were switched off.

MacLeod paused for a moment before describing a genon.

"Genons are relatively small sequences of DNA that reside on either side of a gene. When switched on, they are capable of moving back and forth across a gene to correct any mutations that may be there or have occurred over time. In perfectly normal genes, these genons are constantly checking the gene sequence to make sure the gene remains normal. Let me give you an analogy. Remember the PCs of the early 2000s that had a feature called 'auto spell check' in the Word program? The user had a choice to switch the feature off or on and if they chose to switch it on, it would automatically correct any spelling mistakes. It is the same with genons. Switched on, they will automatically correct any faulty sequences in the gene by deleting them and replacing them with the correct sequence. As a result, they will halt the progress of a disease and in most cases prevent the disease altogether."

Reporters scribbled MacLeod's analogy into their notebooks.

41

"On average, each of us has fifty to one hundred mutations not present in our parents. By extrapolating this back over time, scientists can begin to understand that large numbers of genes stopped functioning for one reason or another. Identifying a gene's genon and restoring its function makes it possible to correct a faulty gene and prevent or even reverse a diseased state."

MacLeod clicked the remote and a new image appeared showing Chromosome 7 and the genon sequence responsible for correcting the faulty CF gene. "This is the very first genon we discovered in 2015 and I believe that as a result of this discovery, cystic fibrosis will be totally eradicated during our lifetime."

He clicked to the next slide, a list of genons and genes appeared on the screen. "Since that first discovery in 2015, we have identified more than twenty other genons related to various diseases of one sort or another, and seven previously unidentified genes." MacLeod sipped on his glass of water before continuing. "I predict that by the time we finish our research we will identify around fifty to sixty thousand genes, more than twice the number stated by the Human Genome Consortium when they published their findings in 2003."

MacLeod looked at the time and said he would just take a few minutes to give them a glimpse of the future as he could see it. He told them to let their imagination run free on the possibilities.

"Apart from correcting mutated genes that pre-dispose people to known genetic disorders such as cystic fibrosis, Alzheimer's, Parkinson's, etc., what if we can identify the genes and genons that are responsible for winter hibernation in bears and other animals? Imagine if an astronaut could hibernate for several years with a resting heart rate of ten to fifteen beats per minute. Or envision having super hearing or perfect eyesight for life. Ladies and gentlemen, the future is no longer science fiction, but merely a challenge to the imagination. And we intend to vigorously pursue this challenge. Thank you for your attention."

The audience applauded loudly.

"Now I'll be happy to answer any questions."

Dozens of hands went up. MacLeod pointed to a young female student.

"Professor MacLeod, your list of new genons and new genes is impressive. Can you tell us more about the function of these recently discovered genes?

MacLeod smiled. "I am afraid not; the discovery of these genes may prove to be proprietary therefore their function and sequences must remain confidential for the time being."

A male professor asked the next question. "Sir Francis, you have identified twenty-three genons, what is the average length of a genon?" And typically, where are they situated?"

MacLeod nodded his head at the question. "Good question. They vary in length as you might expect but on average they are about three hundred base pairs long and situated on either side of the gene."

MacLeod pointed to a reporter from the *Times*.

"Sir Francis, you have just been awarded the Nobel Prize in Physiology and Medicine and earlier in the year you received a Knighthood. Can I ask you what has given you the most satisfaction during your career so far?"

"That's easy to answer. The discovery of genons has allowed many people to lead normal healthy lives who otherwise might be suffering from the severe and debilitating symptoms of a formerly incurable disease. And, I may add, the very exciting prospects for the future of being able to improve the quality of life of those who otherwise may have had to suffer."

A rookie female reporter named Amy from the *Cambridge Evening News* asked the last question. "Sir Francis, what's the next step?"

MacLeod grinned as he responded. "I can tell you this much, if you attend the press conference I am holding tomorrow morning you will get a front-page story for your newspaper. Thanks again, everybody. Good afternoon."

Chapter 7

After the lecture, the five heads of some of the world's largest pharmaceutical companies sat around the oval conference table discussing what they had learned from MacLeod's talk.

"You have to admit for a stiff-upper-lip limey, pardon the expression, Charles, the guy's a genius," Gillespie, the chairman and CEO of Prezfi, Inc. observed.

They all nodded except Anderson, "And a damned ego as big as a hot-air balloon."

"What the hell's wrong with you, Henry?" Gillespie asked. "He's invited us to be in on the ground floor and you're behaving like he's the enemy. Besides, anyone here who doesn't think they have as big an ego, throw the first stone."

Brenda coughed to remind them of her presence as she hovered around, offering each one of them tea, coffee or water.

"Sir Francis should be here in a couple of minutes," she said. "He had to take a call from the Minister of Science and Technology."

Five minutes later, MacLeod arrived, apologizing for being late. Brenda handed him a cup of tea.

"Well, gentlemen, here we are, the big day has arrived! We are ready to start Project GT, so let me give you some details, and then I want to share with you some really exciting stuff that I couldn't reveal in the press conference." He took several sips of tea.

"We are all ears, Francis," Gillespie said.

"Good," MacLeod finished off his tea and pushed the cup and saucer to one side. "On Monday, we are going to set up a new company called Genon plc with an initial capitalization of two hundred and fifty million and that's where you all come in. I need you to put in fifty million each to fund a ten-year project. But realistically, I think we will get the job done in seven to eight years."

"Exactly what is the job?" asked Meier, the president of Tronavis S.A.

MacLeod answered, as he had pointed out in his talk, he believed that less than half of human genes had been identified. He told the group he wanted to go after the other fifty percent. If accomplished, he said, it would have a far greater impact than the mapping of the human genome. He reiterated that he needed a commitment of fifty million pounds from each man to move ahead. He stared at each one of them then slowly said, "I need to have the whole two hundred and fifty million up front, in fact, by midnight Friday."

Henry Anderson, president and COO of SMB Inc., said, "Why do you need all the money up front when you are only going to spend twenty-five million a year?"

"I have seen too many situations in the past where commitments have been dropped or cancelled because of a changing of the guard at the top," MacLeod said. "And I know I will have no problem getting other companies to step in if any of you turn down your first right of refusal."

Anderson, quietly seething, didn't notice Palmer give a slight wink to MacLeod.

"So we each give you fifty million and what do we get in return?" Gillespie asked.

"First rights to our discoveries and equity, each of your companies will hold a five percent stake in Genon for a total of twenty-five percent. Ten percent will go to the university and ten percent divided equally among my key staff. I will own the remaining fifty-five percent."

"Geez!" Gillespie said. "That's a one-billion-pound valuation right out of the chute, about a billion and half dollars. That's a bit heavy, don't you think?"

MacLeod was firm. "It might be a little on the high side, but not unprecedented and I can assure you this is going to be a blockbuster. When the new gene therapies ramp up, you will all make a fortune. So who is in?"

Palmer was first to raise his hand.

Meier followed. "We're in, too."

"And us," Gillespie said.

DeLille nodded.

Anderson, his face flushed, asked to speak to MacLeod outside the conference room.

MacLeod stood up. "Excuse us, gentlemen, this won't take long."

In the corridor, Anderson said, "Francis, SMB has been providing financial support to you for over three years and would like to continue to do that."

"I am glad to hear that, so what's the problem?" MacLeod asked.

"There is no problem except that I cannot get fifty million to you in forty-eight hours. It will take at least a couple of weeks and I don't see what the rush is for anyway."

"Henry, I do appreciate SMB's past support, but these are my conditions and if you want in, you need to transfer the funds by Friday. For heaven's sake, Henry, it's less than one percent of your annual R & D budget and the potential payback is enormous."

"Francis, I don't take over the chairmanship for another three months. Until then I don't have the authority to sign off on a fifty-million-pound investment. Please understand that."

"Not my problem, Henry. We'd better get back to the others."

"You go ahead. I need to talk to the chairman," Anderson said, turning and taking out his phone.

MacLeod called Brenda. "Do you know if Anne has arrived yet? Oh, good. Could you tell her to come over right away and meet me in my office? Thanks."

As he entered the conference room, MacLeod looked towards Palmer and raised his eyebrows as he took his seat back at the table.

Gillespie noticed the exchange. "Everything okay with Henry?" he asked.

"Oh, just a little matter of money. Now where were we? Oh, yes, money. I will have Brenda give you the wiring instructions as soon as we are done here and don't forget that you need to meet Friday's midnight deadline. Next, we need to finalize contracts. I have them all prepared for you, so if you could just look them over and sign and date them, I would appreciate that. And as soon as you have done that, I will tell you something even more exciting."

The men signed the documents quickly, eager to hear what else MacLeod had to say.

MacLeod announced that he had been conducting animal experiments into the possibility of retaining perfect eyesight throughout life. They were having a large measure of success in one area of sight deterioration – glaucoma. So far, using beagles, they had been able to stop the progression of the disease and, in a few cases, had reversed the deterioration, restoring full sight to the dog. They had yet to achieve full success, but it was early days, and he believed that once Genon was up and running, they would succeed not only with glaucoma but other causes of sight defect such as adult macular degeneration (AMD).

Meier jumped in to speak on behalf of the group. "Francis, this is incredible. I have to say that you have taken us all by surprise. I would like to add that you know that this is right up our alley and I'm offering our full resources to take this into human trials as soon as you are ready."

MacLeod acknowledged the offer. "I appreciate that, Hans, but as I said we're not ready yet, we need to do a lot more animal trials before we can experiment with humans. Now, if you could just excuse me again. I'll be back in about twenty minutes."

Anne Benton and MacLeod embraced as soon as he entered his office. "Good to see you again, Anne," he whispered in her ear as he recognized the familiar smell of Chanel No 5 and drew her closer and kissed her. "Still wearing the same perfume, I see."

She nodded. "I wore it today especially for you," she said, stepping away and taking a seat in front of MacLeod's desk.

Anne could barely hold back her excitement when MacLeod explained the project to her and asked her to join the group.

"It would be a privilege, Francis. You know how much I have always admired your work and this latest stuff is mind-boggling." She stood up and hugged MacLeod again. "You will have the money first thing Friday morning."

"I knew I could count on you, Anne, but before we sign any agreement I need to make sure that Henry hasn't been able to come up with the funds, so let me go talk to him. I'll be right back."

Pacing up and down the hallway, shouting into his iPhone, Anderson watched MacLeod approach. "Damn it, Harry, we can't miss out on this. Surely, you can make an exception just this once, after all this was one of your pet projects. Please think it over and I will call you back in an hour." Anderson pocketed his phone.

"Harry won't approve the fifty million investment? That's too bad. The other four didn't hesitate for a second. Henry, I need to know soon. I'll check back with you shortly."

"You set me up, didn't you? You knew Harry wouldn't let me commit fifty million."

"How would I know that, Henry? Don't be so paranoid."

MacLeod returned to his office and asked Anne to join him in the conference room.

"Gentlemen, you all know Anne Benton. I'd like you to welcome her to the group."

Gillespie looked puzzled. "What about Henry and SMB?"

MacLeod shrugged his shoulders. "Unfortunately, they did not want to put up the fifty million, so Anne has stepped in and committed NZA to the project."

He looked at the time. "Now, as it's only a little after five o'clock, you have almost two hours to relax and freshen up. Then we will meet in the Eagle pub at seven for a drink. We have a table booked for dinner at Midsummer House for eight o'clock. Brenda has directions for you."

He left to go back and talk to Henry. "I am sorry, Henry, but you had your chance."

"You son-of-a-bitch. You screwed me, didn't you?" Anderson yelled.

"Your company screwed you, Henry, not me, old chap," MacLeod replied. It had taken more than fifteen years, but he was finally getting his revenge on Anderson for having an affair with Mary Lou.

"Now, if you'll excuse me, I have to go."

The next day when Anderson reported to Harry Sawyer what had happened in Cambridge, it was not MacLeod that Sawyer was upset with. He blamed Anderson for not being able to persuade MacLeod to let SMB participate in the project.

Three months later, Harry Sawyer changed his mind about the chairmanship and appointed someone else as his successor.

Chapter 8

Owned by Corpus Christi College since the late fourteenth century, the Eagle public house at 8 Benet Street is the oldest pub in Cambridge. Opened as a coaching inn in 1525, for centuries, the pub has been the favorite watering hole of countless famous and not-so-famous Cambridge scholars.

In the 1940s, however, following the outbreak of World War II, the bar began attracting a different clientele: British RAF pilots and US Air Force pilots stationed on many of the nearby bases. These fun-loving, rowdy fliers congregated in a particular area of the pub and took to inscribing their names and squadrons on the heavily nicotine-stained ceiling. Standing on chairs and tables in the smoked-filled room, the men used cigarettes, lighters, candle flames, lipstick, and whatever was available to etch initials like DS-SQ2 RAF, PH-SQ8 USAF and AM 14.

The tradition lasted for twenty-five years until, in the late sixties, the owners remodeled and painted the pub, moving the original bar from the next room into this area and renaming it the RAF Bar. The owners preserved the historic ceiling in a coat of resin where it remains as a reminder of history and those who fought in WWII.

Adjacent to the RAF Bar is where the original bar was located, and it was in here on February the twenty-eighth, 1953 that the Eagle was restored to its academic roots when two of its most famous patrons created scientific history. On that cold and blustery February day, Francis Crick burst through the doors and unashamedly declared to all who were within earshot, "We have discovered the secret of life." Crick's younger colleague, the American biologist James D Watson, straggled behind, somewhat embarrassed by Crick's premature bragging about their discovery of the double helix and the structure of DNA.

Although the pub has been remodeled and redecorated several times over the years, the owners preserved the table where Watson and Crick frequently sat for lunch and dinner or to enjoy a few drinks after a hard day's work at the lab. MacLeod had reserved that table for his investor group.

"Charles, what will you have?" MacLeod asked Palmer.

"A gin and tonic would go down rather well, old chap. Bombay Sapphire."

"I'll have the same," MacLeod said to the waiter. "Anne, white wine?"

"Yes, please, medium-dry," she answered.

"Hans?"

Meier was standing in front of the entryway reading about the history of the pub. He turned when he heard his name called. "A Pilsner if they have one. Thanks."

"Alain?"

"Vin rouge, Merci," DeLille replied.

"Fred?"

"Jim Slim on the rocks. Thanks."

"Never heard of it. What is it?" the bartender asked

"Jim Beam and Diet Coke on ice." Gillespie answered.

When the drinks arrived, MacLeod raised his glass and toasted the future. "To Genon plc."

"Genon plc," they all replied.

MacLeod smiled as he observed the others talking with great enthusiasm about what they had learned during the day.

They all laughed and toasted again. "To Genon plc and the GT Project."

They chatted for another twenty minutes and then MacLeod said, "Okay, let's go to dinner, it's only a few minutes' walk from here."

"Hang on a minute," Gillespie said. "Look at the quote on the back of the door here. It's James Watson."

"Yes, that's the very door that Crick burst through in 1953." MacLeod said.

The visitors turned around and read Watson's quote.

"*Incroyable*, it is a little piece of *histoire*," exclaimed DeLille.

"Anne, gentlemen, if you are ready," MacLeod added.

They finished their drinks and took a stroll through the city to Midsummer House on the bank of the river Cam. MacLeod dined there so often that he had a favorite table in the corner, but tonight he had reserved a private room. Anne smiled knowingly at MacLeod as they walked past the table.

The maître d' greeted him with deference and led the group to the room.

"Thanks, Tony," MacLeod said as he gestured to the group to sit down. "I think we'll start with a bottle of your 2015 Dom Perignon, Tony. Thank you."

"Now, lady," he raised his glass to Anne, "and gentlemen, let me outline our immediate plans. By Monday evening, Genon plc will have been established. Our solicitors have been working on this for the past three months. We have the labs almost ready to go. They will be finished over the Christmas holidays. I am going to offer each of my four key scientists a senior position at Genon and I have offered a fifth position to a new chap who will join us in January. By the middle of January, I expect to be fully operational."

"Gee, you haven't let the grass grow under your feet, Francis. That's pretty fast even by our standards," Gillespie said.

The others nodded.

"Onward and upward, as they say," MacLeod responded.

"I'll drink to that," Gillespie added.

After dinner, they walked back across Midsummer Common and made their way to the University Arms, where Palmer's chauffeur was waiting to drive him back to London. They all said good night and the remaining three men went into Parker's Bar for a nightcap. When they were out of sight MacLeod took Anne by the hand and walked her back to the Hilton.

It was almost two a.m. when he got home.

Chapter 9

The next morning, MacLeod gathered his four key scientists, Kathleen, Ian Walton, Darren Richards and Vinjay Gupta to update them on what he had been doing outside the lab recently.

"Yesterday, I met with five pharmaceutical companies and they each agreed to provide substantial funding to launch a new commercial venture to accelerate our genon research. At the beginning of January, we will be opening the doors of a new company called Genon plc and I would like the four of you to join me as founder employees. If you accept, you will receive shares in the company along with a salary significantly higher than you are earning now---"

"If I may ask," Kathleen interrupted, "it sounds like a good opportunity, but what about our academic integrity?"

"Kathleen, always the purist. Apart from you and Darren, we have all dirtied our hands in the commercial world and I can tell you first hand it's not all that bad, especially in a private company where we don't have to answer to outside shareholders. Plus, where else would we get this kind of funding?"

"How much funding?" Kathleen asked.

"Two hundred and fifty million."

The scientists stared at one another. "Geez, that's almost a half-billion dollars. Incredible! Is it over twenty years or something?" Darren asked.

"It's to cover the next ten years but paid in full upfront, in fact by tomorrow night," MacLeod responded. "Anyway, I will explain more about that after the holidays, but let me tell you some other details. The new labs will be completed over the Christmas break in time for us to start work on Monday, January the fourth. In the meantime, you can finish whatever you are doing here and then you can have the rest of the time off until the New Year. We will meet at nine a.m. on the fourth and I will tell you about your salary, stock etc. Trust me, you will not be disappointed. I will also introduce you to your new colleague, Rob Elliott, who comes to us from the NESCI in Newcastle."

"Oh, a stem cell specialist. Interesting," Kathleen said.

"Yes, he is, and not only that, his group has had significant success with adult stem cells, so I think he's a good fit and I am sure you will all like him. Besides, how could you not? He's a Geordie," MacLeod said. "The other thing you should know is that I took VJ into my confidence several weeks ago and he'll be working with the movers to have all of the computer systems and quite a bit of new hardware relocated and up and running by the time we move in."

MacLeod looked at the time. "Well, I think that's about it for now, but you are all welcome to join me in the media room for the ten o'clock video conference. It should be interesting."

MacLeod took his place at the center of the table with Anne Benton, Meier and DeLille flanking him. Palmer was back in London and Gillespie had taken an early morning flight from Heathrow to New York.

The video conference had a live feed into the major media networks. A few local reporters were there in person including Amy Harper from the Cambridge Evening News Online.

MacLeod waited for his cue. The camera lights flashed and zoomed in on MacLeod.

"Welcome everyone. I am here today to share some exciting news with you. Yesterday, five of the world's largest pharmaceutical companies agreed to financially support a new company called Genon plc, which will focus exclusively on the discovery of new genons and perfect the techniques of gene therapy."

Reporters immediately started to ask questions.

MacLeod ignored them and continued. "With me here today are the heads of three of the five companies that are putting up the money for this venture, so let me introduce them to you." The cameras zoomed out as MacLeod called out the names of Benton, Meier and DeLille. "The other two members of the group are the world's largest pharmaceutical companies: Prezfi, Inc. in the US and Britain's own SKG plc. Four out of the five companies have been funding our work for several years, but a new company has now joined the group." MacLeod turned and thanked Anne Benton, Managing Director of Britain's NZA, for agreeing to be part of the venture.

"Now, we will take your questions."

A reporter from *Vector Media* spoke first. "Sir, I understand that SMB was one of the original companies funding your research, but they are not part of this new venture. Can you comment on that?"

MacLeod hadn't wanted to discuss SMB. "Very simple really. We could not reach an agreement with them. As a result, we approached NZA who were more than happy to participate in this new venture. Next?"

"Sir Francis, how much money are these five companies investing?" A reporter from the *Daily Web News* asked.

MacLeod hesitated. "You know, I am not sure that I should share that with you." He turned to look at the three pharmaceutical executives beside him. They shrugged their shoulders. "Okay," he said. "You are probably going to find out sooner or later anyway, so you may as well hear it from the horse's mouth. It's two hundred and fifty million."

The *FT Online* reporter asked the next question. "Sir, two hundred and fifty million is a significant sum, even these days. Can you tell us how the company will be structured?"

"Yes, I will have controlling interest with over fifty percent of the shares and the rest will be split among the five pharmaceutical companies, Cambridge University and key members of my staff."

Darren turned to VJ. "How much do you think we will get?" he whispered.

"Probably three to five percent between us," VJ replied. "No doubt the five investors will get the lion's share, given how much money they are putting in."

"Better than a kick in the ass!" Darren said jokingly, as he dug his right elbow into VJ's left arm.

Amy from the *Cambridge Evening News Online* asked a question. "Sir Francis, during your talk yesterday you asked us to imagine a lifetime of perfect hearing and eyesight. Is this an area of your current research?"

MacLeod smiled. "You are a very perceptive young woman. As a matter of fact, it is and something we intend to work on in the future."

The *FT Online* reporter jumped in with a second question. "Sir, from what we understand your therapies will create a big shift toward preventative medicine, doesn't this mean that the pharmaceutical companies who are funding your work will be putting themselves out of business?"

"That's a very important question," MacLeod said. "The truth is that preventative medicine is the future and it's going to happen regardless, so isn't it better to be part of it rather than fight it? Besides, there will be a lot of money to be made from this alternative form of medicine and in return for their investment these companies will have the option of first right of refusal for the therapies that we develop."

The *Vector Media* reporter asked another question. "Sir, I would like to ask your investors for their perspective, if I may."

"Of course." MacLeod replied.

The reporter addressed Anne Benton. "Ms. Benton, you were not part of this group in the past. Can you tell us why you are prepared to make this investment?"

Anne leaned forward. "I'd be happy to. I have known Sir Francis for a long time and always taken a keen interest in his fascinating work, so when he presented an opportunity for NZA to participate in this new commercial venture, I didn't hesitate. It's good for NZA and it is good for the British pharmaceutical industry, and Sir Francis is right, this is the future of medicine."

MacLeod nodded his agreement.

The reporter then turned to the other two. "Would either of you like to add any further comment?"

Meier moved nearer to the microphone. "Tronavis has been helping fund Sir Francis' research for three years and what he has accomplished in that time is extraordinary, to say the least. Based on his past success, we knew that one day he would approach us to provide the funding for a commercial enterprise where he would have all the resources he needs to expand and accelerate his research in this very important area . . ."

The *Vector Media* reporter interrupted. "Herr Meier, if I may ask, there must be more to it than that because this is a significant investment, even for your company."

"Let me just finish by saying that I have gotten to know Sir Francis extremely well over the past three years and he is a man of the highest integrity, with an unblemished scientific reputation. Thank you." Moments later those remarks streamed across the Internet.

Chapter 10

After the Christmas holidays, MacLeod's key staff members assembled at the brand-new facility, located at the Cambridge Science Park in West Cambridge. They had all arrived before eight thirty a.m., eager to look around their new labs and offices. Each employee had a lab and an office, complete with his or her name on the door. VJ's computer room was completely locked down with special security systems. For all of them, it was very different to the ancient labs and cramped office space at the university.

They were drinking freshly brewed coffee and chatting in the elegant conference room decorated with scientific artwork and a large print of Watson and Crick in front of the double helix. There were a number of pictures of MacLeod taken at Buckingham Palace when he received his Knighthood and from the Nobel Prize ceremonies in Stockholm.

MacLeod and his new recruit arrived just before nine.

"What do you think, team?" MacLeod asked with a broad smile.

"Fabulous," volunteered Kathleen.

"Great," answered Darren.

"I am glad to hear that. Now, let me introduce you to the newest member of the team, Rob Elliot." Everyone shook Rob's hand. MacLeod then suggested that they tell their new colleague a little bit about themselves and asked Kathleen to go first.

"Welcome to the group, Rob. I'm Kathleen Murphy; I was born in Dundalk, Ireland and studied chemistry at Trinity College, Dublin, and then did my PhD in Biochem at Oxford, followed by three years as a post doc there. I joined Sir Francis about eleven years ago."

She turned to Darren.

"Hi, Darren Richards from Encinitas, California. I came from a very modest background and worked my way through a BA in chemistry at Cal State San Diego, and then did my PhD in Molecular Biology at the University of California, Irvine. After that, I did post docs at the University of Bath and then Cambridge. I joined the group nine years ago."

"Welcome, Rob. I'm Ian Walton, born close to here in the market town of Oundle, studied at Oxford, and then did my PhD in Biochem at Cambridge. I worked for Alpha Genetics for six years before coming here just over four years ago, my hobbies are rugby and cricket."

MacLeod looked across the table. "VJ."

"I'm Vinjay Gupta," he said softly. "I was born in Hyderabad, India, did a BSc in math and statistics at Hyderabad University and then went on to do a PhD in engineering at MIT. I was with Microsoft for six years, four in New York, and then two in London. I left the firm a couple of years ago to join Sir Francis. I'm married with two children, and by the way, I often beat the boss at squash."

"We'll see about that. You're on for lunchtime today." MacLeod said. "Now, Rob, if you could tell the group a little about your background."

"Thank you, Sir Francis." Rob went on to tell the group that he came from the north east of England where he did his undergraduate and graduate degrees at Durham University, the latter in Biochem. He had spent the last four years at the North East England Stem Cell Institute (NESCI), working on limbus stem cells to regenerate the corneas of damaged eyes.

"I ride a motorcycle and believe it or not, I am still a die-hard Newcastle United fan, but don't hold that against me."

"Good, good," MacLeod said. "Maybe the four of you could have lunch together today to get acquainted, while I kick VJ's backside at squash. Now, we have a lot to talk about." He passed each of them a sheet of paper with a list of agenda topics: salaries and shares, staffing, project details, blood samples, and security.

Brenda entered the conference room carrying a tray of hot tea and a plate of assorted biscuits.

"Will you need anything else, Sir Francis?"

"No, thank you, Brenda," he replied, then went on to cover the most important topic first; the compensation package. He said they would all be treated equally regardless of their overall experience or how long they had been working for him, because it was about the future and teamwork. They would each receive an annual salary of two hundred thousand pounds a year with an annual increase every January of ten thousand pounds. In addition, they would get a two percent equity position in Genon, which based on the starting valuation of the company, meant on paper at least, that their shares were valued at twenty million. "Keep in mind there is no public market for the shares yet, it's a paper asset only until the company goes public."

Darren asked, "And when do you anticipate going public?"

"You know, Darren, I haven't even thought that far ahead but I'm hoping that your compensation package will ensure you'll see this project through to the finish, and that we'll retire with financial security. My expectations are that in addition to a lot of hard work, and at times possibly long hours, I will have your complete trust and loyalty."

They all nodded.

"Fine, that's all I ask." MacLeod said.

He then told them that each of the four geneticists would randomly be assigned five pairs of chromosomes to work on while he would work on the remaining three. None of them would know which chromosome pairs the others would be working on. The company would provide each of them with two computers. One was for everyday use, e-mails, web searching, etc. The other was for data collection, analysis and transmission directly to the central computer system; it also had a much more secure access feature that required both retinal scanning and their personal security code.

"Make sense so far?"

They all nodded again.

MacLeod continued. "Let me explain why I have decided to keep your work confidential. First of all, rather than have you report your individual progress at monthly staff meetings, I will review all of the data first and then present the overall progress to you as a group. That way, there will be no finger pointing or second guessing about individual contributions to the project. Secondly, if you succeed the way I believe you will, you are going to make some astonishing discoveries, which could possibly put you at risk. So, better to plan ahead and put the systems in place now rather than have to worry about it in the future. Everyone okay with this approach?"

Rob was first to speak. "Sir . . ."

"Sorry, Rob, I meant to mention this to you before: we are all equally important in this team and so from now on I want you to call me Francis, except maybe when we are in the public spotlight, if you know what I mean. Carry on."

"I was just going to say, Sir Fr . . er, Francis, our individual data will obviously be transmitted directly to the mainframe. Will we in turn be able to retrieve other data from the mainframe?"

"No, that would defeat the purpose of the high security we have put in place. When we get on to the final topic on security, I will have VJ explain it to you in more detail."

He looked toward VJ and VJ nodded.

"The next thing I want to talk about is the blood samples we will need for our experiments. I suggest we use pooled blood, from six donors. If we all give 500cc of blood, we can take 250cc of each and pool it to use for genon and gene discovery research; the remaining fifty percent will be stored for future use. I've arranged for a phlebotomist to draw the blood tomorrow afternoon in a private room; it will be very confidential. Each bag of blood will be given a randomly selected five-digit code and the only cross reference will be the appointment time. The blood service will keep the only record, although in the case of an emergency I will be able to access the data through a secure system. And as I will be the last one to give blood, I will collect all of the samples and bring them back to the lab where we will pool the blood and lock it away in the secure freezer. Any questions so far?"

"Yes," Ian said. "I assume at some point in the future we might want to identify individual samples, otherwise there is no point in a cross reference, so I guess we all need to make sure we record our appointment time somewhere safe. Why not just be open about it now instead of all this secrecy?"

"The answer to your first point is, yes, you need to keep that information and you'll be the only one who has it. As to your question, I think it is better this way because we don't know what we are going to find, good or bad. If we do find some genetic predisposition to disease in the pooled blood, I don't want anyone worrying about the possibility it might be their blood and go off on a tangent to find out. So, it's for our own protection and peace of mind. Then, after we have completed the project, if we want to pursue individual blood samples we can. Okay?"

"Sure, I was just asking," Ian said.

MacLeod then covered the last topic on the agenda – security. He explained that the project would be highly secure and confidential because he wanted to make sure that they protected all of their discoveries from any inquisitive outsiders. Over the past few weeks, he and VJ had been working closely on the security systems and between them they would go over this in detail. One matter needed taking care of – the signing of confidentiality and non-disclosure agreements. He had them for the team to review and sign before they left the meeting.

"Okay, VJ, tell them what you have been up to," MacLeod said.

"The first thing I want to tell you about is the retinal scanning systems and the special individual biochip implants (IBIs)," VJ said. "As far as your own labs and offices are concerned, the only security system installed at the moment is the retinal scanning device on your Project GT computers. However, if any of you feel you want a more secure entry and exit system for your labs or offices, please come and talk to me in the next few days. Now, the secure common labs like the sequencing labs have a double security system using a combination of retinal scanning and your own biochip implant. In order to gain access, both must be lined up simultaneously to unlock the secure entryway . . ."

"Excuse me, VJ, what biochip implant?" Rob asked.

"Well, I was coming to that. Tomorrow morning, we have a specialist coming to implant the IBIs, and also do the retinal eye scans, then program the systems . . ."

"Why in the heck do we need biochip implants?" Darren interrupted.

MacLeod took the question. "Well, as you know it's a very commonly used device with high-profile people, just in case they get kidnapped or go missing, and although it's not likely that will happen to us, there may come a time when we need to take precautions. These devices not only have sophisticated tracking capabilities, but they will also include your DNA profile and are an integral part of the overall security system to give you access to the secure areas. They are also extremely miniaturized; you won't even know they are under your skin. Carry on, VJ."

VJ explained that the specialist would be coming in the morning to do the implants and eye scans then complete the systems installation. In answer to Rob's earlier question about data access from the mainframe, he explained how it would work. They would input their new data on a regular basis, say once a week, and at any time they could retrieve their own data but no one else's. The only person who would have access to all of the data would be Francis. A double-locking entryway to the central computer lab would make it virtually impossible for anyone other than VJ and Francis to gain entry. Their biochips had an added security feature that required both of them to stand in front of the first entry door. Once inside and the first door was firmly locked behind them then there would be a period of twenty seconds before the inside door opened.

Laughing, Darren said, "Doo, doo – doo, doo; doo, doo – doo, doo. It's like the Twilight Zone."

MacLeod smiled. "Maybe it seems a little over the top, but for those of you who don't remember the breach of security at SKG five years ago, let me remind you. Two of their key researchers, who had high-level clearance, were able to access and steal trade secrets on cancer drugs and intended to sell the information in China. After that, SKG was the first pharmaceutical company to put the security system in place, similar to the ones we have now adopted. You can't be too careful these days. Anything else, VJ?"

"No, I think that's it for now. We should have everything up and running by the end of the week and if I can help you guys with anything, just let me know."

They all nodded.

"In that case, our first official meeting is over," MacLeod said. "You chaps can go off to lunch now and then this afternoon start to get your labs and offices organized. In the meantime, I'm going to take VJ over to the squash club and humiliate him. See everybody in the morning."

By late morning of the following day, the specialist had completed his work and was sitting with VJ and MacLeod in MacLeod's office, drinking tea. The three of them were discussing technical details about the retinal scanning systems and the biochip implants.

"So, none of the others had any problems when you implanted the biochips into their thighs?" MacLeod asked the specialist.

"Not really, just Ms. Murphy. She was a little bit hesitant, so it took a little bit longer than the others."

VJ stood and put his teacup on a side table then turned to the specialist. "Thanks for doing a good job today. We'll be in touch. See you." The specialist shook hands with MacLeod and VJ, and left the office.

At five thirty p.m., MacLeod returned from the blood center with all six bags of blood and gathered the team in his lab. Kathleen and Darren emptied half of each bag of blood into a container then handed the bag to Ian and Rob who then divided the remaining blood in each bag into five separate fifty cc test tubes to store for the future. VJ put matching labels on each set of test tubes: AB 111; CD 222; EF 333; GH 444; IJ 555; KL 666.

When all the blood samples were stored and locked away in the secure freezer, MacLeod addressed his team. "Francis Crick may well have been premature when he boasted about discovering the 'secret of life' back in 1953, because they had not; but it was a step in the right direction, and now we are embarking on a journey that will turn that boast into a reality. So, let's go and celebrate at the Eagle. The drinks are on me."

Everyone but VJ hurried out the door.

Chapter 11

Convinced MacLeod had pre-conceived his dirty scheme to oust him from the Cambridge group, Henry Anderson, angrier than hell, began to wonder if MacLeod had known all along that he was the one who had had an affair with his wife back in the summer of '03. He had been the leader of a technology transfer team at SMB and spent most of that summer traveling between the east and west coasts to ensure a smooth transfer of a new biotech drug from Genentech, Mary Lou MacLeod was the project coordinator. As she and Anderson got to know each other, they found they had something in common – both their marriages were on the rocks. Mary Lou's husband, Francis, had gone to England for the summer to interview for a professor's job at Cambridge University. After a few weeks, Mary Lou and Henry became lovers.

Every time Anderson thought about being left out of the new venture, his blood boiled; but he kept reminding himself of the adage, 'Don't get mad, get even', and that was what he intended to do. A few days after Anderson found out Sawyer had reneged on his promise to give him the chairman's job, he called a colleague from the past, the former Director of the Department of Genetics at Harvard University. Vince J. Garret was a maverick biologist, one of the most controversial figures in the scientific community. An unruly personality, he had known both great success and failure throughout his career. After the Human Genome Project he began studying viruses and bacterium and had successfully constructed the world's first synthetic genome.

Anderson asked Garret for his opinion on the validity of MacLeod's research.

"To be honest, I haven't paid too much attention to his work because I've been too busy working on my own research," Garret said. "However, from what I've read I don't think we can say his work is incontrovertible; as far as I'm concerned the jury is still out."

"Interesting," replied Anderson. "In that case, are you aware of any research that might contradict his work?"

Garret told Anderson that a study had been started in his department a few years ago, counter to MacLeod's assumptions that there was no such thing as junk DNA, and that DNA had mutated over time. The study had put forward a hypothesis that human DNA evolved from a single cell and independently from all other species. The scientists had suggested that this single cell had evolved slowly over millions of years alongside other species. Then about five hundred thousand years ago, its development accelerated, creating the first hominids and eventually Homo sapiens. They further suggested that human DNA, and genes in particular, were pretty much the same today as they were back then. This was counter to MacLeod's theories. Unfortunately, the group ran out of money and the work never finished or published.

"Both can't be right, can they? Which theory is more plausible?" Anderson asked.

"Actually, maybe neither. There is not enough scientific evidence to prove either at the moment and I suspect what MacLeod's is actually calling genons may well be nothing more than a form of transposons, otherwise known as jumping genes." Garret replied.

"Is there any chance that your Harvard group might have been on to something?" Anderson asked.

"Who knows? I would never rule anything out these days," Garret said. "Why do you ask?"

"If I thought that their work might discredit MacLeod I would fund them right away," Anderson said.

Garret seized on the opportunity and suggested to Anderson that there was nothing to lose, especially as they had already put several years of effort into it. From what he understood, they could probably finish the study in twelve to fifteen months. Anderson agreed to provide whatever funding they needed on condition Garret, given his universal name recognition, agreed to add his name to the study. Garret had no problem having his name on another publication and taking credit for it if it turned out to be of scientific value. As soon as SMB provided the funds, Garret restarted the project. The study, completed twelve months later, was published in the journal *Science*. The paper created a great furor in the scientific community. Harvard University was subject to worldwide ridicule and accusations of deception and fraud because the authors did not present any scientific evidence to substantiate their sensational hypothesis. MacLeod, one of the first and most outspoken critics of the *Science* paper, called it 'Utter rubbish and unworthy of a great institution like Harvard'.

Two years later in 2023, Garret visited Cambridge as a guest speaker at the seventieth anniversary conference of Watson & Crick's discovery of the structure of DNA, the double helix, his first real opportunity to rebuild the credibility of his department at Harvard. And now he had to admit that rather than discredit MacLeod, the Harvard *Science* article and MacLeod's own scientific papers had only enhanced his reputation.

Garret had put his name to the *Science* publication and his reputation had ebbed and flowed in the currents of his scientific breakthroughs and his own overbearing ego; the antithesis of MacLeod who, dedicated, competitive and self-assured, was a solid non-controversial scientist whose research was thorough, well documented, and admired by his more prudent peers. Rumors in scientific circles were that MacLeod's team had made amazing progress and that they had now discovered a significant number of new genons.

Garret swaggered to the podium, greeted with polite applause by no more than half of the audience. After the customary tongue in-cheek, "Thank you for the honor of inviting me to speak at this prestigious event," etc., he stared down at the audience. He made no attempt to apologize for the *Science* paper. There were few scientists, if any, in the room whose research had not been challenged at some point in their careers. Scientists and academics thrive on the challenge of pulling their colleague's research apart, often irreparably damaging reputations and years of work in the process. In the case of the Harvard paper, it was clearly justified.

Garret's research had led to the development of the world's first synthetic genome, the subject of his talk today. However, while viruses and bacterium are clearly useful DNA models in their own right and a synthetic genome is a valuable genetic tool, they are trumped by human DNA. Garret had changed his talk dozens of times over the past couple of months. He wanted to discredit MacLeod's work, brag about his own and enhance Harvard's reputation, but just how much could he get away with on MacLeod's own turf?

As Garret opened his mouth to start his talk, MacLeod walked into the room to loud applause.

Garret paused and then, with a hint of sarcasm said, "Welcome, Francis, glad you could make it."

He looked at the small monitor on the podium in front of him, picked up the remote and quickly clicked through the first nine slides of his presentation. He clicked on slide ten to highlight it and immediately it appeared on the large screens. The slide showed a model of a synthetic genome and Garret began to explain how it could be used for doing thousands of experiments simultaneously. Although he was seething inside, he remained calm, finishing his talk in ten minutes less than his allotted time. The audience was much kinder and gave him a round of applause. He quickly left the podium and disappeared.

The conference chairman stood at the podium scanning the auditorium as he spoke into the microphone. "I would like to thank Dr Garret for his very illuminating talk on the synthetic genome and congratulate him for being the first speaker at this conference to finish his talk ahead of his scheduled time. Dr Garret, if you would please stand." The chairman again scanned the room. "Er, maybe he is taking a bathroom break."

The chairman glanced at his watch. "If any of you need to do the same, now would be a good time as we have seven or eight minutes before our next speaker."

Once back in his hotel, Garret called Anderson, who was eager to hear how the audience had reacted to his challenge of MacLeod's work.

"I skipped that part," Garret told him.

"What? Why in the hell would you do that?" Anderson asked.

"Henry, you have to understand that Harvard University was once considered to be the most prestigious university in the world. However, its reputation has been seriously tarnished in recent years because of the scandals and, of course, last year's paper in *Science,* for which I have to take full responsibility. Trashing MacLeod here could have backfired and added to our problems."

Anderson said, "Damn it, Vince, we're going to have come up with another way because I am not going to give up until we discredit that egotistical bastard."

Chapter 12

Saturday, July 26, 2025

Kathleen's mother and father stood on the doorstep of their modest stone-built cottage on the outskirts of Dundalk, anxious to hug the daughter they had not seen for several years. Tears were forming in Mrs. Murphy's eyes as she watched her only child get out of the rental car and stroll up the pathway toward them.

"Hi, Mom. Hi, Dad," Kathleen said, as if she had been visiting them every weekend for years.

Her mother stepped forward and flung her arms around Kathleen, squeezing her tightly. "'Tis so good to see you, and you looking so well. Your pa has been ready for hours, pacing up and down the living room like he did the day you were born."

Mr. Murphy, an accounting clerk in the city, shy and conservative, was dressed as if on his way to Sunday morning Mass. "Oh woman, be quiet, would yuh? Let me take a good look atcha, Katleen," he said in his distinctive Cork accent. He grabbed her by both hands and looked her up and down, tears welling in his eyes. He hugged Kathleen quickly so she couldn't see him cry.

"Let's go in and I'll boil the kettle and make a cup o' tea while your pa gets your suitcase out of the car. Your bedroom is ready for you."

Over a pot of tea and freshly baked scones, they talked excitedly about the reason that had prompted Kathleen to immediately book a Saturday lunchtime flight to Dublin.

"'Tis such a wonderful blessing for us all," Mrs. Murphy said, as she bowed and made the sign of the cross.

John Patrick Murphy, the Archbishop of Dublin and Kathleen's first cousin and mentor, had been informed a few days earlier that the pope had appointed him to the College of Cardinals. His parents, her father's brother and his wife, had decided on the spur of the moment to hold a family gathering in their home on Saturday to congratulate and honor their son, Cardinal Murphy.

"Dad, you must be so proud that JP is going to be a cardinal." Kathleen said, bursting with pride.

JP was ten years older than Kathleen and the only child of her uncle John and her aunt Nellie. He had entered a seminary soon after his sixteenth birthday. No sooner had the ink dried on his ordination papers eight years later that the word spread of a new and progressive young priest who could give a powerful sermon and keep the congregation spellbound, no matter what he preached about. Handsome, with charisma and a great speaking voice, his presence helped boost the number of women attending mass. It distinguished him, at least in Catholic circles, and there was no shortage of local women who volunteered to be his housekeeper.

Kathleen recalled the family celebration after his ordination when she was fourteen. He had taken her to one side, and invited her to come visit him at his new parish because he wanted to talk to her.

Two weeks later, Kathleen had taken the fifteen-minute bus ride to the other side of Dundalk to have lunch with him. He told her that he had faced a real dilemma when he had graduated with a double major in theology and biology – whether to stay on and become a priest or go to medical school to become a doctor. But in the end, the priesthood was an easy choice for him, his science studies convincing him more than ever of God's existence. But he continued to take a keen interest in science, and that was what he wanted to talk to her about, to convince her to pursue a career in that field. He told her he would help her whenever he could. He had become her mentor, and if it had not been for him she probably would not be where she was now.

JP had become a parish priest at the age of thirty when he was transferred to a small parish outside of Dundalk. As news spread about his preaching, Catholics from other villages traveled the extra distance to attend his church and so began his rapid rise in the Catholic hierarchy: parish priest, bishop, then Archbishop of Dublin, and now cardinal.

Kathleen, very proud of her cousin, felt guilty; she rarely went to church these days.

"JP's saying the six o'clock Mass at St. Pat's tonight and then afterwards we're all going back to John and Nellie's to celebrate," Mrs. Murphy said as she looked at the clock. "It's almost five, so I'm sure you'll want to freshen up, Kathleen, we don't want to be late; the church will be packed."

Kathleen had never seen St. Patrick's as full. When JP mounted the pulpit, and she saw him for the first time in years, she cried with joy.

His deep, velvety voice echoed throughout the cathedral.

"May God bless you, my dear friends, I can think of no better send-off than celebrating in the church I attended throughout my youth and to see so many familiar faces here this evening. No matter where I go from here, I will always treasure the fond memories I have of this church and its congregation and, rest assured, I will never forget you nor will I stop praying for you every single day . . .

. . . I am the good shepherd. I know my sheep and my sheep know me in the same way that the Father knows me and I know

75

the Father; for these sheep I will give my life. I have no other sheep that do not belong to this fold. I must lead them, too, and they shall hear my voice. There shall be one flock, then, one shepherd. Amen."

"Amen," the congregation echoed. Women took out handkerchiefs or tissues and wiped the tears from their eyes.

At the party, JP was constantly surrounded by family members and close friends making it difficult for Kathleen to get more than a few minutes of his time. When she did, JP suggested she come to Dublin on Tuesday. He could make time to see her.

It was a beautiful summer's day and after lunch Kathleen and JP sat on a bench in the flower garden at Phoenix Park.

"Now that I've answered all of your questions I would like to hear everything about this exciting job of yours. From what I hear, one of these days you are going to be the richest member of the family."

Kathleen blushed. "Mom been bragging about her *little girl* again, has she?"

Just then a kiddy's soccer ball rolled towards JP's feet, a noisy six-year old boy with fiery red hair in hot pursuit. He stopped dead in his tracks in front of the strange man in a long black cassock, staring in silence as Ireland's newest cardinal picked up the ball and handed it to him.

The boy just stood there staring until he heard a voice calling out, "Aidan, Aidan."

"Aptly chosen name – *little fiery one*." JP glanced toward Kathleen. "Just like you when you were his age." They both laughed.

"Your mother's calling for you, Aidan," JP said, patting the boy on the head and turning him around to face his mother. Clearly embarrassed, she signaled him to come to her.

"Just as well I'm not wearing my cardinal's red frock yet," he added.

They laughed again as the small boy walked slowly toward his mother turning his head every few paces to look back at the odd couple.

"So?" JP asked.

Kathleen told her cousin all about the genon research, how exciting and cutting edge it was, how it would change the nature of healthcare and improve the quality of life for so many people. She also told him what an absolutely brilliant man MacLeod was.

JP had never seen Kathleen so passionate about anything in the past and he couldn't help but notice that every time she mentioned MacLeod's name, there was excitement in her voice and a twinkle in her eyes.

Chapter 13

Saturday, December 20, 2025

With its striking façade, the four-star De Vere University Arms Hotel, located at the northwest corner of Parker's Common, is one of the many well-known landmarks in the center of Cambridge. Originally built in 1832 as a posting house, its historical links with nineteenth century university town life are still apparent, and it remains the hub of commercial and social activity. In winter time, the blustery winds blow across the common, gusting around the corner to the hotel entrance. This evening was unusually severe, and arriving guests were stamping their feet to get rid of the snow as they hurried through the entrance and out of the cold, bringing with them swirling snowflakes that met their end as they evaporated into eternity.

As the invited guests closed their umbrellas and removed their coats and gloves, they turned to each other in typical English fashion.

"Frightful weather!"

"I'll say so, old chap. A Scotch is the order of the day, I think."

The Parker's Bar next to the banquet room teemed with men trying to get the attention of the two barmen to order their favorite tipple and something for their partners.

With drinks in hand, the guests entered the grand ballroom, its wood-paneled walls, heavy blue drapes, chandeliers and large fireplace flanked by wooden columns exemplifying old-world elegance, now buzzing with activity as more than a hundred and thirty Genon employees and over a hundred guests were celebrating the fifth anniversary of Genon plc. MacLeod sat in the center of the head table flanked by Kathleen and Palmer's wife, Gillian, who were both chatting to the people next to them.

MacLeod's mind was miles away, thinking about how far the company had come in the past five years. He was proud of what he and his company had accomplished. After dessert, MacLeod stood to address the gathering.

"Sir Charles and Lady Palmer, Anne and John, fellow employees and guests, it has been an incredible journey these past five years. In the beginning, we had only discovered twenty-three genons and matched seven of them to known genes. Now we have found more than twenty-seven thousand genons. The progress has exceeded my wildest expectations. In a few short weeks, Genon and one of our pharmaceutical partners will be entering into a new phase of human clinical trials."

The audience clapped loudly.

"I want to take this opportunity to sincerely thank all of the Genon employees for their outstanding work and contribution to the success of the company. Without your hard work and loyalty, we would not be where we are today and, who knows, maybe in a couple of years we will take the company public. But for now, as a token of my appreciation, you will all receive an extra Christmas bonus with next week's pay."

There was instant applause. Several employees stood up and whistled.

MacLeod put his hand up to signal them to quiet down before continuing.

"Let me just thank all of the employees again and wish everyone a very happy holiday season. The dancing will start shortly, so please enjoy the rest of the evening."

People slowly started to take to the dance floor. When the DJ announced the quickstep, Sir Charles took Lady Palmer's arm and led her onto the dance floor followed by Anne Benton and her husband John.

MacLeod turned to Kathleen and said, "Shall we?"

"It would be an honor, sir," she said, pleasantly surprised by his invitation.

MacLeod pulled her chair back and watched her from a few paces behind as she made her way to the dance floor, her red hair a sharp contrast to the form-fitting green cocktail dress, which did wonders to highlight her shapely figure. A few minutes into the dance, Kathleen remarked, "I have to say you are pretty light on your feet, Francis. Where did you learn to dance?"

"Oh, for the four years before I went to Dundee University, my mother insisted that I learn ballroom dancing just in case. I haven't practiced much in recent years, though."

The music changed from the quickstep to a slow waltz and, as they moved across the floor, their cheeks brushed ever so slightly. Kathleen felt MacLeod's hold on her tighten a little and smiled. Still in an embrace when the music stopped, they quickly moved apart when the vibrant beat of the salsa music filled the room. Stepping apart, they looked at each other, shaking their heads. MacLeod led Kathleen back to the table to join the others.

As the evening started to wind down, MacLeod asked Kathleen to dance a final waltz. Half-way through, he nervously asked her if she would join him for a nightcap at his place. "After all, it's on your way home," he said awkwardly. She smiled and accepted.

At home, he took her coat and hung it on a hanger in the hall closet, threw his own coat over a chair and then poured gin and tonics. He confessed to her it was the most enjoyable evening he had had in a longtime.

He handed her the gin and tonic and said, "Cheers."

"Was?" She replied with a mischievous tone. "The night is still young."

He raised his eyebrows, and then pointed a remote at a sound system. As they leisurely danced around his large living room, MacLeod gently kissed Kathleen on her right cheek. She pretended to hesitate then returned the kiss to his cheek and tantalizingly brushed her tongue toward his mouth. Their lips met and they kissed long and passionately. A few minutes later, MacLeod switched off the music and lights and gently led Kathleen up the winding staircase to his bedroom.

At the top of the landing, Kathleen pinned MacLeod to the wall and slowly but deliberately removed his tie and unbuttoned his shirt. She looked up at him with her emerald green eyes. She put her arms inside his shirt and up around his back as she clasped him tightly on the shoulders and pulled him down toward her and began kissing him furiously. MacLeod grappled with the zipper at the back of her dress. Kathleen stepped back and smiled as she tore off MacLeod's shirt, throwing it over her shoulder and down the stairs. She undid the zipper and let her dress fall to the floor.

She wore skimpy white lace and satin underwear, her body more beautiful than he had imagined. Slowly, Kathleen undid his belt, unbuttoned his fly, and dragged his trousers downward. Stepping out of them, he moved her gently yet forcefully toward the bed. She unclasped her bra, threw it on the floor, and slipped between the bed sheets, and watched as he fumbled hurriedly to remove his socks, both of them starting to laugh.

Two hours later, exhausted, they fell asleep in each other's arms.

MacLeod woke first, Kathleen still sleeping peacefully. He sat up and stared at her half-naked body. She looked remarkably young for forty-five. An attractive woman with shiny, shoulder-length red hair and a trim figure on her five-foot eight frame.

He got out of bed, slipped on his silk dressing gown and went downstairs to prepare a breakfast of orange juice, cereals, whole grain bread, hot tea and coffee and waited for Kathleen in the kitchen. While he waited, he powered-up the wall display and caught up with the news.

When Kathleen awoke, she sleepily glanced around MacLeod's bedroom. The room had a masculine feel. Tastefully decorated, it looked more like a suite at the Ritz. Impressed by its coziness, she got up, wrapped a bed sheet around her body and stood for a few seconds reflecting on what had been a totally unexpected and incredible evening. Her feelings, bottled up for years, had erupted in a night of passion with a man she thought could never be hers. Kathleen realized she was in love.

She entered the kitchen and saw MacLeod sitting at the table. Without hesitating, she swiftly sat on his lap, facing him, opening up the bed sheet and curling it around him, her warm naked body pressed firmly against his torso. She untied his dressing gown and worked her hand into his pajama pants. When he was erect, she eased him inside her and with her hands firmly planted on his shoulders, began slowly and rhythmically moving up and down. Neither of them said a word. After a while, she increased her rhythm, thrusting and slowing until their bodies moved together, the chair bouncing noisily across the kitchen floor. A few minutes later, just as they reached a simultaneous climax, the chair fell backward, lodged against the pantry door and slid slowly down to the floor, MacLeod's head bumping several times against the wooden door.

"Wow . . . wow," he yelled as he instinctively kicked the chair across the kitchen floor, Kathleen's body came to full rest on top of him. Still locked in position, Kathleen pressed the palms of her hands on the floor and raised her head a few inches to look at him. "Oh, my God," she shouted, "Francis MacLeod . . . no . . . Sir Francis MacLeod, who would ever have imagined that you have that much passion. That was incredible. Wait till I tell the others." She burst out laughing.

MacLeod playfully slapped her bottom. "Don't even think about it."

They lay there in silence, holding onto each other for several minutes before Kathleen got up.

"Is it okay if I take a shower?" she asked.

"Of course, use the main bathroom," MacLeod replied.

After Kathleen went upstairs, MacLeod sat up and leaned back against the pantry door, reliving every minute of what had just taken place; then he noticed the deep scratch marks on the polished wooden floor. He would have to get rid of them. What would his housekeeper think?

Sweat and the tingling feeling in his joystick, made him flashback to when he first met Mary Lou, the spur-of-the-moment sexual encounters he thought would last a lifetime, then jolted to the present by the sobering reality of the throbbing at the back of his head. He stood, took an ice-pack from the refrigerator and placed it on the lump before going upstairs.

MacLeod showered with a broad and satisfied grin on his face. It quickly disappeared when he thought of what had happened. He had mixed emotions. He had never imagined that sex could be that good again nor that he could be that unabashed and wild, but she was his employee. He had just spent the past twelve hours screwing around with one of his key staff members. He wondered how Kathleen felt about it and whether it was just a one-time fling to her. He hoped not but either way, it was going to change their relationship. He stood there under the warm jet of water thinking about his reputation as an upstanding knight of the realm and a Nobel laureate at that. What would people think? He laughed aloud. One thing was for sure; he had certainly been upstanding last night and this morning. He turned off the shower and broke into song, "When Irish eyes are smiling . . ." He toweled himself down and was back in the kitchen before Kathleen.

When she appeared, MacLeod asked her rather mischievously, "Coffee, tea or me?"

"Well there's a difficult choice, but right now I think I need tea, please," she said with a smile as she sat down opposite him.

They stared across the table at each other, then MacLeod leaned across and kissed her gently.

"You have certainly made me feel a lot younger, that's for sure. Last night, I became alive again and this morning, that was just incredible, and in the kitchen of all places." MacLeod glanced at the scratch marks on the floor. "In fact, as a permanent reminder, from now on when you misbehave, I will call you, Kitchen."

Kathleen shook her head and laughed. "Kitchen? Not a very romantic name, but as long as I don't have to cook."

"Well, not in a traditional sense anyway." They both smiled then MacLeod added, "I hope this is just the beginning."

Kathleen stretched across, held his hand tightly and said, "Oh, so there is a chance that this may be more than a meaningful, one-night stand?"

Francis laughed. "That's funny. Well I just hope that it develops into a long-term meaningful relationship, that's if you feel the same way."

"Absolutely I do, Francis."

MacLeod began to speak, but Kathleen put her forefinger over his lips and changed the subject.

"You seemed very pleased with yourself last night, what with all that upbeat news about Genon. You must be pretty excited about the new clinical trials."

"Well, to tell you the truth, I am excited" he paused . . . "but apprehensive. Tronavis have been pushing very hard to get started, I would have preferred to have conducted a few more animal experiments before conducting human trials on glaucoma gene therapy."

"But you have repeatedly proven the efficacy of the protocol, haven't you?"

"Oh, yes, it is well over eighty percent – a success rate of five out of six, but that still leaves a one-in-six chance of failure. Maybe I am just getting more risk-averse as I get older."

Kathleen balked at the last comment. "Francis, you are not getting older, you are fitter than most men half your age. My God, you have certainly proved that."

"If you say so, Kitchen."

Chapter 14

January, 2026

It had been seven years since MacLeod had discovered the genons for the genes related to early onset glaucoma and adult macular degeneration (AMD). When a glaucoma gene is mutated, the resulting protein can produce excess fluid, which in turn creates internal pressure leading to glaucoma.

Since the formation of Genon plc, Rob Elliott had carried out most of the animal studies on these genons because of his experience in cornea stem cell research.

Rob was a stereotypical Geordie, down to earth with a good sense of humor. An avid sports fan, he played soccer and cricket. His first loves, though, were Newcastle United and his motorcycle. He had an on-off eight-year relationship with his girlfriend Mary. Rob had been born in Gosforth Park, Newcastle-upon-Tyne, and spent all of his life in the city until moving to Cambridge to work for MacLeod.

For the past six months, Rob had been traveling to Basel, Switzerland to work closely with the Tronavis team who would be conducting the upcoming human trials on glaucoma gene therapy. He was there in mid-January to go over the protocol when Meier asked him to stop by before flying back to London.

Hans Meier was not a stereotypical Swiss German. He was as precise as Swiss clockwork, yes, and was always dressed immaculately, but driven by ambition, he was a consummate risk-taker. He learned English and French in high school. At eighteen, he did his two years in the Swiss Military, then attended the Université de Genève, graduating with honors in Biochemistry, followed by a two-year Master's degree in Pharmacology. His upbringing in St. Gallen had been very conservative compared to the cosmopolitan lifestyle he experienced during his five years in Geneva. By the time he had finished his education, he spoke fluent German, French, English, and Italian. He had rapidly climbed the ranks of Tronavis.

"Good to see you again, Rob. Please, have a seat," Meier said as Rob was ushered in by Anna. "How was your flight?"

"It landed on time and more importantly, it landed. Never been too keen on flying!"

"And how is Francis?"

"Seems in really good spirits these days. Something or someone is making him happy."

"That's good to hear. Well, the big day has arrived, not soon enough as far as I am concerned; I have been pushing Francis for years to get started on these trials."

"I know only too well about that," Rob said.

"So, tell me, Rob, forget Francis' conservatism for the moment. How confident are you about the protocol? After all, you must have conducted hundreds, if not thousands, of animal tests."

"I am very confident, especially if everybody follows the protocol to the letter, just as we have been doing back in Cambridge. The results on the beagles are probably as high a success rate of any trial I have ever been involved in, close to a ninety percent success rate is still not that common for any kind of trial."

"I agree," replied Meier. "I wish I could say that about some of our other trials. Well, in a few short months we'll know for sure if the genon protocols can fix these diseases." He shook

Rob's hand. "Say hello to Francis for me and we'll see you in a couple of months. Auf Wiedersehen."

On the flight back to London, Rob lay back in his seat with his eyes half-closed, thinking about Mary. They had met at the stem cell institute when they both worked there. A few weeks before Rob went to work for MacLeod, they talked about getting married. Neither of them had lived outside the northeast of England before, and it seemed that the talk of marriage would create a stronger bond, even though they would be apart. Almost every weekend after he first moved to Cambridge, Rob rode his motor-cycle north to spend the weekend with her. Some weekends, Mary would catch a train from Newcastle and spend the weekend with him in Cambridge. The visits became less frequent and, after six months, they broke up. A year later, they got back together; then broke up again. They had gotten back together again and then parted again a few months ago. But now he missed her and decided to travel up north this weekend.

He sat up in his seat with his eyes wide open when Meier's last few words popped into his head. 'Protocols, diseases. Plural?' What the hell did that mean? He settled back and reassured himself that glaucoma is a series of diseases, so that's probably what he meant; or maybe it was just simply the language difference.

Chapter 15

Basel, Switzerland

Two months later, Brenda received a call from Anna who asked if Rob was available, saying Meier urgently needed to talk to him. Rob was not in yet but Brenda said she would give him a message as soon as he arrived.

"Hans? Rob here. What can I do for you?"

"Get the first plane out to Basel. We need to talk," Meier said.

"What's going on?" Rob asked.

"Can't talk on the phone. Just get here as fast as you can."

Rob was in Meier's office by three o'clock; Meier looked ill. "How was your flight?"

"Never mind my flight. What's going on?" Rob asked.

Meier spoke deliberately. "I have some really good news and some really bad news. The glaucoma patients are doing well. In fact, in fifty percent of the subjects, we have a hundred percent sight-restoration success rate; the others are all heading in the same direction. However, in the case of the macular degeneration trials . . ."

"Macular degeneration . . . Macular degeneration trials, what in the hell are you talking about? You didn't. Don't tell me . . . ."

Meier just sat there.

" . . . Don't tell me you experimented with the AMD protocol."

89

Meier nodded.

"Shit, no . . . What exactly did you do?" Rob said.

"Well, when we screened the candidates for the glaucoma trials, about a third of them had either AMD or a combination of AMD and glaucoma and as you seemed so confident about the efficacies of the protocols we thought we could kill two birds with one stone, as it were, and decided to do a parallel trial on AMD."

"That's why you used the plural when I was here the last time; it bothered me when I thought about it later. Bloody hell, I should have figured it out."

"Plural, what are you talking about?" Meier asked.

"Forget it, it's not important. And so what happened?"

Meier told him. "But I am sure we can sort it out," he said with little conviction.

"That's not the bloody point! You were supposed to concentrate on glaucoma and nothing else. Wait 'til MacLeod hears about this. He'll hit the bloody roof."

"Well, that's why I asked you to come here, so I could tell you first and I was hoping you would be the one to tell Francis."

"Not on your bloody life, mate. And take the blame for you? He'll assume I must have known about it all along, but you didn't even hint to me that you planned to do that. And I can't believe you did it, especially when you know how cautious he has been about human trials." Rob shook his head. "This is a bloody night-mare!"

"What are we going to do, Rob?"

"We? You are going to tell Francis to his face, that's what! I dunno. Maybe I should call him and ask him to fly out here to review the results, and then we can meet with him together while you deliver the bad news. It won't be pretty."

After Rob called MacLeod, he insisted that Meier take him to see the blind man.

"This is Dr Elliott from the UK," Meier said as he introduced Rob to the blind man.

The blind man sat up in the bed and raised his arm in the direction of the visitors. Tears were forming in his eyes as he said something in Swiss German.

Rob turned to Meier. "What did he say?"

"He said, 'Can you help me, doctor?' Merde." Meier answered.

Rob winced as he scribbled some notes in his lab book and quickly left the room.

MacLeod arrived in Basel just before lunch the following day. He was ecstatic when he heard about the results of the glaucoma trial.

"I thought you would be pleased, Francis."

MacLeod looked over the report on the glaucoma trial that Meier had handed to him.

"Very impressive, Hans, better than I could hope for and such a relief because I have to say I was a little apprehensive. But this is just great, well done, let's go for lunch and celebrate."

Rob stared at Meier, who was avoiding eye contact.

Meier stood up and looked at his watch, hesitating, "Yes, lunch sounds good. Do you want to eat in the executive dining room or go into town?"

Rob was losing his patience; he wanted to get it over with, whatever *it* was going to be.

"Hans, tell him."

Meier started walking toward the door. "Let's eat first and discuss that after lunch."

"Tell me what?" MacLeod inquired.

"Tell him, Hans," Rob said.

When MacLeod heard the news, he turned white, sank back in his chair.

After a while, he said, "You stupid, stupid man, you have completely ruined my career and reputation." He stood up as if he was going to throw a punch at Meier but Rob grabbed him. MacLeod shook him off and lunged at Meier across his desk. Meier's chair fell backward and crashed to the floor. Meier's head banged against the chair-back and he rolled off the chair onto the floor, unconscious.

"Damn fool," MacLeod shouted.

Rob pushed MacLeod to one side and knelt down to check Meier – he was still breathing. Rob righted the chair and carefully eased Meier into a sitting position. When Meier came round a few minutes later, MacLeod was still seething.

"You had to push the damned envelope, didn't you? Despite all my caution. Well, you are just going to have to make this go away completely."

Rob stood between them ready to restrain MacLeod.

"Where are these people now? And who knows about this?" MacLeod demanded.

Meier, still shocked by MacLeod's violent behavior, rubbed the back of his head.

"The woman's family have taken her body for burial. They were perfectly reasonable and had been planning to put her into a special home for the blind, when they heard about the clinical trial. As part of the trial terms, there is an insurance clause, which of course we will be paying out to them."

"And what about the blind man?" MacLeod asked.

"He is still in our clinic and apart from us and the trials team nobody knows about it, except that he has been talking to a solicitor."

MacLeod paced up and down the room. "A solicitor? Hell's bells, that's all we damn well need. And what are we going to do about him?"

"I am not sure yet. Our legal team are trying to negotiate a temporary confidentiality agreement with him to see if we can come to some kind of settlement, but they are screaming medical negligence and demanding a full inquiry."

"If that happens, that's the end of Genon and everything I have worked for, all because of your damned stupidity."

"Let's take a walk, boss, and get a cup of coffee," Rob said as he opened Meier's office door.

Rob led MacLeod to the restaurant in the visitor's center and ordered a pot of tea for MacLeod and a cappuccino for himself. Before he even sat down, MacLeod unleashed on Rob.

"You had to know about this ahead of time and you said nothing; you are just as guilty as he is."

"I swear to you, Francis, I knew nothing about this before yesterday afternoon. It was as much of a shock to me as it is to you that Meier would do this without consulting either of us."

"Balderdash! I don't buy it for a minute," MacLeod said angrily.

"Listen, boss, you are wrong, but that's not important, what is important is how we fix it, or at least how Meier is going to fix it, so when we are finished let's go and talk in a civilized manner and make sure he does fix it."

When they got back to Meier's office, MacLeod had calmed down, but only a little.

"What options do we have?" he demanded.

Meier was ready with an answer. "I have thought about that and the only option is to negotiate a substantial settlement with his counsel as soon as possible."

"Damn it, Hans. Within another six months to a year, we probably could have cured him anyway if it hadn't been for your damned impatience. Do you think he will settle?"

"I believe he will, if we act soon."

"Okay. Do whatever it takes, and it's all on your nickel. And what are you going to do to prevent this from leaking out?"

"Well, fortunately, he lives in a very small mountain village about a hundred kilometers south of Basel, and those people don't get around all that much, so he shouldn't be a problem, as long as we can keep his solicitor from talking," Meier replied.

"This could turn out to be a right royal cock-up if word does ever get out. You talk about a damaged reputation, and you of all people. Weren't you the one who suggested to the media that I had an unblemished scientific reputation? Well, probably not for much longer!"

"Francis, I'll fix it!" Meier said.

"You damn well better."

Chapter 16

October 2026

The genon discovery program was moving along rapidly. Every Friday afternoon, MacLeod and VJ locked themselves in the central computer room to review any new research data. While VJ downloaded the new data from the researchers, MacLeod downloaded it onto his own database to analyze the new genons. One by one, he inserted the DNA sequences into their correct place on the chromosomes; it was like working on several very large jigsaw puzzles at the same time.

MacLeod looked at the latest data. Something was beginning to bother him. Most of the chromosomes were more than eighty percent complete. But there were two chromosome pairs that were only about fifty percent complete. Statistically, this was odd. He needed an explanation.

"We have a problem," MacLeod told VJ.

"What kind of problem?" VJ asked.

"Either missing data or lack of effort."

"I don't think it can be the latter, these guys are working around the clock."

"That's what I was afraid of. Somebody is holding back for some reason," MacLeod said.

After the setback with Tronavis on the AMD protocol, and despite MacLeod's conservative approach, the company was a great success; the glaucoma program had taken off quickly and the AMD therapy shortly followed.

However, the negotiations with the blind man's counsel dragged on. The greater the success of the genon therapy programs the greater the demand from the blind man's solicitor, who argued that Tronavis would not be enjoying such success if it were not at the expense of his client.

MacLeod watched the blind man walking slowly toward him with a white stick, then stumble and fall flat on his face. He tried to rush forward to help him, he couldn't. His legs wouldn't move. The blind man gingerly got back up on his feet and then waved his stick angrily in MacLeod's direction, who said, 'I am sorry, so sorry'.

"No, no, no," MacLeod screamed.

"Francis, what's the matter?" Kathleen woke up, startled by the outburst. "Are you okay?"

"I don't know, maybe something I ate at dinner, I am sorry I woke you."

Soaked in sweat and unable to get back to sleep, the failure of the unauthorized AMD trial still haunted MacLeod, who was painfully aware that no settlement had been reached with the blind man's solicitor.

For several months after the tragedy, MacLeod and Rob poured over the clinical trial data to determine what had gone wrong. They checked and re-checked the protocols to make sure that their carefully constructed procedures had been carried out to the letter.

"It's obvious what happened here," MacLeod said to Rob. "They mixed them up. The AMD protocol was trying to correct the faulty glaucoma gene, while the glaucoma protocol was trying to correct the faulty AMD gene. Instead of each gene being corrected, they became more defective, accelerating both diseases and causing death and premature blindness."

"Well, it's a relief to know it wasn't the protocols after all, but rather a sloppy mistake by the people carrying out the trial."

"That may be so," MacLeod responded, "but we are going to have to keep this to ourselves. If the blind man's solicitor discovers that Tronavis *has* been negligent, the world's media will have a field day."

"Agreed," Rob replied.

After the successful glaucoma trials, MacLeod approved a carefully constructed AMD clinical trial. The trial was a resounding success with the reversal of AMD in nine of the ten patients and a seventy-five percent recovery in the tenth. The second trial a few months later was equally successful.

In addition to the glaucoma and AMD programs, MacLeod's team extended the cystic fibrosis therapy program to patients clearly suffering from acute symptoms. Soon after the second AMD trial at Tronavis, the two companies negotiated a worldwide co-exclusive license agreement allowing Tronavis to commercially practice both glaucoma and AMD genon therapies. Genon would retain a sub-license to use the two protocols for non-commercial use. Tronavis paid Genon a ten-million-pound upfront license fee for each protocol with a ten percent royalty stream on future revenues

As news spread about the positive results of these new protocols, Tronavis, inundated with prospective patients wanting to be placed on a waiting list, capitalized on this opportunity by building a new genon/gene therapy clinic and spa in a mountainside resort not far from Basel. On opening day, MacLeod cut the ribbon and unveiled a plaque reading, 'The MacLeod Genon Clinic'. In June, the first forty patients arrived, each paying thirty thousand pounds for a six-day stay. At the end of June, Tronavis steadily increased the weekly intake to around a hundred patients a week, with an estimated eventual capacity of between two hundred and fifty to three hundred patients. By the end of October, they had already generated enough profit to offset the cost of the upfront license fees.

Genon received twenty million in license fees and £3.4 million in royalties from Tronavis, plus, by the year-end another £3.6 million in royalties. The company had also negotiated a ten million license deal with Prezfi for the cystic fibrosis protocol, bringing their income for the year to a projected thirty-seven million.

With Prezfi planning to start its own genon therapy program for cystic fibrosis in early 2027 and several more license deals in the making in addition to an increasing royalty stream, Genon forecast an income of around a hundred million in 2027.

The *Financial Times* ran a full-length feature article on the company, titled, *Genons, Going for Gold?* '*Genon, a Cambridge genetics company started by Noble laureate and entrepreneur, Sir Francis MacLeod, is on the verge of entering the big league with its exciting genon discovery and therapy programs*'.

Within hours of the story going live, MacLeod's phone was ringing off the hook from financial institutions wishing to meet with him to discuss an initial public offering (IPO). He and the financial director, Peter Coleman, together with the company's legal counsel, held several meetings with most of the top firms and eventually decided to go with KPMG.

The firm's senior consultant and his two auditors were looking at pictures on the wall of the conference room when MacLeod and Coleman, with Brenda tagging behind, entered.

"Nice to see you again, Sir Francis," the consultant said, as everyone introduced themselves. He quickly got down to business. "What are your projections for the next three to five years?"

"Next year, I believe we can expect income to be close to a hundred million and after that we will probably at least double every year or so," Coleman said.

"So, in two to three years your income should be in the five to six hundred million range? That's excellent," remarked one of the auditors.

"What does that mean in terms of how much money we can raise and the valuation of the company?" MacLeod asked.

"That depends on how much of the company you are willing to give up and at what share price. But with that level of income in a few years, I would put the valuation as high as ten times revenues or around five to six billion pounds. We can probably raise say, five hundred million at fifty pounds per share, and you would still own fifty percent of the shares."

"That means I would no longer have controlling interest in the company," MacLeod said. "I would prefer for that not to happen, if possible."

The auditor was fast on his feet. "Not a problem, sir. We could limit the raise to four hundred and fifty million, so that you would hang on to fifty-one percent."

"That sounds like a better plan to me. What do you think, Peter?"

"Whatever keeps you happy, sir," Coleman replied.

The senior consultant asked, "Sir Francis, can I ask why it is important for you to keep controlling interest? After all, you will be a very rich man when the IPO closes."

"In the next few years, I want to set up the clinics as joint ventures so that there is an equal share of the profits to fund new clinics, starting in Europe and the United States, and wherever they are needed. After that, I would like to set up non-profit clinics in third-world countries. If I lose controlling interest, I may not be able to get shareholder approval for non-profit investments. It's that simple, really."

"I see, okay, and of course the numbers that my guys are throwing around here are just ballpark figures because the final valuation and offering price will be determined shortly before we complete the final documentation, and how close you come to your forecast income. So let me move on to logistics and what role we will all be playing in this project." He went on to explain all of the information that they would need: research programs, milestones, patent valuations, key personnel profiles, financial projections, litigations, etc., a complete and thorough due diligence of the company's affairs.

When the meeting was over, MacLeod asked Brenda to book a table at Midsummer House for seven o'clock so that he could share the good news of the IPO with his staff.

Chapter 17

"Bring us a bottle of the 2020 Dom Perignon, please, Tony," MacLeod asked the Maître d' after the group had taken their seats at the table.

They toasted each other, and MacLeod explained all he had learned that afternoon about IPOs and what their role in it would be.

"KPMG's auditors will be conducting a thorough due diligence, whereby apart from examining the books etc., they will be spending a lot of time with each of us asking about our work and future research milestones and the like. But let me tell you what they believe the company valuation could be when we do the offering." MacLeod tapped his fingers on the table, faking a drum roll. "Between five and six billion pounds, which means each of you will be worth more than a hundred million on paper. Not bad for a few years of hard work."

They looked at each other in shock, and then Rob said, "A hundred million quid! That's . . . er . . . incredible!"

He and Darren high-fived while the others slapped each other on the back and shook hands with MacLeod.

After dinner, Darren asked everyone if they would like to stop by the Eagle for a celebratory nightcap. Ian declined, saying that he had promised to be home around nine. VJ said 'no' as he didn't drink anyway, and of course MacLeod and Kathleen were headed off to his place - they had told the others about their relationship six months ago.

That left Rob, who said, "Hey, I'll go, got nothing better to do anyway." And off they went to the Eagle with broad grins on their faces and arms across each other's shoulders.

Darren ordered two pints at the bar and carried them across to the table. "Cheers," he said to Rob.

"Cheers, mate," Rob replied. They both took a sip of beer and started laughing. The champagne, dinner wine and the general euphoria of the evening had made them giggly.

"Say, buddy, did you ever think when you were younger that one day you would be worth this much money?"

"Not in a hundred million years," Rob answered.

"That's funny. A hundred million. Sounds good, doesn't it? One - hundred - million."

"I know, it's surreal. I mean you hear about people winning that kind of money in the lottery but you never dream that one day you might be that rich, I get goose bumps thinking about it."

"I know what you mean. What are you going to do with it when you get it?" Darren asked.

"Well, it's not like I haven't thought about it. After all we were already sitting on twenty mill, at least on paper, but the first thing I will do as soon as some of the money hits my account will be to order a top-of-the-line Harley hog and then maybe a Jag, or even a Bentley or a Rolls."

Darren laughed. "Yeah, yeah, I can just see you driving through Geordie Land, past your old mates' houses, in a brand-spanking new Roller. That'll be a sight to see."

"Yeah, you're right; I should probably just stick to the Hog and Jag." They laughed again at the absurdity of it all. "Of course I will probably buy a new bungalow with all mod cons for my parents. How about you?"

"You know, when I was a kid growing up in Encinitas, my folks would often take me and my sister to La Jolla or San Diego on weekends and I would watch all those rich folks with their big yachts and large homes on the hillside. It was if they were from a different planet. I always dreamed of one day owning a seventy-footer, so that's going to be my first purchase, probably followed by a house on the hill," Darren mused. They both chuckled.

Rob went to the bar and brought back two more pints. "Hey Darren, there is something I have been meaning to ask for a while now, but I didn't want to show my ignorance in the meetings. If the company received two hundred and fifty million from the pharmaceuticals, and now will get another four hundred and fifty million from outside investors, that's seven hundred million. How can the company be valued at five to six billion?"

"It's easy, really. Whatever was the last price paid for the shares times all of the shares outstanding is the valuation. If people pay fifty pounds per share for ten million shares, then the previous issued shares, in this case a hundred million, are also worth fifty pounds per share, so a hundred and ten million in total times fifty pounds equals five and a half billion, it's that simple."

"Okay, I see. Thanks. I certainly didn't want to ask the auditors, either. So what's your take on what these guys will be doing around here and what will they need from us?" Rob asked.

"Oh, the usual things, digging into the science and checking out the company's intellectual property portfolio, what R and D milestones you are working toward, where you are at, and checking that you are keeping good records in your lab book, that kind of stuff, and making sure there are no hidden surprises."

Those last two words made the color drain from Rob's face.

"What's the matter, buddy? Are you all right?" Darren asked.

"Just a skeleton in the closet and if it gets out it may ruin it for all of us."

"What the hell are you talking about, – skeleton in the closet? What skeleton?"

"Can't say," Rob said.

"Hang on a minute." Darren went to the bar, brought back a brandy and gave it to Rob. "Down this."

Rob took the glass and finished off the brandy in one gulp.

"Okay Rob, we're a team here. If you know something that could catch me off guard, you better in the hell tell me."

"I can't. MacLeod swore me to secrecy. Besides, I probably overreacted."

"Bullshit. You're not leaving here until you tell me what in the hell is going on."

Feeling the effect of the brandy on top of the other drinks, Rob slurred, "Listen, Darren, if I tell you, you have to swear to God that you will not tell another living soul."

"I promise, I promise. Now what in the hell is it? Besides, you don't think for a moment I am going to risk a two hundred-million-dollar payday, do you? Now stop screwing around and tell me."

Slow and hesitant, Rob said, "Well, about eighteen months ago when we did the first glaucoma trials at Tronavis, unbeknownst to us, they did a parallel macular degeneration trial, and it went wrong."

"What do you mean, it went wrong?"

Rob had a grim expression on his face as he whispered into Darren's ear. "A seventy-five-year-old woman died and a fifty-three-year-old man went prematurely blind."

"Shit, they did? How?"

"The Tronavis people did an unauthorized AMD trial, and to make it worse they mixed up the protocols."

"And what happened?" Darren asked, moving in closer.

"Well, Tronavis paid off the woman's family with the insurance money but the blind man has a solicitor and he's threatening to sue for medical negligence."

Darren shook his head. "Shit, so why don't they settle and get it behind them?"

"They would, but he's playing hardball and keeps upping the ante; it's no secret, the success Tronavis is having."

"Look, I am sure Tronavis will settle it soon, there's too much to lose, and besides, the auditors aren't going to find out."

"They will if they go through my lab books."

Chapter 18

March 2027

Something about the results did not seem right to MacLeod. Most of the chromosomes were now almost complete – except for the same two. He asked VJ to meet him at the lab on Saturday morning so he could get into the computer room to analyze the data.

VJ was leaning up against the wall cleaning his fingernails with a small screwdriver when MacLeod appeared a few minutes after nine. They lined up in front of the automatic-entry door and pressed the button. A few seconds later, it unlocked and they stepped inside the interlock chamber as the entry door closed behind them. They waited for the customary twenty seconds for the inside door to open. Nothing happened.

"Strange," VJ said. "That has never happened before." He kept pressing the green button.

They exchanged a look.

VJ was nervous. "Let's try changing positions."

Still nothing happened.

MacLeod frowned. "So how in the hell do we get out of here?"

Starting to perspire, VJ pointed to a small intercom on the wall. "Call the lab for help."

"But nobody's around on Saturday. So now what?"

"Let me think for a minute. Maybe one of our chips has a low signal. The receptor chip is about five feet up the door frame, so if we can position our thighs two feet higher there might just be enough signal to open the door. Here, I'll go first, cup your hands and give me a leg up."

VJ removed his shoes, stepped on MacLeod's hands and lined up with the receptor. Nothing happened.

"Okay, let's switch places," VJ said as he cupped his hands for MacLeod to stand on.

"This is ridiculous," MacLeod said as he took off his shoes and stepped onto VJ's hands. After about ten seconds, the door clicked open. VJ sighed with relief.

"Okay, explain to me what happened. I'd be pretty upset if I suffered from claustrophobia."

"*Lucky you don't,*" VJ said under his breath. "I think the electromagnetic waves from all the equipment may have weakened our chips, and particularly yours because you have spent more time in here than me. We should probably order new ones."

MacLeod nodded then entered the secure code to access information about which pairs of chromosomes had been allocated to which scientists. Within seconds the groupings appeared. He stared at the screen. The two suspect chromosomes both had Darren's name alongside them, but the other three chromosomes in Darren's group were all over ninety-five percent complete.

He got up, walked across to VJ's work station, "How can I get into Darren's computer?"

"Only by getting a duplicate copy of his biochip and retinal scan," VJ answered. "Why?"

MacLeod hesitated. "Something's wrong, I need to take a quick peek at his data."

"Why not ask him? There may be a very simple explanation. Besides wouldn't you be going back on your word?"

"Yes, yes," MacLeod said. "Can you do it?"

"I can ask the specialist to make us a copy of his retinal scan and order another chip when I order new ones for us, but it will take a couple of weeks."

"Perfect, Darren is going over to a conference in San Diego in a couple of weeks. But before you order them come and see me in my office on Monday morning. I would like to add some features to our chips. Now, how are we going to get out of here?" MacLeod asked.

VJ laughed nervously. "I think we can get out, but we won't be able to get back in again until we get the new chips."

"Okay, and when you have them, I want you to look at the data entry patterns from the beginning, both by scientist and chromosomes."

"You're giving me access to all of the data? I thought you wanted to keep that to yourself."

"VJ, if I cannot trust you after all these years, who can I trust?"

"I'll take that as a vote of confidence."

"Good, let's get out of here."

Chapter 19

San Diego, April 2027

Darren arrived over the weekend to stay at his parents' home in Encinitas, recover from jetlag and rehearse the talk he was to give at the conference. He wanted to make some last-minute changes but knew he couldn't; MacLeod had crossed every 't' and dotted every 'i' before he left Cambridge.

On the Monday morning, as he mounted the stage and walked toward the podium, Darren looked out at the packed hall. He recognized former colleagues and friends in the audience. "Don't screw up," he said to himself.

He scanned the first row. MacLeod aside – it was the A-list of international geneticists.

The title of his talk - *Genons: Their Role and Functionality* – filled the large screens.

Matt Price watched from a distance and waited patiently until Darren finally broke free from the after-talk questions and made his way to the cafeteria for lunch. Matt approached Darren's table with a food tray and asked whether the seat was taken.

"No, it's all yours, buddy."

"Thanks, I'm Matt. Matt Price. Interesting talk you gave. I am curious, though, you never said how many genons you guys have discovered so far, is it a lot?"

Darren looked up from his food. "Sshh, it's a big secret, but nice try."

"Well, there are a lot of people interested in what you guys are doing and you're certainly generating a lot of buzz around here."

Darren looked up again. "Just for the record, who are *you*?"

"I'm an assistant professor at Harvard. I work for Vince Garret, the director of the Genetics Institute. You've heard of him, no doubt?"

"Of course, who hasn't? Always been a bit of a maverick, from what I've heard."

"Yeah, a lot of people think that but he's fun to work for and he still gets plenty of funding."

"So, how did you come to work for him?"

"I joined his second start-up company straight out of Harvard grad school and was one of the founder employees. Thanks to him I made a small fortune when the company went public. After that he went back to Harvard and offered me my current position and I accepted so that I could focus on my own research."

"What field?"

"Bacterial genetics."

"Hmm," Darren mumbled.

"Say, do you have any plans tonight? I'd like to buy you dinner."

"Nothing concrete," Darren answered, then suggested they meet at Happy Harry's, a restaurant bar he used to go to with his college friends when he attended CSUSD.

Happy Harry's, overlooking the marina, bustled with the young and the rich.

"Cool place," Matt remarked as he approached Darren, leaning on the veranda railing with a beer in hand, looking out at the ocean and the setting sun. Seagulls, swirling above, squealed loudly. Matt shook Darren's hand, and then pointed to the beer. "Another one?"

"Sure, thanks."

110

"So, how did you end up working for Genon?" Matt asked when he returned with two beers.

"Luck, I guess. My old professor at UCI got me a post-doc at Bath University. When that was finished, I managed to get a transfer to Cambridge and ended up working for MacLeod. Then he took me and my co-workers with him when he formed the company."

"I've heard a rumor that the company is going public in a few months, is it true?"

"Where did you hear that?"

"I'm not sure, but that kind of thing always leaks out."

"I guess it does, but you didn't hear it from me, okay?"

"Of course not. I guess you guys are going to make a lot of money when it happens?"

"So they say," Darren said smiling.

"That's great. Can I ask how much?"

"Around two hundred million dollars each and billions in MacLeod's case."

Matt had just taken a mouthful of beer. It went down the wrong way and he coughed and spluttered. "Two - hundred - million - dollars? Wow, I thought I had made out like a bandit when I got three mill."

"Well, it's only on paper for now, but hopefully it will all work out."

"And when it does, you'll spend it, no doubt."

Darren pointed to a yacht in the marina. "You see that seventy-footer? That's my dream right there."

"So, why don't you buy it? Surely you can borrow money against your future assets."

"I don't know anything about that and wouldn't know where to start. Anyway, all being well, in about six months from now I should have all the money I need. Another beer? And then maybe we can eat. The food is pretty good here." He went to the bar to get two more beers.

Matt, deep in thought, looked across the ocean at the sun sinking below the horizon.

Chapter 20

The next morning, Matt scanned the main conference hall, spotted Darren, and waited outside in the hallway to intercept him at the morning coffee break.

"Can we do dinner again tonight? I have something very interesting to tell you."

"About what?"

"Sorry, I don't have time right now. How about I meet you at Happy Harry's at seven?"

"Okay, seven it is then."

When Darren arrived, he saw Matt talking to someone on the verandah.

"Oh, hi, let me introduce you to Joe."

Darren and Joe exchanged greetings.

"Joe is going to show us around *your* yacht," Matt added.

"Yeah, right."

The yacht, more opulent than either Matt or Darren could have imagined, looked like a luxury hotel. Inside they found a first-class galley, dining room and lounge, all the rooms smelling of rich dark mahogany.

"It's magnificent, wouldn't mind this myself." Matt remarked.

Joe said, "It's only eighteen months old and hardly been used. The owner was diagnosed with pancreatic cancer four months after he bought it and died a few months later. His widow wants to get rid of it as soon as possible, memories you know, which is why the price is so reasonable."

In the master bedroom, Darren flopped onto the large circular bed, looked at his reflection in the mirrored ceiling, and imagined cruising around South America and the Caribbean with his buddies, and maybe a girl or two. His youthful fantasies could soon be a reality.

"So?" Matt asked.

"Oh, just day-dreaming," he jumped up quickly and thanked Joe. "One day, maybe."

"Dreams can come true," Matt offered, regretting the phrase as soon as he said it.

"Yep, maybe so. Let's get a beer and you can tell me what you were so secretive about this morning."

"Well, I talked to some people who advance money to insiders in exchange for IPO shares. They are willing to give you twenty million dollars in return for twenty million of Genon stock at the time of the IPO."

Darren smiled awkwardly at Matt. "Well, thanks, I appreciate you doing that, but I think I can wait for another six months."

"Sure is a nice vessel," Matt remarked. "Why wait?

"Twenty million dollars, you said. It's tempting. I could buy the yacht and a house now, but why would anyone risk that kind of money? What's the catch?"

Matt started to reel him in. "There isn't any, except that you will have to sign an agreement to deliver twenty million dollars of shares within thirty days after the IPO. After that, you just have to give them first option on any other future liquidation of your shares. As for the details, as soon as you review the agreement and sign it, the funds will be available within forty-eight hours."

Darren asked, "Tell me, why would anyone want to lay out that kind of money, six months ahead of time and at no interest, when they could purchase shares on the open market at the time of the IPO?"

"You see, that's the thing. The IPO is being brokered in England and usually the firm's own clients get first dibs on the offering shares, so it is more than likely that nobody else will get in on it. Besides, these people are gamblers and risk-takers. They obviously feel that the Genon stock will be worth having, betting that the stock will appreciate after the IPO."

"I don't know, Matt. I would love to own a yacht like that, but I'm not comfortable trading my Genon shares, I'm not even sure it's legal."

"Listen, tomorrow morning go to the Bank of America offices downtown. There will be an agreement all ready for you to sign. Here's the bank officer's name." He handed Darren a piece of paper. "He'll go over it with you and if you're satisfied, open up your own account. By Friday, the money will be deposited in your name and the yacht could be yours by the weekend."

"I don't know, Matt, let me think about it and I'll call you tomorrow."

Darren's father didn't know the answer to the question but he gave him the name of an attorney friend. "Tell him who you are and he'll give you some free advice."

Darren hung up the phone after talking to the attorney, his mind working overtime.

He couldn't sleep. Several times during the night, he switched on the TV trying to take his mind off the yacht. It was a waste of time. He got up before five, dressed, made a cup of coffee and headed down to the marina.

At seven, he called Matt. "I talked to an attorney last night. He told me the only way to do this legitimately is in the form of a promissory note and in the note I promise to pay back the twenty million dollars in cash or equivalent; the equivalent in this case being Genon shares. So that part might be doable. But the bad news is, after an IPO there is a lock-up period of ninety days for insiders, so the offer as it stands is not possible."

"I understand. Let me work on that after breakfast then I'll call you."

Two hours later, Matt called back. "Darren, you outsmarted the big boys. They agree to ninety days because they don't want any trouble with the SEC, so they are going to instruct the bank to make the changes. All you have to do is go there later today and get the ball rolling."

By late Friday afternoon, the paperwork was complete and Saturday morning Darren would take possession. He spent the rest of Friday calling as many of his friends and family as he could reach, inviting them to a party on Saturday evening. He also invited Matt.

A group of close friends and family members stood on the deck drinking beer and wine and munching on chips and salsa as Darren led them in groups of four or five to tour the inside of the vessel. The five guest cabins were decorated in different themes, replicas of rooms at some of the world's finest hotels: George V, Paris; Gleneagles, Scotland; Oriental, Bangkok; Raffles, Singapore; and Mount Nelson, Cape Town. Finally, Darren showed them the master suite.

"Looks like the presidential suite at the Ritz Carlton in Dana Point," One of the guests said.

"Stayed there, have you?" another asked.

"Yeah, several times, but that was a long time ago, in the good old days of the dot-com boom."

Darren led the last group back to the deck and grabbed himself a beer, weary of the phony 'oohs' and 'aahs' and references to posh hotels.

Small groups gathered in intimate conversation with a common theme. How could their former surfer-buddy suddenly afford such a classy toy?

Matt blended into the background but overheard the main topic of conversation.

In a matter of minutes the sun faded and ominous dark clouds appeared.

Darren clanged a bell for attention. "Looks like some unusual weather heading our way, so we'd better get this over quickly."

He had asked his mother if she would carry out the ceremonial re-naming of the vessel.

His father turned to his wife and said, "I'll bet he's going to name it after you."

"Vicky? I doubt it," she replied.

"Not Vicky, but Victoria – like royalty. Very appropriate I think."

Taking his mother's hand, Darren led her down the gangplank onto the quayside. She nervously stepped forward as he released the rope with the bottle of French vintage champagne tied to it and placed it in her cupped hands. He then took a carefully prepared speech out of his shirt pocket and held it up for her to read. Guests stretched their necks over the railings to watch.

Darren's mother shook her head as she handed the bottle back to him while she took out a pair of reading glasses and put them on.

She stepped forward again and gingerly grasped the bottle of champagne. She read the speech out aloud. "I name this ship *Eagle II*. May God bless her and all who sail in her." She propelled the bottle toward the bow. There were muted gasps when the bottle didn't break.

Chapter 21

Two weeks after VJ had ordered the new biochips, the specialist came by Genon to implant them.

VJ examined the tiny microchips. "These are so much smaller than the others. They do have the added features that MacLeod requested, right?"

The specialist nodded. "That's modern technology for you. Smaller is better; well, at least in this case."

"Ha, okay, let's go to MacLeod's office and get this over with."

After the implants were inserted in their upper left shoulders and the specialist left, MacLeod asked VJ, "Do you have Darren's yet?"

"His chip? Yes, but not the retinal scan, it's complicated. Probably another week."

"I see. Then let's make good use of our time."

They spent the next three days in the central computer room. VJ worked on the new algorithm while MacLeod studied the data. "By my calculation we have now accounted for around ninety percent of human DNA. It would be more if it wasn't for those two chromosomes. What in the heck is Darren up to?"

"We'll know soon enough."

By the third morning, VJ had finished the algorithm and was ready to run the program. They both stared curiously as the time-based graphs came to life on the screen. Twenty-one of the twenty-three chromosome pairs showed a consistent pattern toward completion.

MacLeod shook his head as he pointed to the screen. "Look at that, all twenty-three were tracking together until about a year ago. It's odd. Can you run the algorithm for each scientist?"

"Sure," VJ clicked to another program.

Again, they stared at the screen. The data from all of the scientists were similar in the earlier years, but then Darren's data started to trail off.

"Well, there is only one way to find out and that is to get into his computer and see if there is any other data there. When does he return from San Diego?"

"Wednesday, I believe, and back into work on Thursday."

"Okay, as soon as you get a copy of his scan we'll take a look."

* * * * *

While the others were out to lunch on Monday, MacLeod and VJ sneaked in to Darren's office. VJ lined up the biochip and the retinal scan. It only took him a few seconds to get into Darren's database and start downloading it into the central computer.

"Will Darren know that we have downloaded his data?" MacLeod asked.

"No, not at all, because it will still be there on his hard drive. He won't even know his computer has been switched on while he was gone," VJ said.

"Come on, come on," MacLeod said.

VJ gave a thumbs-up. They hurried out of Darren's office and headed back to the central computer room, passing Rob and Ian on the way.

"Good lunch?" MacLeod asked.

"Yeah, pot pie and a pint at the Eagle," Ian answered.

MacLeod watched as the data appeared. He was shocked by what he saw. Darren's two chromosomes started to fall into line with all of the others, showing a ninety-five percent completion rate.

"He has deliberately withheld this. But why?" MacLeod spent hours poring over the data.

VJ shrugged his shoulders as he looked at the time. "How much longer are you going to be? Imelda is expecting me home for dinner by seven."

"It's probably going to take me several more hours, it can wait until tomorrow. Meanwhile I want to see his lab books. Do you know where they are?"

"In his office safe. Before you ask, yes, I can get access."

"In that case, let's retrieve them so I can take them with me."

* * * * *

When MacLeod arrived home, Kathleen had dinner and a bottle of red wine waiting. Over the meal, MacLeod confessed to her what he'd been doing in the lab.

"I was reluctant to do it but it became obvious he was hiding something. Any idea why he would?"

"It doesn't seem like him," she said. "There obviously has to be a good reason."

After dinner, MacLeod went into his study to read Darren's five lab books. He scanned each lab book quickly until he got to number three, which he studied closely.

He jumped out of his chair and opened the study door. "Kathleen, come in here, I think I know what's going on." He showed her the notes in the lab book.

"There are two things. First, the sneaky bugger has identified two whole new groups of genons associated with

120

testosterone and DHT regulation. He might have found the genetic remedy to male hair loss and erectile dysfunction."

"Really? That would be huge."

"Maybe, but why withhold the data?"

"It's always possible he has been checking and double checking his work to make absolutely sure before he passed it on."

"I don't think that's the explanation. Perhaps he is secretly developing the genon therapy for his own use."

"Could be," Kathleen said. "After all, he has started to thin out on top."

MacLeod smiled as he unconsciously brushed his fingers through his hair, and then said, "It seems he has also had his group doing a lot of experiments on the testosterone and DHT genons with mice. I certainly didn't know about that, did you?"

"Why would I? All of our groups are working independently. You said there were two things, what's the other?"

MacLeod frowned. "The second thing is far more serious. Someone in the blood pool has two mutated copies of the Parkinson's gene, which means one of us is at high risk of getting the disease."

"Oh, my God, that's awful, I wonder who. Are you going to say anything to the others?"

"Probably not, we are still a long away off with a Parkinson's therapy. Look, I am going to spend a couple of hours in here going through his notes. If you want to stay and have an early night, I'll see you at breakfast."

As soon as Kathleen left the study, MacLeod started poring over Darren's records; he kept studying the Parkinson's data, odds of one in six, he had his suspicions but there was nothing he could do about that right now. He focused on the other data and was surprised how well Darren's team had demonstrated the successful regulation of testosterone and DHT levels. There were photographs of old mice with thick crops of hair and other physical signs of a successful genon therapy trial. Really good work, he thought to himself. There was no apparent explanation why Darren had kept this to himself. All he could do was to wait until Darren returned on Thursday and confront him.

The following morning, MacLeod gave Darren's lab books back to VJ to return to the safe, and then he spent the rest of the day and all day Wednesday studying his almost complete human genon jigsaw puzzle. It confirmed his original hypothesis. Between them they had discovered no fewer than fifty thousand genons, so there must be the same number of genes. He did the calculation: the combined sequences of DNA for both genons and genes and other DNA sequences, such as transposons, would eventually account for ninety percent of human DNA.

In deep thought, he leaned back in his chair, drumming his fingers on the desk. His mind, like a pin ball machine, resounded and rebounded with thoughts he couldn't quite grasp. "It will come." He made a phone call, allowed himself a self-satisfied smile, got up, and strolled down the corridor to see Kathleen.

She looked up from her paperwork. "You are looking pleased with yourself, what's up?"

"I think a celebration is in order so I have booked a table at Midsummer House for seven."

"Tell me what kind of celebration,"

"Later."

At the restaurant, Tony poured champagne, and after they had clinked glasses MacLeod smiled at Kathleen and said, "I was right all along. Every piece of DNA has a purpose and by the time we are finished we will prove it."

"I never doubted it for a moment, a complete genetic code."

"Clang, clang," he could hear the sound of the pin ball machine in his head. He grasped it.

"What is it?" Kathleen frowned.

"We're on the verge of having the recipe for perfect DNA."

"Jesus, Mary and Joseph. I didn't see the implications, does that mean that one day it might be possible to make a perfect human being?"

"Not one day, but soon."

Kathleen's jaw dropped as she stared across the table at MacLeod. It was one of those rare moments; her mouth was wide open but there was no sound.

Chapter 22

After dinner, they went back to his place. MacLeod wasn't the least bit tired. He wanted to review his notes one more time. Kathleen, yawning, went off to bed. It was after midnight when MacLeod finally entered the bedroom and saw Kathleen sound asleep. He quietly crept into bed and tried to settle in but he couldn't; he was fidgety and kept tossing and turning. He could not get the enormity of his discovery out of his head.

His restlessness woke Kathleen. "Are you okay?"

"Can't sleep."

Kathleen stroked his cheek and he put his arm around her shoulder. She kissed him gently; they made love and then fell asleep.

MacLeod woke suddenly at six thirty a.m. and quietly got up. He put on his sweats and a T-shirt to go for a jog. When he returned, Kathleen was sitting at the breakfast table. MacLeod kissed her then went to the fridge and poured himself a glass of orange juice. He sat down beside her.

Kathleen spoke first, "I have been sitting here thinking about what you told me last night. It's incredible to believe that perfect DNA can exist."

MacLeod nodded. "I know, but there is no other way to explain the fifty thousand genons that we have discovered so far. They can only exist if there is the same number of genes."

"My first biology professor Dr Silverman would readily agree with you. He taught with great conviction the belief at the time. 'One gene, one protein,' He was never the same after the government published the results of the Human Genome Project. There was no scientist on this planet more shocked than he was. I wish he was still around to witness this, he was a terrific scientist and a great tutor."

"I believe it. I was at Genentech; everybody was surprised at the findings."

"But do you know what amazes me?" Kathleen said, "People just blindly assumed that because it was a government-backed project the conclusions must be true. What BS. Jesus, you talk about a modern flat-earth society, this was far worse."

"Well, it's not the first time and I am sure it'll not be the last."

"I'll bet you can't wait to tell the others."

MacLeod got up, poured himself a cup of coffee and put some whole-wheat bread in the toaster. He leaned against the kitchen sink, stared at the scratch marks on the floor and smiled. "I am thinking of taking the staff away this weekend as a celebration of the progress we've made, so I'll probably wait until then to tell them."

"And what about Darren?"

"Yes, I need to deal with that first." He kissed her again and went upstairs to shower.

Kathleen stood up and cleared the table.

Chapter 23

"Welcome back, Darren. How was the conference?" MacLeod asked.

Taking a quick gulp of coffee, Darren told him that his talk had generated a lot of interest in their work.

"Let me get right to the point. I need an update from you on the chromosome data. How much have you downloaded so far?" MacLeod asked.

Darren's face turned red. "Not all of it, I was holding back some data for further verification."

"Okay, Darren, I am going to say this one time. We are a team here and if you ever do anything like that again I am going to throw your arse into the river Cam and you can forget about your Genon stock. Have I made myself clear?" MacLeod said.

Darren's mouth was bone dry and his voice croaked when he spoke. "Yes, very clear. How did you know?"

"Go straight back to your office and download all your data to the central computer. Everything. Now, if you don't mind, I have other things to attend to."

Once outside of MacLeod's office, Darren took a deep breath, relieved that MacLeod had not found out the real reason why he had withheld the data on the testosterone and DHT genons.

MacLeod called Brenda into his office and told her to reserve rooms at the Bell Hotel in Thetford for Saturday night and a conference room for Sunday morning.

"Tell everyone we will meet in the bar for cocktails at seven and then dinner. Oh, and while you're at it, book a table for six in the King James Restaurant for eight o'clock. Thanks."

MacLeod called VJ and told him to meet him at the central computer lab to review Darren's work again. He was tempted to share his new hypothesis with VJ, but he controlled that impulse. After all, he hadn't made up his mind whether the others should know.

Later that evening, Darren, sprawled out on his sofa at home drinking beer, debated whether he should make the call to the US. It was after nine o'clock local time and after four on the East Coast when he decided. A secretary told him that her boss was on another call but she would have him call when finished.

Ten minutes later, Darren's phone rang. "Hello, Darren, how are you?"

"Fine, thanks. Listen, the reason I was calling, was to tell you that I had no choice but to download the testosterone and DHT data to MacLeod today; he figured out that I was holding back on him."

"Man, that guy really gets in my craw, but one of these days he is going to fall from that lofty pedestal of his. How did he find out?" the caller asked.

"To be honest, I think it was pure guesswork, but he doesn't know about all of the successful mice experiments because that information is in my lab book and locked in the safe," Darren said.

"Well, at least that's something. When can I see that stuff? There is nothing I'd like better than to kill two birds with one stone; embarrass MacLeod and ruin Prezfi's Viagra market."

"I don't know, but now is not the right time. You need to be a little more patient. I know you're eager to start human trials, but I cannot risk MacLeod finding out. There's too much at stake."

"I know, I know, okay. By the way, how was San Diego? I'm sorry I couldn't make it this time to see you."

"It was great. My talk seemed to go down very well; there was a lot of interest in Genon."

"I am sure there was, and what about the rest of your stay?" the caller asked.

"It was great, family and friends and that sort of thing, relaxing," Darren answered.

"Good for you, and don't forget I am anxious to see that data." The caller hung up.

"Damn!" Darren picked up a cushion from the sofa and rapidly hammered his fist into it then threw it across the room in a fit of temper. It had not been a good day.

Chapter 24

When Francis and Kathleen entered the bar at 7.25 on Saturday evening, the others were already there. Ian was telling them some of the history of the hotel.

"This old coaching inn dates back to the fifteenth century and is one of the most haunted sites in England," he said. "In 1750, Betty Radcliffe, the landlady at the time, committed suicide after a tiff with her lover. Many hotel guests claim to have seen her ghost roaming through a nearby corridor, wringing her hands in a state of anguish and utter misery. The inn has been on TV a lot, paranormal investigations and that sort of thing; not that I personally believe in any of that nonsense."

"Doo, doo – doo, doo; doo, doo – doo, doo; it's déjà-vu all over again," Darren said.

Kathleen turned to MacLeod with raised eyebrows. "Wait until they hear what you are going to tell them tomorrow."

* * * * *

MacLeod got up early the next morning and went for a jog through the surrounding villages.

Kathleen got up shortly after and went to Mass, something she hadn't done in years. During the dreary sermon at St. Mary's Catholic Church, she stared up above the altar at the impressive 1835 painting of the Nativity by James Parry. She

129

knew why she had come to church today. It was the dream she'd had in the middle of the night. In it, she was standing before the priest in a beautiful handmade white satin and lace dress, making her first communion at the age of seven. Her mother and father were smiling behind her. It caused her to pause. Her parents were now in their late seventies, and she hadn't visited them since JP had been made a cardinal.

After the IPO, she thought to herself, she would be able to repay them for everything they had done. Repay some of the money they had spent on her studies. She felt guilty that they had very little left to spend on themselves.

She shuffled in her seat then glanced at her watch. The priest was only three or four minutes into his sermon, droning on and on. This was one of the reasons she didn't go to church very often these days. When they were not making a pitch for money, which happened all too often, the priests seemed to pick one theme like, 'Why did Jesus Christ die on the cross for you?' then dissect that question ten different ways. By the time they were only half-way through, most of the congregation had switched off.

Kathleen thought about her older cousin JP – Cardinal John Patrick Murphy – who not long after his fifty-third birthday, was transferred to Rome. And then, just six months later, he was the only cardinal to be a member of the Pontifical Academy of Sciences. Kathleen was very proud of her cousin, but would he be proud of her? Probably not. After all, this was only the second or third time she had been to Mass since she last saw him.

Her eyes closed in reflection, Kathleen's mind wandered from religion to science and then back to religion. Jesus Christ died on the cross for our sins. Did he? According to the New Testament he did, but what proof do we have? He performed miracles. Were they really miracles or was he a clever magician? Was he really the son of God? He was crucified for his teachings, we are told, but again, where's the proof? The Shroud of Turin has the bloody image of a crucified man; was it Christ's image? It is so controversial and one of life's greatest mysteries. Is it real? Kathleen was skeptical. Was that heresy?

She looked up at the pulpit but had no idea what the priest was talking about. She looked down to hide her uneasiness.

The priest interrupted her embarrassment when he said loudly, "We believe in one God . . ." The beginning of the Creed.

Before the final blessing, Kathleen got up from the pew, bowed her head and genuflected. She dipped her fingers in the font, quickly made the sign of the cross and hurried out of the church. She got back to the hotel just as MacLeod finished breakfast. She joined him for a cup of coffee.

Darren, Ian and Rob, hung over from the night before, hurried into the restaurant around eight thirty and helped themselves to a full English breakfast with lots of tea.

By a few minutes after nine, everyone assembled in a small conference room in the older part of the building.

MacLeod sat at the far end with Kathleen directly opposite. "There is something I shared with Kathleen a few nights ago ---"

Darren leaned over and whispered into Rob's ear, "His bed."

Rob snickered.

MacLeod continued, "And now I want to share this with the rest of you. First of all, with all of the latest downloads now in the system," he glanced toward Darren, "It looks like we have discovered well over ninety-five percent of the estimated genons. I have spent a lot of time looking at the data and what I am about to tell you now is rather extraordinary, but credible."

MacLeod restated his original hypothesis that all DNA must have a purpose, which contradicted everything the

131

scientific community had been saying for more than twenty-five years.

"Since the Human Genome Project we know that one gene can produce several different proteins and on average about five, which accounts for approximately a hundred thousand proteins. However, we now know there are fifty thousand genons and based on our belief of one genon, one gene, there has to be the same number of genes. However, we have a little problem because so far we have only matched between three to four thousands of them to known genes and only forty to fifty to new genes. This last piece of data is not statistically significant, so our next challenge is to identify more new genes. But let me come back to that later."

MacLeod took a sip of water. "If we assume we are right and we extrapolate the average number of base pairs of genes and genons, together with transposons, etc., their total will account for ninety percent of human DNA. And the reason most of it is not functioning in its present form is because it has changed or been mutilated over time. However, if with time, we can correct all mutated genes with our genon therapy, we will have a fully functional human genome with extraordinary powers and capabilities."

He paused for a moment to let it sink in, deciding to hold back on his hypothesis and instead focus on the fact that there was no such thing as junk DNA.

"Lady and gentlemen, every piece of DNA has a specific purpose."

They were quiet as they absorbed what MacLeod had just said. Rob broke the silence.

"And what is your definition of a specific purpose?"

"That every single piece of human DNA has a dedicated function."

"And?" Kathleen was waiting for the punch line.

MacLeod ignored her.

"Francis, we're waiting."

The others looked at each other with blank expressions.

MacLeod ignored her for a second time as he unscrewed the cap from a bottle of sparkling Malvern water and filled his glass. He watched the bubbles floating to the top, and then stood up. He handed each of them a copy of two lists that he had prepared for the meeting.

"Let's examine these."

I

a) Ability to spend several hours under water.

b) Hibernate for months.

c) Run faster than a racehorse.

d) See in the dark.

e) Fly.

"There are other species that can do these things!"

II

a) Hear conversations hundreds of yards away.

b) Be in two places at the same time.

c) Read other people's thoughts.

d) Teleport.

e) Levitate.

"There are people who claim that they can do these things!"

"The point is, that through the natural process of evolution man may achieve some or all of these capabilities, and many more, in the years to come. I believe, however, that we have the means to accomplish these things in the near future, and that puts a huge responsibility on our shoulders."

Kathleen leaned over to VJ and whispered in his ear, "I would like to talk to you after the meeting." VJ nodded

MacLeod continued. "However, before we can convince everyone that all DNA has a purpose, we need to identify more new genes, at least several thousand. So, for the next few months I want you to put your genon discovery programs on hold and focus all of your staff's attention on gene discovery."

"Wow, hours under water without an oxygen tank, how cool would that be?" Darren said.

"Or read other people's thoughts," Rob added, "and get inside that crazy head of yours!"

"And you'd find out how much brighter I am than you, smart ass."

As the others were jibing back and forth and packing up their things to go to lunch Kathleen took MacLeod to one side.

"Why didn't you tell them about your real hypothesis?"

"I am not sure, really. Maybe I will over lunch."

* * * * *

Everyone was talking at once about MacLeod's revelations, and then halfway through lunch, Kathleen shouted a little too loudly.

"Jesus Christ, Jesus Christ!"

MacLeod, slightly embarrassed, quickly interrupted her. "You shouldn't be taking the Lord's name in vain, especially in public."

"Let me explain, Francis. What I was going to say was Jesus Christ single-handedly changed the course of religion and now billions of people around the world follow his teachings. And for over a thousand years, his more zealous followers have been trying to find the chalice from the Last Supper. In recent times their attention has turned to what was in the chalice – his blood, and theories abound that there may be a bloodline. Some even suggest that Jesus Christ married Mary Magdalene and they had a child."

134

"So what?" Ian said, shrugging his shoulders.

She ignored him and continued. "These zealots have all missed the point. It's not the chalice, nor is it what was in the chalice – his blood. It's what was in his blood – his DNA. If we now believe that there is such a thing as perfect DNA – then that's it. Perfect DNA, a flawless genetic code. *Jesus Christ."*

MacLeod stared at her, thinking, "How dare she reveal *my* hypothesis of perfect DNA."

"So what are you implying?" Ian said.

"I am not implying anything other than the fact that if perfect DNA does exist then Jesus Christ was the human manifestation of it."

"What a load of balls. How could his DNA be perfect?" Ian countered. "I can buy into the idea that if you believe in God, Christ's DNA might have been fifty percent perfect because he inherited one copy of DNA from his father but the other half from his mother. His genome would therefore be a combination of divine DNA and human DNA, which may explain that if *He* did have divine powers, he also had human weaknesses."

This time, MacLeod interrupted, clearly irritated with Kathleen. "Okay, you two; stop the squabbling. It's a fascinating topic and I am sure it's going to open a whole new can of worms, but that debate is for another time and another place."

MacLeod got up from the dining table and stormed out. Kathleen raised her eyebrows.

After lunch, she took VJ to one side to talk to him about the Hindu Siddha tradition, and the legends of yogis being able to transport themselves to other places, stay under water for long periods, use powers of telepathy, to read thoughts and communicate with birds and animals.

VJ admitted that he did not have any personal experience but recounted a tale of a cousin who had taken a boat across a lake to an island to visit an old chapel. His cousin and a friend had hired a boat from the local village and rowed the half-mile journey to the island to visit the sacred chapel inhabited by a solitary yogi. He gave them a tour and pointed out various venerable artifacts and holy paintings, and then sat with them in meditation for fifteen minutes. When the tour was over, the yogi waved them goodbye and closed the chapel door behind them. They headed straight to the shore and rowed back to the village. As they walked up the ramp from the jetty, there he was, the same yogi sitting on a bench some fifty yards ahead of them.

"My cousin was flabbergasted, but her friend said that yogis could do that sort of thing, bi-locate and teleport themselves. My cousin swears to this day that there was no other explanation."

"Did you believe her? Kathleen asked.

"As a matter of fact I did. When I was a little boy in Hyderabad my grandfather told me about tales of the yogis and all of their mystical powers. But why are you all of a sudden interested in the Hindu religion and Siddhis?"

"Well, since Francis's revelation this morning and the potential of us having undiscovered genes that may give us extraordinary capabilities, I cannot get perfect DNA and Jesus Christ out of my head."

"I have to admit," VJ said, "your hypothesis completely blew the wind out of Francis' sails. He seemed to be a bit ticked off that you revealed, then trumped his hypothesis."

"Well, he shouldn't be, because what I am suggesting is based on his work. Anyway, I appreciate this discussion and I would like to talk to you in more depth over the next few weeks, after we have satisfied Francis."

"Sure," VJ replied. "Any time. It's an exciting subject, genetics, religion and the paranormal, and as Francis said, it's probably going to open up a whole new can of worms."

Kathleen smiled. "Better go, Francis is mad enough at me already."

Chapter 25

Kathleen tried several times to apologize and make up to Francis for upstaging him in front of his staff. MacLeod ignored her attempts, suggesting he was far too busy to get involved in any further arguments and didn't want to discuss it. She knew what that meant.

Kathleen desperately needed someone as a sounding board to have a meaningful discussion, or to be more exact, to listen to her point of view about her conclusion that if perfect DNA does exist, Jesus Christ was the human manifestation of it. But who? Ian is an Atheist, VJ is a Hindu and Darren and Rob are not interested in religion and would just mock her as usual.

Then it dawned on her, who better than her mentor and cousin JP now a cardinal and a member of the prestigious and secular Pontifical Academy of Sciences.

The PAS, as it is known, has its roots in the original Academia dei Lincei, founded in Rome in 1603 by Prince Federico Cesi; it is the oldest scientific academy in the world. But, despite the fact that it received international recognition, especially with the appointment of Galileo Galilei as a member in 1610, it did not survive the death of Federico Cesi. However, more than two hundred years later in 1847, and within one year of becoming pope, Pius IX reestablished the Academy, renaming it the Pontifical Academy of New Lynxes. Then in 1936 Pope Pius XI renewed and reconstituted the Academy and gave it its present name, the Pontifical Academy of Sciences.

Since the early 1900s it has had over fifty Nobel laureates who have served as members, names such as Lord Ernest Rutherford (Chemistry), Guglielmo Marconi (Physics) and Sir Alexander Fleming (Physiology). In recent times eighty men and women constitute an elected body of Academicians, these have included David Baltimore (Biologist), Stephen Hawking (Physicist) and Francis Collins (Geneticist), the former Director of The Human Genome Project.

JP couldn't have been happier when he was elected as a member of the PAS, six months after arriving in Rome. It gave him the opportunity to immerse himself in science, and in particular his passion for biology, attending PAS meetings with internationally acclaimed Academicians and conversing with them after the formal meetings about the latest developments in their field of interest. JP became a prolific writer of scientific papers focusing mainly on the interaction and education of the public's understanding of science and its relationship to religious values. After fifteen months as a member he was promoted, and appointed by the Holy Father, to Chancellor of the Academy. Together with the Academic President, who is also appointed by the Holy Father to a four-year term, they are responsible for setting the goals and agenda of the Academy.

Although they had exchanged letters from time to time, discussing mainly family and job-related matters - JP was always very interested to hear the latest on her work and relationship with MacLeod - Kathleen was unaware of her cousin's latest appointment.

Kathleen called her cousin and got his voicemail, she left a message saying she wanted to discuss a scientific matter with him, she didn't want to alarm him that it might be a family illness. He called back several hours later. Kathleen was just getting out of the shower when her phone rang, she answered and when she realized it was JP she immediately grabbed a towel and wrapped herself, she couldn't speak to a cardinal while standing naked, even if he was her cousin. She told him if it was okay with him she would call back in seven or eight minutes, he agreed.

JP was reading in his study when Kathleen called back and said, "Sorry about that, I was just getting out of the shower. Anyway, how are you?"

"Very well, thanks, and pretty busy, especially with a PAS conference scheduled for next week, how about you, have you set a date yet?"

"Afraid not, but hopefully one of these fine days." Kathleen quickly changed the subject. "So what is the topic for next week's conference, anything interesting?"

"Yes, I think so, it is titled, 'How to Further the Participation and Benefits of Science and Technology into Third World Countries.' The Church feels that the developed world is not doing enough in places like Africa to reduce disease and develop a better quality of healthcare, so the people live longer and happier lives."

"It sounds like an interesting topic and the trick will be trying to get commitments to do something at long last, it has been an issue for decades, and it doesn't seem any further forward."

"I agree, but at least we are trying. So, how are things at your end? Is the job still as exciting as it was and are you making good progress? You said in your voice message that you had a scientific matter to discuss with me, what is it?"

"The job is still exciting and we have now transferred quite a few protocols to Switzerland and patients are being treated and even cured, in fact, apparently, it is going so well that people are lined up to participate in the program."

JP got straight to the matter at hand. "And the reason you wanted to talk to me?"

Kathleen hesitated, she now felt a little foolish asking her cousin if he believed in Divine DNA and if he thought Jesus

139

Christ might be the manifestation of it. "Do you know what, I have taken enough of your time; perhaps it would be better if we left it to the next time we meet face to face, I know you are very busy at the moment preparing for next week's conference?"

"Well true, I am co-chair of the conference, along with the President of the Academy."

"Still a mover and shaker, I see." Kathleen added, glad she hadn't discussed her subject.

"You probably didn't know this but I am now the Chancellor of the Academy, been in the job since the beginning of the year."

"Congratulations, I had no idea, Mom or Dad didn't mention it."

"Well, I did not tell my parents, as they really don't understand what it means."

"I will write to you soon, I promise, and I hope to hear from you even if it is only occasionally; bye." Kathleen ended the call.

Chapter 26

Exhausted after weeks of long hours at the lab, Ian was having difficulty getting a good night's sleep, his mind constantly thinking about perfect DNA.

"Get away for the weekend," his girlfriend Angela had suggested. "Go visit your parents, you owe them a visit. You are always more relaxed when you are there."

The next day, Ian sat at an outside table at Beans Café, in the center of the ancient market town of Oundle. From here, he could see north up New Street and east along Market Street. Apart from open market day every Thursday, Saturday morning was usually one of the busiest times of the week. Ian had slept late for the first time in months, got up and strolled into town. He sipped on a latté and watched the passers-by hurrying from ATM machines to the post office, in and out of the butcher's and baker's, stopping briefly to chat to friends and neighbors. He felt at home in the town where he had spent the first eighteen years of his life.

Shortly after his mother became pregnant, his parents, both of whom were medical doctors, had moved back to Oundle to ensure a place for their son at the town's public school. Founded by the Oundle-born Lord Mayor of London, Sir William Laxton, Oundle, England's third largest public school after Eton and Millfield, housing more than a thousand pupils dominates the town, not only with its Oxford-like architecture, but because it remains a driving force behind most of the town's cultural activities. Ian's father attended the school in the '60s.

Ian savored the last few drops of coffee, stood and stretched in the warmth of the mid-day sun. He looked down Market Street and then headed up New Street, pausing at the Talbot Hotel, where he had enjoyed his first pint of beer with some school friends when he was only seventeen. He had not been in the place for over twenty years. He crossed the cobble courtyard underneath the stone archway and entered the bar.

"A pint of IPA shandy," he asked the Polish barmaid. "It's a beautiful day?"

"It certainly is, sir," she replied, pouring beer and lemonade into a pint glass.

Ian paid for his shandy, took a sip then climbed the stairs of this old market town inn looking for something his father had first pointed out to him when he was nine years old. His father had told him that the inn, founded in 638 AD by a group of monks as a hostel, was rebuilt with stones from ruins of Fotheringhay Castle, where on February the seventh, 1587, Mary Queen of Scots was executed. After the death of Mary, the castle fell into disrepair and was eventually demolished in 1628. Stone from the ruins were used to rebuild the hotel and other properties in the surrounding villages. In 1638, the hotel added a staircase; it had led to the top room of the castle where Mary had been imprisoned. It took him over five minutes to find what he was searching for; the outline of a crown in the polished wood of the balustrade, made by a ring on Mary's hand as she was dragged down the staircase to her death. The image of the Scottish Queen fighting for her life on that very staircase as she was led away to have her head chopped off, had frightened Ian.

Ian placed his shandy on the window sill and looked through the great horn windows, which also came from the castle, and now overlooked the Talbot courtyard. He was deep in thought about the past few weeks and how hectic it had been – a much faster pace of life. Yet, here on this old wooden staircase hardly anything had changed in almost four hundred years. He carried the half-full glass back downstairs and placed it on the bar.

"Thanks," he said to the barmaid as he hurried out into the bright sunshine and ambled along New Street on his way to his old school.

Ian spent seven happy years there from age eleven to eighteen and in his final year captained the First XV rugby team as well as being an oarsman on the rowing team. At five-foot ten, he was not a tall man, but he packed a solid body on his two hundred and thirty-pound frame. Despite the fact that his home was close by, his parents felt very strongly that their young son should board at the school to build up his independence. His memory of those first few days in Fischer House, the oldest of the school's houses, was vivid in his mind. But he adjusted well and now considered it the best time in his life.

Ian stopped at the corner of Milton and Glapthorn Roads and looked across at the Sir Peter Scott building where he had studied mathematics and biology. He leaned on the perimeter wall thinking about his rather eccentric and feisty biology teacher, Dr Watts-Russell, who had a long red pointed nose that hissed in an erratic manner as if he had permanent summer allergies. It was Watts-Russell, with his unusual and entertaining experiments, who had piqued Ian's interest in biology in the first place. He wondered whether his old teacher was still alive. After a few minutes reminiscing, Ian strolled toward the chapel where he had attended the six-fifteen pm service every Saturday. The chapel, built in the twentieth century and designed to fit in with the surroundings, its architecture matching that of the school, was an impressive but welcoming edifice, a sanctuary for thousands of Oundle pupils.

Ian opened the wooden gate and stepped onto the gravel walkway surrounded by lush lawns dotted with daisies. He stopped in front of the west entrance, with 'God Grant Grace' chiseled in stone above the heavy door. Inside, he looked at the inscription reading, '1914 - 1918 To the Glory of God and in memory of those who died.' Standing next to the first row of chairs, he studied the stained-glass windows surrounding the church at eye level. They were modern depictions rendered in brilliant colors of traditional scenes such as the Sermon on the Mount or the Last Supper. Some looked more suitable for a modern art museum than a chapel, Ian thought. He had always liked that they were different. When the sun shone through the stained-glass windows, reflections danced on the scratched wooden floor of the church. Ian quietly made his way to the seventh row and sat down on the chair that bore the inscription, JM Walton, his father. He removed the hymn book from the metal holder attached to the back of the chair and smiled when he saw that after twenty-five years his handiwork still lived on. When he was sixteen, he had used a black fiber-tip pen to heavily inscribe the name I Walton 2002 on the bottom of the hymnbook holder, his reasoning being that just because the chapel had ceased the practice of inscribing chairs before he had arrived was no good reason why his name, like his father's, should not be there for posterity.

The chairs, incredibly uncomfortable, forced students to sit up straight. Ian wondered what became of the boys whose names were inscribed on the chairs. How many had children and grandchildren who were still alive? How many who had sat there before him also yearned for answers? He liked looking up at the chancel where nine huge stained-glass windows featured the nine figures of Christ. He could relate most to the three on the right, the ones that depicted Christ the Judge, Teacher and Good Shepherd. The others seemed too abstract.

He got up and walked to his favorite part of the chapel, the area behind the altar, which was somewhat of a mausoleum. Plaques honored Oundle students who had died, such as the fifteen-year-old killed by a train in 1907 in front of his brother and cousin. The ashes of one of the school's most revered headmasters were there. Frederick William Sanderson had led the school from 1892 to 1922 and had been credited with reviving the ancient school and enhancing its reputation. The school itself was considered to be his memorial. Ian's conscience was kicking in again.

He stopped in front of one of the chapel's two organs, a Copeman Hart, situated near the altar, the one used most frequently to accompany the chapel choir, and at times, the whole school. Ian always got goose bumps every time he heard the unofficial school song – adapted from William Blake's hymn *Jerusalem* sung at rugby matches and other sporting events.

> *And did those feet in ancient time*
> *walk upon England's mountains green?*
> *And was the holy Lamb of God*
> *on England's pleasant pastures seen?*

The original poem had been created from a mythical idea in the Book of Revelation about the second coming of Christ and a medieval account that the young Jesus Christ, accompanied by Joseph of Arimathea, had visited the English town of Glastonbury. Supposedly, Joseph had returned to Glastonbury thirty years after the death of Jesus and, at his request, the first Christian church was built there to house the Holy Grail. As a result, there are many who believe the town to be the birthplace of Christianity in Great Britain. Local folklore claims that the Holy Grail is buried deep in the spring at Glastonbury Tor, a venerated hill, five-hundred feet above sea level.

Several times during his years at Oundle School, Ian had gone on field trips to Glastonbury and spent hours at the remains of Glastonbury Abbey and St. Michael's Church at the summit of Glastonbury Tor, contemplating God, the Holy Grail, the Shroud and the 'meaning of life'. Once he had gone up to Oxford, where he discovered willing girls and uninhibited sex, his interest in religion had waned. Since then, he had doubted the existence of God and labeled himself an atheist. But now he had doubts about his doubts.

As soon as he had finished his undergraduate degree in microbiology at Oxford, he went on to Cambridge to complete a PhD in molecular biology. He then joined Alpha Genetics as a research scientist studying the genetics of degenerative diseases. Soon after joining the company, he met his girlfriend Angela. They had been living together ever since. Ian left the company after six years to join MacLeod's lab and had worked for him now for ten years.

He had convinced himself since his Oxford days that God did not exist. Then why now, all of a sudden, was he losing sleep over Kathleen's illogical conclusion that just because there might be such a thing as perfect DNA, Christ was its true form?

For the first eighteen years of his life, Ian had been a practicing Roman Catholic and had gone to church every Sunday. As a teenager, he was consumed with the mysteries of life and artifacts like the Shroud of Turin and fables of the Holy Grail. He had thrown all of that to one side when he went to university and had been content with his atheistic viewpoint ever since. When he was young, he had always thought that one day he would use science to prove the existence of God. Now, tossing and turning every night, his mind in turmoil, Kathleen's comments changed all that, and he felt he had no choice but to use science to prove that God did not exist.

Chapter 27

Henry Anderson's obsession with MacLeod had reached a new fervor. He had contacted Garret about a new scheme and needed Matt's help, who he thought, had done a splendid job persuading Darren to sell some of his Genon shares. He had asked Garret to arrange a two-month assignment for Matt at Cambridge University, all expenses paid by SMB.

It took Garret just one telephone call to his counterparts in the Department of Genetics to initiate a summer exchange. When Matt was first told about the assignment he was thrilled.

The idea of spending a couple of months at Cambridge was something he had always dreamed of and maybe it would open the door to a more permanent position, he thought. He had visited England and parts of Europe many times when he was younger but had never been to Cambridge.

In the summer of 2008, Matt graduated from high school with a 3.92 GPA. Delighted, his father rewarded Matt with a one-month trip to Europe, his first overseas visit without his parents. He and his three eighteen-year-old companions were booked into the Selfridges Hotel on Oxford Street, in the heart of London, where Matt and his parents had always stayed in the past.

Matt recalled the first night of that trip. After showering and freshening up for a night on the town, they exited the back entrance of the hotel on Duke St. and made a beeline for the Henry Holland pub across the street. Matt knew that Henry

Holland, a famous eighteenth Century English architect, worked on Woburn Abbey in Bedfordshire for fifteen years and spent two years working on Althorp House in Northamptonshire, where Princess Diana is now buried.

The four friends, all members of the high school football team, stood at the small crowded bar, giddy with the legitimacy of being able to order alcohol at eighteen and in anticipation of creating testosterone-driven mayhem across Europe.

Matt raised his glass. "Gentlemen, and I use that term rather loosely but mainly in deference to the country that is hosting us; to Europe, beer and girls."

They noisily chinked each other's beer glasses. "To Europe, beer and girls," they all shouted.

Three hours later, Matt said, "Let's find another bar with more women." Apart from a drunken old hag at the end of the bar, who bore witness to the deleterious effects of too much alcohol, there were no females in the Henry Holland.

The quarterback was already half-asleep with his elbows propping up his head on the bar.

"Grab one side and I'll grab the other," the defensive linesman hollered as they staggered out of the bar and weaved in and out of other pedestrians on Oxford Street. They managed a hundred yards in five minutes flat before unceremoniously dumping the quarterback at the entrance of the first bar that came toward them like a double-decker bus. That was the beginning of a night-long pub crawl and Matt's first and last hangover. He had enduring memories of that night in England.

Garret told Matt that Anderson wanted him to research MacLeod's past. "It's a free trip, so humor him." But Matt had to question the reasons. Garret had also told him that Anderson had also said, "Leave no stone unturned, from the time his father's sperm entered his mother and everything since."

148

"What kind of person uses a phrase like that?" Matt had asked at the time. "A damned nutcase, that's who. What's going on with these two guys, anyway?"

"They're arch-rivals with a long history and I wouldn't worry about it. You're not going to find anything on MacLeod anyway, so go enjoy yourself for a couple of months."

Matt still expressed his concern that what he was being asked to do might be unethical. Garret was no stranger to ethical issues; he had straddled the ethical line many times in his career. He told Matt there was nothing unethical about it; in fact, anyone can research another person's background. People had been doing that on the Internet for more than forty years.

That's exactly where Matt started, on the Internet. He had ten days to go before he took up his assignment in Cambridge, so he began to build a profile of MacLeod. After a few days, he had a reasonable framework of MacLeod's career history, and though there were many gaps, there was some useful stuff for him to research.

He had found out that MacLeod had once lived in the United Sates, worked for Genentech and had been married for four years. He decided to start with MacLeod's ex-wife. He traced Mary Lou Bell from Genentech to Stanford and then Berkeley where she was now Chair of Biochemistry. He offered to fly out to meet with her, but she felt that it was unnecessary; whatever it was he wanted to talk to her about, they could do it over the phone.

"Can you tell me what this is all about?" Mary Lou asked.

Matt explained he was doing an assignment on famous geneticists for Harvard University, and her ex-husband was on the list.

"Oh, I see. Well, first of all, Francis is a charming English gentleman and we fell in love when we first met, but as it turned out, we were both deeply in love with genetics and that's what had attracted us to each other in the first place."

149

"So, what happened?"

"Don't get me wrong, I still admire him, but under that veneer of English charm, Francis can be very aggressive, and he can be quite irritating at times. There is only one way to do things in his book and that's the MacLeod way. And now that he is *Sir Francis* and a *Nobel laureate,* I am sure that hasn't suppressed his ego any."

"Was he ever aggressive with you?"

"No, of course not. I didn't mean it in that sense."

"With others, perhaps?" Matt was clutching at straws.

"Not really, although he did land a rather nice left hook on a fellow researcher one time, early in our marriage. We were in a bar and the other guy was persistently hitting on me. It got Francis mad so he let him have one; floored the guy. It was quite chivalrous I thought at the time."

Matt laughed. "Good old English gallantry at its best, coming to the defense of a young maiden."

Mary Lou let out a chuckle. "Young, at the time maybe, but not a maiden. After all, I have lived in the spirit of San Francisco my whole life."

"Do you have any contact with him these days?"

"No, very little. Maybe once a year, if I read something interesting about him in the press, usually related to his work."

"Sounds to me like a good guy all round," Matt said.

"In a nutshell, yes," Mary Lou replied.

"Well, thanks, Ms Bell, good talking to you."

Matt was feeling a whole lot better about his assignment for Anderson. Maybe MacLeod was the *real deal* and no matter how many layers of onion he peeled back, he would only find more onion. He hoped so.

Chapter 28

MacLeod was ecstatic. After only three weeks, his scientists had used the genon sequences to discover and match more than two thousand new genes, more than twice the number he had hoped for. Of course, determining their function would be a much harder and more time-consuming task.

He sat staring at his computer on Friday afternoon, probing the three-dimensional images of the various chromosomes and the locations of the newly found genes. In one sense, he felt exhilaration that his hypothesis had been right all along; first, that there is no such thing as 'junk DNA' and, secondly, that perfect DNA did exist. It was also a huge responsibility to open the world to the awesome possibilities of man's ultimate destiny.

VJ looked across and saw the consternation on his MacLeod's face. "Are you okay, Francis?"

It took several seconds for MacLeod to answer. "VJ, I am not sure, to be honest with you. I am just sitting here trying to make sense of this. It is one thing to correct a faulty gene that could cause blindness, but it is a totally different matter if we have discovered dormant or non-functioning genes that are capable of giving us superhuman powers."

"I am not following you. What do you mean by superhuman powers?" VJ said.

"Well, that's the thing. I don't really know, but what if, for example, there are some genes that would allow us to transcend normal human performance – it seems incomprehensible, and yet."

"This is eerie," VJ thought, first Kathleen and now MacLeod. "Are you saying what I think you are saying; that within the human genome there is the potential to attain God-like powers?"

"Well, I wouldn't go that far, but if you think about it, look at the differences in capabilities between man and species such as a mouse, cat or dog. If they were capable of thought, we would probably seem God-like to them."

"I suppose you are right about that."

"Chimpanzee and human DNA have a ninety-six percent correlation, yet we are by far the superior species. Look how far we have evolved from apes to what we are today, in what is a relatively short period of time in the scheme of things. It's not hard to imagine that in the future, as man continues to evolve, his capabilities and powers will be much greater than they are today."

"Yes, but that's just natural evolution and nature taking its course, isn't it?" VJ asked.

"True, but what if we now have the tools to accelerate or manipulate that naturally evolving process? It's an awesome burden of responsibility."

"Have you talked to Kathleen about this?" VJ asked.

MacLeod glared at him, not understanding the relevance of the question. "No. Why?"

"After the Thetford meeting, she took me to one side and asked me about the yogis and the legends of their mystical powers. It just seemed too much of a coincidence that this discussion is so similar." VJ smiled and tried to change the subject. "So what did you think about her conclusion about perfect DNA and Jesus Christ?"

"I don't have time for that. I have enough on my plate trying to deal with the scientific implications and ethical issues of our genon research without getting distracted by the science against religion debate. I have a lot to think about this weekend. In fact, I could do with clearing my head." MacLeod looked at the wall clock; it was three minutes after four. "How about we wrap up here and see if we can get a court?"

"Okay," VJ said. "But as long as we're done by six to six-thirty."

They shut down their computers and followed the usual routine to exit the computer room through the interlocking doors. MacLeod told his immediate staff he would be holding a meeting first thing Monday morning. He and VJ headed over to the squash club.

MacLeod had held a significant lead in the number of matches won. But that had started to change in the past six to seven months with VJ invariably winning two out of every three matches.

After the usual five-minute warm-up, VJ served first and quickly won three points in a row. Then after a long rally MacLeod won the serve and notched up four points. They went back and forth until the game was tied at eight-eight. Then VJ won the next point and took the first game. In the second game it was a totally different MacLeod, like his old self; he hardly had to move from mid-court as he angled superb shot after superb shot into every corner with precision. VJ, on the other hand, ran around the court, dripping in sweat, as if he were trying to swat a fast and furious wasp. The game ended nine-one in MacLeod's favor.

They both grabbed their towels to wipe off the sweat but when MacLeod temporarily closed his eyes to wipe his face he was acutely aware of the darkness, and thought about how terrible it must be to be blind. An image of a blind man appeared in his head and sent a cold shiver down his spine. VJ won the third game nine-three.

VJ didn't say anything other than, "Good match; thanks," but he knew MacLeod had completely lost his focus in the last game. They both showered, changed and said goodbye. MacLeod went to the bar, ordered a beer shandy and sat down at an empty table in the corner. He drank about a quarter of the pint in one swallow, then called Sir Charles Palmer.

"Francis, what a surprise. Is everything all right?"

"I need to talk to you, Charles. Are you available anytime tomorrow?"

"I am for most of the day, apart from hosting a dinner party tomorrow evening at seven-thirty for eight guests. In fact, we have room for another two, so why don't you and Kathleen join us?"

"That's very kind of you, Charles, but there is something very important I want to talk to you about, without Kathleen being there."

"Don't tell me you're planning to pop the question, old chap, are you?"

MacLeod felt his cheeks flush. "No, nothing like that. It's about Genon and a very critical decision that I need to make and I want to be sure it is the right one."

"Look, come down around four. We'll play a couple of sets of tennis; then we can discuss your problem, whatever it is, over a drink. You can still join us for dinner and stay overnight. We have plenty of room."

"That's not necessary, Charles. Besides, I would be the odd one out, so I'll leave before your dinner guests arrive."

"Nonsense, old chap, you're staying; it'll do you good to get away, even if it's only for twenty-four hours. I'll have Gill invite one of her single friends to even up the group. And talking about Gill, there is something very personal and confidential I would like to talk to you about. So see you at four."

The eight-bedroom sixteenth century Tudor manor on the outskirts of Henley-on-Thames had been carefully restored on the outside to its original condition. The grounds of the five-acre estate, the epitome of a traditional English garden, were cared for with a meticulous neatness. The back of the house featured a lap pool, a grass tennis court with several bench seats, and a good-sized gazebo, often used by the musicians who entertained at the Palmers' frequent summer garden parties.

MacLeod was no match for Palmer on the tennis court despite his superior overall fitness and skills at racket sports. Palmer won six-two, six-three puzzled by his opponent's lack of enthusiasm during the game.

"Clearly, you have something significant on your mind, Francis. Let me get us a drink and we'll talk, G and T?"

"No, I'll take a shandy, if you don't mind. Thanks."

MacLeod told Palmer the dilemma he faced. In a couple of months, they would be initiating the public offering but there was something that had happened in the first clinical trials at Tronavis that he had not reported to the GT group. MacLeod went on to tell Palmer about the two patients, the woman who had died and the man who had gone blind. He told him about the solicitor threatening to expose Tronavis for medical negligence, who had refused every settlement they had offered. MacLeod was very concerned that the solicitor would use the IPO to get maximum publicity and a much bigger settlement and ruin his and Genon's reputation.

Palmer listened to the whole story until almost seven and then said, "Francis, I wish you had told me this at the time, because maybe there was something I could have done to help. What a bloody fool Meier was to do that AMD trial behind your back. But as they say, it's no use crying over spilled milk. I can see that you're agonizing over this decision, but under the circumstances I think you have no other choice but to postpone the IPO, even though you are going to upset a lot of people." He looked at his watch. "We need to shower and get ready for dinner. So let's do that and we can both sleep on it and talk again over breakfast."

Many of the original walls of the manor had been removed or altered to make way for modern amenities but the medieval ambiance had been preserved and the interior remained opulent yet tasteful. Gill's sophisticated taste was apparent throughout the home. At dinner, MacLeod was seated next to an elegant widow in her early fifties. He was amused by Gill's choice of dinner partners for him, but it was an ideal diversion from the difficult decision that was weighing on him.

The widow hugged and kissed him on the cheek when she left. "Maybe we could have dinner some time," she whispered in his ear.

He smiled and said, "It was nice to meet you."

The next morning at breakfast, MacLeod confirmed with Palmer that his mind was made up. He would postpone the IPO until Tronavis had settled with the blind man's counsel and would give other reasons to his staff for the postponement. Palmer agreed that the fewer people who knew, the less likely it would get out to the media.

"Now, Francis, what I want to talk to you about in confidence is Gill. We received some bad news a few weeks ago. Gill has been diagnosed with early stage Alzheimer's and, while she is doing fine so far, we both know only too well what's in store. We have talked about it every night since we found out, and in the end, we both agreed that I would talk to you to see how far away you are from an Alzheimer's genon therapy."

"To be perfectly frank with you, Charles, we have yet to match the Alzheimer's genon, but I have every confidence we will before next April and I assure you when we do, I'll give the clinical trials top priority."

"Well, all we can hope for is that you discover it sooner rather than later, for both Gill's sake and mine."

Chapter 29

At nine a.m. on Monday, MacLeod addressed his immediate staff.

"You have all done a fantastic job these past three weeks, discovering more than two thousand new genes. This clearly proves, beyond a shadow of a doubt, that our hypothesis has been correct all along. As a result, I have made two decisions. The first is that we are going to buy three more sets of the latest sequencing machines, with the goal of discovering the remaining genes within the next eight to nine months. And before I discuss the second decision I want to explain some of the conclusions I have come to in the past few days."

He sat down and took a drink of water. "I decided to accelerate the gene discovery program in order to complete the project by next March and present our findings at the seventy-fifth Watson and Crick Anniversary Symposium in April."

"That'll be great," Kathleen said.

MacLeod smiled. "I am glad you think so, Kathleen. Unfortunately, we will have to disclose the results to the IPO auditors, which means the world will find out long before the symposium and that could cause us all a lot of grief. Consequently, I have decided to postpone the IPO until next May."

There was little to no reaction from Kathleen, Rob, Ian or VJ, but Darren said, "What! You can't do that! The IPO is only a couple of months away."

"I can and I will . . . what you do not seem to understand, Darren, is that when the world finds out that there really *are* more than fifty thousand genes, as was believed before the Human Genome Project, everyone is going to scramble to get in on the act. I do not want to take the risk of some shady opportunists getting their hands on the data. That could put us all in danger," said MacLeod.

"Francis, we have worked our asses off for you these past seven years; and even longer for most of us. We were all motivated not only by the work but the promised rewards, and now you are going back on your word. It is so unlike you. And besides, why do you have to even mention either your perfect DNA hypothesis or the number of genes for that matter? The IPO is based on genon discovery, isn't it?"

"If we do not disclose everything, and the stock does not appreciate, should the investors find out we could end up with a shareholder lawsuit on our hands. It's just not worth the risk."

Rob asked. "What's the difference between going public on the data now versus next April?"

"There's a big difference," MacLeod responded, lowering his voice a half-octave. "For one thing, by next April we will have identified all of the genes and will go public with the data in an academic environment where everyone will have equal access. On the other hand, if we only have about fifteen to twenty percent of the genes identified at the time of the offering, you can bet that some other commercial enterprise will jump in and try to get those new genes for themselves. You were all too young in the 1990s but that's exactly what happened when Vince J Garret jumped into the race to map the human genome in competition with the government-sponsored Human Genome Project."

Although Darren was the only one who had taken the news badly so far, MacLeod knew the others would mull it over and

159

start to question his judgment, which he had to admit had been a little shaky lately. Everyone could do with a break.

"You have all worked extremely hard these past several months, and made tremendous progress, I might add. So I have decided that everyone should take a month's vacation. This will also allow us to remodel and update the lab and get the new machines delivered and installed."

That evening after work, as Kathleen was driving over to MacLeod's house, her iPhone rang. It was Darren calling from the Eagle. He sounded terrible. He appeared to be drunk and told her he had been there since after lunch. Rob had joined him about an hour before. He asked whether she wanted to stop by.

"Let me talk to Francis then go home and change. I'll grab a taxi and should be there in about thirty minutes." She called Francis and told him she was going to the Eagle to meet Darren and Rob. He said he understood. She disconnected the phone and threw it on the passenger seat.

The next morning, Kathleen had a splitting headache. She lay in bed for most of the day and in the afternoon called her parents to tell them that she would be visiting them soon for a week.

MacLeod flew to Basel.

Rob went into work on Wednesday and Thursday and he and VJ briefly chatted about the postponed IPO. But Rob was thinking about something else. It had now been six and a half years since he left NESCI and the northeast of England to join Genon. He had Mary on his mind. By Thursday evening he knew what he was going to do. It was the biggest decision of his life; this weekend he would ask Mary to marry him. On Friday, he loaded up his bike and headed north.

That same day, Darren caught a flight to Los Angeles en route to San Diego. He had received a message that Matt would be arriving over the weekend to start a two-month summer

160

exchange at Cambridge. He was not ready to face the questions about the postponed IPO. He needed time to think.

Chapter 30

Kathleen and VJ were surprised to see each other at the lab on Friday. Not that it was problem for her, she was glad to have the opportunity to talk to VJ when no one else was around.

Kathleen explained to him what had been occupying her mind since Francis had revealed his 'perfect DNA' hypothesis and she had related it to Jesus Christ. "I know this is going to sound crazy, but I think I have an idea how the 'immaculate conception' may have come about."

VJ shook his head. "This I have to hear."

Kathleen reminded him about the discussion at Thetford three weeks earlier, and her theory that Jesus Christ was the manifestation of perfect DNA. "The most tantalizing question is how the Virgin Mary became impregnated with divine DNA? Don't you agree?"

VJ shrugged.

Kathleen continued, "Well, by all biblical accounts, '*Mary was awakened by a bright flash of light*'. What if the divine DNA was in the form of light? In other words, a complete spectral copy of divine DNA that penetrated her womb and fertilized an egg."

"That makes no sense at all," VJ replied. "Isn't DNA a substance, like protein?"

Kathleen smiled. "You're pulling my leg, right? DNA is made up of nucleotides. DNA is just a recipe for making the proteins that we are all made of. I know you are just a computer

162

jock but I'd have thought you would have picked up that much by osmosis."

"I have but I just wanted to make sure I understood what you were getting at. Anyway, it's another interesting hypothesis about the 'immaculate conception' and nobody can prove you are wrong and you cannot prove you are right, so, c'est la vie!" VJ said.

"But this is the thing, VJ; I think we can conduct some scientific experiments that might suggest it is possible."

"Scientific experiments to prove a two thousand-year-old miraculous event took place? What are you going to use for evidence? You're nuts."

"Maybe, maybe not. Just hear me out and bear with me for a minute. We know that the universe was created from one single atom that exploded fourteen-billion years ago and everything in our universe stems from that 'big bang.' As a result, we are biologically connected to every other living thing on our planet, chemically connected to every other star and planet in our universe, and atomically connected to that one single atom that exploded so long ago. *We are literally made up of stardust*. Given the wonder of all that, is it that far-fetched to imagine that spectral DNA is at least a possibility?"

"Well, I guess when you put it like that, anything is possible," VJ acknowledged. "But proving it, well, that's another matter."

Undeterred, Kathleen continued, "Let's just assume for a moment that DNA can be transmitted in the form of light, and we will come back to that shortly. But first, let me ask you a question. You are a Hindu; what does your faith say happens to you after you die?"

"We are reincarnated as we move forward to a higher level on our journey to Nirvana, like most religions."

163

"And just how do you get from the human form to some other form to journey toward Nirvana and God?" Kathleen asked.

"How would I know? Nobody has ever come back to tell me, or anyone else I know, for that matter. And, actually, that is something I wanted to discuss with you."

"OK, maybe, but for now let's focus and get back to what we were talking about. Given then, that you are not sure, will you at least concede that maybe it is in the form of light?"

"Again, anything is possible."

"When a human form dies and disintegrates, there is only one thing left that truly represents that particular individual. Like to guess?" Kathleen asked.

"Well, you're implying . . . its DNA. You are going to say, that when we die a copy of our DNA leaves the body in the form of a spectral image, aren't you?"

"Exactly. 'And the light went on'; excuse the pun." Kathleen now had VJ's full attention. "Consider accounts of people who have had a near-death experience. They invariably say they saw a bright white light, and eye witnesses of death often claim to have observed a flash of light when a person died. Light in all of these cases is a common denominator. So what do you think?"

"Fascinating theory, but as I said before, a theory is one thing but proving it is another."

"I have already thought of a series of experiments we could do to test the theory. Let me tell you what I have in mind."

Kathleen explained to him her idea of contacting all of the local hospitals to find out how many people were being kept alive on life support systems and which ones were likely to have the plugs pulled in the near future. Further, if the relatives were even slightly religious, they might be willing to let their loved ones participate in a religious/scientific experiment to provide evidence of an afterlife, a fitting final act in the name of God before they expire.

Assuming they could identify at least a few candidates, they would then have a special casket made so they could carry out a series of experiments, including the detection of light, both before and during the time of death.

"So will you help?" Kathleen asked VJ.

VJ thought for a moment about something he had intended to look into while everyone was away for a month, but there was no rush and Kathleen's experiments sounded interesting. "Okay, I'll help you. By the way, have you talked to Ian about this?"

"Ian? Of course not. He's an atheist," Kathleen said.

"I suggest that you do. He's not taking a month off. He's going to set up some experiments of his own to prove you are wrong."

"What? What kind of experiments?"

"I am not sure, but if you want my advice it might be better if you joined forces rather than getting into a peeing contest."

"Okay, I'll talk to him."

Kathleen explained to Ian what kind of experiments she had in mind. He immediately expressed interest. "Fascinating," he responded.

"VJ told me that you were going to be doing some experiments of your own, what about them?" said Kathleen.

"Trust me; they now seem boring compared to yours. Besides, if yours fail I will have proved my point. In fact, I'll set up the experiments for you if you want."

"That would be great," Kathleen said.

While Kathleen visited her parents for a week, Ian and VJ identified twenty-seven patients within a fifty-mile radius of Cambridge on life-support systems. A combination of improved technology and a dramatic increase in durable power of attorney on health decisions resulted in more family disputes and

165

patients being kept alive longer. One patient at Addenbrooke's Hospital had been on life support for more than a year but was scheduled to have the ventilator switched off in seventy-two hours.

This didn't give Ian and VJ enough time to get a special casket ready; they would need at least seven days. They talked to the hospital and close family members and after several hours were able to convince the patient's daughter to keep her father alive for another week. Ian offered to pay for all additional expenses and the funeral, plus a donation to the daughter's chosen charity.

The patient had been on his way home from work on the M11 when a sudden patch of fog had drifted across the motorway, causing a multiple car pile-up. His car had been crushed between the car in front and a petrol tanker behind; it took three and a half hours to extract his limp body from the wreckage. He was rushed to Addenbrooke's and immediately put on a ventilator. While there were no external signs of physical injury, it was apparent that significant trauma to the spine and brain had caused complete paralysis.

At first, the physicians had given the family hope. While the odds were against any realistic recovery, it was worth keeping him artificially alive, at least for a short while. That was enough for the patient's wife. Her daughter, on the other hand, could not bear the thought of seeing her father lying there, day after day, totally helpless and lifeless. It was legally the daughter's decision because her father and mother, as part of their will, had signed over power of attorney to the daughter. Mother and daughter fell out. After a year, the courts had ruled in the daughter's favor.

Ian had already researched the type of casket he would need for the experiments and he could get one within forty-eight hours. The modifications and testing, however, would take several more days. The casket was made of metal. He had inquired about ordering one without the side-wall linings and with the interior painted completely in a matte black. He would then have a sliding view port installed directly above where the head would be positioned, and a cut-out in the entry door to allow the life-support lines and monitor cables to pass through.

The one thing he had yet to figure out was where to position the photodiodes that detected any emission of light. He knew a photonics expert at the university whom he could talk to.

Chapter 31

Because of a family wedding on Saturday morning, Matt left Boston later that evening on an overnight flight to Heathrow Airport. From there, he took an underground train on the Piccadilly line to London's King's Cross station. He stepped off the Tube, walked briskly to the turnstile and put his ticket into the slot. The stile opened but his luggage was too wide to pull through. He yanked it onto his shoulder and stumbled out on to the concourse. For a Sunday morning, it was surprisingly busy with holidaymakers scurrying about like ants and dragging skate-wheeled luggage in their wake. He had read that seven thousand people pass through the station every hour. He believed it; he bumped into most of them. He spotted a Prêt à Manger. 'Handmade natural food and a hundred percent organic coffee'; he remembered the slogan from his past visits to London. Sitting with a large latté, he admired the futuristic design of the remodeled station with its sixteen perimeter columns and twelve hundred solid pipes and a thousand and twenty glass triangular panels forming a giant honeycomb-like ceiling. It had been completely refurbished in time for the 2012 Olympics, transformed into a magnificently modern and efficient concourse inside with a restored 1852 façade outside.

Matt saw a large sign across the hall, 'Tickets for Cambridge and all other destinations this way'. "Cambridge and all others? How utterly royal and plebeian." He said under his breath, as he tried to imitate a snooty English accent.

Smiling and refreshed, he ambled to the ticket machine and purchased a one-way ticket. The train left on time at nine fifteen a.m. and arrived forty-five minutes later at Cambridge Station. Outside, he took a taxi for the short ride to Pembroke College. The taxi driver jumped out and dropped Matt's luggage on the ground in front of the college.

"That'll be fifteen pounds, squire."

"Keep the change," Matt said generously, handing the cabbie a twenty-pound note.

He took a deep breath as he stared at his surroundings on a glorious English summer morning; it was almost as if he could taste the rich cultural and academic history of the city. Pembroke College, established on Christmas Eve, 1347 was the third oldest college in Cambridge. Matt had read that settlements had existed in the area since before the Roman Empire with archaeological evidence dating back to the late Bronze Age, around 1000 BC.

He grabbed his suitcase and wheeled it up to the porter's lodge. A rather rotund man in his sixties, dressed in a dark navy standard-issue porter's suit, peered over the top of his glasses as Matt approached. "Can I help you?" the man asked in a Welsh accent.

"I hope so," Matt responded as he handed the man his passport, "I believe I am expected."

"Ah, yes, Dr Price, indeed you are," the porter answered, reaching into the centuries-old wooden mail slot with the letter 'P' above it. "This package is for you. Welcome to Pembroke College, sir."

"Thanks, may I ask your name?"

"Llewellyn Williams, sir, but call me Lew for short. You're in room two one six, I'll show you the way," He took a card from a drawer and placed it on the desk. It said, 'Back in five minutes.'

After the porter left, Matt sat on the bed, opened the package and shuffled through the contents. A staff ID pass, a layout of the Department of Genetics with a lab number, a map of the city, and a 'Brief history of Cambridge.'

Matt filled the kettle from the sink to make a cup of tea then lay on the bed to peruse the booklet. 'Cambridge was occupied by the Romans shortly after the death of Christ until about AD 400. After the Romans left, the Saxons took over until the Vikings arrived in 875 then the Saxons took over again for a few decades until 1068 after William of Normandy had conquered England in 1066. Cambridge is rich in Roman, Saxon and Norman architecture. St. Benet's Church in Benet Street was built by the Saxons in 1025. The distinctive Round Church was built fifty years later by the Normans. The university was formed in 1209 by students from Oxford who fled to Cambridge fleeing from the hostile townspeople in England's oldest university town.'

Matt marveled at the deep-rooted history of the University. Harvard, the most prestigious American university paled in comparison, he thought to himself. After finishing a cup of tea, Matt studied the city map and decided where he would go first. He ran down the stairs and across the courtyard, waving to Lew as he exited on to Trumpington Street, turned the corner into Pembroke Street then hurried along Downing Street to the Genetics Building. The labs seemed well-equipped, as good as any back at Harvard. Satisfied, he back-tracked along Downing Street, turned right on Free School Lane, made a left on Benet Street, passing the Eagle pub without noticing it, and onto King's Parade. There, before him, stood King's College, founded by Henry VI in 1441. Its magnificent medieval architecture was all the more stunning as it preened itself in sun-drenched splendor. He was quickly surrounded by foreign students, each one of them eager to sell him a boat ride ticket.

One student from the Czech Republic shouted, "Sir, it's a beautiful day for a river tour, would you like to buy a ticket?"

"No, thanks, maybe some other time. What's your name?"

"Jan, sir. Come to me when you want to go punting."

Matt waved as he crossed the Parade to the college.

A security guard stopped him as he attempted to walk through the gatehouse. Matt fumbled into his back pocket and showed the guard his new ID. The guard allowed him in with a polite, "Thank you, Dr Price." Once inside, he stopped in his tracks and stared around the quadrangle with its impeccably manicured lawns and ancient buildings. Breathtakingly medieval, he told himself as he slowly strolled around the gravel path past the south building, passing Clare College on his right, finally arriving at the banks of the River Cam.

Matt stood on the bridge and looked back toward the other nearby colleges, including Queens and Trinity, in awe of their history. He studied each in the booklet. Hearing noises below, he leaned over the side of the bridge. Underneath him, scores of boaters were punting along the river. It was easy to pick out the experts; not only by their straw hats, but the way they skillfully handled their flat-bottomed boat, steering clear of trouble on the narrow river. Many of the self-hire customers, not used to a punting pole, precariously wobbled on the back of the boat, bouncing from side to side as they hit other vessels, their friends laughing and ridiculing as they enjoyed the boat ride through this idyllic setting.

Doubling back to King's Parade, Matt crossed the road to where the hordes of students had surrounded him.

"Jan," he shouted. The Czech student came running toward him, ticket at the ready, and ushered Matt to the entrance of St. Benet's, where six other people were waiting. A few minutes later, Jan led the group of passengers down the jetty for the forty-five-minute tour of the 'Backs' a one-mile stretch of River

Cam boasting nine unique bridges and eight of Cambridge's earliest colleges.

Matt stretched out in the front of the punt; he had watched people sitting at the back of other boats frequently splashed with water. The punter/guide steered his vessel north past King's College and King's College Chapel, which took over a hundred years to build, and was completed in 1547, the guide explained.

"It has one of the finest collections of medieval stained glass in all of Britain, and as a precaution at the beginning of WWII all of the glass was removed and put into storage, even though Hitler had promised not to bomb Cambridge. It was rumored that once he had conquered Europe, he might wish to set up a home here. The re-installation of the glass took years and was eventually completed in 1948."

They passed an oncoming chauffeured punt with a group of young children repeatedly singing at the top of their voices, probably the only boating song they knew.

'Row, row, row your boat, gently down the stream.
Merrily, merrily, merrily, merrily, life is but a dream.'

Matt applauded and waved at the youngsters.

They boated past Clare, Trinity, St. John's and Magdalene College and Bridge then turned around and headed south. The turning point was crowded and Matt laughed at one group of boaters who had dropped their pole and were frantically using their hands as paddles to maneuver their punt to get it.

Matt was glad he was in the hands of an expert who not only steered well but gave the passengers well-rehearsed tidbits of information about the history of the colleges.

Once back past King's, they saw St. Catherine's and Queens' College, which sits on both sides of the Cam. It is connected by the infamous Mathematical Bridge. The well-rehearsed talk continued.

"There are plenty of baseless stories that the Mathematical Bridge was built by Sir Isaac Newton. However, Newton had been dead for twenty-two years when it was built in 1749 by James Essex the Younger."

Once back at the jetty, Matt gave the punter a good tip and told him how much he appreciated the ride and excellent commentary on the history of all of the colleges on either side of the Cam.

He was delighted to be here. 'This is great,' he thought to himself as he casually strolled back through the college grounds and turned left onto King's Parade in search of a pub for lunch.

Chapter 32

Matt visited the lab the next morning around nine o'clock and acquainted himself with the only people who were there, a post-doc and two students. It was summer and, like most of Europe, things here came to a standstill. He went to the lecture hall fifteen minutes early and met the head of the department who was setting up his welcome and introductory lecture on bacterial genetics. Matt introduced himself and was invited to lunch in the staff room after the lecture.

Over lunch with the department head and one of his colleagues from the department of genomics, he learned quite a bit about MacLeod, not surprising since he was considered a modern-day equivalent of Watson and Crick. Clearly, his peers held MacLeod in the highest regard.

After lunch, Matt called Genon. A receptionist put him through to VJ.

"Hello, Gupta here. Can I help you?" VJ asked.

"Hi, my name is Matt Price and I'm calling to speak with Darren Richards. Is he in?" Matt inquired.

"I'm afraid not. We are closed for a month and Darren is on holiday in the States until the end of the month, I believe."

"Oh, I see. Well, thank you, anyway. I'll call again when he gets back."

Matt thought it strange that Darren hadn't told him he would be gone for a month.

On Tuesday, Matt spent several hours on the Internet researching MacLeod's life, starting with the Scottish Registry of births and deaths. He reminded himself of Anderson's bizarre words. "From the time his father's sperm entered his mother and everything since."

He entered Francis James MacLeod into the search box. The name popped up asking for a date of birth and date of death. Matt entered the twenty-third of April 1969 in the DOB box and left the DOD blank. Two new boxes appeared, one asking for the mother's name and the other the father's name. He entered Anne MacLeod and left the other box blank. It appeared Anne MacLeod was the daughter of John MacLeod, a Scottish politician, born in 1897 and died in 1974. His wife's name was Elizabeth. John MacLeod's father and Anne MacLeod's grandfather, William Robert MacLeod, had served as the Provincial Governor of Bengal in the 1880s under the Earl of Dufferin, Viceroy of India. He had met his wife Sushma, the daughter of a local Indian politician, while there.

"Interesting, some Indian blood in the family," he thought as he double-clicked on the father's name box and a name appeared, 'James Ewan MacLeod'.

Francis James MacLeod, son of James Ewan MacLeod and Anne MacLeod. "Good, now we're getting somewhere," he said under his breath.

He copied and pasted 'James Ewan MacLeod/1900 to present' into several different genealogy sites but came up blank every time. Then he searched several marriage record sites and again came up blank. He went back to Anne MacLeod's mother and father and researched their backgrounds; they were from Kinross, where Anne MacLeod had been born, perhaps married there too.

By Thursday, Matt had been unable to find anything new on James Ewan MacLeod and decided to go to Kinross and research the local archives.

After spending a few hours in the lab on Friday morning, he took the train to Edinburgh, picked up a rental car and drove north across the Forth Bridge and headed up to Kinross. It was an exceptional summer's evening and as he turned off the motorway toward his destination, the reflection of the sun on the rippling waters of Loch Leven almost blinded him.

The next morning, he got up and had a full Scottish breakfast of bacon, eggs, sausage, beans, mushrooms and tomatoes, with toast and coffee. After breakfast, he drove thirty-five miles to Dundee University, MacLeod's alma mater, believing it might be better to start there and work backward. He showed his Cambridge University staff pass and gained easy access to the university library where he spent a couple of hours researching MacLeod in their records. He pulled up MacLeod's files and confirmed that he had attended the university from 1987 – 1990 and had completed a bachelor's degree in biology – 'Summa Cum Laude'. The records confirmed that MacLeod had been born in Kinross on the twenty-third of April 1969 and his parents' names were James Ewan and Anne Marie MacLeod.

Satisfied, Matt drove back to Kinross, stopping briefly for lunch on the way. Back in Kinross, he went straight to the library to study the local newspapers from the twenty-third of April 1969 and onward. After a few minutes, he found what he was looking for – a birth announcement dated the twenty-seventh of April 1969. It read:

Born to James Ewan MacLeod and Anne Marie MacLeod on 23 April 1969, a son, Francis James, weight 8lb 11oz. Mother and child doing well.

Matt left the library and walked the few hundred yards to the local church. He wandered through the cemetery with its tombstones scattered amongst the overgrown grass and weeds.

He stopped intermittently and read the Scottish names and dates going back to the sixteenth century. At the back of the church, there was a small cottage, in desperate need of repair. He gingerly knocked on the door and waited. An old man in disheveled clothing appeared, looking as if he had just been resurrected from one of the graves.

"Vicar?"

"Aye."

"My name is Matt Price from Harvard University. I'm doing research on Sir Francis MacLeod. Could I possibly look at your church records?"

"Aye, aye, han' on a minit, laddie," the man said in an accent as thick as Scottish oats.

The vicar grabbed a key and led Matt to the church, mumbling away in what might as well have been a foreign language. Matt nodded his head, saying yes and no according to the man's body language. The vicar opened the creaky wooden church door and headed straight for the vestry with Matt in tow. He unlocked the vestry door and pointed to a glass cabinet filled with leather-bound records.

"Help yersel', laddie," he said, leaving Matt alone to his task.

Matt grabbed the ledger with 1900-2000 on the spine, dusted it off, and searched through the records of births, deaths and marriages. He quickly found the entry of MacLeod's birth in 1969, then his mother's birth in 1935. He turned to the marriage records and went back as far as 1950.

He found no entry of a marriage between James Ewan MacLeod and Anne Marie MacLeod; she obviously did not get married in her home town, but that would not be unusual in those days.

Then he thought of something.

"Wait a minute, what if they were not married?" he said to himself. "If not, it would be one hell of a coincidence that MacLeod's father and mother both had the same name."

Intrigued, he went back through the birth records and studied them more closely. Going back to the beginning of the ledger, he found nothing of interest. To be thorough, he took down the ledger for 1800-1900, blew off even more dust and thumbed through it. He found what he was looking for, an entry for James Ewan MacLeod. The problem was it was dated 1816, one hundred and fifty years before Francis MacLeod was born.

It was now clear to Matt that the entry of father's name on MacLeod's birth certificate had been fabricated. Why? He could understand that MacLeod's mother would want to give the appearance she was married when her son was born, but why go to the length of digging up an old ancestor's name? What was she trying to hide? Who was his real father? Maybe it was somebody well-known; or even one of her own relatives, incest perhaps? And if the truth got out it could have started a scandal. There was only one way to find out – local knowledge – and if that meant spending some time in the village pub on a Saturday night --- Oh well, a man has to do what a man has to do, Matt thought.

He put the ledgers back in the cabinet and strolled back to the vicar's cottage. The vicar was standing at the front door with a mug of tea in his hand.

"Find what yer were looking for, did yer?"

"Yes, thanks, it was very helpful."

The vicar coughed. Matt took the hint and pulled a twenty pound note out of his pocket.

"Thank you, laddie, I'll say a wee prayer for ye."

Back at his hotel, Matt called the village inn and booked a table for one for seven-thirty p.m. It was just as well. By eight p.m. the restaurant was packed. After chicken liver pâté, poached Scottish salmon and fresh vegetables, followed by a cup of coffee, Matt made his way into the bar and ordered a pint of local ale. He struck up a conversation with the landlord, a portly man in his mid-fifties, who picked up on Matt's American accent.

"So what part of the States are you from?" he asked.

"I was actually born in Trumbull, Connecticut, but I now live in the Boston area and work at Harvard University. But I'm on an exchange to Cambridge this summer. I'm here to research the backgrounds of Sir Francis MacLeod, and Watson and Crick. Is there anyone here I could talk to about Sir Francis's early childhood?"

The landlord laughed. "It'll cost you a pint but the man you need to talk to is auld McGregor, sitting at the end of the bar there."

"In that case, pour a pint of his usual poison, Landlord."

Matt paid for the beer and carried it across the bar. "Good evening, sir, can I offer you a drink?"

"That's very kind of ye, laddie," the old man answered in a deep, raspy voice.

"Cheers," Matt said raising his glass to the local wearing a ragged gray beard, tan corduroy jacket with leather patches on the elbows, dark brown trousers and wellington boots.

"Cheers," replied McGregor. "What can I do for ye?"

"Well, I am doing research on Sir Francis MacLeod and the landlord told me that you are the person to talk to."

"Did he now?" he replied, eyeing Matt up and down out of the corner of his eye, as he swallowed the rest of his beer. Slamming his empty glass on the bar, he wiped a sleeve across his mouth and winked at Matt. "Tek it from me, laddie, that's the finest ale in all of Scotland and I have a thirst as big as Loch Leven. Sir Francis, did yer say?"

Matt held a twenty pound note and watched the Scotsman lick his lips. "Did you know his mother and father?"

"Aye, in a manner of speaking," McGregor answered, tilting his head from the money towards the landlord.

"Landlord," Matt called. "The same again for my friend here. So you did know them?"

The old man grabbed the drink and took a sip.

"Well at least his mother, Annie MacLeod, a very attractive lady; she was about ten years older than me, not that she looked it. I was about twenty-five when she came back home to have wee Francis. It had been a number of years before that the last time I had seen her around here."

"What about his father? How well did you know him?" Matt asked.

"Well, that's the thing, ye see, laddie, I never met his father. In fact no one around here knew that she was even married," McGregor said, taking a big mouthful of beer. "He did visit here a couple of times though, after wee Francis was born, but never came into the pub or anything like that. I think the only person ever to see him was the postmistress when he stopped by there to buy a few stamps."

"Oh, I see. Do you think I could talk to her?" Matt asked.

"I dunno, laddie, talk to the dead, can ye? She's been gone these past twenty-five years," McGregor said with a wry smile.

"Did she ever tell you what he was like?"

"All I can remember her saying was that he was a tall thin man." McGregor replied.

"Did you see much of her after that?" Matt asked.

"Oh, aye, she was here for about three months after the wee one was born, and after that every other weekend and holidays. You see, wee Francis stayed here with his grandparents until he was about five years old. Never heard of the father ever coming back though, everyone assumed they both had important jobs in London or somewhere."

Matt left the exact change for a pint of beer on the bar, said thanks, and left the pub.

Chapter 33

The two delivery men wheeled the heavy shipment into the lab and maneuvered it into the spot Ian pointed to. As soon as they left, Ian and VJ started ripping the Styrofoam packing apart like little kids opening Christmas presents. It was an unconventional metal coffin, cylindrical in shape, with a flat bottom and a hydraulic platform to allow height adjustment. The manufacturer had painted the outside a warm cream color to soften the harshness of its purpose.

Ian plugged in the power cord and lights began flickering on the control panel. He slid the cover from the porthole on top of the casket and peered into the dark chamber below, where the patient's head would be positioned.

VJ took a quick look into the porthole. "Gives me the creeps."

When Ian pressed a green button marked 'open/close', the semi-circular entry door elevated slowly and a roller system, supporting a mattress frame, came sliding out of the chamber. Inside, the chamber was painted matte black, and when completely closed was hermetically sealed.

The casket had been modified exactly according to Ian's instructions.

"We have about forty-eight hours to set up and test the apparatus," Ian said to VJ, "and Kathleen will be back from her trip tonight, just in time."

VJ got to work immediately, unplugged the power, and began installing and connecting the data devices and monitoring programs. "It will only take an hour or two to fit and check the photodiodes and do some initial testing," he said.

"Great. While you work on that I'll check out the life support system and then tomorrow the fun can begin," Ian said as he walked out the lab.

"What do you mean, fun?" VJ shouted.

"You'll see," Ian shouted back.

When Ian returned, he explained to VJ what he had meant by *fun*. "We need a guinea pig to lie inside the chamber while we test everything and as there are only two of us to choose from, I think you're the better choice."

"Absolutely not, no way," VJ responded. "I'm claustrophobic. I cannot get in there."

"Well, I am certainly not going to fit in there with all of the modifications, not with my two hundred and thirty pounds of lard."

"If it's not going to be you or me, I'll volunteer Kathleen."

"Fine, Kathleen it is. It's her experiment anyway."

"Now what about the life support system?" VJ asked.

"Ready to test; then when that's done, we can start the first live experiment, excuse the pun."

"Nice!" VJ said.

"The first thing we need to do is to check out the oxygen supply, temperature control and monitoring devices. If we get that done today, tomorrow we can experiment with Kathleen inside."

Ian plugged in the chamber and adjusted the temperature control and oxygen flow settings.

* * * * *

182

The following morning, Kathleen showed up shortly after nine and saw Ian and VJ hovering around a metal casket. "Making progress?" she asked.

"Yes, we are, as you will see for yourself shortly," Ian answered.

The apparatus had maintained a steady temperature and oxygen level on the overnight run; they were ready to test it with Kathleen inside.

Ian pressed the button to slide out the mattress platform, placed a disposable foam mattress on it, and told Kathleen to climb on and lie down.

"In the name of Jesus, why me?"

"I'm too big, he's too scared. You're the only one left, so on you go," Ian said with a grin.

Kathleen kicked off her shoes, jumped onto the platform and lay full-stretch on the mattress. Ian connected her to the life support systems and monitoring devices, then handed her a flashlight.

"When we're ready, I will tap on the outside of the chamber and that will be the signal for you to flick the flashlight on and off, okay?"

Kathleen nodded.

Ian pressed the green button and Kathleen disappeared inside the chamber. He waited for ten minutes to let her adjust to the unfamiliar surroundings and then checked that all of the medical monitors were functioning. He then adjusted the oxygen and temperature controls. Remarkably, by now Kathleen's heart rate was a slow sixty beats per minute. Satisfied, he gently tapped on the casket and observed the peak response on the monitor; the photodiodes were working. Ian removed the photographic plate and looked at the negative; it clearly indicated a flash of light.

For the next thirty minutes, Ian wrote up the details of this initial experiment in a lab book. When he was finished, he looked through the porthole and saw she was fast asleep – she certainly didn't suffer from claustrophobia – and even more noteworthy, her heart rate had dropped to a mere fifty-two beats per minute, slow for a woman.

Before Ian opened the chamber, he tapped on the casket to awaken Kathleen. She reacted instinctively and switched the flashlight on and off. Ian observed another peak on the monitor. He pressed the button and Kathleen came sliding out.

"Well?" she asked.

"All systems go," Ian remarked. "Feel like a stiff, do you?"

"Very funny. So, what's next?"

"We'll set it up at the hospital this weekend and arrange to have the life support system disconnected one day next week."

By late Monday morning, the patient's wife and daughter, the physician and Ian, Kathleen and VJ stood around the casket while two nurses gently positioned the patient on the mattress.

Kathleen explained the experiment to the mother and daughter. "We have light monitors on the inside of the chamber and we expect to detect activity at the time of death, hopefully in the form of light." The family nodded without asking any questions.

Once the man was in place, Ian pressed the button and the platform slid slowly into the chamber.

"Stop, stop," the patient's wife shouted as her husband had half-disappeared from view. Ian pressed the button and the platform slowed to a halt.

The woman leaned over and kissed her husband on the forehead, tears streaming down her cheeks. Her daughter put her arm around her and led her to a chair.

"Here, Mom, sit down, it's for the best." She nodded to Ian who re-pressed the button. The casket closed completely.

The next day, Ian and VJ checked all of the monitors and once satisfied that everything was working okay, told the physician they were ready to start the experiment. The daughter willingly signed three sets of release forms and left the room as the nurse switched off the life support.

Ian, Kathleen and VJ stared at the monitors. Nothing changed.

After the first twenty-four hours, Ian asked the physician how long he expected the patient to live without life support. "Anywhere from a few days to a few weeks."

"A few weeks. Gosh, I hope not, for everybody's sake."

Ian and VJ agreed on four-hour shifts to monitor the experiment. Kathleen could come and go as she pleased.

After two days, they both noticed that the patient's vitals were slowly starting to deteriorate, but it was not until early Saturday morning that the physician indicated to them that he thought death would occur within the following twenty-four hours. Ian, Kathleen and VJ decided to remain by the casket and take catnaps.

Ian and Kathleen were fast asleep in the bedside chairs late Saturday night when VJ suddenly heard the intermittent beep from the heart-rate monitor change to a steady tone, signaling the patient's death. He quickly focused his attention on the photodiode monitor as he shook Ian and Kathleen awake. They all stared – nothing!

Ian had a big grin on his face but refrained from saying, "I told you so."

Kathleen shook her head in disappointment. "I was sure we would see something. Wait a minute, let's check the plate."

Ian removed the photographic plate. "Shit!"

"What's wrong?" Kathleen asked.

Ian went red. "I'm sorry, but I forgot to put a new plate in after the lab test."

Kathleen was furious. "Jesus, Mary and Joseph, you bloody idiot, we don't have an unlimited supply of comatose patients!"

VJ kept his head down and fiddled with the controls of the monitor as he reviewed the images at the time of death.

185

"And what the hell are you doing?" she asked.

"Adjusting the gain and sensitivity controls." Then, just as he approached the highest sensitivity level, he saw something for a fleeting second. He turned to Kathleen. "Did you see that?"

"No. What?"

"I don't know. Let's take another look."

Kathleen stared intensely at the screen and there it was. The narrowest of peaks, with an intensity level that was off the charts.

"Can you separate the peaks?" she asked.

"Should be able to, give me a second." VJ adjusted the horizontal axis to separate the peaks from each of the six diodes, but at the monitor's maximum limit there was still only one very narrow peak. VJ froze the signal on the screen.

"There's just this one peak," he said to Kathleen. "I don't understand it. This equipment is supposed to be able to measure the speed of light."

Kathleen shook her head. "Apparently not, it's got to be an extraneous signal. If it were light, there would be separate peaks for the upper and lower photodiodes. Good try, though."

"So, what now?" VJ asked her. "And what are we going to say to the man's family?"

"We're going to carry on." Kathleen glanced toward Ian. "We'll re-test the apparatus and make sure we have a bloody photographic plate in place the next time and conduct the experiment at least three or four more times. As for the poor sod's family, we'll tell them we did get a signal, and it's the first data point, and we will let them know what we find out when we're done."

Ian grinned at Kathleen. "It's a waste of time. We're not going to see anything. Why don't you just accept that?"

"Well, we won't if you keep trying to sabotage my efforts. Beside one experiment proves nothing. Wait a minute."

Kathleen said. "Maybe there is another explanation. What is the maximum sensitivity of your measuring equipment?"

"10^{-7}, why?" VJ answered.

"That could be it. The monitor is not sensitive enough. That's only one-tenth of a millionth of a second. We need to measure one billionth of a second."

VJ grabbed his calculator. "The distance between the photodiodes is exactly twelve inches, and as light travels at a speed of a hundred eighty-six thousand miles per second, that means it'll take approximately one billionth of a second to transverse one foot," he showed Kathleen the display. "You're right."

Kathleen smiled. "No wonder we couldn't see any separation between the peaks. What you need to do is find a more sensitive device, and when you do, we'll re-test everything."

* * * * *

The following week, Ian and VJ checked out all the monitoring equipment, except this time VJ had replaced the photodiode monitor with a later model one hundred times more sensitive.

When they tested the second patient, they observed two very intense peaks, one grid apart.

"How sensitive did you say this equipment is?" Kathleen asked VJ.

"10^{-9}, a hundred times more sensitive than the other."

"So, that's one over one billion – one billionth of a second. It worked! Can you believe this, VJ? It worked."

"Huh." Ian's mind was working overtime as he stared at the monitor and struggled to come up with a more logical explanation.

"Kathleen, the first experiment worked too. The monitor was capable of measuring the speed of light," VJ said.

"What are you talking about? It wasn't sensitive enough. There was no separation of peaks," Kathleen said.

"Look at this," VJ said, pointing to the screen. "You see the peaks on the horizontal axis? They are only one grid apart and as there are a hundred grids on the axis; that means the peaks are actually only one hundredth of one billionth of a second apart."

"Jesus!" Kathleen shouted. "That's one hundred times faster than the speed of light." Kathleen knew of only one phenomenon when this had occurred before and that was at the beginning of time, when a tiny atom exploded and separated faster than the speed of light: the '*big bang*'.

A few minutes later, they carefully removed the photographic plate.

"Bugger me," Ian said as he stared at a small burn hole, surrounded by a halo, scorched on the film. There was no doubt about it, a light of very high intensity was the cause.

Over the next few weeks, they repeated the experiment with a third and then a fourth patient and got the same results.

"Do you know what this means?" Kathleen asked VJ.

"No, tell me."

"It's as I predicted. When the body shuts down, the body's energy condenses into a tiny force that travels at tremendous speed on a journey to--- well, that's something we are going to have to figure out."

"Nirvana, perhaps?" VJ suggested.

"Perhaps, but for now I am not going to concern myself with where the energy goes but focus on proving the theory that Mary, the mother of *Jesus,* was impregnated with a light-form of divine DNA, and at death our individual DNA departs the body in the same manner."

"Interesting," VJ said. "I have to say that I have never heard of any other scientific explanation that comes anywhere close to what you have hypothesized. So what are you going to call this phenomenon of a force traveling faster than the speed of light?"

"Oh, I dunno, perhaps universal light and we could say that this energy or force leaves the body at the speed – of – universal – light."

* * * * *

Since the results of the final experiments, Ian had had trouble sleeping. He tossed and turned in his bed every night, only falling asleep when exhausted. The results of the light experiments had taken him totally by surprise. He argued to himself that maybe there was a burst of energy in the form light that leaves the body at death, so what? That still didn't prove anything. It was just a form of energy, part of the universe.

He reflected on how much simpler it had been when he was a believer. Ever since he was a teenager, he had thought about the mysteries of the Immaculate Conception, the Holy Grail and the Shroud of Turin. And now here he was, twenty-five years later, trying to disprove their authenticity.

Ian got out of bed and stared out of the bedroom window. It was a clear crystal night, stars flickering like distant lighthouses; most of them having been extinguished billions of years ago. What did it all mean? He recalled the many hours he had spent at Glastonbury Tor wrestling with the mysteries of life. He once dreamed of being *the* scientist to solve the mystery of the Shroud. He had repeatedly wrestled with the carbon-14 dating controversy. How could the image of a crucified man from two thousand years ago be imprinted on a cloth only seven hundred years old? They obviously couldn't both be right. Or could they?

189

While at Cambridge, he had read a number of books on the Shroud of Turin and the Holy Grail: Ian Wilson's *The Blood and the Shroud* and *The Holy Blood and the Holy Grail* and a number of fiction books on the same subjects, many of which had an almost cult-like following, convincing readers that they were based on real facts, when in reality they were all fiction.

"It's all fiction promulgated by the church to instill fear and retribution into the minds of the faithful," he preached to an imaginary audience in the garden below.

He climbed back into bed, drifting off to sleep as he tried to convince himself he was right. But the same old nightmare kept waking him. It became more vivid every time it occurred. He was in a dimly-lit room two thousand years ago with the other ten apostles, staring at his own hand dripping blood after he had remove it from the spear wound in Jesus' side.

He *was* Thomas and he would awaken with a start as Christ stared into his eyes and said, "*Blessed are those who have not seen and yet believe.*"

Chapter 34

When Kathleen arrived at work one morning and walked past VJ's office, on her way to the lab, she saw him at his desk with his head buried in papers. She knocked on his door. He pressed a button and it opened about six to seven inches. She stuck her head in the opening and said. "Sorry, a couple of weeks ago you said something was bothering you and you wanted to talk to me."

"Not bothering me, more a question of curiosity and your opinions on a few things."

"Okay, how about now, and a cup of coffee in the cafeteria?"

VJ stood up and shuffled the papers on his desk. "Yeah fine, I'll join you there in a couple of minutes." He neatly sorted out the papers and put some of them in a file cabinet and then locked the drawer. He made sure his office was secure and then joined Kathleen in the company café.

"So what is it you want to talk about?" Kathleen asked.

"Well, when you asked me how I thought we get to Nirvana from here, I didn't have an answer so I wanted to ask you the same question, and also learn a little more about your religious beliefs."

Kathleen laughed. "Let me answer your second question and then I'll get to your first question. I was brought up strict Roman Catholic and went to mass every Sunday with my parents and my father's brother and family. In fact, my only cousin became a priest, and is now a cardinal and lives in Rome?"

"I did hear some rumors about that, are you close?"

"Yes, very close considering, and I actually called him recently to discuss the conclusions of Divine DNA, but in the end I didn't have the nerve and put it off. Of course he is ten years older than me and went into a seminary when I was six, but he did teach me to ride a bicycle when I was five." Kathleen smiled and then grimaced. "In fact, I had a bad accident the first time he put me on the bike, I crashed and had to be stitched up. But he has always been there for me and we would meet up whenever he came home on holidays, he is also my mentor and has a sound knowledge of biology; he double-majored in Biology and Theology, and chose the latter as a career or more to the point, 'vocation'."

"I guess if you have a cousin who is a cardinal you are obliged to practice your religion?"

"Well not really, I have had my moments when my faith has been very shaky and missed mass frequently; especially after all of the scandals in Ireland."

"Oh, what happened?"

"In the mid to late nineties, just before I went to college, all hell broke loose in Ireland when the extent of pedophile priests was exposed, abusing young innocent boys and girls, and reports of several bishops who had fathered children. It had been rumored for years that a lot of catholic priests had secret mistresses, more often than not their willing housekeepers. But that was just the tip of the iceberg, the eventual revelations and how widespread it was, shocked most practicing Catholics to the core, me included, Jesus, Mary and Joseph, the dirty dogs, preaching one thing and doing another. It's not surprising that hundreds of thousands of priests and millions of Catholics worldwide left the church, which is why the Church now concentrates it missionary recruitments in third-world countries in Africa, South America and East Asia. Provide clothes and food to those without on a regular basis and you can easily get their attention, let's just hope those vulnerable people are not subject to the same kind of abuse. Anyway, you got me on my soapbox so I think that's enough about religion, so let's get to your first question. You can guess my answer to that since our experiments proved an intense light leaves the body at death and I can only assume it goes back to our maker, whoever he is or they are."

VJ looked puzzled. "What are you implying, 'whoever they are?' you think God might be more than one person?"

"Well, although I am a fervent believer in God I am capable of thinking outside of the box. For example, is it too far-fetched to think that there might be another civilization somewhere in the Universe who are thousands of years ahead of us and much further advanced, and responsible for our existence on this earth?"

"Interesting." VJ changed the subject, not wanting to pursue that particular avenue. "Do you have any experience or knowledge of spirits coming back to visit family members after they have passed away?"

"I have heard lots of stories, particularly from the Irish, who always tend to embellish anyway, but I cannot say I have come across any evidence, what about you?"

"No, only the stuff I told you about my cousin's experience and what my grandfather told me, but that was a little different. I don't know of any proven cases of dead people returning. Don't you think that if there is an afterlife, someone, somewhere would have returned to prove it?"

"Maybe not, if you think about it, our experiments proved that intense light leaves the body at ten times the speed of ordinary light, which means it can travel outside of our atmosphere and into space in less than one hundredth of a second. I don't think it would be bouncing around near the earth for too long, and besides once it is in the form of spectral DNA, I don't feel it is feasible that it would appear as a lifeform."

"I guess that seems logical. So coming back to what you said about our spectral DNA going back to our maker, if you believe that, it begs the question, why are we here? What is our purpose? Do you have an answer?"

"No, I don't have an answer, but I do have an opinion as you would expect, and that is if we do have a return ticket I have to believe our *raison d'etre* is to further the knowledge of mankind in any way that we can, and I think you and I are doing just that with the kind of groundbreaking research we are doing with MacLeod."

VJ shook his head. "I don't know, I think that is a pretty simplistic point of view. Have you discussed this with Ian?"

"No, why?"

"Well, I think your experiments have thrown him a curve, he seems to be struggling with his own beliefs right now."

Chapter 35

The week after his trip to Scotland, Matt attended the two weekly lectures and spent a few hours every day in the lab organizing his bench space and getting to know Gary Cook, the only post-doc working during summer. Gary was in his second year of a four-year post-doctoral study in the field of microbial genetics. Matt was familiar with Gary's research and stopped to chat with him each time he saw him in the lab.

Twice during the week, Matt went to the Cavendish labs – relocated in the 1970s to a new site a few miles away from the original building – to research the Watson and Crick era. He had made the acquaintance of an administrative assistant; she smiled as he approached her desk.

"I think I have found what you are looking for, Dr Price. Here is a list of names of scientists and technicians who were working there during that period."

"That's great," Matt replied as he took the sheet of paper from her and glanced at it.

Back at the university library, he systematically went through every name on the list. Most were now dead, but three were still alive. One, an eighty-four-year-old professor had been twenty-six-year-old the year MacLeod was born. Matt then discovered that he had been a post-doc student of MacLeod's mother at the time. Perfect.

Professor Alan Merchant had left Cambridge in 1972 to take an assistant professor's job in the biochemistry department at Oxford University. He rose to chairman of the department, a position he retired from nine years ago. He now lived in the Cotswold's, a two-hour car journey from Cambridge.

Matt tracked down the professor's telephone number through the university faculty alumni association. He called him and explained about the research on Watson, Crick and MacLeod and asked if he could visit him to seek his help.

"What did you say your name was?" Merchant hollered down the phone.

"Matthew. Matthew Price, from Harvard," Matt shouted back.

"Harvard. In that case, you'd better come. Lunch on Saturday, twelve sharp." Merchant hung up.

On Saturday morning, Matt rented a Land Rover LRX and set off to see the professor. After ninety minutes, he reached the outskirts of Stratford upon Avon and continued south on the A429 and into the Cotswold's. He drove through Moreton-in-Marsh, Stow-on-the-Wold and into Bourton-on-the-Water, where he stopped for a cup of coffee and asked for directions. Fifteen minutes later, he arrived in Little Fotherington. The village was like a picture postcard peppered with quaint thatched cottages that were built in the 1600s and 1700s, that could only be matched by imaginary places like Brigadoon.

Matt nervously maneuvered his rental car around parked vehicles and local pedestrians crisscrossing the streets from one shop to another.

He looked at the clock on the dashboard, eleven forty-five, and thought, 'Why's the traffic moving so slowly?' Everyone in front of him was slowing down to watch something in the village square. What? He shook his head. 'You have to be kidding,' he said aloud. Grown men dressed in matching bright-colored medieval costumes danced around like fairies with sticks in their hands, weaving around each other in some sort of ancient dance ritual. He rolled the window down and heard the sound of the jingle bells sewn to leather pads wrapped around their legs. One of Shakespeare's plays described such a group of dancers – he couldn't remember the play or the name of the prancing fairies.

At five minutes after twelve, he found a place to park and identified the house. Merchant's thatched cottage stood at one end of a cul-de-sac. The outside walls, painted a traditional off white, contrasted with the dark brown woodwork. Matt lifted the unhinged gate, carefully replaced it behind him, hurried to the front door and rang the bell.

The professor's housekeeper, a small plump woman with a reddish face and a welcoming smile, opened the old oak front door.

"Dr Price, please come in. He's expecting you."

Matt banged his forehead on the frame, causing a red mark to appear just below his hairline.

"And mind your head," she added.

"Thanks," he said, as he followed her into the living room, padding a handkerchief on his forehead to see if there was any blood.

Professor Merchant, standing by the fireplace, dressed in beige trousers, a blue open-neck shirt and a buttoned-up navy blazer; looked more like someone out of the 1980s than the present time. Matt felt underdressed in his slacks and short-sleeved shirt. He glanced around. Dark brown beams crossed the ceiling, while a mahogany chair rail separated busy floral-patterned wallpaper on the bottom and a cream painted wall on the upper half. Books were scattered everywhere.

"Dr Price, welcome," the professor said, pointing to a comfortable armchair.

"Thank you, professor," Matt replied. "First of all, I would like to thank---"

The professor raised his hand as he walked toward a liquor cabinet.

"First things first, Dr Price. What is your poison?"

"Oh, I'll have whatever you are having, thank you."

"I will have my usual aperitif, a glass of Dalwhinnie."

"That's fine," Matt responded, not realizing Dalwhinnie is a whisky – he hated whisky – but now was not the time to decline his host's hospitality.

The professor sat in the other armchair opposite Matt and said, "Cheers."

"Cheers," Matt responded, then took a minuscule mouthful of the Dalwhinnie. He winced a little as the smooth droplets slid down his throat. To his surprise it tasted nothing like the very few blended whiskies he had tried in the past.

"Now, Dr Price, tell me about this research project of yours."

Matt told the professor about his research. "Can you help me?"

"Perhaps," Merchant replied. "I did have the good fortune to know all three of these very fine gentlemen. What would you like to know?"

"I know you worked in the labs at Cambridge when Watson and Crick were there. Maybe you could start by telling me what kind of people they were and what the atmosphere was like after they had discovered the double helix and won the Nobel Prize."

"Gladly," the professor replied, finishing the whisky in one gulp. "But let's first have lunch."

He got up and led Matt into the adjoining dining room where the professor's housekeeper was waiting to serve them. The first course of avocado and prawns in a Marie Rose sauce was already on the table. As they took their seats, the professor nodded to his housekeeper who immediately poured each of them a glass of white Burgundy. Matt noticed a bottle of Bordeaux already open on the table.

The professor took a rather large sip of wine as he demolished the avocado and prawns and then proceeded to tell all he knew about Watson and Crick. He was still talking about them two glasses of wine later when his housekeeper served the main course of cold beef and salad.

He grabbed the bottle of Bordeaux. "Red?"

"No, thanks, I'll stay on white."

"With beef?"

"Yes, 'fraid so. I like red wine, but my constitution prefers white."

Merchant picked up the empty Burgundy bottle, banged it on the table and yelled, "another bottle of white for our guest." He filled his glass to the brim with red.

"Fascinating about the early years," Matt said to the professor. "Now, as you know, I am particularly interested in Francis MacLeod and I understand that you were one of his mother's post-doctoral students. Is that correct?"

The professor took a gulp from his fourth glass of wine. Matt was not far behind on his third glass.

"Yes, that's right. I studied under Anne MacLeod for four years; a fine woman and a first-rate scientist."

"She was your post-doc professor when MacLeod was born in 1969?"

"Yes, that's right."

"What about her husband? How well did you know him?"

"Well, I didn't. You see, she wasn't married, although there was some speculation at the time about who fathered the child. It was not the sort of thing one discussed, really. All I know is she took a six-month sabbatical in the winter of 1968 and returned in the summer of 1969. I believe Francis was born sometime in the spring."

"Yes, in April. The twenty-third, to be exact. I take it from what you have said that you know who his father was?"

Merchant lowered his head, looked over the top of his glasses and stared at Matt. The professor took another gulp of wine and then said. "Isn't it obvious?"

"What do you mean, obvious?"

"Well, MacLeod's first name."

Matt stared at the professor.

"You're joking. Francis. You mean Francis--- Francis Crick?"

"I don't know for sure, so, please, whatever you do, don't quote me. But that was one of the rumors at the time."

"A tall, thin man," Matt muttered.

"Yes, he was," the professor said.

"No, that's not what I meant," Matt replied. "Well, yes, it is, I suppose. When I was in Scotland doing research last weekend, a local resident of Anne MacLeod's home town told me that a tall thin man had visited a couple of times soon after her son was born."

"Please keep in mind it was only a rumor and never verified. I don't think young Francis was aware of the rumor and nor does he need to hear it now. Let's go back into the living room and have coffee and a digestif."

Afterwards, Matt thanked the professor for his hospitality and then turned to his housekeeper to thank her, the professor already nodding off in his armchair. The housekeeper winked as she let him out the front door.

"And mind your head this time," she said.

As Matt left the house and stepped into the hot summer afternoon, his head started to spin. It was only then he realized how much alcohol he had consumed. In no state to drive, he pulled the key out of his pocket and scrolled his thumb across the screen to open the driver's door. The door opened and he crawled into the back seat and immediately fell asleep. He woke up after two hours and looked at the time, four thirty. The shops would close at five p.m. He had thirty minutes to find a cup of strong coffee before heading back to Cambridge.

On the drive back, he kept thinking about what he had just learned from the professor. It was no big deal. Nobody cares whether a person was born out of wedlock – more than fifty percent were these days. No need to tell Anderson either. How would he react? So MacLeod's a bastard. Anderson had already called him that. As he thought about how much time he had spent trying to find out who had fathered MacLeod, Matt realized what a waste of time it had been. What purpose would it serve anyway? Anderson and his perverted instructions, 'From the time his father's sperm entered his mother'.

He wondered what drove Anderson. Professional jealousy maybe? Had something happened between him and MacLeod in the past? It was very strange for a guy in Anderson's position to have such a vendetta.

Matt reminded himself that he wasn't doing this for Anderson. He was doing it out of loyalty to Garret. After all, Anderson and SMB had always been a primary source of funding for the Institute. And what did Garret say to him before he left? 'I wouldn't worry about it; you're not going find anything on MacLeod anyway, so go enjoy yourself for a couple of months'.

Chapter 36

Kathleen was sitting with Ian and VJ in a coffee shop a week after her conclusion about the speed of universal light.

Ian, silent, looked like he hadn't slept in days.

VJ asked. "Okay, so you are convinced by your experiments, but how would you go about swaying a skeptic like me?"

"You were there. You witnessed what happened to the photographic plates, you saw the peaks on the monitor. 'Blessed are those who have not seen, and yet---' " Kathleen said.

Ian went pale. "Bloody hell!"

"What's wrong?" Kathleen asked.

"You've broken my bad dream . . . nightmares," Ian said. "That phrase . . . that's what's wrong."

"What on earth are you talking about?" VJ asked.

Ian went on to explain that since the experiments, he had been tossing and turning every night, having nightmares about being the apostle Doubting Thomas.

"I was a devout Catholic before college, but an atheist since. Why I am having this persistent nightmare and waking up to that phrase ringing in my ears?"

"Ah, ha," Kathleen said, "A battle of conscience. Having doubts about your atheistic beliefs. You know you are in a minority, even among scientists. The believers outnumber the non-believers by more than twenty to one."

"I don't need a sermon, Kathleen. I am a scientist. Let's get serious; I'll need a lot more evidence before I am convinced about any of this stuff."

"You're a bleeding Doubting Thomas!" Kathleen responded, poking her index finger into Ian's arm. "The only evidence I have so far is what we have already talked about. But think about the laws of conservation of energy. Energy is always conserved when it is transformed from one form to another. And the body's energy is not just made up of body heat, but chemical and spiritual energy too – a life force."

"So?" Ian said.

"In addition to heat dissipation at the time of death, we know there is another form of energy that condenses into light and leaves the body at a much faster speed than either heat or light. I know we need more evidence to convince skeptics like you and VJ, but I believe we can get it."

VJ laughed. "What are you going to do next, scientifically prove the existence of God? Get real."

"Maybe it's not out of the question."

VJ shook his head. "Here we go again, another bright idea. What now?"

"I have to admit that I have been thinking about this a lot during the past week; the existence of God, Jesus Christ, the Son of God, and Christianity."

"That's pretty obvious; I just hope that you're not turning into a religious nut."

Kathleen answered. "I don't think so, but when I was young I was constantly looking for answers to age-old questions, such as the existence of God? Was Jesus Christ really the Son of God? What is the meaning of life? Is there such a place as heaven?"

"So did I," said Ian, "but by the time I got to university, I had given up on those questions, which is why I gave up religion altogether."

203

"I can understand that," VJ joined in.

A group of five students sat down at the table next to them. They were young – first years – brimming with enthusiasm and babbling about an English lit assignment.

Ian raised his cup and took a gulp of coffee. "I wish I was young and artsy and oblivious to the mysteries of life."

VJ smiled. "What fun would that be?"

"I don't know about fun, but I'm sure I'd get a better night's sleep."

Kathleen waved a hand across the front of their eyes. "Okay, boys, let's focus."

"Yes Ms Bossy Boots," VJ said. "What I wanted to add, is that I think most people reflect on those questions at some point in their lives and then conclude there aren't any answers, so it becomes a question of faith. That's what religion is all about: faith. You either have it or you don't and Hinduism is no different from Christianity in that regard. So what's really behind this religious epiphany of yours?"

"The great debate – the congruence of religion and science – and Francis's belief that perfect DNA exists, that's what really hit a nerve with me. And if it does, I have to believe that perfect DNA is the same thing as divine DNA, and the issue is how to prove it."

VJ smiled. "You've thought of another scientific experiment, haven't you?"

"Maybe. We have the scientific tools and Francis's hypothesis has certainly made me think that some of these mysteries can be explained by science. There is just one problem. My original idea was to obtain a sample of Christ's blood so we could test His DNA – but there is no blood sample from Jesus Christ."

VJ nodded.

"Unless," Ian said, "Jesus Christ did marry and have children, as many people believe. His bloodline might still exist

204

today. Maybe you can track down a descendent of Christ, and then check their DNA."

"That's a myth," said Kathleen, "but I do remember reading a book when I was a teenager where the authors claimed that very thing; convinced a lot of people at the time. I can't remember the name, *The Blood and the Holy Grail*, or something like that."

"Yeah, *The Holy Blood and the Holy Grail*," Ian said, "by Baigent, Leigh and Lincoln. They suggested Mary Magdalene had a daughter named Sarah and that Jesus Christ was her father. The legendary Knights Templar kept the secret hidden for hundreds of years. The authors claimed that not only did the bloodline exist in a line of French royalty named the Merovingian family but that this bloodline was the Holy Grail."

VJ was tapping numbers on his iPhone. "Even if such a person or persons are alive today and you manage to trace them, wouldn't Christ's DNA be too diluted to be meaningful now?"

Ian asked. "What are you getting at?"

"Well, it's two thousand years since Christ, and if you say each generation is about thirty to forty years, then that's about fifty to sixty generations. With each passing generation His portion would be diluted by half, which means any person carrying Christ's DNA today will have far less than one percent of the original DNA."

Kathleen said. "Jesus, that's a good point; I didn't even think about that."

"Then, I guess that's another fine idea out of the window," VJ added.

"Maybe not. I have just thought of the something," Kathleen said. "The Shroud of Turin."

"What's that?" VJ asked.

"Don't tell me you haven't heard of the Shroud of Turin. It's the linen cloth Christ was buried in. It bears an image of his crucified body, blood and all."

"Never heard of it. You seem to forget that I am not a Christian."

"When Christ was taken down from the cross after his crucifixion he was prepared for burial by Joseph of Arimathea, who wrapped the body in a fine linen shroud. After Christ's resurrection on the third day, His body was no longer in the tomb, but the cloth was still there lying on the floor. Then it disappeared and wasn't seen again for another five hundred years."

The conversation at the next table died as the five students listened to what Kathleen was saying.

"When the Shroud was discovered in the city walls of Edessa in the sixth century, it bore a miraculous image of the crucified Christ with traces of blood from his wounds caused by whip lashings, a crown of thorns and a Roman spear. The Shroud became a symbol of Christianity and was displayed to the faithful as evidence that Jesus Christ was truly the Son of God. It has had a spotty history, appearing and disappearing for long periods of time throughout the Holy Land and Europe, until it eventually reappeared in the fourteenth century. But since then its whereabouts have always been known."

Kathleen stopped when she noticed she had a larger audience than intended. "Want a history lesson, do you?" She asked the students. They responded by turning their chairs to face her.

Kathleen continued as if she were giving one of her lectures. "It is without doubt the most researched and controversial religious relic in history. Millions believe it is genuine and an equal number think it is a fake. For over a hundred years, it has been the subject of the most rigorous scientific research, and in just about every new scientific study, a new controversy unfolds. When Secondo Pia took the first photograph of the Shroud in 1898, he was shocked to see that the image was negative, later confirmed by many others with more sophisticated cameras. Many years later, the Shroud was made available for further scientific testing that identified human blood. Then, in 1988, the most controversial scientific testing was carried out when three different labs conducted carbon-14 dating on fragments of the Shroud. Their findings stunned the believers when they reported that the actual cloth only dated back to between 1260 and 1390."

One of the students raised her hand. "The carbon-14 dating proved beyond a doubt that the Shroud is a fake, end of story."

"Really, and you are qualified to make that determination?"

The student hesitated. "Well, I'm not a scientist, but from what I have read, it is a well-established technology."

"Yes, it is, but what if the testing labs were given bad samples to test?" Kathleen didn't wait for a response. "Those who thought the Shroud was a fake had a field day and all kinds of theories were put forward on how the image was made. One belief was that it is actually a hoax created by Leonardo da Vinci in the fourteenth century."

Kathleen paused to take a sip of coffee and turned her attention back to VJ.

"You would think that the carbon-14 results would have been a huge setback for the Catholic Church, and many feared that the Church would never allow the Shroud to be subjected to further scientific scrutiny, but that has not been the case. They have periodically allowed access to prominent international scientists. The believers have not been silenced either and have led a vigorous campaign to prove that the carbon-14 dating was flawed, either through instrumental error or testing fragments of the cloth that had been repaired by nuns in the sixteenth century. The controversy still rages today."

Ian nodded with a thin smile. "It was the carbon-14 dating that convinced me in the end that the Shroud is a fake. Three different labs all with the same results can't all be wrong."

"It's still fascinating," VJ commented. "I would like to learn more about it; can't beat a good scientific mystery."

"You should," Ian said. "In fact, I believe I still have an old copy of *The Blood and the Shroud* lying around at home, I'll bring it in tomorrow."

"Thanks, I'll look forward to reading it."

Kathleen continued. "There are labs that still have some blood samples taken from the Shroud a few years ago. If we could get some of their blood to test, we'll be in business."

"Why would they give you some of their precious samples?" Ian asked.

"In exchange for scientific evidence that solves the controversy of the Shroud."

"Another scientific experiment?"

"Exactly." Kathleen nodded.

"What kind?"

"I'll tell you what, Ian," Kathleen said. "Like me, you have spent a lot of time in the past searching for answers to the mysteries of life, but the difference now is that I still want to prove the existence of God, while you want to disprove it. So why don't I come up with some new experiments and have you carry them out, and then when we analyze the results, it will be from two different perspectives." She patted him on the shoulder. "And I do trust your scientific expertise."

"Okay, it's a deal," he said, shaking Kathleen's hand.

"Teamwork, how delightful," VJ said. "So, do you need me?"

"Not for a few days. Ian and I need to set up the experiments first."

"Good, I have some research of my own I need to do before the others get back."

208

Chapter 37

While Kathleen and Ian were doing preliminary lab work, VJ spent several days on a puzzle that made him glad he'd ordered two sets of the new biochips.

Using his own and MacLeod's biochip he could now access the central computer room without MacLeod being present. He carefully studied Darren's data. Someone in the blood pool had two mutated copies of the Parkinson's gene – but who?

Parkinson's genes were located on chromosomes 4 and 13. He stared at the mutated gene on chromosome 13 – unlucky for someone, he thought. He was not a geneticist, but he had spent enough time reviewing data with MacLeod to understand what he was looking at.

The only way to find the mutated gene carrier was to test all the blood. He retrieved the six samples from the -70°C freezer and took a few milliliters of each. He packed the vials into a cold box and arranged for a local company to pick them up for genetic testing.

He expected answers within forty-eight hours, but they called him with the results the following morning. No question about it: blood sample KL 666 tested positive for the mutated Parkinson's gene. Now all he had to do was find out whose it was.

He hacked into the database of MacLeod's computer, found the right file, but there was no information cross-linking the samples to individual team members. He remembered MacLeod saying that the information would be held by the company that drew the blood, and he would be the only other person to have access. As much as VJ tried, he could not access the password for the secure system.

He thought of another solution, called the genetic testing company and asked them if they had blood-typed the samples. They had not, so he asked them to blood-type sample KL 666.

* * * * *

When Ian was doing research at Alpha Genetics, it had dawned on him that the answer to the Shroud puzzle was staring him in the face. However, at the time, he had lost interest in religion and he was so busy doing research into the genetics of degenerative diseases that he had no time for anything else. Now he had both the time and the technical resources to conduct his experiments. But there was a difference. He no longer cared about the credit he might receive. It was now a means to an end and one of much bigger proportions – proving whether or not Jesus Christ was the Son of God.

Kathleen and Ian had designed a series of preliminary experiments, each one building on the next until the final experiment. Like any other research Ian was accustomed to doing, he took a new lab book, titled and dated it, then wrote up a list of all the items he would need. In this case, he did not need a single piece of modern-day apparatus. After all, he was trying to re-create something that had occurred a long time ago.

One of the most important items was linen, and although it would be virtually impossible to find very old linen – similar to that used in the Middle-Ages – most modern linen had the same herringbone weave used for thousands of years in its manufacture. The only other items he needed were a flat wooden board, small nails, water and blood. The latter was no problem as he had access to half a pint of his own blood in the -70°C freezer.

He cut two pieces of linen six inches square from the roll of cloth, then splattered some small spots of blood on one and left it to dry overnight.

The next morning, Ian studied the blood stains. They had completely dried out and diffused into the linen. The spots were larger than they had been the day before. He took the other piece of linen and laid it flat on the bottom of a twelve-inch square dish securing it with tape. He laid the first linen face down on top of it and then poured liquid into the dish to cover them. He left the dish on a lab bench to dry out overnight.

On the third day, Ian carefully separated the pieces of linen and stared at the faint stains on the lower cloth. The experiment was inconclusive. He photographed the two pieces of linen, taped them to blank pages of his lab book and made some notes alongside.

He called VJ and asked him for his help with a second experiment. They agreed to meet at the squash club at lunchtime the following day.

An hour before he was due to meet Ian, VJ received a call from the genetic testing company with the blood type of sample KL 666: it was AB. His blood type. He knew AB was the rarest of the four blood groups. Only one in thirty Caucasians had this blood type, but it was three times more prevalent in Indians than Caucasians. VJ was devastated. His grandmother had died of Parkinson's disease in her early fifties, and it was a sad and humiliating death.

He sat staring at his computer screen, thinking about his wife Imelda and his two children. What kind of future would they have dealing with a father suffering from Parkinson's? VJ looked at his watch – eleven thirty a.m. He had reserved a court as Ian requested and was waiting in the locker room of the squash club with his chin in his hands staring into space when Ian arrived.

"Hi, are you okay?" Ian asked.

"Yeah, yeah, fine. Nothing a good game of squash won't cure," VJ replied.

"Want to talk about it?"

VJ shook his head. "I didn't know that you played squash."

"I don't. I haven't played since I was at university," Ian said. "So, don't worry, I am looking forward to you beating the pants off me."

"Fine by me. I haven't played since Francis left for Switzerland and I need the exercise. I am surprised we haven't heard from him."

"Did he tell you what he was going to be doing there?"

"No, not a word." VJ started hitting the small black rubber ball against the back wall.

After just a few minutes, VJ had Ian running all over the court. Ian had barely managed to get a shot back.

VJ stopped playing and said, "Why are you here?"

Ian panted, trying to catch his breath. "Simple, really. I need to work up a good sweat. I'll explain to you on the way back to the lab, but for now just give me your best shots."

VJ shrugged and after thirty minutes, VJ was making all the shots, dragging Ian around the court.

When they had finished, Ian dripped from head to toe with sweat, and he intended to leave it that way until he got back to the lab. Ian had not trimmed his beard or hair for over a week. He was disheveled and exhausted, but happy.

"Thanks, pal. That was a heck of a workout."

Laughing, VJ said, "You look like a vagrant. So, what do you want me to do?"

"I'll explain back at the lab."

Ian took a one cc syringe full of his own blood from the refrigerator and handed it to VJ, then sat on a chair.

"I want you to carefully place eight to ten spots of blood across the top of my head then observe what happens."

VJ watched the blood form little rivulets down Ian's forehead. "It's trickling down your face."

"I know, I can feel it. It's ticklish, tell me when it's about to reach my eyebrows."

After a few minutes VJ said, "Okay, what now?"

"Take that piece of cloth and put it over my face," Ian answered as he lay down on the lab floor.

VJ placed the two-foot square piece of linen cloth across Ian's face and gently positioned it around his hair, eyes, nose, mouth and beard. Ian lay there motionless as the blood intermingled with facial fluids and sweat diffused into the cloth. After forty-five minutes, VJ carefully removed the cloth, placing it face up on the lab bench. They looked at it. It was a surprisingly adequate outline of Ian's bloodied face with salty sweat marks, pore oils and blood spatter on it. They left it on the bench to dry overnight.

The following day, they placed the wooden board on a lab bench. Stretching a new piece of linen flat across the board, they fastened it with small nails. Next, they took the linen with the image of Ian's face and stretched it face down on top of the first piece of linen. VJ secured the second piece of linen by nailing strips of wood along all four sides of the cloths.

Ian filled a flask with ice-cubes and a heaped spoonful of salt, added cold water, then carefully poured it into the framed area so that both linens were entirely soaked.

VJ stood watching. "So what are you actually trying to do here?"

"When I was an undergrad we did some experiments using an outdated technique called 'Western Blot'. It was a biological method for separating and then transferring proteins from one membrane to another. Then, when I was at Alpha Genetics it occurred to me that maybe that could explain the controversy of

213

the Shroud, a two thousand-year-old image of a crucified man transferred onto medieval cloth. We'll soon know if it's a feasible theory."

They left the linens to dry for three days.

Kathleen joined them as Ian and VJ carefully separated the two linens and lay them face up on the lab bench. Ian shook his head as he looked at the faint stains on the bottom cloth.

"Not as well defined as I had hoped for."

VJ just studied both linens. "But some transfer has definitely taken place. What if you use hot water instead?"

"No, the heat would just denature the blood."

Kathleen added, "Maybe there is some element you are missing?"

Ian nodded. "Perhaps. I will have to rethink it through."

Chapter 38

1352 Mont-Saint-Michel, France

For several weeks during the cold winter nights Benedictine alchemist Paolo Aquinas and his young assistant, Gabriel, studied the waves swishing back and forth over the rocks in the moonlight off the Normandy coast. They had hammered two posts, one meter apart, firmly into the shoreline to carefully measure the average height of the evening tides. Satisfied with the data, Aquinas instructed Gabriel to position two more posts, in line with the first two but four meters apart. Together they fixed a flat wooden board onto the posts making sure it was level. Early one evening they stretched some very fine three-to-one weaved herringbone twill linen across the full length of the board and secured it. Carefully handling the Shroud, they placed it face down on the bottom cloth and smoothed it out before nailing wooden strips along all four sides.

Aquinas, aware that if the experiment didn't work it could be the end of his career, perhaps even his life; sat on a rock for several hours and watched the icy-cold seawater gently sweep back and forth across the linens, covering them by no more than two to three centimeters. At eight p.m. he turned in for the night. He was suddenly awakened at two a.m. by booms of thunder that reverberated around the walls of his stark living quarters. He jumped up and looked out the small window as jagged flashes of lightning darted out of the heavy sky striking the shoreline below.

Meter-high waves were lashing angrily against the makeshift platform. Panicking, he banged on Gabriel's door and the two of them ran down the monastery steps and out into the freezing night. Waist high in the icy water they struggled to free the board supporting the precious linen. Exhausted, they carried the heavily soaked board into the chapel and laid it on the stone floor in front of the altar. Aquinas fell to his knees and prayed. At sunrise he and Gabriel moved the board into the dungeon and locked the door.

A week went by and Aquinas could wait no longer. He and Gabriel wrapped the board in cloth and loaded it across two mules and set off on the long and arduous journey to Lirey, the home of Geoffrey de Charny.

Aquinas explained to de Charny what had taken place the night they had set up the experiment as he and Gabriel placed the board on the floor of the Great Hall and removed the protective cloth. De Charny knelt down beside the board to examine it more closely. He touched the linens - they were now dry - but he noticed something odd.

"What are these scorched nails?" he asked.

Aquinas moved closer and knelt beside de Charny, observing the charred nails for the first time. "The only explanation is lightning," he answered, fearing now that even more damage had been done to the Shroud.

"Separate the linens!" De Charny ordered.

Aquinas and his assistant cautiously peeled the linens apart and laid them out side by side.

They stepped back and all three gazed at the two cloths in astonishment.

Visibly relieved, Aquinas fell to his knees and prayed over the linens.

Blood, body fluids, pollens, fibrils, shards, insects and other extraneous debris had separated from the upper linen and transferred onto the bottom cloth. Heavier elements in blood such as iron, assisted by gravity, were in higher concentrations on the bottom linen. This would, centuries later, lead some scientists to claim that the Shroud was a painted forgery due to iron oxide concentrations similar to those of pigments used in paint in the Middle-Ages.

Less intense than the original Shroud image, the lower linen showed an exact replica but *mirror image* of the Shroud. Five and a half centuries later, one of the world's early photographers, Secondo Pia took the first photograph of the Shroud of Turin and noticed that it was a photographic negative, the rights and lefts reversed, baffling scientists for years to come.

Chapter 39

Matt was having coffee in the department tearoom at the Genetics Institute with Gary Cook – discussing bacterial genetics – when the subject of Genon came up.

"So you know those guys over there?" Matt asked.

"Who doesn't? Not that I am close to any of them, but we do cross paths at seminars and conferences."

"Do you know Darren Richards?"

"Yes, I have had a drink with him a few times. Do you know Darren?"

"I do. We met in the States and I was fully expecting to see him when I arrived here, but apparently he has gone back there."

"Oh, he has? They did close the place for a month, I do know that."

"It must be nice being able to close a business down for a month's vacation in the summer, just like academia. It certainly would never happen with a business in the US."

Gary smiled. "It's not that usual here, either, but something happened and the managing director, MacLeod, decided to give everyone a month off with pay."

"What do you mean, something happened? Like what?" Matt fired back quickly.

"Well, I had heard that they were going to be having an IPO soon and they all expected to get rich, very rich, but it's rumored that MacLeod postponed the IPO."

"He did? Why?"

"I don't know; you need to talk to someone at Genon."

"I will. I'll ask Darren, but I don't think he gets back for another week or so."

"You could always talk to Brenda," Gary suggested.

"Who's she?"

"Brenda Thompson. She's MacLeod's assistant, and I know she's around because I just saw her in the city yesterday."

"Do you happen to know her telephone number?"

"I don't, but I know someone who does, I can get it for you."

"Thanks, that would be great," Matt said. "She probably knows when Darren and the others are coming back."

* * * * *

Brenda had been on a two-week vacation with a friend who owned a condominium in the south of Spain; she took Brenda there at least once a year.

Brenda did not recognize the number that appeared on her iPhone and was even more surprised when she heard the American accent.

"Hi, there, is this Brenda Thompson?" Matt asked.

"Er, yes. Who is this?"

"You don't know me, ma'am, my name is Matt Price. I am here at Cambridge University on a two-month summer exchange from Harvard and I am a friend of Darren Richards."

"Oh, I see. Darren is in the States right now," Brenda said.

"Yes, I know. I was wondering if you know when he will be returning."

"I am not absolutely sure, but I believe at the end of next week. If you need to know exactly, I can go into the office and look at the calendar."

"That's okay; he's going to be back when he's back, so to speak."

Brenda laughed. "That's very true."

Matt thought carefully before saying, "Ms. Thompson, can I take you into my confidence? Part of my assignment here is to do research on the life of Sir Francis MacLeod. Harvard intends to honor him next year. Would it be possible to meet you and discuss his life and career?"

Brenda hesitated. "Er--- can I ask you how you got my phone number?"

"Gary Cook got it for me, from a mutual friend."

She paused. "All right, I know Gary Cook. What did you have in mind?"

"Maybe coffee or lunch," Matt chose to be decisive. "How about lunch tomorrow?"

"I suppose I can do that. We can meet at the Eagle pub. Do you know it?"

"No, I don't. Where is it?"

"It's in Benet Street on the city side of King's College. Do you know where that is?"

"King's College? I sure do. It's the first place I visited when I got here. I'll find the pub okay. So, what time?"

"How about noon? I'll wait for you outside the entrance. I'll wear a white dress. Look forward to meeting you, Dr Price."

Matt was pleasantly surprised when he arrived at the Eagle pub and met Brenda. She was wearing a flattering white cotton dress that highlighted her dark hair and golden suntan.

"Ms. Thompson, I presume?"

"Yes. Dr Price? Please call me Brenda."

They shook hands. "And I'm Matt. After you."

Brenda walked ahead through the pub and made her way to the Watson and Crick room. Three people sat at the famous table. She pointed to a table for two. "Is this okay?"

"Sure, that's fine. What can I get you to drink?"

"Just a lemonade, please."

Matt returned with lemonade for Brenda and a pint of local ale for himself. "Neat place," he said, as he scanned the surroundings.

"I am surprised you haven't been here before. It's the oldest and most famous pub in the city, and this is the famed Watson and Crick room."

It took Matt a second or two before it dawned on him. "You mean this is the actual pub where Watson and Crick announced that they had discovered the secret of life?"

"The very same one. There's a statement by Watson over there on the door."

Matt got up and walked across to read Watson's comments.

FRANCIS CRICK'S BRAG IN
THE EAGLE, THE PUB WHERE WE HABITUALLY
ATE LUNCH, THAT WE HAD INDEED DISCOVERED
THE SECRET OF LIFE, STRUCK ME AS SOMEWHAT
IMMODEST, ESPECIALLY IN ENGLAND,
WHERE UNDERSTATEMENT
IS A WAY OF LIFE

JAMES WATSON.

When he sat back down, he said, "Gee, this is great. Thanks for thinking of this place; it gives me goose bumps just to think I might be sitting on a seat that Watson or Crick sat on seventy years ago. Amazing. Cheers."

"Cheers. So how can I help you, Matt?"

"Let me explain. I don't have to tell *you* how well your boss is respected in the scientific community, and especially in the field of genetics. A group of geneticists at Harvard have decided to compile a book on the history of genetics at Cambridge, and it will largely be devoted to Watson, Crick and MacLeod." He hated himself for making up the lie. He took a

221

mouthful of beer. "They are planning to have it finished by April in time for next year's Watson and Crick Seventy-Fifth Anniversary Symposium. As your boss is the only one still alive, they would like to present him with the first copy at the conference."

"Oh, I see. That's nice. So do you want me to set up an interview with Sir Francis for you?" Brenda asked.

"No, no, we don't want him to know. It's a surprise, so I need your confidentiality on this. Let's order some food and then I will tell you how you can help."

During lunch, Matt was very attentive, asking Brenda questions about herself, her family, her job and her interests and making other small talk. She answered happily.

Brenda thought Matt charming with a mischievous twinkle in his eye. She guessed that they were about the same age, although she thought that he might be one or two years older.

"Sorry, Matt, I am doing all the talking and you haven't told me anything about yourself," she said feeling like a teenager again.

"Trust me, you are far more interesting than a boring scientist like me," Matt said with a grin.

After lunch, with the small talk behind them, Matt got down to business.

"I have done quite a bit of research on MacLeod's early life, family background, education and that sort of thing, and I have even spoken to his ex-wife. But what I don't know much about is the last ten or fifteen years, apart from his knighthood and Nobel Prize, of course. So I was hoping you would be a good source for me. You have worked for him a good part of that time, from what you have told me."

"Yes, twelve years to be exact," Brenda offered. "What sort of thing do you need to know?"

"Anything that might be of interest to the reader. For example, his reaction to receiving the knighthood and the Nobel

222

Prize, the founding of Genon plc, the success of the company, the IPO and things like that."

"I see. I don't know everything but I can give you some non-confidential insights into his achievements and what a remarkable person he is. And by the way, the IPO has been postponed."

"It has? Why?" Matt said.

"Well, what Sir Francis told me was that he has made this important discovery and he did not want to reveal it until next year's conference. Something about telling academia first."

"Interesting. His staff must be ticked off. Are they?"

"I don't think so, apart from Darren, that is."

"I guess that's not a surprise. From what he told me, he expected to make a lot of money, so who wouldn't be upset? Say, Brenda, could you set aside some time in the next few days so that I can ask you some questions? You have a real insight into the man himself and what drives him and makes him tick, so to speak. We could meet in my lab, if that's not too inconvenient for you."

"I'm sure that would be okay. I don't go back to work until Sir Francis returns."

"Where is he now? On vacation?"

"He's in Basel, Switzerland, a combination of work and holiday, but knowing him, I am sure it will be all work. You know he has a clinic there called the MacLeod Genon Clinic, built by Tronavis. It's been very successful."

"Oh, I didn't know that. Good for him. Okay, Brenda, I appreciate your time and cooperation. I better get back and do some work in the lab, but maybe we could meet tomorrow."

"I have a lunch appointment. How about after that, say one thirty?"

"That would be great. By the way, do you have a boyfriend? Or a husband?" Matt asked.

Brenda's face reddened a little. "Why do you ask?"

"Oh, I was hoping you might let me buy you dinner this weekend as a way of thanking you for your help."

"It's very kind of you. I'll have to let you know."

"Sure, hopefully see you at one thirty then." With that, Matt left the pub.

Brenda called her friend Kate.

"So what do you think? Should I accept?"

"Whoa, what's got into you? Slow down there, you've only just met him, but sure, why not?

"Well, he lives in the States and he's only here for another month or so!"

"Hey, if he is half as interested as you obviously are, have a fling. You have nothing to lose. Besides it's about time you did it, instead of just thinking about it all the time."

"I do not! Well sometimes maybe, but this is different."

Kate sighed. "Brenda, cut the BS and enjoy a fling for a change."

Chapter 40

Rob Elliott returned to Cambridge after three and a half weeks in the north of England. As he parked his motorcycle, he noticed Kathleen's BMW in her parking spot. He grabbed a cup of coffee and went straight to her office.

Kathleen nodded hello while she talked on the phone. Rob waited and then decided to leave but Kathleen gestured for him to wait, raised one finger in the air, indicating she would only be about a minute. He plopped down on a chair as Kathleen continued her conversation.

"Yes, they're both fine and were so happy to see me. I did, and they sent their love to you, too." Kathleen's face reddened. "I miss you, too, and can't wait to see you at the weekend. Better go, Rob's here to see me. Love you, bye."

"Francis?" Rob asked.

Kathleen nodded with a smile on her face.

"So, how was Ireland?"

"Really good. You know that is the longest time I have spent with my parents since I left Ireland over twenty years ago. In the past, it was just a couple of days here and a couple of days there. It made me realize what's important. They struggled for over twenty years to bring me up and put me through college, then what did I do? Leave. It made them so happy that I was spending quality time with them, rather than just rushing in and rushing out again.

"I know what you mean."

"I also got a lot of research done. I took a lot of books with me. So, how was it up north?"

"Oh, good, but I think I might have made a big mistake." Rob said.

"Like what?"

"Well, the first night I was there I took Mary out to dinner and proposed to her. She didn't hesitate, she accepted immediately, which surprised me. I really thought that given our on-and-off relationship, she would take some persuading, so in a way it was a nice surprise."

Kathleen smiled. "Congratulations. So, what was the mistake?"

"Well, I moved into her place right away and the first week was great. Then the second week all she wanted to do was talk about preparing for a wedding in the spring, which was earlier than I had in my mind. By the third week, she was making decisions on everything and bossing me around. I have never experienced that with her before. I felt like I was suffocating and just had to get back, and now I am wondering if I did the right thing."

"Buyer's remorse? So soon? That's too bad."

"Regrettably, it is. What about you? What else have you been up to?"

"Oh, as you know, Francis went off to Basel for a month, so since coming back from my parents' I have just been busying myself around the lab and in the libraries. You know, I really miss him. He's a good man and a real gentleman and very kind and caring, so I am keeping my fingers crossed that one of these days –well, you heard, I can't wait to see him on Sunday night."

Rob nodded, "Have you heard from Darren? He was ticked off about the IPO."

"No, I haven't, but you saw the state he was in the night we were at the Eagle."

"Tell me about it. After you left, I had to carry him back to his place. He never stopped talking about it, kept repeating, 'What am I going to do?' He kept punching the walls, bruised all of his knuckles. I have never seen him behave like that before. He was out of control. And I had no idea what he was talking about."

"Oh, I have seen him behave strangely a few times in the past. In fact, I've always thought he had an aggressive side."

"A bit like you, you mean?"

Kathleen laughed. "I guess . . . if the cap fits!"

"Just joking. Anyway as far as the IPO is concerned, when I was up north I was thinking about it, and you know what, Francis has every right to postpone it. After all, if it wasn't for him there wouldn't be an IPO. He's been good to all of us, he pays us well, we have stock in the company and he's a man of high integrity."

Kathleen nodded. "You're right. And the other thing is, we have waited this long. Surely we can wait another six months."

Chapter 41

Over the weekend, Darren planned to fly back from Los Angeles to London Heathrow. While packing, he thought about the great sailing trip he had made to Central America with his buddies. They had sailed all the way down to Costa Rica and back. It was smooth sailing all the way, with the yacht more than living up to his expectations. He was at last captain of his own vessel, the *Eagle II*. But for how long? He still hadn't figured out what he was going to do. The agreement stated that he had to deliver twenty million dollars' worth of Genon stock within ninety days of the scheduled IPO, or return the twenty million with interest within a hundred and twenty days. He wondered who had put up the money and whether they would give him a six-month extension. After all, it wasn't his fault MacLeod postponed the IPO.

* * * * *

MacLeod walked into the conference room on Monday morning and greeted his team for the first time in over a month. "Good morning, everyone."

Kathleen had a big smile on her face, reliving the night before.

"Welcome back," VJ said, seemingly happy to see MacLeod again.

The others were equally as cordial except for Darren. He didn't acknowledge his boss.

MacLeod's face tightened a little. "Darren, I know you are upset that I postponed the IPO, but I didn't have a choice. And quite frankly, I didn't tell you all of the reasons at the time. My big concern about announcing to the world that there are more than fifty thousand genes is that dirty politics and big money will rear their ugly heads. But, if we wait until we have identified all of the genes and disclose them next April to academia, it will be a fait accompli and an even playing field for everyone."

"Dirty politics and big money. What does that mean?" Darren asked.

"Self-interest groups, pushing their own agendas and applying pressure for the research to be focused on specific genes and diseases of their choice. It's happened so often in the past."

"I guess that makes sense," Ian said, unsure that he understood what MacLeod was implying.

MacLeod moved on. "As you know I have spent the past month in Switzerland and most of my time at the clinic and at Tronavis. I want to share with you some exciting developments in their cryobiology department. I have been aware of their research programs for some time but in the past didn't pay close attention to them because we have been so focused on the genon therapy protocols. But one of their programs is so exciting and cutting edge that I have been working on it with them. And, before I left I signed a new collaboration agreement with them. You have all heard of desert resurrection plants, nematodes and tardigrades, I assume?"

They all nodded except VJ. "Er, no, afraid not."

For VJ's benefit, MacLeod explained that these desert plants and creatures have the ability to put their lives on hold during a drought, only to come back to life years later when water becomes available. They have the ability to stay in a dry, death-like state for decades.

"For decades?" VJ questioned.

"There is actually a recorded case of some tardigrades at the British Museum in London that had been in dry suspension for a hundred and twenty years when they were accidentally moistened and came to life and literally staggered around for a while, before they died, destroyed by oxygen. There are also records of nematodes that were still revivable after fifty years or more."

Rob turned to VJ. "It's a fact that dehydrated animation allows these creatures to leap into the future and continue to exist well beyond their normal life spans."

"The point is," MacLeod continued, "Tronavis have been doing research in this area for the past ten years, having started with some alpine resurrection plants with one key difference. Instead of dehydration being the trigger, these plants have the ability to shut down when there is a rapid drop in temperature, and then years later come back to life when the weather heats up."

"Fascinating," VJ observed.

"It is," MacLeod said, "After a couple of years working on alpine resurrection plants and nematodes, their researchers discovered the mechanisms which makes this possible, and started experimenting with mice. It turns out that a combination of zinc ions and sugars protect proteins during dehydration, so seven years ago they injected a hundred mice with these cryoprotectants. Then they rapidly froze the live mice and put them in ten separate cryogenic chambers. Each year since, they have revived the mice from one of the containers and in seven years, only one mouse didn't survive. That was in the first year and the post mortem showed the mouse had a weak heart."

"Hans told me about that program but I didn't realize they were that far along," Rob said.

"There's more," MacLeod continued. "Five years ago, they began experimenting with small dogs and then three years ago with small chimpanzees."

"And?" VJ asked.

"There was a problem with the dogs at first. After year one, two of them died. You see, when they went from mice to dogs, they weren't sure what concentrations they should use because of the difference in size of the animal. So, they decided to give two dogs a full dose and the other two a three-quarter dose. The latter two dogs did not survive because the dose was not strong enough to protect them. They froze to death. However, since then, all of the dogs have survived. Even better news, so far, so have all of the chimps."

"Let me get this right," VJ leaned forward. "Are you saying that they have mice that have come back to life after six years, and dogs and chimps after several years?"

"Exactly," MacLeod answered.

"How does it affect us? And what's this agreement?" Kathleen asked.

"Well, there is tremendous potential for this scientific breakthrough. For example, we can place people who are waiting for an organ transplant in suspended animation until the right organ match becomes available. Long distance space travel could be another use. Imagine being able to put an astronaut's life on hold for twenty-five years while he travels to a far distant planet, revive him while he's there, then suspend him again for the twenty-five-year journey back to Earth."

"Welcome to the twenty-second century, seventy years early," Rob said.

MacLeod continued. "As for the agreement, you know I am very concerned about the dilemma of disclosing all of these new genes before we have a genon therapy in place to correct specific mutated genes. However, what the Tronavis technology might allow us to do in the future is to put potential genon therapy patients in suspended animation indefinitely, until we have perfected the therapies that may cure them."

"Didn't Walt Disney and others undergo cryonic freezing in the last century?" Ian asked.

"So they say, but the big difference is that they were dead when they were frozen, and they will still be dead when their chambers are eventually opened. In this case, people will be frozen while they are still alive, and they will become alive again when their chambers are opened."

Something about MacLeod's body language disturbed Kathleen.

Before he left Basel, MacLeod and Meier had agreed on two things: the next genon protocol they would take into clinical trials would be for Parkinson's, and Meier would have an extra cryogenic chamber made. Meier agreed to ship it to MacLeod's lab at Addenbrooke's between Christmas and New Year, normally one of the slow periods of the year.

After the meeting, MacLeod called Palmer, he had something very important to tell him.

Chapter 42

Matt had taken Brenda to dinner the previous Saturday in appreciation of her providing him with background information on MacLeod. They had hit it off almost immediately. Halfway through dinner and, after only one glass of wine, Matt could see in Brenda's eyes that she was attracted to him. He was equally attracted to her. When they left the restaurant, he walked her to her car and told her he had enjoyed the evening. He said goodbye and walked away.

She called after him. "Matt, do you like Gilbert and Sullivan, by any chance?"

He stopped and turned. "Never heard of them. Are they musicians?"

"Oh, never mind, it was just a thought," she said, feeling embarrassed.

He walked back toward her. "Please, forgive my ignorance. What were you going to say?"

"I have two tickets for next Saturday night at the Arts Theatre. The Cambridge Operatic Society is performing Gilbert and Sullivan's *Pirates of Penzance*. It's a comic opera, but if that's not your sort of thing I can take my friend Kate."

"I would love to go. A new experience, that's what it's all about, being here."

She kissed him on the cheek and got into her car. "I'll call you."

They had dinner in the theatre restaurant before going into the show, and although Matt found parts of it boring, he enjoyed a few laughs here and there. Afterward, they went back to her place, where Matt spent the night. It had been a while for both of them.

Now, on Monday evening, the same day that everyone had returned to work, they were having dinner in a cozy little Italian restaurant in the center of the city.

"So, your boss was back at work today? How is he?"

"He looked fit and well but he did seem a little tense, at least when he went into the staff meeting. However, when he came back after the meeting he was in a good mood. Then I heard some of his staff talking about some new research at Tronavis that he was excited about."

"Really? So, he wasn't just over there on vacation? He was working too?"

"Absolutely. He works too hard if you ask me, and of course he spends time at his clinic overseeing the genon therapy programs."

"Oh, I'm glad you mentioned that. Do you think you can arrange for me to visit the clinic? I'd like to talk to the staff to get their opinions of MacLeod's genon technology."

"Sure, I can talk to Francis tomorrow and he can---"

"No, no, Brenda, please don't talk to MacLeod. Remember, I told you the book is to be a complete surprise. I don't want to take the chance of him finding out."

These lies disturbed him. Matt had lied to enough people about why he was in Cambridge, and now he was lying to a woman he had become attached to.

"Not a problem, I will call Anna, Hans Meier's personal assistant, she can make all of the arrangements. When would you like to go?'

"Any time in the next couple of weeks, whenever it's convenient for them."

Brenda leaned across the table and kissed Matt on the lips. "Consider it done, Detective Price."

"Yeah, right. If you only knew how inept I am at that."

"So, this book that Harvard is putting together, when is it going to be presented to Francis?"

"I have just found out that MacLeod is going to be giving the keynote lecture at next year's Watson and Crick. So probably a week before that we will approach the conference chairman and ask him if Harvard can present MacLeod with the first edition of the book after his keynote address."

"Brilliant, he'll be delighted," Brenda said.

"Everything okay?" Matt asked.

Brenda gave a sullen smile. "I was just thinking, you'll be going back to the States in a few more weeks, and I was wondering what will become of us."

"Let's see how we feel when I leave. If things are still working out, I don't see why we won't be able to see each other from time to time. After all, it's only a six-hour flight from the East Coast to here."

Brenda's face lit up. "Good answer. By the way, I was meaning to ask you. Have you been in touch with Darren yet?"

"No, not since he returned, but I am hoping to catch up with him in the next couple of days. Why do you ask?"

"Oh, only because you said that you knew him from his trips to the States. Of all the staff, I get the impression that he seems to be the one who is most upset about the postponed IPO."

"Really? I wonder why that is? I guess it's just human nature. Most people would feel disappointed if an expected windfall was postponed."

That evening, Matt called Anderson to bring him up to date on what he had learned during his month in Cambridge. He told him that he had been to Scotland to look into MacLeod's ancestry and learned that his great grandfather had worked in

India and had married a local politician's daughter. He also talked to an old professor who had worked for MacLeod's mother in the 1960s and, apparently, she was a very capable scientist. Anderson did not ask about MacLeod's father so Matt decided not to tell him about the rumors and switched topics quickly. He told Anderson that the scheduled IPO had been postponed until next May.

"It has, has it? Next May, very interesting. That means that Darren is going to default on the terms of the agreement. We will have him just where we want him. Have you talked to him yet?"

"No, but I will in the next couple of days. How do you want me to handle it? He's bound to ask me for advice since I was the intermediary."

"Let's see what he says first, then you can always say that you will contact the investors in the US and find out what they intend to do. Let him sweat a little. There's nothing like fear to get someone's attention. Anything else? I am holding up a meeting."

"That's about it so far, but I am planning to go to MacLeod's clinic in Basel next week and talk to the folks there about him, so we'll see."

"Good, keep at it." Anderson hung up.

Relieved the call was over, Matt couldn't help thinking there was something different about Anderson, less aggressive, distracted. Maybe he had another scheme up his sleeve.

The next day, Matt phoned Darren. They agreed to meet at the Eagle for a drink after work.

Matt carried two pints from the bar and handed one to Darren. "Cheers. It's good to see you again. So how was the great American vacation?"

"Fantastic. Spent most of it on the yacht, traveling down the coastline to Central America. It's a great yacht. I just loved it.

And all thanks to you. If you hadn't put that deal together I would have been twiddling my thumbs at my parents' house."

"That's great. Glad I could help."

"I have a little problem, though. MacLeod has postponed the IPO until May, so that means I won't be able to deliver the Genon stock on time. I was hoping with your help we could work something out with the investors."

"I have to be honest with you, Darren, I have been out with Brenda a few times and she did tell me about the postponed IPO and that you were upset about it."

"You're a sly one. Brenda, eh?" Interesting combo, Darren thought to himself. "So you have had some time to think about this. What do you think I should do? Do you think they will give me an extension? After all I have no control over MacLeod's decision, and quite frankly I do not understand the logic behind it. But you know he marches to his own drum."

Matt genuinely liked Darren and did not want to jeopardize their friendship but Anderson was paying his way in Cambridge and had given clear instructions. 'Let him sweat a little'.

"Darren, if you want my opinion, these guys are businessmen first and nice guys second. They gamble, they deal, they expect to win, and time is money. We need to come up with a winning scenario for them." He paused for effect.

Darren's lips tightened. "So what do you suggest?"

"If I were you, I would go on the offensive, suggest to them that in light of the six-month delay, if they are prepared to give you a six-month extension you will make it up in additional Genon stock. It would be a straightforward calculation based on the interest you would owe them. You have enough stock anyway, and it'll get you off the hook."

"Matt, you're a genius. Will you put the proposal together for me?" Darren said.

"Sure, what are friends for? But please keep in mind, as I said, these guys are tough businessmen and they may not go along with it. If they think they have leverage they will use it to their advantage, understand?"

Darren nodded. "Of course."

"Okay, I will put it to them as soon as I get back to Harvard and let's see how they respond."

Darren got up to go to the bar to order two more pints. "This is such a relief. I owe you one."

Chapter 43

Ian and VJ sipped at large mochas in the company cafe. VJ handed the copy of *The Blood and The Shroud* back to Ian. "Here, thanks."

"So, what did you think of it?"

"Fascinating, it certainly covers the controversial issues very thoroughly. Although I might have found it more interesting if I hadn't known your theory on the Shroud, because it made a lot of those older ideas and experiments look a little amateurish. Those experiments where they had made metal busts, heated them up and then stretched linen over them to burn in an image were rather silly, I thought. But nevertheless they got published in *Science* and *Nature*."

Ian raised his eyebrows. "I wouldn't ridicule them for that, because there were a lot of scientists who did feel that the image on the Shroud looked like it had been burnt onto the linen."

"No doubt," VJ responded. "That reminds me. When I was thinking about your experiment, it raised a question. If you do get it to work, and prove the cloth in Turin may be a copy, where is the original Shroud now?"

"It's a good question, and I don't have an answer," Ian said. "Perhaps they hid it, just as others had done so many times in the past. After all, it was hidden in a city wall in Edessa for hundreds of years."

"Another thing that struck me, if the last Savoy king, whatever his name was, bequeathed the Shroud to Pope John

Paul II and his successors, why didn't the pope transfer it to the Vatican archives?"

"That's another good question that I don't have an answer for," Ian replied.

VJ laughed sarcastically.

"Why are you laughing?" Ian asked.

"Two questions in a row and you don't have answers. That's a first. Seriously, though, I know that you have spent a lot of time researching this stuff and I think your 'Western Blot' idea makes a lot more sense than the others. The point is, where do you go from here?"

"I need to talk to Kathleen. She's got some other experiments she wants me to do."

"Like what?" VJ asked.

Before Ian had a chance to answer, Kathleen walked into the cafe and looked across at their table.

"Hi. What's going on? You two always seem to be in a huddle these days. Planning to rob a bank or something?"

"Yes, exactly," Ian replied. "We need to do something now that the IPO has been cancelled."

Kathleen raised her eyes to the ceiling. "Postponed, not cancelled. There is a big difference."

"Yes, Dr Murphy. If you say so, Dr Murphy," VJ mocked her.

Kathleen stuck her tongue out at VJ then went to the counter to get a cup of coffee. She came back and sat down beside them.

Ian said to her, "I was telling VJ that you have some other experiments you want to do."

"I do, as a matter of fact, if we can get a sample of blood from the Shroud and we can test it. Who knows what it might show?"

"Christ's blood? But I read in Ian Wilson's book that they have already done DNA testing on blood samples taken from the Shroud?" VJ remarked.

"Yes, they did, but the last time was almost forty years ago. They didn't have the powerful amplification and sequencing technology that we have today. It's a different ball game now."

"That's true," VJ acknowledged. "So you believe you are going to prove that Jesus Christ was the Son of God?"

Kathleen nodded. "I do. Not only that, before I am through, I intend to get answers to those other questions that have puzzled me since I was a kid."

"All of them?" VJ asked.

Kathleen smiled at VJ. "You mock me, so let me ask you a hypothetical question."

"Okay, go ahead."

"If an angel appeared before you and gave you a choice of three questions and you could only select one, which would you choose? 1) Does God exist? 2) What is the purpose of life? 3) Is there life after death?"

"Hmm," VJ nodded. "Interesting, but obvious!"

"Okay, which one?" Kathleen asked.

"What is the purpose of life?" VJ answered without hesitation.

"Well done. That's the right answer. So tell me why you chose that question?"

"For starters, if an angel appeared before me it would prove that God does exist and, that being the case, that He created us and put us on this Earth. If He did that, it would seem more than likely that He will take us back after death. So, the obvious question is. Why are we here? What is our purpose?"

"That, my friend is the sixty-four-thousand-dollar question that I intend to answer."

"I'll wait with bated breath. Just make sure you do it in my lifetime so that I fulfill *my* purpose," VJ said.

Kathleen detected a little sarcasm. "Here we go again. So you don't believe we can solve that mystery?"

"With all due respect, Dr Murphy, there are literally thousands of very intelligent people over the past several thousands of years who have tried to find the answer to that question. Some of them spent their whole life doing so. What makes you so confident that you will be the one to come up with the right answers?"

"You'll see, ye of little faith. I seem to recall that you were skeptical when we started the experiments on dying people. But I was right; there is an intense light force that leaves the body at death. We proved it scientifically and you witnessed that. We also solved one of the mysteries of the Shroud of Turin, and we demonstrated it scientifically, and you were part of that. But that's okay. It just makes me more determined."

"You're right," VJ admitted. "I was skeptical and so far you have been right, but you have to admit this is a little different. For heaven's sake, Plato, way back when, spent an inordinate amount of time contemplating this question. In fact, that's how the word originated, with – thought – Plato, contemplate. Since then some of the best minds in history have wrestled with this question, so please forgive me for being a little dubious."

Ian grinned and winked at VJ. "She's playing right into my hands. If we can get a sample from the Shroud, I will prove once and for all, if it is human blood, it will be just regular old blood and nothing divine about it."

"We'll see," Kathleen said. "I've just thought of something. You know I was at Oxford for six years when Professor Howard Corrigan was in the Department of Molecular Biology. Corrigan's lab was one of those chosen to do the last series of testing on the Shroud in the early two thousands. They were given samples of blood from the Shroud. He taught one of my classes and I got to know him quite well."

"Does he still have some sample left?" Ian asked.

242

"I don't know, and if he did I am sure he doesn't want to part with it."

"Isn't he a keen Shroud enthusiast?"

"Yes, why?"

"What if we offer to share our 'Western Blot' experiments with him and let him repeat them, and if he succeeds let him publish in exchange for a small blood sample from the cloth? We can also tell him that although his testing was inconclusive back then, we now have more sophisticated machines in our labs, so even a few cells of blood would be enough."

"All right, let me call him when I get back to the office."

A couple of hours later, Kathleen called Ian and told him that Corrigan had a few small samples left, but didn't want to part with them. However, he agreed to have lunch with them the next day and hear what they had to say about the Shroud experiments.

Kathleen offered to drive and picked up Ian just before ten the following morning. It took them two hours to make the hundred-mile journey to Oxford. After they parked the car, Kathleen looked at the time. It was only a couple of minutes after twelve.

"Want to grab a cup of coffee?" She asked Ian. "We're not meeting Corrigan until twelve thirty."

"Actually, I wouldn't mind stretching my legs, plus I haven't been here for a number of years."

As they slowly strolled through the streets, Kathleen reminisced about the happy days she had spent at Trinity College, both as a grad student and post-doc.

"That's right, you did your PhD here, didn't you? And your bachelor's at Trinity in Dublin? What's with you and colleges called Trinity?"

"Mere coincidence."

As they walked through the gates of the college, Kathleen pointed up to the West Tower.

"Here's a trivia question for you. You see the four female statues on the top of the tower. Do you know what they represent?"

"As a matter of fact I do: Astronomy, Geometry, Medicine, and Theology."

Kathleen raised her eyebrows in surprise. "I am impressed, a Cambridge man knowing that! What is the world coming to?"

"When I was a student at Cambridge, Oxford was the visiting team for *University Challenge* and that was one of the final round questions given to our side. Funny how some things stick."

"Did your chap get it right?"

"Of course, and before you ask, yes, Oxford won."

"Obviously," Kathleen said as they reached the entrance of the building and pointed to the stairs. "Corrigan's office is on the second floor."

Corrigan was sitting behind an extremely cluttered desk. He stood up. "Kathleen, how nice to see you after all this time. How are you?"

"Terrific, thanks. This is my colleague from work, Ian Walton."

"Nice to meet you, Ian. That's right, I forgot you're commercial these days," he said, looking back at Kathleen.

Over lunch, Kathleen and Ian told Professor Corrigan that they had almost scientifically solved one of the mysteries of the Shroud of Turin. They hoped he'd give them a small sample of blood from the Shroud so they could test it on Ian's instruments. Corrigan insisted that they tell him details before he would give him a blood sample.

Ian looked at Kathleen and shook his head. He knew if they did that they would lose any advantage they had.

Corrigan had three small blood samples in his freezer left over from his previous testing. At the time he had been very disappointed with the results and had to publicly admit that he

244

could not be certain that the samples were of human blood, although he suspected that they were.

Ian saw an in, and emphasized that in his lab he had the most up-to-date and sophisticated testing equipment. If in fact it was human blood, his machines would prove it. In addition, he would only need a minuscule sample. He also made a promise that he would share the test results with him before he shared them with anyone else, and if he wished, they could publish the results together as co-authors. Corrigan reluctantly agreed and gave them a small amount of dried blood from one of his samples.

Two days later, as Ian and Kathleen stared anxiously at the display; the results of the DNA testing on Corrigan's small blood sample came through.

Kathleen's jaw dropped. "What does that mean?"

"Hell, no!" Ian exclaimed. "It means we have a contaminated sample."

"So, what now?" Kathleen asked.

"Tell Corrigan we need to test his other two samples."

When Ian showed Corrigan the result, he was just as puzzled as Ian. He agreed to provide two more samples.

When Ian and Kathleen saw the results of the two new samples appear on the screen they turned to each other, astonished.

"Holy shit!" Ian said.

Kathleen was at a loss for words.

It was human blood. But it didn't make sense. XX – just like the first sample. Two X chromosomes – female!

"Jesus, Mary and Joseph, how can that be? The image on the cloth is clearly that of a man," Kathleen said.

"I don't want to say I told you so, but I am right. The Shroud is a forgery. Female blood!"

Kathleen stared at the screen, shaking her head. "I can understand one sample being contaminated, but not all three. They were from different sections of the Shroud."

She remembered reading that in 1532, the Shroud had almost been destroyed by a fire and was subsequently repaired by the nuns of St. Clare. Like many other aspects of the Shroud there was a lot of controversy about whether one of the nuns had pricked her finger and spilled blood on the cloth. But for the same nun to spill blood in three separate places on the fourteen-foot-long cloth was improbable. There had to be some other explanation for the female blood, she thought. Kathleen felt defeated and a little foolish.

"At least I am glad that only you and VJ know about my Shroud theory. Can you imagine if we had rushed to publish our experiments then these blood tests became public? We would be ridiculed, and rightly so. There has to be an explanation for this."

"Oh, trust me, there is. The Shroud must be a forgery after all, despite the fact that in my heart I was rather hoping you might be right. But you have to accept that these results mean that the Shroud was probably created between the thirteenth and fifteenth centuries as many scientists have claimed, since that is what the carbon-14 dating showed."

Kathleen shook her head. "But that doesn't make sense either. If it is a forgery why would the forger use female blood instead of male blood to create an image of Christ?"

"Because it wouldn't matter back then, blood was blood. In the middle-ages, they didn't know there was any difference between male and female blood. That was only discovered hundreds of years later. The forger, whoever he was – probably a nobleman or a da Vinci type – could have taken blood from a female servant and used it to add a little authenticity to the faked image of Jesus Christ."

When Kathleen reported their latest findings to Corrigan, the professor was equally puzzled at first. But after thinking about it, he told her that it really didn't surprise him after all, given that the Shroud of Turin has defied all other reasonable explanation. The image on the cloth is a mirror image where lefts and rights are reversed and it is also a photographic negative. In fact, every aspect of the Shroud is unusual. It contradicts not only conventional wisdom but scientific testing as well. So why should it be surprising that the blood is female instead of male, opposite of what they would expect?

"It truly is an enigma in every respect," Corrigan sighed. "So what is your theory on the Shroud that you were going to share with me?"

Kathleen was embarrassed to tell Corrigan now that they knew it was female blood on the cloth. She reluctantly told him about the 'Western Blot' experiments that Ian had carried out and then opened the file that she had brought.

Corrigan looked at the two pieces of linen with the faint blood stained images of Ian's face and said nothing.

Every second seemed like a minute to Kathleen as she fidgeted nervously in her seat until she couldn't take it anymore and ventured, "Well?" she said.

"Bloody brilliant! Why didn't I think of this? Or a million other scientists for that matter? But I know why. It is so simple and elegant and obvious. We scientists don't think like that. We prefer to deal with more complex problems if we think there is a solution. It's our own arrogance that blinds us to the simple straightforward explanations. Well done, this is very innovative."

Kathleen was stunned by how effusive Corrigan was and stuttered, "But, but, what about the female blood suggesting it is a forgery and probably from the fourteenth or fifteenth century, which ties in with the carbon-14 dating?"

"I am not concerned about that right now," Corrigan replied. "I think we should go ahead and publish your work as soon as possible. It explains most of the anomalies that scientists have been trying to figure out for so long. As far as the blood is concerned, we can keep that to ourselves for now. Why cast any doubts on what could be an important scientific paper?"

"But don't you think we should wait until we figure out an explanation for the blood? And, the other thing that bothers me is that they are going to do further carbon-14 dating on the cloth because of the claims that the previous tests were done with samples from the repaired edges. What if the new dating says the cloth is from around two thousand years ago?"

"It is no longer relevant what the carbon-14 dating says anymore," Corrigan said, with a grin. "Whether the image transfer was done deliberately in the fourteenth century, as you surmise, or by accident two thousand years ago doesn't matter. Either way you have solved the mystery."

"What do you mean? By accident?"

"Well, it is always possible that two thousand years ago, the Shroud could have got very wet, say exposed to heavy rain or dropped in the sea by accident and in order to dry it, they wrapped it in two pieces of linen and left it to dry, with a similar result to your organized experiment. In fact, the more I think about that, the more likely I think that's what might have happened. Can you imagine back then if after the cloth dried and they opened it up to find two images? Their immediate reaction would be that it was a miracle. Maybe that's how the holy relic with miraculous powers came to be in the first place."

Kathleen didn't want to rush into a publication without being certain of the scientific evidence. The female blood result had thrown her a curve. They argued back and forth for an hour, and while there was no doubt in Kathleen's mind that the professor was very fervent about his belief in the authenticity of the Shroud, she was still uneasy.

Ian felt the same.

Then Corrigan shouted out. "I've got it. I have an explanation for the female blood! You said you believe there are two cloths, the one in Turin, where my blood samples came from and another one somewhere else. I suggest that what happened is the maternal human blood transferred onto the new cloth while the paternal blood, whose properties would be totally different from human blood, remained on the original cloth." Corrigan put his hand on Kathleen's back and patted it several times. "There's your answer, young lady."

Kathleen let the implications of what the professor had just said sink in. It just didn't make sense, none of it. Maternal DNA transferred to the new cloth. Who is he trying to kid? His judgment was obviously clouded by his obsessive desire to solve the Shroud's mystery. Yes, she would like to believe that was an explanation, but she was not some blind follower of the church. She was a scientist. She had hoped by testing a sample of blood from the Shroud she would be able to prove that at least half of Christ's DNA was divine DNA as she had theorized months earlier. But she now felt she had been robbed of the opportunity of proving once and for all that Jesus Christ was the son of God.

Ian said nothing. He merely raised his eyebrows when Kathleen looked across at him.

She resisted the temptation to tell him to wipe the smug look from his face.

Chapter 44

Brenda had contacted Meier's assistant, Anna, and asked her to arrange for Matt to visit the Tronavis corporate headquarters in Basel and the MacLeod Genon Clinic, a few miles south.

The Tronavis site, ideally located in the heart of biotechnology valley along the banks of the Rheine, close to the German and French borders, had been completely transformed in the last twenty years. A huge complex of more than fifty buildings, designed to encourage communication and creativity, it housed more than two thousand scientists and technologists.

Just before lunch, Anna greeted Matt as his taxi pulled up at the main gate. After Matt signed in, she pinned a class C security badge on his lapel, then walked him to the visitor's center and called Peter Fischer. Peter would host Matt during the two-day visit. He showed up a few minutes later with a file of papers under his arm.

Anna left, and Peter took Matt straight to one of the visitors' restaurants for something to eat.

"We can't do a three-hour tour without something in the belly," Peter laughed.

That was fine by Matt because lunch gave him a chance to ask questions. Peter told him that he had been a member of the team that did the original genon trials and was now in charge of the technology transfer group coordinating the transfer of new protocols from Tronavis to the clinic; one of the reasons he had been chosen to chaperone Matt.

Matt explained he was there to learn as much as he could about how MacLeod's technology from Genon found its way to Tronavis and then into the clinic, where it was obviously having a great impact on people's lives.

"It's a noble cause, which is why Harvard would like to recognize his scientific contributions in a book they are putting together about him and Watson and Crick." Matt lied. "So I am all ears to every detail."

Peter smiled. "I was told about it. I have arranged a tour of Tronavis this afternoon and then tomorrow we will spend all morning at the clinic, so you will know as much as me by the time we are done. Well, almost as much."

After they had finished eating and were sipping coffee, Peter opened his file, took out two copies of the company's confidentiality agreement and asked Matt to sign them. He then opened an extensive sitemap of the Tronavis complex.

"Obviously, most of these buildings are where drug discovery takes place, which will not be of interest to you," he said, and then pointed to a highlighted line that connected three of the buildings out of the dozens on the map. "These are the places that we will be visiting this afternoon. Human Genetics, Plant Genetics and the Cryobiology Research Center."

"Plant Genetics and Cryobiology Research? Why those?" Matt asked.

"You'll see," Peter replied. "I think you will find them very interesting. Let's go, we'll start with Genetics. It's about a ten-minute walk from here."

Peter took Matt on a tour of the building starting on the top floor. The labs were modern and well-equipped. After touring the sixth and fifth floors, Peter suggested that they skip the fourth floor because that was where they were doing bacterial and viral genetics, something Matt already knew a lot about.

"Oh, if we've got time I would like to include it. It's always interesting to compare one's work with others in the same field."

"Okay," Peter reluctantly agreed.

After being shown around the labs, Matt got into a conversation with one of the scientists. She was using Garret's synthetic genome model for her research and commented that it was working well now despite some early problems. Matt acknowledged that Garret had glossed over some of the shortfalls in the protocols when he had first published his scientific papers, but they had all been resolved since then. He exchanged business cards with the researcher in case she ever needed help or advice.

Peter looked at the time. Matt had been talking to her for almost thirty minutes. "We'd better get moving. We're running behind, and we're only halfway through the first building."

The third floor was where the genon testing laboratories were located. "This is where we do all of the clinical trials for the new genon protocols," Peter explained. "Once new disease protocols are released from MacLeod's labs, they are tested and re-tested here before they go into human trials. Then when they go into Phase III trials, my group gets involved in the final testing before we transfer the new protocols to the clinic."

They moved down to the second floor. "This way," Peter said. "Let me show you what we do here. Follow me." Peter gave him a tour of all the labs on the second floor. "Since the clinic opened six months ago with the AMD and glaucoma protocols, we have transferred three new protocols, with a lot more scheduled in the next six months."

Matt was impressed. "Remarkable!" he said.

After the tour of the Human Genetics facility, they walked over to Plant Genetics, talking on the way.

Matt asked, "Why are there so many labs involved? It seems to me that if you combined some of them you could commercialize the protocols a lot faster."

Peter nodded. "Yes, you are right, but MacLeod was paranoid about not making any mistakes when we started treating patients. He spent quite a lot of time here going over everything. He still does"

"Oh, really? What made him so paranoid?" Matt asked casually.

"Well, there was a bit of a setback during the original trials."

Matt sensed he was on to something. "What happened?"

Peter frowned. "It's not important. Let's drop it. I've said too much already."

"Wait a minute, Peter," Matt said. "If the story about MacLeod is to be accurate, and in the interests of full disclosure, I need to include everything that is relevant. I am sure you understand that."

"I said drop it, Matt. I have only known you a couple of hours. We're not going to talk about it anymore."

"Okay, okay, whatever you say," Matt said, convinced there was some sort of cover-up.

They arrived at the entrance of Plant Genetics and Peter stopped in front of the two eight story buildings that were joined by crosswalks every two stories. Matt stared at the two large buildings and wondered why Plant Genetics was more than twice the size of Human Genetics.

"The building on the left, PG 1, is where they do conventional plant genetics studying global herbs and botanicals from places like the Amazon, Australia, Africa, and China." Peter gestured to the other building. "We are going to tour the building on the right, PG 2, where they are doing research on resurrection plants, which I am sure you are familiar with?"

"Desert resurrection plants? Sure, in fact, UC Davis used to do a lot of work in that area. I read a number of their papers."

"Well, similar sort of thing, but here they are working on alpine resurrection plants, which instead of shutting down in a drought and then being revived by water like the desert variety, shut down in extreme cold and are revived by heat. These labs hold the key to the future of medicine. Let's go in."

Peter led Matt into an impressive entry hall made of Italian marble and granite.

"Geez, what is this? An art museum?" He stared at the oil paintings covering the walls then looked down at the medallion on the floor, he recognized the symbolism.

"Apoptosis?"

"Exactly." Peter answered, looking down at the floor and then up to the ceiling. "It's what we do here."

Peter took Matt on a tour of the labs as he explained that an Italian botanist at the University of Geneva had first discovered the alpine resurrection plants fifteen years earlier and Tronavis had funded his work ten years ago, during the rebuilding of the complex, they had built this facility exclusively to develop the technology and now had nearly fifty scientists working on it.

"It's going to lead to so many new natural medicines and techniques and completely change healthcare as we know it," Peter said.

They stopped at one lab where scientists had modified plant cryoprotectants to produce a natural sedative that would eventually replace general anesthetics. The sedative slowed down the heart rate and induced a deep sleep for several hours so that the patient could undergo surgery without feeling anything, and with none of the side effects of anesthetics.

In another lab, scientists had developed a natural compound designed specifically to put patients suffering from deep anxiety to sleep for one to two weeks and allow their bodies to relax and recover from the stress. Each lab they toured was working on a different aspect of the alpine resurrection plant phenomena.

In the last lab they visited, the team had developed a cryoprotectant cocktail that allowed the freezing of small live animals.

"They can be frozen for years at a time and then we revive them by gradually bringing them back to normal body temperature."

"You can't be serious," Matt said.

"Absolutely, but we're running late, so let's head over to the Cryobiology Center and you'll see for yourself."

As they entered the Cryobiology Center, Matt recognized the familiar smell of an animal house. Peter showed him the ten cryogenic chambers used for the animal hibernation experiments. He explained to Matt that seven years ago, they froze a hundred mice and each year revived ten of them. Only one had not recovered so far. They had since experimented with dogs and small chimps and were having equal success.

"I had no idea that this kind of work was being done. This is a well-kept secret," Matt said. "So where is this all leading to? And what is the connection with MacLeod?"

"There wasn't one until fairly recently, when MacLeod realized that this technology could add a whole new dimension to his genon therapy. One of the biggest issues we have at the clinic is the enormous demand from people for therapies that we have simply not perfected yet such as Parkinson's, Huntingdon's, multiple sclerosis, and just about every other genetic disease you can imagine. Some of these people are desperate, and as soon as they are told they have a possible life-threatening genetic disease, they will go to any measure to find a cure."

"Understandably," Matt nodded.

Peter continued. "Given the success so far of the animal experiments, it may not be too far off before we start human trials. And if they work, the clinic will be able to offer potential patients an opportunity to put their lives on hold until the new therapy is available."

"I thought we had come a long way in the last twenty years or so, but this is amazing stuff."

Peter looked at the wall clock; it was after five p.m. "I thought you would find it interesting. Anyway, that's it for today. I will take you to your hotel and then pick you up in the morning around eight thirty and take you to the clinic."

Matt hesitated and then asked, "Would you care to join me for dinner?"

"You know I had planned to take you out to dinner but something came up at the last minute. I hope you don't mind?"

"No, not at all. I understand." In fact, Matt understood very well. Peter's demeanor had changed dramatically after he had let slip about a setback in the original trials. Matt had pushed too hard to get Peter to expand on his comments and Peter was not going to take the risk of further interrogation. Matt spent all evening trying to figure out what the secret might be.

Chapter 45

The MacLeod Genon Clinic was set in picturesque surroundings and looked like a luxurious resort. The ground floor included a grand reception area, lounges, a restaurant, a coffee shop, a gymnasium, a spa, a swimming pool, and administrative offices. The second floor contained the medical testing lab, technology transfer lab and physicians' offices. The remaining six floors each contained fifty private rooms, fully equipped to administer the genon therapy protocols and closely monitor every patient. As Matt and Peter toured the ground floor and arrived at the backend of the building, Peter pointed out the window at a new building under construction.

"It's a three hundred-bed wing, due to open within three to four months. It also has three floors below ground," he said.

Peter led Matt up the stairs to the second floor.

"The clinic is consistently doing two hundred and fifty therapies a week, but there is a significant waiting list and it's only going to get bigger as more and more people become aware of these successful therapies."

They didn't spend much time on the second floor. Matt peered through the window into a fairly typical diagnostic testing lab and then they did a quick walk through of the technology transfer lab, which was a much smaller version of Peter's lab at Tronavis.

They took the stairs to the third floor and as they toured the hallways on all of the floors and looked in the rooms Matt was surprised to find people of all ages, from young children to the elderly. Although most of them were connected to a drip, they appeared as if they were just lounging around in a hotel room, listening to music, watching TV or reading a book.

Peter explained that patients usually arrived on a Monday. On Tuesday, they were put through a battery of clinical evaluations and if everything was okay, genon therapy started on Wednesday for three days. If everything went according to plan, they were released on Saturday.

"Do many have to stay longer than that?" Matt asked.

"Yes, in a few cases, which is why we do not fill all of the beds at any one time. Some patients need an extra few days of therapy. Generally, though, it is either the older patients or those who have had more severe symptoms for some time. But over ninety percent leave after the six-day stay."

"Remarkable results," Matt said.

On the drive back to Tronavis, where Matt would take a taxi to the airport, Peter asked him if his visit had been worthwhile and if he had learned what he needed for the book.

"It's very impressive what you guys have accomplished, especially when you think it takes pharmaceutical companies an average of twelve to fifteen years to bring a new drug to market and then the drug usually just relieves symptoms. In this case, in less than half of the time, you have working therapies that not only relieve symptoms but actually cure genetic disorders. I think you are right when you say in the next twenty years existing pharmaceuticals will be replaced by this new kind of preventative technique."

Peter nodded. "We believe it, which is why Tronavis has invested so much. It's the future."

"I knew quite a lot about MacLeod's work before I came here but I had no idea of the extent of the progress that has been made. Major kudos to him. It's definitely been very informative for me," Matt paused. "There is something I need to tell you,

Peter. When I get back to Harvard they are going to ask me if I found out anything in his past that may prevent them from including him in the book. I will have to tell them what you said yesterday and I am sure it cannot be that bad, whatever it is. Can you a least give me a hint?"

"Listen, Matt, you seem to be a nice guy, but there is no way I am going to tell you anything. If I did and Meier ever found out, I would be fired on the spot. All I can suggest is that you talk to MacLeod and if he wants to be in the book then he can decide whether to tell you."

"I can't do that," Matt said "I told you MacLeod doesn't know about the book. It's a surprise."

"I will give you another name but you have to promise never to mention my name."

"Promise," Matt replied.

"Okay, his name is Rob Elliott."

"Rob Elliott? Who in the hell is he?"

"He works for MacLeod at Genon. He was the coordinator on the original trials, but as I said, that didn't come from me."

Rob Elliott? Funny, Matt thought, I don't remember Brenda mentioning his name.

"Thanks, Peter, I appreciate it."

They arrived at Tronavis and Matt grabbed a taxi and headed to the airport.

When he arrived back in Cambridge, he called Brenda and asked about Rob. She arranged to bring Rob to the Eagle straight after work to introduce them.

As Brenda left, she kissed Matt on the cheek and said, "I'll see you at the restaurant at seven thirty. Bye for now. Bye, Rob."

Matt and Rob watched as Brenda left the pub.

"So, you are the guy she's been seeing recently," Rob commented. "That's great. I have never seen her so happy. Harvard, eh? So how can I help you?"

Matt blushed a little. "We are working on a book about the history of genetics at Cambridge, it includes MacLeod. It's a surprise, and he will be presented with the first copy at next year's Watson and Crick conference. I am here on a fact-finding assignment about him."

"Oh, I see," Rob responded, taking the first sip of his pint. "What can I tell you?"

"Well, I have learned a lot of great things about him and his work in the past two months, but I understand that there was a setback in the original trials."

"What in the hell?" Rob was flabbergasted. He stood up as if he was about to leave.

"Hold on," Matt pleaded.

"I don't know who the hell you are or what the hell you are up to--- it was bloody Darren, wasn't it? The bloody idiot." He stormed out of the pub.

Matt, shocked at how quickly Rob had become angry, sat there bewildered. What was it Rob had said? "It was bloody Darren, wasn't it? The bloody idiot." Darren must also know this closely guarded secret. It's got to be something bad for everyone around MacLeod to circle the wagons like that, he thought.

When Matt joined Brenda at their favorite Italian restaurant, she asked him how he had gotten on with Rob.

"Fine," he said, straightening his cutlery.

It was Matt's last night before flying back to Boston and Harvard. Brenda felt comfortable with Matt and liked having him around. She had even told him how attached she was, and after a couple of drinks one night, admitted she thought she was in love with him. As she sipped her wine and gazed at him with tearful eyes, she told him she was really going to miss him.

Matt reassured her that he had grown attached to her, too, and that he would be back to see her sooner than she thought. While she appreciated his sincerity, it didn't escape her that he did a convincing job of expressing his mutual feelings, but at the same time avoided the four-letter word like the plague. Men, she thought, but quickly cleared her negative thoughts. After all, he was the best thing that had happened to her in years and she didn't want to ruin it.

The next morning, Matt and Brenda stood on her doorstep saying goodbye before he left for Boston. She whispered in his ear that she was going to miss him a lot and asked him to call her as soon as he got back home.

"I will. Don't worry. I think I am going to be coming back here a lot sooner than you think."

Chapter 46

September 2027, Rome, Italy

For the third time in less than fifteen years, over a billion Catholics around the world were mourning the passing of a pope. All three popes had been in their seventies when elected. Benedict XVI, at age seventy-eight the oldest; he was pope for eight years before resigning in 2013 at the age of eighty-six. He was followed by Pope Francis, born in Buenos Aires, Argentina, who was seventy-six when he was elected pope in 2013. The most recent one, Pope Adrian VII, was pontiff for less than three years. His unexpected death caused cardinals from around the world to make their way to Rome to attend the pope's funeral and join the College of Cardinals to elect a new pope.

Pope Adrian VII lay in state for four days before his funeral. Funeral rites and celebrations continued for another four days. Six days later, the thousand-year-old tradition of the 'conclave' began. In the morning, the cardinals celebrated Mass then walked in procession to the Sistine Chapel where they shut themselves off from the outside world. They banned all lines of communication: iPhones, radios, TVs, computers, newspapers and magazines, until they decided on the election of a new pope.

More than two hundred thousand people filled St. Peter's Square and the surrounding areas, many willing to camp out until a new pope was elected, which in the recent past had usually been decided within three or four days.

Officially in charge of the election process, the Cardinal Camerlengo, or Chamberlain's, first responsibility was to ensure that no one apart from the one hundred and twenty eligible cardinals was present in the chapel. He conducted the customary headcount – there were one hundred and twenty-one cardinals. Then he spotted the ninety-three-year-old Cardinal Bertolucci asleep at the back of the chapel. He signaled to the cardinal sitting next to him, who grabbed the old cardinal's arm – Bertolucci was well past the eighty-year-old voting age limit – and ushered him out of the chapel. Once the large doors were closed again, the chamberlain conducted a new head count.

With that out of the way, he proceeded to go over the voting process, usually done for the benefit of those who had not participated in previous elections. This time it was redundant – all of the cardinals in the room had voted in earlier conclaves. However, he did remind them that on each day they would hold two ballots in the morning and two in the afternoon until they had elected a new pope.

During the fifteen days between the death of Pope Adrian VII and the beginning of the conclave, rumors spread among the cardinals that it would be a tight race between an Italian, Spanish and African cardinal. There was a lot of buzz about the possibility of the first black pope. Knowing this, the chamberlain decided to have a single ballot on the first afternoon, a straw poll, to give them the chance to sleep on the results.

The cardinals in charge handed each cardinal a rectangular ballot paper with the words *Eligio in Summum Pontificem* – I elect as Supreme Pontiff – on the top, and a space below to write in their choice. They folded the paper twice and then waited their turn to put it in the ballot box.

One by one, each cardinal, in predetermined order, walked up to the altar carrying his ballot above his head for all to see, and then placed it in the urn. When the last cardinal had placed his ballot, the overseers emptied all of the ballots from the urn and shuffled them, ready for the count.

One cardinal called out the name from each individual ballot paper and then handed it to another who pierced it with a needle and thread, stringing all of the ballots together. Other than when the names were being called out, an eerie silence pervaded the chapel. There was one name being called out at a greater frequency than all of the others. After all the ballots had been accounted for, three cardinals dutifully counted the votes for each candidate, but everyone knew the outcome. Ninety-seven of them had voted for the same candidate – a modernist. He had received sixteen votes more than the required 'two-thirds plus one' majority and for the first time in over a hundred years, the College of Cardinals had elected a new pope on the first ballot.

A few minutes later, St. Peter's Square erupted when 'fumata bianca' – white smoke – billowed out of the chimney from the burning ballot papers. At that same moment, the bells of St. Peter's Basilica echoed throughout Vatican City. The crowd chanted, 'Papa, Papa', eager to learn the name of the new pontiff.

The Dean of the College of Cardinals asked the new pope-to-be if he accepted his election as Supreme Pontiff. After giving his consent, he was asked by what name he wished to be called.

He responded without hesitation. After each cardinal bowed before him and pledged his obedience, the new pope entered the 'Room of Tears' to be fitted with his papal robes, ready for his introduction to the world.

The Cardinal Dean, surrounded by a handful of cardinals, stepped onto the balcony of the Basilica and announced,

"Annuntio vobis guadium magnum. Habemus papam." – "I announce to you a great joy. We have a pope."

He paused, then said, "Papa Giovanni Paulo III."

At that moment, Pope John Paul III stepped briskly onto the balcony and waved to the hundreds of thousands of followers assembled below in St. Peter's Square. After ten minutes of tumultuous applause, the new pope gestured to the crowd to settle down as he said his first words as pontiff and gave the traditional blessing, "Urbi et Orbi"; "To the city and the world."

A few hours later, in the confines of the papal quarters, the Cardinal Dean hung a cross-shaped key around the new pope's neck, the same key he had removed from the neck of Pope Adrian VII minutes after he had died. As Cardinal Dean, one of his secret responsibilities was to ensure that the key passed from one pope to the next. It was part of the 'Giuramento del Decano' – 'the oath of the Dean' – that he had sworn to when appointed to his position. The Dean bowed to the new pope and left the room, leaving him to a private ritual handed down to every new pope for the past seven hundred years.

Pope John Paul III sat in an armchair for a few moments of reflection. He was only the third cardinal in the last hundred years, after Pope Paul VI and Pope Benedict XVI, who was a sitting member of the Pontifical Academy of Sciences. More importantly, at fifty-five years old, he was the youngest pope elected in the last hundred and fifty years. The College of Cardinals had made a statement by electing him. It was time for change. The church needed to move with the times; it could no longer be led by the 'old school'.

He toyed with the key around his neck. It opened a safe in the altar of *his* private chapel.

Within it, a message from his predecessor, a tradition in many societies such as the Knights of the Templar, Academia dei Lincei, the Masons, and, more recently, Opus Dei and the presidency of the United States. He got up, went to the safe, put the key in the lock, and turned it. He peered into the safe and saw a casket. He lifted it out, placed it on the altar and casually opened it. Inside was a pouch lying on top of a folded cloth. The pouch contained two envelopes and a parchment. Both envelopes bore the seal of Pope Adrian VII. He removed the two envelopes and sat back down in the chair. He opened one of the envelopes and started to read. It was a letter from Pope Clement VI giving instructions to all future popes on the need to protect the Secret of the Shroud, which was explained in the enclosed parchment.

"The folded cloth was the Shroud?" he asked himself quietly. "How could that be? The Shroud is in Turin."

Pope John Paul III leaned back in his chair fascinated by the revelation. He had become a believer in Jesus Christ as a teenager, mainly because his parents had brought him up in a traditional Catholic home where faith was never questioned. It was such blind faith that gave him the fortitude and vocation to enter the priesthood.

He opened up the pouch, took out the parchment and carefully unrolled it. He read the Latin text slowly and deliberately and glanced at the signatures and date at the bottom – Clement VI, Paulo Aquinas, Geoffrey de Charny, 1352.

There were two Shrouds? The Shroud of Turin – a copy? The original Shroud that Jesus Christ was buried in two thousand years ago was lying here before his very own eyes. And he was now the sole custodian of this miraculous relic. No other person alive knew this secret. Pope John Paul III fell to his knees and humbly submitted himself to the Divine will of God and prayed that he would be given the strength to carry the burden of the papal office with dignity and piety.

The pope rolled up the parchment and placed it back in the pouch, sealed Pope Clement VI's letter in a new envelope and scribbled his signature across it. He kissed the folded Shroud and prepared to put the casket back in the safe when he realized he had not opened the second letter.

John Paul III sat down once again, opened the second letter and began to read it. He froze in astonishment.

He put the half-read letter down on his lap for a moment and said, "Holy Shillelagh!"

The new pope got up and walked around the room, trying to absorb what he had read so far. John Paul II, whom he greatly admired, and whose symbolic name he had taken, had actually seen Jesus Christ in the flesh almost forty-five years ago, and was told by Him that He would return on the fiftieth anniversary of this occasion – five years from now.

He sat down again in the armchair to finish reading the account. It was even more astonishing. Jesus Christ had actually spilled new blood on the Shroud in the presence of John Paul II. "Real physical evidence. It cannot be?" As a scientist, he knew that could not be the case. He got up and walked over to examine the Shroud. He dropped it on the altar like a hot Irish potato, "Holy Shi--- lleleagh!" He gasped for air as he looked down at the three splattered bloodstains. They were more recent than the faded dark brown markings on the rest of the cloth.

If it had been any pope but John Paul II, he might have had doubts, but he had been *his* pope for twenty-seven years of his life – his role model. He knew exactly what to do. Modern techniques that were now available would allow him to establish the authenticity of the bloodspots.

Chapter 47

Kathleen looked at the number of the incoming call. It was her parents' number. And they never called her. She always called them. She glanced at the time – nine thirty p.m. And this late? It was her father. "Dad, is everything okay? Mom?"

"Everybody's fine. What do think of the great news?"

She heard loud music, singing and shouting in the background. Her father was in a pub, which was so unusual. "What news?" she said, rather puzzled.

"You really haven't heard? JP has been elected pope! The first Irish pope in history! All of Ireland is going wild tonight."

Kathleen was speechless. Her own cousin, John Patrick Murphy, was now Supreme Pontiff of the Catholic Church?

"Isn't it just wonderful?" her dad shouted above the noise. "And guess what? Your uncle John got a call from the Vatican tonight and we have all been invited to the official ceremonies in Rome on Sunday."

"You have to be kidding. Really? Dad, as soon as you get more information, call me right away and I will book my flights. I wouldn't miss this for the world. Give my love to Mom. We'll see you both soon. Oh, and congratulate Uncle John for me. He must be so proud! Bye."

Kathleen pumped her fist in the air and shouted, "Yes, yes!" She wasn't sure why she did that or what to do next. Celebrate? After all she was Irish. She called Mary. "You'll never believe what I have to tell you." Mary had already heard but had not made the connection to Kathleen.

Three days later, Kathleen, her parents and JP's parents stood outside their hotel waiting to be picked up. A black car pulled up to the curbside. It had a white license plate with the red letters SCV 33: one of the pope's personal plates. They saw a yellow and white pennant bearing a coat of arms on the white portion. They all stared at it. It was the familiar green and red family crest of the Murphy clan. John nudged her father with a proud smile on his face.

As the car neared the Vatican, a long line of cars on the inside lane patiently edged their way forward toward the entrance. Their driver cruised passed the line of cars in the outside lane as the line of polizia directing traffic waved them through toward St. Anne's Gate. A Swiss Guard dressed in a plain blue duty uniform with a brown leather belt and black beret saluted to the driver and beckoned him to go through without stopping. The people in the line of cars strained their necks to see if they could recognize the dignitaries in the pontifical car.

Unlike inaugurations in recent years, when the ceremonies had been held outside in St. Peter's Square, these were being held inside of St. Peter's Basilica because of predicted thunderstorms. This limited the invitees to around fifteen thousand. The pope told the Master of Liturgical Ceremonies to find a place for his family in one of the first three rows of the pews reserved for royalty and heads of state. He wanted to be able to see them during the ceremonies and for them to be able to see him. There is a very rigid protocol for such occasions, but not wanting to displease the pope on his first request, the MLC considered what he should do. If he put them in the first row, it would seem he was too anxious to please. However, if he put them in the third row, it would appear as if he was being a little defiant.

The Murphy family sat in the second row, center aisle seats amidst international dignitaries and celebrities. Kathleen saw the King and Queen of Britain, and the President of the United States and her husband sitting across the other side of the aisle in the same row. Princess Madeleine of Sweden and her husband sat in the row behind with other royals. She also saw Cardinal O'Leary who had succeeded her cousin as Archbishop of Dublin, sitting among the two hundred and twenty-four cardinals.

Although looking smart in their best Sunday outfits, it was clear that Kathleen and her family were in a different class. As she looked around and admired the well-tailored clothes, she wished Francis were with her. He would certainly fit in well with the people surrounding her.

Suddenly, the pontifical choir burst into song and with great pomp and fanfare the inauguration of a new pope – *her first cousin* – John Patrick, now Pope John Paul III, began. She cried with joy.

When it was time for the new pope to take the papal oath – the so-called oath against modernism – he declined, just as Pope John Paul I, Pope John Paul II and Pope Benedict XVI had before him. Although the others had not taken the oath, not much had changed; they continued the tradition of strict conservatism. His conviction, however, in refusing to take the oath against modernism was because *he* intended to modernize the Catholic Church. It was long overdue. With the mandate he had from the College of Cardinals, he would gradually implement the changes he thought necessary.

The new pope's mind wandered away from the ceremonies and he thought about what he wanted to achieve as pope. In the few days since his election, he had prepared a five-year plan of where he intended to lead the church. His mission was clear – to bring as many lapsed Catholics as possible back into the fold by

2033, the year Jesus Christ told Pope John Paul II He would return.

JP III would allow priests to marry. After all, there were millions of mature married men around the world who would embrace a final career as a priest. Besides, this was not such an extraordinary concept. In the few hundred years after Christ's death, most of the clergy had been married – even the popes. But Pope Gregory had changed all that. Many people also believe that Jesus Christ had been married to Mary Magdalene.

Next, he would change the rules on contraception. Millions were dying in Africa and elsewhere because of sexually transmitted diseases, especially AIDS. Imagine the positive impact it would have on the Roman Catholic Church if it carried out such a humanitarian act as distributing condoms throughout Africa.

The *Roman* Catholic Church; that was something else he intended to change. He would drop the word *Roman* and replace it with either *Christian* or *Universal*, probably *Christian Catholic Church,* would be the most appropriate. After all, the word *'catholic'* literally meant 'universal'. No, the other way round would be better, *Catholic Christian Church.* 'Yes, that's it,' he thought. He also intended to decentralize power from the Vatican. He would establish five regional popes, one each for Europe, North America, South America, Africa, and Asia and Australasia, and they would become the five candidates for his replacement. That certainly would give every ethnicity a better chance in future elections.

He knew it would be very tricky, if not impossible, to get the College of Cardinals to embrace any form of decentralization of power. It would certainly ruffle the 'old guard's' feathers. But he would not let that deter him. He would make the decision immediately while the cardinals were still in Rome. He had already decided on the likely candidates; all were his contemporaries. The oldest was fifty-five.

271

This was just the beginning, because given the history and tradition of the Church it would take all of his persuasive powers to make changes, perhaps a little time. But he was resolute.

Early the next morning, Kathleen received a personal message from the Vatican, summoning her to a private audience with the new pope.

The pope's secretary led her into the pope's private quarters and closed the door. Kathleen, unsure of herself, bowed her head and said, "Your Holiness."

Pope John Paul III laughed. "Kathleen, shame on you. It's still me, JP" He approached her, kissed her on the cheek and hugged her tightly. "Who would ever have believed that one day you and I would be sitting here in these surroundings and circumstances?"

"I know. It hasn't really sunk in yet, at least for me, although I am sure you are taking it all in your stride, as usual?"

JP smiled. "Well, I wouldn't go as far to say that. I mean, I had hoped one day, maybe, but not as soon as this."

They continued chatting back and forth for fifteen to twenty minutes. The pope's reassuring charm reminded Kathleen of her days as a teenager when women from all over County Louth would go to his church just to see him and listen to him. She shook her head and clenched her teeth in a forced smile as she thought about the impact this attractive and charismatic leader was going to have on the faithful around the world. He certainly did not fit the customary mold of any other pope during her lifetime.

"I am sure you have more important things to do than sit here and chat with me," Kathleen said. "But I know you asked me here for some reason. Is there something you want me to do for you?"

"No, not at all." The pope smiled. "I just know that this will probably be one of the few occasions that I will be able to sit and have a chat with you in private, so I wanted to make the most of it. Besides I didn't write as I had promised, so tell me what have you been up to these past few years?"

"Really? You want to know what I've been up to and here you are, one of the most powerful men in the world."

The pope nodded and smiled again.

Kathleen tried to be as brief as possible as she gave her cousin an update on the work at Genon and the clinics with Sir Francis MacLeod and his team of researchers.

The pope, still smiling, interrupted her for the first time. "Yes, you told me about MacLeod a few years ago in Phoenix Park, remember? A very clever man, you said."

"Brilliant!" Kathleen couldn't help herself saying. "Sorry."

"No, that's all right, you and he are--- er?"

Kathleen blushed. "Yes, we're, er, in love, and I hope to marry him some day."

"Well good for the two of you, Kathleen. Let me know when the big day arrives. So what else have you been up to?"

"Er---" Kathleen blushed as a vivid image of her and Francis having sex on one of his kitchen chairs on that first Sunday morning came into her head. On a Sunday of all days, she should have been at church. She tried hard to put it out of her mind.

"There is something else I wanted to talk to you about," she paused, the image still in her head. What would the pope think of her? Does he know? She wondered. Of course he doesn't, how could he? Thank God she had started going to church again.

"I must confess," she blurted out. 'Oh God no, what a stupid phrase to use to the pope." She coughed nervously, embarrassed that she couldn't get her words out. She coughed again. The pope rose and went to the credenza. Kathleen stared at his back. God, he knows. How could he? He's not omniscient. He's not God. Then she reminded herself that she

273

was with John Patrick, her cousin, her mentor. John Paul III, but he was still JP to her.

He turned and handed her a glass of water. She took a few small sips and said, "Thank you. For some reason my throat dried up,"

"You were saying?" The pope asked patiently.

Kathleen hesitated, "Well, a few months ago myself and a colleague did a series of experiments – you'll laugh at this – to prove that there is life after death."

The pope didn't laugh, far from it. He listened intently to every single word that she had to say without a comment or a single question.

She was about to tell him about the blood samples from the Shroud they had tested, but stopped herself in time when she realized how embarrassing it would be to tell the leader of the Catholic Church that the Shroud of Turin may not be the original, but rather a copy.

He wanted to discuss something with her but he hesitated and, at that moment, there was a knock on the door. He looked at the time. An hour had flown by.

His private secretary stood with the Prefect of the Pontifical Household, a jovial Irish bishop, who had served at the Vatican for more than eight years, with him were the pope's parents and Kathleen's parents.

"We're ready to do the tour," Bishop Keegan said.

Kathleen stepped out of the pope's study and joined her parents and aunt and uncle. JP had arranged for a private tour of the Vatican of all the places, well almost all, that most visitors don't even know exist, let alone get the chance to see.

The pope kissed his mother and aunt on the cheek and hugged his father and uncle. "See you all at lunch."

His secretary handed him some papers to sign, which he did without reading them. He had more important things on his mind. He briefly thought about what he had intended to discuss

274

with Kathleen, and on second thought he realized it was probably just as well he hadn't. There was no need to rush into something that important. And besides, right now, he had other more practical things to attend to, the first meeting of the five carefully selected cardinals, none of whom had any idea what was in store for them. But he knew they would understand. After all, they were of his generation.

The new pope addressed the chosen five. Before he told them about their new roles, he told them they had been selected for two reasons. First, because they were among the youngest members of the College of Cardinals, and second because they represented the continents on which they lived. There was a cardinal from New York, a Brazilian, a Nigerian, a Filipino, and a Frenchman.

JP III reminded them of some of the most critical issues facing the Church, including the declining number of clergy, the continuing scandals of homosexual and pedophile priests, the need to modernize the Church and convert more people to Catholicism, and the need to bring millions of lapsed Catholics back into the fold.

He shocked them with what he said next. "I want to pose a hypothetical question to you. How prepared is the Catholic Church for a second coming of Christ?"

They looked at each other, shaking their heads as they did so.

Cardinal Montrachet summed it up on behalf of them. "Pas du tout." – Not at all.

"Then, it's something I want you to think about because it will be a topic of one of our future meetings," the pope responded, "and on that subject, I intend for us to meet every three months. Let me give you some of my other thoughts. I intend to change some long-standing traditions. I will require future popes to retire at the age of seventy-five. It was so painful for me to watch John Paul II suffer so much with

275

Parkinson's in the latter years of his papacy. Which is also why in the future, no cardinal aged sixty-five or older will be eligible to be elected as pope."

Several of them raised their eyebrows. Then he dropped the biggest bombshell of all.

"If anything happens to me before I finish out my term, at age seventy-five," he said, "one of you will succeed me, because as of today I am appointing you to the new positions of regional popes. In the future the new pope will still be chosen by the College of Cardinals, but there will only be five candidates – regional popes."

Only the Nigerian candidate was afraid of the prospect.

As soon as he closed the meeting JP III summoned the Master of Liturgical Ceremonies to tell him to prepare for the inauguration of five new regional popes. The pope then went into his private dining room to wait for his family members to return from their tour.

They had visited the Vatican secret archives where documents such as the petition on behalf of Henry VIII requesting an annulment of his marriage to Catherine of Aragon are stored. The petition was denied and, as a result, Henry broke away from Rome and established the Church of England. In workshops, artists restored precious paintings and marble statues. In one room, Franciscan sisters repaired tapestries from the Renaissance. Some of the nuns had been doing the same monotonous and painstaking work for more than twenty years.

They were also shown around the barracks of the Swiss Guard who have protected popes for six hundred years. The barracks, also a museum of the history of the Guard, had rows of medieval armory and uniforms. Some guards polished their helmets, while others were changing into their traditional uniforms made with blue, orange, yellow and red pieces of material in a style reminiscent of a fifteenth century court jester, to prepare for the day's ceremonies.

As Kathleen and her family went back upstairs and back through the galleries she nodded and smiled at the dedicated young Swiss Catholic men who give up several years of their life to fulfill the vocation of being a Guardsman. As they walked back toward the papal quarters, she couldn't help but notice the upside-down images of the guards in the highly polished marble floors; they were as clear as any reflection in a still pool.

Bishop Keegan opened a door and ushered them through. They were all taken by surprise when they found themselves standing in the Sistine Chapel. As they walked passed the altar, Kathleen stared at the back wall and studied Michelangelo's '*Last Judgment*'. She scanned the fresco, her eyes settling on the demons with huge bulging eyes.

She knelt down at the altar rail and quietly made an act of confession

Chapter 48

With the latest state-of-the-art sequencers churning away twenty-four hours a day every day of the week, MacLeod's staff were making rapid progress and, on average, identifying over a hundred new genes a day. He was confident his team would finish the job well in advance of the April target.

With the gene discovery program going so well, MacLeod's visits to Switzerland became more frequent, usually three or four days every other week. He told his staff he was keeping a close eye on the genon therapy programs and the cryobiology research at Tronavis. Kathleen, however, could not help thinking there was another reason why Francis was spending so much time in Basel. Maybe it was just a woman's intuition.

VJ had asked MacLeod if he could join him on one of his trips to Tronavis to meet the people there and see for himself the progress being made with the Genon therapy program. MacLeod told VJ that he usually had a busy schedule when he was there and said it would probably be better for him to go at his own convenience. VJ sensed that MacLeod had some agenda that he didn't want to share, which was fine with him because he had his own hidden agenda for the visit.

Brenda contacted Anna and made the same arrangements for VJ as she had previously made for Matt and once again Peter Fischer was assigned to showing the guest around the Tronavis campus. They met in the visitor center.

"Welcome," Peter said to VJ as they shook hands. "I gave your colleague, Matt Price, a similar tour a while back."

VJ was puzzled. Matt Price, Brenda's new boyfriend? What was he doing here? "Okay."

"We will start with Human Genetics, Plant Genetics and then do a tour of the Cryobiology Research Center."

The tour of the Human Genetics facilities took only about half the time it had taken with Matt. VJ hardly asked any questions. It was a different story when they arrived at the entry hall of the Plant Genetics building. VJ stared at the opulence of the marble surroundings.

Above him, he saw a domed ceiling with a fresco of the Resurrection of Christ by fashionable Italian artist Giuseppe Butturini. In the center of the circular marble floor, a medallion depicting an oak tree with gold leaves and one leaf floating down to earth. An inscription in Italian around the outer edge read, *non cade foglia che Dio non voglia*.

VJ looked up at Peter. "I don't speak Italian," he said. "What does the inscription mean?"

"It is a popular Italian saying, *No leaf falls unless God wants it to*," Peter answered as he pressed the elevator button. "Apoptosis – *a falling leaf* on the floor and Renaissance – *rebirth* on the ceiling. It's what we do here," he added.

Suspending life and bringing it back later. VJ was eager to learn more.

As they toured the various labs, VJ became fascinated by the fact that these alpine resurrection plants might hold the key to the future of health, including his. In the Cryobiology Center, he bombarded Peter with questions about the success of the various animal trials. He was very curious about future human trials. Peter told him that MacLeod was making regular visits to Tronavis and the Genon Clinic, and had a keen interest in the cryobiology program. And tomorrow, when he showed him around the clinic, he would see that they had very quickly finished the underground floors. They were in the process of equipping one of the floors and getting it ready for future patients.

"Herr Meier does not waste time when he sees a business opportunity," Peter added.

"So, when do you expect to start taking in patients?"

"Maybe in about one year, but we will probably start some preliminary trials in about three months or so."

"What sort of preliminary trials?"

"Apparently, word got out about future plans and the clinic already has quite a long waiting list of people who are willing to be guinea pigs. I guess their quality of life is so poor that they are willing to try anything that might give them some hope. We will probably start by suspending them for about six months at a time and then gradually progress to longer and longer periods."

"Interesting,"

"Yes, it is. You'll see the progress we have made in the morning," Peter said.

"Good, looking forward to it. By the way, are you available to join me for dinner tonight?"

"As a matter of fact, I was going to invite you out to one of my favorite restaurants," Peter laughed, more at ease with VJ than he had been with Matt.

Peter took him to the Kunsthalle Restaurant in downtown Basel. It consisted of two rooms, one more exclusive than the other, catering for business people and those wanting finer dining. The other, a brasserie, was a lot noisier and alive with young people. Both rooms offered French and Italian cuisine. Peter led VJ into the brasserie and shoved his way to the bar. Over the din, he shouted that they would have a drink there and then move into the other room to eat. He pushed his way back through the crowds, handed VJ a Coke and said, "Cheers" as he put a large glass of pilsner to his lips.

Over dinner, VJ quizzed Peter about the preliminary trials and asked about the criteria used to decide which patients would be accepted first.

"Oh, that will be up to MacLeod and Meier."

The following morning, VJ was given a tour of the MacLeod Genon Clinic just as Matt had been given a few months earlier.

"Impressive facilities," he remarked. "It's more like a holiday resort."

As they toured all the floors, VJ stopped and talked to at least one patient on each floor and asked them about their stay at the clinic and how they felt while they were undergoing therapy. With the exception of one little girl who had an advanced case of cystic fibrosis, they all seemed to be in good spirits and felt no discomfort from the therapy. The little girl had breathing difficulties and VJ couldn't tell whether that was her normal state or a result of the treatment.

After the tour of the clinic, they walked across the back patio to the new three-hundred-bed wing. Dozens of contractors worked on every floor installing plumbing, electrical, carpets, tiles, cabinets, beds, various types of monitoring devices, medical testing equipment etc. Urgency was in the air.

They didn't tour the upper floors but rather at VJ's request went straight downstairs to the underground facilities. When Peter pushed open the interlocking entry doors, a gust of cold air swept past their faces. VJ took a step back before he recovered and followed Peter inside.

When he looked around all he could say was, "Wow!"

It was if they had walked into the entrance of a magnificent and ancient marble mausoleum.

VJ stared at the Italian frescos on the surrounding walls depicting some of the most uplifting scenes from the paintings of Michelangelo, Raphael and Leonardo De Vinci. The center pieces on the ceiling and floor were identical to those in the entryway of the Plant Genetics building, the *Resurrection* and the *Falling Leaf*.

Opposite the entrance, a central corridor with individual rooms off to either side, the rooms all contained two rows of three seven by three by three-foot cryonic chambers, each designed to house a single patient. VJ found himself doing a quick calculation: six patients per room and twenty rooms per floor, three floors; a total of three hundred and sixty patients at any one time. They *are* serious about this.

Peter pointed to a digital thermometer. "At the moment the temperature in the rooms is the same as the rest of the building, about 12°C, at least for the time being, as none of the chambers are occupied. Once the program starts the room temperature will be regulated to 4°C."

VJ made his decision. He just had to figure out how to pull it off. By the time his flight landed at Stansted, he knew what he had to do.

Chapter 49

Less than two months after her cousin JP had been inaugurated as the new pope, Kathleen received a call from the Vatican inviting her to have lunch with him.

She was greeted at the airport by Bishop Keegan.

"Nice to see you again, Dr Murphy, I do hope you had a pleasant flight."

"An uneventful flight, which is always the best kind, and thanks for meeting me."

"Not at all, not at all," the grinning Irish Bishop replied as he opened the rear door of the black chauffeur-driven car with her cousin's pennant on the front.

In the car on their way to the Vatican, they chatted about the last and only time they had met before. The conversation was mainly about the Vatican Secret Archives below the museums.

"There is one other question I would like to ask you. Do you believe that my cousin as current pope is part of an unbroken line of Vicars of Christ?"

"Yes, it goes without saying, my dear. It is that continuity within the Church, which goes back to St Peter; that makes the Roman Catholic Church the one true Christian faith."

"Including the immoral popes like Alexander VI, who fathered numerous illegitimate children and lived openly with his mistress?"

"Hmm, quite so," the bishop stuttered. "But you see, Kathleen, if I may call you that?" She nodded. "A lot of those stories are exaggerated, but we do acknowledge that there were some wayward popes in the past. Otherwise, we would not have had the Reformation in the sixteenth century, for which we are all better off today."

"I am sorry, Bishop, if that was an embarrassing question for you."

"Not at all, not at all," the bishop replied, as they were waved through St Anne's Gate by the Swiss Guard, the bishop more than happy to hand over the responsibility for this inquisitive woman to the pope.

"Kathleen," the pope called out as the bishop bowed and closed the door behind him.

"Your Holiness," Kathleen answered, as they walked toward each other laughing. They hugged and then he pulled out a chair from the dining table.

It didn't take him long to get to the point. "What I want to talk to you about is the Holy Shroud."

Kathleen blinked. "How can you possibly know about that? That was the other thing I wanted to talk to you about when I was here the last time."

"I see. But I don't think I am quite following you."

"You know about the testing we did on the Shroud?"

"Er, no. Maybe you could tell me,"

"One of my colleagues and I recently tested blood samples from the Shroud of Turin."

"And?"

"Two X chromosomes. *Female*. The Shroud of Turin is probably a fake." Kathleen waited for a reaction

"Well, I wouldn't quite go that far," JP said. "A copy maybe."

Now Kathleen was perplexed. "A copy? I don't understand."

284

JP gave her a thin smile. "There are two Shrouds."

Kathleen's jaw dropped. That's what Ian had concluded. Anxious to hear what her cousin was going to say next, she didn't say a word.

"I am going to be breaking a seven hundred-year-old tradition of secrecy with what I am about to tell you, so you have to understand that it must be in the strictest confidence."

The pope leaned forward, elbows on his thighs, steepling his fingers, as he revealed what he had learned to Kathleen.

Chapter 50

When the papacy moved back to Rome from Avignon in 1377, Pope Gregory XI had a safe built behind the altar in the pope's private chapel. The Holy Shroud and documents relating to it have been kept there for more than six hundred years. Since 1377, and within hours of the election of a new pope, a private ceremony is held in the pope's quarters. A cross-shaped key is hung around his neck. It is the key to the Holy Shroud safe. The pope is then left on his own for an hour to open the safe and remove the casket and documents.

After the pope reads the letter handed down from Pope Clement VI and examines the parchment, he puts the letter into a new envelope and closes it with his seal. He then places the Holy Shroud on the altar, where he kisses it in one corner and then prays in silence. He kisses it again and returns it to the safe. This ritual is carried out every Easter Sunday to honor the resurrection of Christ.

Whenever there is a crisis in the Catholic Church, the pope kneels before his private altar and prays to the Lord to strengthen his faith and his resolve. He is comforted in the knowledge that he is praying within a few feet of the irrefutable proof of the risen Christ.

Such a crisis occurred in 1988, when three separate carbon-14 dating laboratories published the results of their independent analysis and declared that the cloth was manufactured between 1260 and 1390. The Shroud of Turin was a forgery, most likely created in the Middle-Ages, possibly by Leonardo da Vinci using a hundred to two-hundred-year-old linen. John Paul II had his reasons for not revealing that the Church was in possession of the original Shroud. He was the only person in the Catholic Church who knew the truth. If he had admitted the church possessed the Holy Shroud, it would have caused serious problems, from the outside world, the church hierarchy, and Catholics everywhere. The public would think it had been concocted to explain the embarrassing carbon-14 dating results, or a huge cover-up that would imply the church had something more revealing to hide. The press would have had a field day. With all the attempts to steal or destroy the Shroud of Turin, Pope John Paul II couldn't take that kind of risk with the Holy Shroud.

Yet, despite the very damaging carbon-14 dating results, the church continued to allow testing of the Shroud. John Paul II knew in his heart that he had nothing to lose. The image on the Shroud of Turin was the true image of Jesus Christ, and one day science would prove it. For now, the Church would just have to live with the consequences of the carbon-14 dating results on the other cloth.

The most recent private owner of the Shroud of Turin had been Umberto II, the last Savoy King of Italy, exiled to Portugal. When he died in 1983, he bequeathed the Shroud to the pope and his successors. However, Pope John Paul II decreed that the Shroud should remain in the custody of the Bishop of Turin and housed at the Cathedral of St. John the Baptist. This came as a great surprise to Rome's Catholic hierarchy, as all of the church's greatest relics and records were housed in the underground archives in Vatican City.

John Paul II's private secretary relayed the gossip circulating among the Vatican's cardinals, telling him that the cardinals were concerned about his decision to leave the Shroud in Turin and not bring it back to Rome; that they felt this may send a message that he was not convinced of its authenticity.

John Paul II explained that the Shroud had been in Turin for hundreds of years and that it was well protected there, and had survived many attempts to destroy it by fire and various other means. There was no need to move it at this time.

Kathleen listened intently, unsure as to where this story had come from and fascinated as to where it was leading.

JP stood and walked around the room, occasionally looking out of the window. He continued.

On Easter Sunday 1983, Pope John Paul II had his head bowed in prayer in front of the Holy Shroud when he was startled by a bright white light. He looked up in astonishment. Rising out of the Holy Shroud was Jesus Christ, the crucified, in the same pose in which he had died on the cross, only no cross supported Him. He stared in wonderment. Jesus Christ was there above him, full-sized and in actual flesh and blood, wearing only a loin cloth. Small droplets of blood dripped from His side and splattered onto the Shroud below. John Paul II nervously uttered, "My Lord and My God," and then lay prostrate before the altar, listening to the words of Christ.

When he looked up again, Christ was no longer there. The bright light slowly faded downward, as if it were being drawn back into the cloth below. John Paul II pushed himself back up to a kneeling position, closed his eyes, and began praying rapidly, unaware of the passing time.

There was a knock on the door. It was a Swiss Guard. The pontiff had been in the chapel for almost two hours, twice as long as usual. John Paul II either did not hear the knock or ignored it. There was a second knock a few minutes later. Again, John Paul II did not respond. After a third knock and no reply, the guard ran down the corridor to the office of John Paul II's private secretary and explained.

The secretary got up from his desk and they both hurried to the chapel. The secretary knocked loudly on the chapel door.

"Papa, Papa. Are you in there? Are you all right?"

The pope slowly got up from his knees and opened the door. He told his secretary that he would be out in a few minutes. He went back to the altar to pick up the Holy Shroud and lock it away in the safe. He hesitated and just stared at the cloth. The blood drops on the Shroud were still wet. *They were real*. He had proof of what he had just witnessed – *Divine Blood*. He felt very alone. His heart was pounding.

John Paul II was faced with the most difficult dilemma of his papacy. No one else in this world knew of the existence of the Holy Shroud and its sanctuary in the altar of the pope's private chapel. Now he faced the decision of either upholding the secret of the Shroud, which had only been known to one living person at a time since Innocent VI in the 1350s, the sitting pope of the Catholic Church, or once and for all, put to rest the doubts and myths about the authenticity of Jesus Christ, the Son of God. It was no secret that the church was going through a rocky period and even the staunchest of Catholics were having doubts about their faith. The church was losing parishioners by the million. Was this a sign or an act to strengthen Christianity?

He needed to think, *alone*. He carefully put the Shroud back into the safe, slowly and gently moving it from the altar, making sure he did not disturb the blood samples in any way. He shut the safe, took the key from around his neck and locked the door. He summoned the Swiss Guard and told him he was going to his study and was not to be disturbed for a couple of hours. The obedient servant took up his new position outside of the pope's study.

John Paul II slumped into an armchair, rested his right elbow on the armrest and cradled his forehead in his palm, deep in thought and prayer. His left hand trembled as it had done on

289

several other occasions recently. He sighed aloud once or twice. He looked upward and then in a whisper repeated word for word, over and over again, what Christ had said to him.

'*Your faith has been tested to the full, but you will remain strong, and I will protect you.*

Your work here is not yet done. I will return on the fiftieth anniversary of this day in the full glory of He who was, is, and forever will be.'

The memory of the assassination attempt two years earlier flashed through his mind. He had forgiven the Turk, Mehmet Ali Agca, for trying to end his life, and even forgave him personally when he visited him in prison. At the time he had thought that his life was over, but he soon realized he was going to face greater challenges ahead. At sixty-one years old and only three years into his papacy, he had not yet earned his place in Heaven.

John Paul II got up, sat at his desk and wrote a detailed account of what had taken place and the words that Christ had spoken to him. He sealed the document then went back to the chapel and placed it in the pouch along with the parchments. The promised second coming of Jesus Christ would occur in fifty years. The date was precise – Easter Sunday 2033, the two thousandth anniversary of Christ's Resurrection in 33AD – and he would not witness it.

In the true tradition of the papacy, when confronted with an apparent miracle, it would be left to a future pope. Maybe, with God's blessing, JP acknowledged, the task might fall to him to decide on the authenticity of what had been witnessed on that day.

Fifteen years later, as he looked back on his twenty years as pope, John Paul II knew he had been right about one thing, and that was that the attempt on his life paled in comparison with all of the other challenges he had faced. The most burdensome was keeping the visitation of Christ in 1983 and the secret of the Shroud to himself, especially in light of all of the negative press the church was encountering. None more than the unbelievable stories emerging out of the UK and United States about the widespread child abuse by Catholic clergy. Not only that, but the controversy about the authenticity of the Shroud of Turin had reached a fever pitch, thanks in part to a new book by Ian Wilson, *The Blood and the Shroud:* (New Evidence That the World's Most Sacred Relic is Real).

The Shroud believers were now on the attack and strongly challenged the carbon-14 dating conclusions, claiming that the portions of the cloth that were tested came from the outer edges, which were actually strands of medieval cloth woven into the original cloth by nuns in 1532 to repair the Shroud after it had almost been destroyed in a fire.

The Vatican's Pontifical Academy of Sciences was inundated with requests to weigh in on the new scientific explanations for and against the authenticity of the shroud.

A response was deferred to John Paul II, who, in May 1998, on a pastoral visit to the Turin Saint-John the Baptist Cathedral gave an address and made the following statement:

'The Church has no specific competence to pronounce on these questions. She entrusts to scientists the task of continuing to investigate, so that satisfactory answers may be found to the questions connected with the Shroud.'

After making this statement, Pope John Paul II retreated to the chapel with Cardinal Bishop Sodano and prayed with him in front of the holy relic that was the subject of so much controversy.

As he walked from the altar, he said to himself in Italian, *"Sono come son."* 'It is as is'.

"Now you know." JP said as he clapped his hands. Kathleen jumped. Immersed in the story, she had forgotten where she was.

Chapter 51

Stunned by what JP had just told her, Kathleen blurted out, "Jesus, Mary and Joseph," as she hurriedly made the sign of the cross. "Sorry!"

"Astonishing, isn't it? I have hardly stopped thinking about it these past few months. Can you imagine the impact if it was proven that the two sets of bloodstains on the cloth are authentic? I can understand why popes in the past were probably very reluctant to publicize the existence of the Shroud; after all, they had no real proof it was genuine. But given John Paul II's account of a visit by Our Lord, I don't understand why popes since him have not shared this, at least with the College of Cardinals."

"Neither have you. Didn't you say that all popes were sworn to secrecy?"

"Yes, on the Secret of the Shroud, but hardly John Paul's letter."

"But why are you telling me? I am a lay person."

"Because you are the only person on this Earth that I can trust to do something extremely important and confidential for me." JP paused. "I would like to have the old bloodstains and the recent ones tested to see if they match."

"This is unbelievable," Kathleen got up and stared out of the window at the grounds below. She turned around to face JP again.

"Well?" Her cousin asked.

She hesitated. "There is one small problem. I cannot do it by myself. I would need the help of my colleague."

"This colleague of yours, I'd like to talk to him. Can he be trusted?"

"Absolutely. Like you, he is trying to use science to get to the truth, except the difference is, you and I are on the same team, but he's on the other team. What we want to prove he wants to disprove."

"Perfect."

"It is?"

"Didn't they teach you in college that opposing viewpoints are the only way to get to the real truth?"

Kathleen smiled.

"Well, that's settled, then. I would like you to come back here with him as soon as possible, and please don't tell him anything. I will take care of that when you get here."

They hugged, and then Kathleen left JP to his private thoughts.

As she sat in back of the black chauffeur-driven car on her way to the airport, Kathleen reflected on what had taken place in the past hour with JP she talked to herself under her breath. "It's like a dream. It's so unreal. Wait until Ian finds out that he has been invited to the Vatican to meet the pope."

Kathleen's Monday afternoon flight from Rome touched down at Stansted Airport just a few minutes behind schedule. After quickly passing through customs and immigration, she made her way to the short-term parking lot. As soon as she got into her car she called Ian at the lab and explained that she needed to meet with him in private as soon as possible, preferably that evening.

"Okay, can you tell me what this is all about?"

"Not on the phone. You'll find out soon enough. And, I don't want to meet at the lab, but somewhere private. I should be home between six and six thirty, can you come to my place around seven?"

Ian stroked his beard trying to figure out what in the world Kathleen was up to. He knew her cousin was now the pope and she had gone to Rome that morning. There had to be a connection, but what?

"Sure, no problem," he said. "See you at seven then."

She started the car then pulled out of the parking lot and followed the signs to the M11 on her way north to Cambridge.

* * * * *

Relaxing by the fireplace, drinking locally-brewed ale, Kathleen heard the knock on her front door. She put the drink down and went to let Ian in. They kissed on the cheek.

"Drink?" she offered Ian as she led him into the sitting room.

Ian nodded. "Same as you would be great, thanks."

She didn't waste any time. "I had a one-hour private luncheon with the pope today, and he wants to meet you as soon as possible."

"Me?" Ian stammered. "He does? What for? He doesn't know me from Adam. You must have mentioned my name. Why?"

"As a matter of fact, I did tell him about you. That's why he wants to see you. And I am sworn to secrecy not to tell you what it is about. He'll do that himself. Can you fly to Rome on Saturday morning for an overnight stay?"

"How could I turn it down? It's so intriguing and mysterious. Count me in," Ian said.

Chapter 52

Just before eight on Saturday evening, the pope's private secretary escorted Kathleen and Ian to the pope's private quarters. He pointed to two chairs and then offered them an aperitif. At first, they hesitated, looking back and forth at each other. Then Kathleen discreetly mouthed "Why not?" to Ian. The secretary walked across the room and opened the doors to a drinks cabinet. She spotted the Martini Rosso.

"We'll take a glass of sweet vermouth on the rocks, grazie."

The secretary left and told them that the pope would be along in a few minutes.

"This is surreal," Ian said as he looked nervously around the pope's quarters. "We're about to have a private dinner with the pope in the Vatican. Remarkable."

The door opened and in walked Pope John Paul III. He hugged Kathleen, shook Ian's hand and then led them to the dining table. After they were seated, he pressed a button under his side of the table to signal the staff to start serving dinner. After the servers put the first course on the table and left the room, the pope asked Ian to tell him about his background and career.

"Well, I had a typical Catholic upbringing and as a young man I was fascinated with the stories of the Holy Grail and the Shroud of Turin. I was determined that one day I would use my scientific knowledge to resolve these centuries-old mysteries."

The pope asked more questions and he and Ian became engrossed in a spirited discussion, almost ignoring Kathleen. He had also forgotten to press the button for the servers to clear the plates and serve the main course.

Kathleen looked at her watch; it was almost nine already.

JP turned to Kathleen and said, "Sorry, I'll call the servers in right away, but this is fascinating stuff. I had no idea."

Over the main course, Ian told the pope about his theory on the controversy surrounding the Shroud of Turin – a two thousand-year-old image on medieval cloth – and the experiments he and Kathleen had conducted over the summer.

"I believe there are two Shrouds. The original and the Shroud of Turin, a copy," Ian said.

The pope dropped his knife and fork and looked incredulously at Kathleen. He then turned and stared straight at Ian, clearly deep in thought.

The Secret of the Shroud had only been known to one living person for seven hundred years, and this English scientist had figured out what really happened back then.

"That's a very interesting theory on the Shroud of Turin," the pope said at last. "How do you intend to prove it?"

Ian laughed. "I don't suppose we ever will."

Kathleen knew Ian was trying to play up to the pope and hide the fact he was a non-believer.

She chirped in. "Ian, he knows, and he's okay with it."

Ian blushed.

JP smiled and winked at Kathleen, then pressed the call button. Two servers came in, cleared the table and brought back a selection of desserts, fruit, cheese and crackers and a pot of coffee.

As soon as they were gone, the pope turned to Ian. "I invited you and Kathleen to the Vatican because I need a couple of thorough scientists to work on a highly confidential project. But you must understand, Ian, and you also, Kathleen, that

297

under no circumstances whatsoever can you discuss or disclose the nature of the work that I am going to ask you to do."

"Absolutely," they both answered and Ian added, "You have my word, your Holiness."

"Good to hear that, Ian. I know I can count on you. Now before I talk about the project, Kathleen tells me that you tested some blood samples from the Shroud of Turin with some rather interesting results."

For the first time since the beginning of dinner, Ian felt a little uneasy. "Er, yes. The tests showed the blood to be female."

"Yes, I understand that. Kathleen told me already, and your explanation?" the pope asked.

"I don't have one, other than the one put forward by Professor Corrigan at Oxford University who gave me the samples to test. He believes that when the image transferred from one cloth to the other, the paternal DNA remained on the old cloth while the maternal DNA was transferred to the new cloth, the Shroud of Turin. I personally don't agree with him."

"Interesting concept. Well, maybe there is another explanation. We'll see what our project reveals."

Ian glanced across at Kathleen with a puzzled expression on his face. *There's a connection between our testing of Shroud samples and the pope's project?*

The pope noticed Ian's puzzled look. "Let me put your mind at rest and tell you what this is all about."

He then went on to explain what he had shared with Kathleen earlier in the week.

Ian sat there with his mouth wide open as the pope told him about the original Shroud, the parchment signed by Paulo Aquinas, Geoffrey de Charny and Pope Clement VI, together with the pope's letter. *Was this a dream? Or was he actually sitting in the pope's private dining room listening to this incredible story?* He had been right all along. Hair was standing up on his arms. Then, when the pope told him about Christ's visit to John Paul II and the blood drops he left behind, a cold shiver ran down his spine.

The pope offered Kathleen and Ian coffee, and then continued, "I would like you both to come back early in the morning to take blood samples from the Shroud and take them back to your lab and find out if the old and new match." The pope looked at the wall clock. It was well past ten.

"See you first thing."

At the hotel, Ian marched straight to the bar. "I need a drink." He was shaking and could hardly contain his excitement. They sat at a table in a quiet corner of the bar.

"These past few months have been some of the most exciting times in my life, but tonight's experience has just been the most incredible thing I could ever imagine," he said. "I mean, here we are, apart from your cousin, the only two people in the world who know about the Secret of the Shroud. And to think about what he revealed to us about the visit of Jesus Christ to John Paul II, and the fresh blood drops, and he is going to give us samples of the old and new to test. It's just so mind-boggling and hard to absorb. I'm sorry, I am probably rambling."

"Hang on a minute, am I hearing right? You're an atheist, a non-believer. You're here to give the project perspective, as JP put it, opposing viewpoints to get to the real truth."

Ian shuffled in his seat, then picked up his beer and took a sip while he thought of a suitable answer. "Well, er--- agnostic is probably a better description of my current thinking."

"Ah, ha! Doubting Thomas now doubts his own 'doubting' label?"

"We'll see. It's hard not to be 'on the team' when you're in those surroundings, isn't it?"

"I know what you mean. I feel the same way, as if someone needs to pinch me. My cousin is the pope, for Heaven's sake!

And he reveals all of these centuries-old secrets and stuff to us. It *is* mind-boggling."

"I agree completely, and by the way, I've just thought of something. How are we going to collect samples from the Shroud? We didn't bring anything with us."

"Trust me; knowing my cousin, I am sure he has already taken care of that."

Early the following morning, Kathleen and Ian knelt next to John Paul III in front of his private altar as he led them in morning prayers.

"Amen," they said together when he had finished. They all stood up and the pope went around to the back of the altar and unlocked the safe.

Kathleen and Ian watched as he opened a casket and carefully removed a few documents and a folded cloth, which he laid on the altar, kissed, and then stepped back and made the sign of the cross. Kathleen and Ian also blessed themselves.

The pope pointed to three splatters of blood on the top of the folded cloth. "These blood drops materialized in 1983 during a visitation of Jesus Christ to John Paul II."

Ian could not help observing that the pope did not use words such as 'apparently' or 'supposedly' before the word 'materialized', but had made his comment with true conviction.

John Paul III then opened a plastic bag and took out six vials, a roll of medical sticky tape, surgical gloves, laboratory tweezers and a pair of scissors and placed them on the altar beside the Shroud. He stepped back and gestured to Ian to take a sample from each of the blood drops. Ian put on the gloves then cut a strip of the sticky tape.

While he was doing that, Kathleen made a sketch of the locations of each blood drop on the Shroud and labeled them NB1, NB2 and NB3. She marked up three vials with the same labeling.

Ian took the piece of sticky tape, gently placed it over the first blood drop in position NB1 and firmly pressed it into the cloth, holding it there for about one minute. He then took the tweezers, carefully peeled the tape from the cloth and put it in the first vial. He repeated the same procedure for samples NB2 and NB3.

When he had finished, the pope put on a pair of surgical gloves and then he and Ian slowly unfolded the cloth across the length of the altar, exposing a faint but positive image of the bloody outline of a man. Ian had seen images of the Shroud in books, but this was very different. It was not a dark negative as the Shroud of Turin appears, but a positive image and consistent with his experiments using the Western Blot technique. Because the density of the blood pattern was much paler than the image on the Shroud of Turin, where scientists in the past had only been allowed to take blood samples from around the edges of the cloth, the pope carefully chose the more dense bloodied areas. He pointed to three areas on the cloth in the main body of the image: the forehead where thorn wounds had created rivulets of blood, the rib cage where the lance had penetrated and the wrists where the nails had fastened Christ to the wooden cross.

Ian and Kathleen went through the same routine to collect the old blood samples, this time labeling the samples and vials OB1, OB2 and OB3.

When done, Ian and John Paul III refolded the cloth and gently placed it back into the casket. The pope was about to return the documents but hesitated and then handed the medieval parchment to Ian to look at. Ian's Latin was a little rusty but he could translate a few sentences here and there. 'Lightning, an electrical charge – the missing element,' he said to Kathleen. And there was no doubt about the signatures at the bottom – Clement VI, Paulo Aquinas, Geoffrey de Charny, 1352. He rolled up the parchment and handed it back.

Kathleen placed the six precious vials in a separate plastic bag and sealed it. She then hugged her cousin and said her goodbyes. He told her to wait while he wrote something on a piece of paper.

"It's my private iPhone number; call me as soon as you have finished the testing."

He turned to Ian and said, "Good luck, it was nice to meet you." He rang for his secretary to escort Kathleen and Ian off the premises.

They went back to the hotel, packed their bags and checked out. After a leisurely lunch, they caught an afternoon flight back to Stansted. On the drive back to Cambridge, Ian told Kathleen he would start the testing after dinner on Monday evening when everyone had left the lab for the day, and should have some results by Tuesday morning.

Chapter 53

Shortly after eight on Monday night, Ian took the six vials out of the plastic bag and laid them out neatly in a row on his lab bench. He had mixed feelings; doubt, awe, the awesome burden of testing blood samples for the pope, which may or may not prove the truth about Jesus Christ.

He was still at the lab at six on Tuesday morning after getting the results two hours earlier. He had thought about calling Kathleen immediately, but instead decided to wait until around seven, her usual time for getting up for work. He looked at the time. He just couldn't wait any longer. He called Kathleen's iPhone.

"Hello?" Kathleen answered with a throaty morning voice, looking at the time on her phone, it displayed six twenty-one "Who is this?"

"Kathleen, it's me," Ian answered.

"Oh, so how's it going? You have the results already?"

"Er, yes."

"And?" Kathleen said sleepily.

There was a long pause at the other end of the line. "I would rather not talk about this over the phone. Can we meet for breakfast somewhere at seven?"

Kathleen swung her legs out of the bed onto the floor. "If you insist. How about Caffè Nero on Market Street?"

"That's fine. See you there." Ian put the printouts in a file and headed to the men's room for a quick shower. It had been a long night, testing and re-testing, researching the Internet and always with the same results.

Ian was halfway through a large Café Mocha and a bacon sandwich when Kathleen showed up ten minutes late. He got up to order her something, but she stopped him and said,

"It's okay, finish yours. I'll get something later."

Ian opened the file and pushed it toward Kathleen. She read the top page, then looked up at him and grinned.

"JP will be thrilled when he sees these results. So the old and the new blood samples are a match. All six samples are from the same source – that's remarkable."

Ian nodded. "It is, but not as remarkable as the results on the second page."

Kathleen removed the top sheet and stared at the next page. She didn't recognize the sex phenotype. She had never seen or read about this one. "Three Y chromosomes. This means the blood is definitely not female, but it's not male either."

"I know – it's bizarre, isn't it? I have never heard of YYYs. For the past several hours I have been on the Internet researching this. There is nothing. There are plenty of examples of poly-X and Y chromosomes like XXX, XXY and XYY, but not one example of three Ys."

"Oh, my God! It's like a combination of three pairs of YY phenotype in one. Like three persons in one. Isn't this proof of divine DNA?" Kathleen whispered.

"Of course not. I am sure there is a logical explanation, so I am going to do a complete DNA sequence and prove that despite the fact that the tests showed it is triple poly-Y phenotype, that it is probably just an anomaly. In a few weeks, I will have the sequence and I'll prove to you once and for all that you are wrong," Ian whispered back.

"Yeah, right! But I need to call my cousin right away to tell him that the old and new blood samples match, just as he hoped."

JP was having breakfast in his private quarters when he received Kathleen's call. He listened carefully then simply said, "Thank you, Kathleen, I knew I could count on you."

Several weeks later, Ian sat in his office in a reflective mood. On his desk was the scientific proof that Kathleen's hypothesis on Divine DNA was correct. In less than three weeks, using the most recent blood samples from the Shroud and ultra-fast sequencing, he had finished the task of sequencing the complete genome. The several-thousand-page printout, each with thousands of sequences of the four nitrogen-rich bases A, G, T and C, was unlike any other DNA sequence he had ever seen; it was nothing like the human genome.

He didn't need to study the whole document sequence by sequence, it was obvious to him. As he flicked through the pages, there was remarkable symmetry and scientific elegance about it. It reminded him of a classical symphony.

He thought back to several months ago when MacLeod had put forward his hypothesis about perfect DNA and when Kathleen concluded that perhaps Jesus Christ was the human manifestation of it. He now realized he faced a huge dilemma. What if he had been wrong all along and now had actual proof of Divine DNA – *the Holy Grail?*

He clasped his hands and rested them on top of the huge document, knowing that at that moment he was the only person on earth who knew the real truth about the Holy Grail. Should he keep this secret to himself or hand it over to the pope?

As he fell deeper and deeper in thought, he found himself humming the old school song.

> *And did those feet in ancient time*
> *walk upon England's mountains green?*
> *And was the holy Lamb of God*
> *on England's pleasant pastures seen?*

In the space of six months – much to his surprise – he had obtained answers to most of the questions that he had wrestled with when younger: the existence of God, the Holy Grail and the Shroud of Turin. Though, he still had to figure out the 'purpose of life'.

He was confused. He had believed everything he had been taught when younger and then he went to college, studied science and became a 'doubter'. It's true he was probably very close to being an atheist, but agnostic was probably more accurate, at least that had been his position in recent weeks. But now, for the first time in his life, it became remarkably clear to him.

Of course there is a God – there always has been and there always will be – and he created man – and man created organized religion – and that's when the confusion began.

He thought back through the ages and the number of wars – and lives lost – in the cause of religious beliefs: the Egyptians, the Greeks, the Romans, the Jews, the Muslims, Christians, and on and on, had all taken up arms to fight against or defend a religion. Why? There was only one reason – power! It sickened him to think of those who wanted to instill fear into people had hijacked God's name.

And the other nonsense. Christ did not preach to his followers that they must be celibate. That was Paul many years after Christ's death. After all, many popes were not celibate. Even St. Peter, the first Vicar of Christ, was married. Many other popes were adulterers or had mistresses.

'Do not miss Mass'. 'Do not eat meat on a Friday'. 'Do not use birth control'. 'And if you do, do penance for these sins'. And the Catholic Church claims it is the one true religion? How arrogant. No, all of these mandates were put in place long after Christ, by men who ruled through fear. Most people believe in God but they have been brainwashed into believing their own religion comes first.

They have it the wrong way around.

That evening, Ian sat out in the back garden, drinking a glass of beer and staring up at the sky. It was close to winter and the weather, although mild, was cold and dry. It was a clear night, the heavens filled with stars and as he scanned the panoramic view above him, similar patterns emerged. All over the sky, he could see groups of stars in Y formations. He looked north at the Great Bear and Perseus and then south at Aquarius and Orion. The more he stared, the more vivid they seemed. Was his mind playing tricks on him? Or was it just that he had never noticed these Y formations in the past?

"What is the true purpose of life?" he asked himself for the thousandth time.

His mind was all over the place, reflecting on the events of the past few months and the astonishing results he had obtained. Now he had to decide what he should do with them.

An hour later, he shivered with cold. He had made his decision. Despite his past cynicism about religion, he now knew that he had been wrong all these years and was once again a true believer. He would ask Kathleen to hand-deliver the DNA sequence of the Shroud blood to Pope John Paul III.

Chapter 54

December 28, 2027, Cambridge

MacLeod, a little curious why Kathleen was going to the Vatican again, decided not to comment and Kathleen was glad Francis had not asked her why she was going for the fourth time in as many months.

A large white pharmaceutical delivery van with the name Tronavis Pharmaceuticals on the side pulled up at the rear entrance of Addenbrooke's hospital. Although it looked ordinary on the outside, the inside looked like a sophisticated refrigerated transport vehicle with an added bank of instruments and monitors.

The driver jumped out of the cabin and asked where he could find a Sir Francis MacLeod. Two technicians got out of the vehicle, opened the rear doors and started to unload their unusual consignment. The driver returned with MacLeod, who watched as they wheeled a prototype human cryonic chamber down the ramp. It had been custom-designed and built for Tronavis.

Once it was safely out of the van and on firm ground, MacLeod said, "Follow me."

He led them to his lab and opened the door to the new walk-in cold room he had installed. The technicians rolled the chamber into position and prepared it for overnight testing. MacLeod left them to it. They removed a large pouch from inside the chamber and put it to one side, then hooked up the chamber to the liquid nitrogen cylinders, turned the valves, and switched on the vacuum pumps. A few minutes later, satisfied that they had done their job, they all left to check into a local hotel in the city center.

The following morning, the technicians returned to MacLeod's lab and examined the chamber. The temperature was steady at -170°C, and all the monitors seemed to be working properly. MacLeod signed off and gave one of the technicians a spare set of keys to the lab and the cold room to take back to Meier.

That evening, MacLeod called Palmer to tell him that the prototype chamber was installed and he would be starting preliminary testing as soon as suitable bodies became available. If things went well, he hoped they would be able to cryogenically freeze Gill in about six months.

Meanwhile, Kathleen visited the Vatican delivering the complete sequence of the new blood samples taken from the Shroud and sequenced by Ian.

JP studied the voluminous book and said nothing as he flicked through page after page.

"Extraordinary," he said as he looked across at Kathleen sitting quietly on the other side of the table. "However, I don't remember giving Ian permission to do a DNA sequence. It's one thing having matched the old and new blood samples but to go on and sequence the genome adds a whole new burden of responsibility. Who else has seen this?"

"No one. I have not even seen it. He simply bound and wrapped it for me to deliver to you."

"I see. So you are sure that apart from me, he is the only other person who has seen this?"

"Yes. Is that a problem?"

It took a few seconds before the pope answered, "Maybe."

Kathleen seemed surprised by the pope's response.

"You know, JP, as far as Ian was concerned, he was expecting to prove that it was just a straightforward human genome. Then he would have said to me, 'I told you so'. He wouldn't have even shared it with you. It's because he was so surprised at the outcome of his discovery that he asked me to hand-deliver the sequence. Are you upset with him?"

Again the pope hesitated. "I need to think about the potential risk of having someone like him knowing the genetic sequence of Christ's blood. I realize now that I took a big risk sharing with him the 'Secret of the Shroud' and the new samples of Christ's blood. But, it never occurred to me that he might sequence the blood and make such an extraordinary discovery. Do you fully understand what this means?"

She didn't know why, but for the first time in her life, Kathleen felt a little unnerved in the presence of her cousin.

"I would prefer not to guess. I would rather have you tell me."

"Think about it, Kathleen. If somebody announced that they had found the Holy Grail and it was something tangible, people would go to any lengths or pay any price to get their hands on it." The pope tapped his fingers on the book. "This book, if word got out, would become the most sought-after and priceless treasure in history. In fact, one page would be worth millions. Kathleen this is the genetic sequence of the Son of God."

* * * * *

Several weeks later, MacLeod received a phone call from Simpson to let him know that a body was available. It was a middle-aged man who had died of a heart attack and had no known next of kin. MacLeod arranged for the body to be brought over to his lab where two technicians quickly put the man in a linen body-wrap, then into an extra-large freezer bag with a vacuum tube attachment. They sealed the bag, attached the tube to a vacuum pump and sucked out all of the air. They placed the wrapped body in the cryogenic chamber, then opened the valves and rapidly brought the chamber temperature down to -170°C.

A week later, the technicians turned everything off and the next morning checked the body temperature. It had not warmed up to the cold room temperature of 4°C. It was still well below zero. MacLeod told them to put the body onto a lab bench to let it warm up to room temperature.

A few days later, the technicians took the body out of the freezer bag and removed the linen body-wrap. MacLeod examined the body from head to toe. It looked perfectly normal except for some slight freezer burns on the elbows and knees. The linen had been stretched too tight over the bony protrusions; he would solve that problem the next time by slipping foam sleeves over the arms and legs. And next time, he would extend the cryogenic freezing period to one month.

Chapter 55

Darren had not talked to Matt since he had left Cambridge at the end of August, although he had received two e-mails from him, one in late September telling him that the investors were annoyed that the IPO had been postponed and wanted time to think about it. Well, at least they are not making any outrageous demands, he thought at the time. The second e-mail arrived in mid-December and it was a different story. Matt told Darren that the investors were playing hardball and wanted a lot more than just the interest covered. They wanted a much bigger cut of his Genon stock if they were going to extend the loan. How much they didn't say, but the tone of the e-mail was enough to make Darren sweat a little every time he thought about it.

Matt and Brenda had kept in touch, talking to each other at least twice a week. Matt had invited her to Boston in November to spend five days with him over the Thanksgiving weekend. She had had a wonderful time and couldn't wait to see him again. He was beginning to realize that she meant a lot to him.

He had called her on Christmas Day to wish her Merry Christmas and asked her what she was going to be doing during the holidays and in particular, what she planned to do for New Year's Eve.

"Oh, I am very excited, my girlfriends and I decided to splash out this year and get tickets for a New Year's Eve bash in London."

"That sounds great," he paused. "Would it be possible to get another ticket, for me?"

"You mean you might come here for New Year?"

"Only if you want me to, and you can get another ticket."

Brenda flushed a little. "That would be the best Christmas present I could think of."

He said he would arrive a few days beforehand and then probably stay for another week. He needed to make another trip to Tronavis, could she arrange that for him? She could hardly contain herself. She had fallen head over heels and would do anything for him.

"Also, if you could let Darren know that I will be in Cambridge and would like to talk to him after New Year's. Can't wait to see you in a few days. Love you."

Brenda was ecstatic. Matt had never even hinted at those words before.

The New Year's Eve party at O2, the former Millennium Dome, was the biggest bash Matt had ever attended. He had once gone to Times Square with some buddies when he was younger and stood around freezing his ass off for what seemed an eternity, just to watch a big ball slowly drift to the ground at midnight. This was different. It was indoors with thousands of people dancing in the electrifying atmosphere to the thumping music of big-name live bands.

At the stroke of midnight, after he and Brenda kissed, Matt reached into his pocket and took out a small box and handed it to her.

"Go on, open it."

Brenda opened the box and burst into tears at the sight of the beautiful diamond cluster. She was speechless. She looked straight into Matt's eyes.

Above the din, he shouted in her ear, "Will you marry me?"

"Yes, yes," she hugged him tightly. "Oh, Matt, I don't know what to say. I love you with all my heart."

A few days later, Matt arranged to have lunch with Darren at the Eagle.

"I heard the good news. Congratulations! I wish you and Brenda a lot of happiness. She is a very nice lady." It was obvious by Darren's tone that he was anxious.

"Darren, I won't beat around the bush. They are willing to extend the loan period until July but I'm afraid it's going to be a much bigger hit on you than what I had proposed. They want twice as much stock as before."

"What? That's insane. That could be the equivalent of as much as forty million dollars for a twelve-month advance of twenty million dollars. Who in the hell are these guys anyway?"

"I would rather not say, but hey, I know it's not as sweet as we thought, but you will still be very rich after the IPO."

"That's not the damned point. I don't like getting screwed by anybody, and clearly they are out to screw me, whoever they are."

"There is another option," Matt said.

"And that is?"

"Information." Matt hesitated. "I understand there was a major setback during the first genon clinical trials. Something went wrong and it was covered up."

"How in the hell did you ever find out about that? And why would that be of interest to anyone? And what makes you think I know anything about that anyway?"

"Rob told me."

"You're shitting me, right? Rob? That's not possible. Why would he tell you that I knew something? He was the one who told me in the first place and then swore me to secrecy."

"I don't think it was intentional. I accidentally found out about the cover-up at Tronavis and when I asked Rob about it, he assumed you were the one who told me because you and I know each other."

"Now something is starting to make sense. We had a big row a few months ago when he chewed me out for spilling the beans. I told him I didn't know what the hell he was talking about and that I had never discussed it with anyone. We didn't speak for about a month."

"Well, let's not worry about that right now. The point is, they are interested in finding out what actually happened and I believe if I can tell them you were the one to come up with the facts, they will probably give you an extension without any further demands."

Darren was trying to make sense of all this. Why would his investors be interested in something that happened in a past clinical trial? Then it dawned on him. They were after MacLeod! He slowly began to put two and two together. Anderson?

He narrowed his eyes as he looked at Matt. "I think I have an idea what is going on here. It's Anderson, isn't it?"

"What makes you think that?"

"Because he has made it quite obvious to me over the past few years that he is still very upset with MacLeod since he cut him out of the Genon deal. In fact, he and I made our own little deal before the Genon IPO opportunity came along. I should have figured it out when you first offered to get me the loan. You were a plant all along, weren't you?"

"Darren, I'm sorry, but you have to understand that I had no choice. I was told by Garret that I had to carry out this assignment for Anderson. You see, SMB is the largest single contributor of research funds to Garret and Harvard. But please, keep me out of it. After all, you did figure it out on your own."

"Well, at least I know where I stand, and if you can get Anderson off my back I will tell you what little I know. And as for the original deal I made with him, all bets are off now."

"What kind of deal was that?" Matt asked.

"Okay, as we are both coming clean here, I'll tell you, but the same rules apply. You didn't hear it from me."

"Agreed."

"In return for future royalties, I was going to give Anderson some genon protocols for stuff MacLeod wasn't interested in, protocols for testosterone and DHT regulation. But he can forget that now. I don't want to hurt MacLeod in any way but I do want to get Anderson off my back. As far as the clinical trial problem is concerned, all I know is that something went wrong, an elderly female patient died and a male patient went prematurely blind. I don't know his name or where he lives, except that I believe he is Swiss."

"Geez, no wonder they want to keep it quiet. If I can prove that it will definitely get you off the hook with Anderson."

This time when Matt arrived at Basel Airport, he picked up a rental car and drove himself to Tronavis. Peter Fischer welcomed him again and took him straight to lunch. Matt explained to Peter that when he got back to Harvard and told his superiors about some sort of setback at the MacLeod Clinic, they emphasized the need for full disclosure. They had sent him back to Cambridge with the mission of finding out exactly what it was. He had since learned that a female patient had died and a male patient had gone prematurely blind during the first trial.

"Who told you that?" Peter asked.

"I can't answer that and all I ask is for you to give me some information on the individual so I can check it out."

Peter led Matt to his office and said, "Look, I shouldn't be doing this, but I'm going to leave for fifteen minutes to get a cup of coffee." He clicked on a computer file. "Here, take a seat at my computer. If you happen to get bored while I am gone and decide to review my records, so be it."

Matt nodded and as soon as Peter stepped out of the office, he started scanning the files of the first genon trial. After a few minutes, the list of participants appeared. He scanned the list of females and saw the name of a patient with the outcome column marked, 'deceased'. There was a footnote, which he didn't bother to read. He clicked onto the male patient file and scanned the list of patients. Next to patient number six he saw the word 'blind' in the outcome column. The fifty-three-year-old male had been diagnosed with early AMD and glaucoma. He wrote the man's details on a piece of paper and stuffed it into his pocket. He closed the file and sat back in a chair to wait for Peter.

When Peter returned, Matt stood up and said he appreciated his time and would be on his way. "How long do you think it will take me to drive to Hohgant?" he asked.

"About one hour south to Bern and then about forty-five minutes south east to Hohgant – just under two hours in all."

"In that case, I will probably stay there overnight. And thanks again for everything."

It was almost dark when Matt arrived at the alpine village and checked in to the local Gasthof. After dinner, he had a beer in the bar and got talking to the barman. It didn't take long to find out where the blind man lived.

Shortly after nine the next day, Matt pulled up outside a single-story house. He read the nameplate, Jürgen Roeck, and rang the bell. A few minutes later, he heard someone shuffling toward the door and the sound of a cane tapping on a wooden floor. The door opened slowly and a blind man appeared.

"Ja."

"Herr Roeck, do you speak English?" Matt asked haltingly.

"Nein," the man answered.

It had not occurred to Matt when he drove here that the man might not speak English. Matt knew a little French from his previous trips to Europe with his parents, so he tried again. "Parlez-vous Français?"

"Oui, un petit peu," the man answered, "Qui êtes vous?" Who are you?

Matt quickly made up a story in his mediocre French, that he was writing an article for a magazine and wanted to interview the man about his experience in the genon clinical trial.

Herr Roeck was agreeable and invited him in. Matt soon realized why. It was obvious that he was lonely and didn't get many visitors these days. He was very bitter and had been advised by his attorney that he could expect a big settlement because of Tronavis' negligence.

Now Matt realized why everyone was trying to hush this up. If word ever got out that Tronavis and the Genon Clinic were going to be sued for medical malpractice it would ruin MacLeod's reputation and slash the valuation of Genon. He was satisfied he had learned enough.

"Au revoir et merci," he said as he walked to his car.

As soon as Matt got back to Cambridge, he called Darren and arranged to meet him for a cup of coffee. He told him what he had learned in Switzerland and that he no longer wanted to be involved with Anderson. As far as he was concerned, he had done his job by finding out what Anderson was after and justified the trip.

"I think it would be better all-around if you called Anderson and told him the story about Herr Roeck," Matt said.

Darren was hesitant. "I don't know, Matt. What do you suppose Anderson will do with the information?"

"Well, all I know is that something happened between Anderson and MacLeod a long time ago. I have no idea what it was, but there is definitely bad blood between them. That's why MacLeod squeezed him out of the Genon deal and then Anderson was passed over for the top job at SMB because of that, so who wouldn't be upset? But more to the point, I think, is the fact that SMB funded a lot of MacLeod's research, so it's understandable that Anderson believes SMB has a right to share his technology. He's looking for some kind of leverage to use against MacLeod to get back into the deal."

"What does that mean? You're not suggesting he's going to blackmail MacLeod, are you?" Darren asked.

"Well, that's not what Anderson calls it. He said it's more like information sharing. If he has some incriminating information on MacLeod, that information is power and he will be able to negotiate with MacLeod. That's why he has been paying me to try to find a skeleton in MacLeod's closet, as it were."

"And the screwed-up clinical trial is certainly something MacLeod doesn't want to become public knowledge, so I am sure it would put Anderson in a strong bargaining position."

"You can leverage the information to get a better deal for yourself, so will you call him and tell him?" Matt asked.

"Okay, I'll call him and if he doesn't agree to extend the repayment terms, I won't tell him about Herr Roeck."

Anderson was surprised to get a phone call from Darren and even more surprised when he told him he had figured out that Anderson was behind the loan for his yacht and home. Darren then told him that he had something on MacLeod that he might be interested in, but before he told him, Anderson would have to agree to the loan extension.

Anderson laughed. "Quite frankly, I don't give a rat's ass about that. Its peanuts compared to the hundreds of millions we'll make from MacLeod's technology. So, if you have got something worthwhile on MacLeod, I will extend the loan."

Darren told him about the clinical trials that had gone wrong.

"A dead woman and a blind man from a screwed-up clinical trial? That's better than anything I expected. I'll extend the loan."

"Thanks."

319

Anderson had a smug smile on his face when he put the phone down.

* * * * *

Matt felt a great burden had been lifted from his shoulders because the more he had gotten to know MacLeod and the deeper he had fallen for Brenda, the greater the guilt he felt about his assignment for Anderson. He wondered how they would react if they knew, particularly Brenda, because he had lied to her. He winced at the thought. It had taken longer for his feelings for her to develop but he was now deeply in love and couldn't imagine a future without her. He decided that if they were to have a trusting relationship, he had no choice but to confess everything to her.

On Saturday evening at dinner, he explained to Brenda what he had done. He told her that the idea of the book about MacLeod and his predecessors was just a cover so that he could spend time in the UK to try and dig up some dirt. He personally had never felt comfortable about the assignment and he was only doing it out of loyalty to his boss.

Brenda was flabbergasted. "How could you lie to me and use me like that?" she blurted out as she burst into tears and stormed out of the restaurant.

Matt ran after her, grabbed her by the arm and swung her around toward him. He grabbed her other arm and breathing heavily said, "Brenda, I am so sorry, please let me explain and then I promise I will personally apologize to MacLeod."

"Let go of me, you liar." Brenda tore herself away and left Matt standing in the middle of the pavement. He spent most of the next day trying to call Brenda on her iPhone but she ignored every call.

On Monday morning, Matt showed up at Genon and asked to see MacLeod. Brenda ignored him and refused to let him in to see her boss. Matt was not about to give up so he sat in the lobby all morning until MacLeod appeared on his way to lunch. Matt stood up and introduced himself. After explaining to MacLeod that he was Brenda's fiancé, MacLeod agreed to see him after lunch.

At first, MacLeod was upset with Matt but understood that his actions were done out of pure loyalty to his boss and loyalty had always been high on MacLeod's list.

"So, what did you find?" MacLeod asked.

Matt could not bring himself to tell MacLeod that he knew about the botched clinical trial and the blind man. "Very little. In fact, before I left Harvard, Garret said to me, 'You're not going find anything on MacLeod, so go enjoy yourself for a couple of months'. He was right."

MacLeod called Brenda into his office. "Brenda, I have never seen you as happy as you have been these past few months. Don't throw that away. Matt is a good man."

Brenda burst into tears. Matt got up and embraced her. She hugged him tightly.

Chapter 56

Easter Thursday, April 13, 2028

MacLeod and VJ entered the central computer room shortly after ten. They had a full night's work ahead of them. MacLeod poured himself a cup of coffee and carried it to his desk. He sat in front of his computer screen and studied the jigsaw puzzle of more than one hundred thousand sets of genes and genons.

His team had lived up to the task and completed the sequencing in time for the Watson and Crick Conference. They had identified the genes and genons of every single genetic disorder known to man and tens of thousands of genes that they knew little about. But time would solve that too.

MacLeod stared at the screen as he scrolled through the reams of data confirming the existence of perfect DNA. He was 'high' and likened it to the 'rush' an archeologist must get with the discovery of some ancient artifact. He swallowed a quarter of a cup of black coffee.

Recent events, though, had caused him to pause, and he had decided that he must protect his years of research by taking some drastic steps. He had asked VJ to join him at the lab late at night to make copies of all the files from the hard-drive.

After several hours, he told VJ to download the data onto two separate 512GB storage devices. When VJ completed this, he safely removed the devices one at a time, then re-inserted them and opened them. MacLeod then scanned the data to make sure all the information had been completely transferred from the hard-drive onto the devices. Satisfied, he took one more look before he told VJ to wipe the files from the hard-drive. When that was done, VJ accessed all of the research team's computers and deleted all their files.

The only record that now existed of perfect DNA was on the two 512GB storage devices. MacLeod slipped them into two cylindrical gold lockets on fine gold chains then put one around his neck and snapped the clasp closed. He handed the other to VJ who did the same.

Before they left, VJ asked MacLeod to sign three copies of the same letter. MacLeod barely looked at the papers.

"What's this?"

"It's a letter to document for future reference that you and I agreed to do this, just in case anything happens to one of us and the other has some explaining to do."

MacLeod quickly read the top copy, "We, Francis J. MacLeod and Vinjay Gupta declare that we voluntarily---"

He scribbled his signature at the bottom of all three pages. VJ then gave MacLeod the top copy, filed the second copy, folded the bottom copy and put it in his pocket, relieved that MacLeod hadn't noticed that the bottom copy was different.

MacLeod got home just before six-thirty. He lay down on top of the bed and rested for an hour. He got up, showered, had breakfast, and headed out again for a nine o'clock appointment with his solicitor. He entered the six-story building, got in the elevator and pressed the button for the top floor offices of Hodges, Rowley & Hatton. Stephen Hatton had been MacLeod's solicitor since he had moved back to Cambridge from the States in 2004. Hatton and his two older partners had founded the firm thirty-seven years ago, but they had both since retired and he was getting ready to retire in two years. A cautious man, a little on the plump side, bald on top with thick white hair on the back and sides, Hatton wore horned-rimmed glasses with lenses as thick as the bottom of a jam jar.

After the usual small talk, Hatton got down to business. "You mentioned on the phone that you wanted me to take care of something for you. Do you want to make changes to your will?"

"No, my will's fine the way it is." MacLeod opened a blue folder he had brought with him and took out two envelopes. One was addressed to Stephen Hatton Esq., the other to Professor Richard Simpson. He handed them both to Hatton. "I would like you to hold on to these for me for one week and I'll come by and pick them up next Friday, unopened," he added.

Hatton seemed puzzled. "And the reason you need me to hold on to these for one week?"

"Well, if something should happen to me in the meantime, my instructions are in there for you." MacLeod pointed to the envelope with Hatton's name on it. "The other envelope I want you to get to Richard right away."

"What do you mean, if something happens to you? I must admit you don't look like your usual self. Are you ill?"

"Not really. I haven't slept for several nights and last night I spent the whole night at the lab," MacLeod replied, instinctively fidgeting with the gold locket around his neck.

Hatton noticed. "When did you start wearing jewelry?"

MacLeod hesitated for a second before holding up the gold locket. "This, old chap, contains the Secret of Life."

"What is going on, Francis? I think you'd better start at the beginning."

"On one condition; when I tell you I know exactly what advice you are going to give me and the answer will be no, understood?"

Hatton had known MacLeod long enough to know there was no point in arguing. He nodded.

"You know that when I came here from the States I had recently been divorced, but what I didn't tell you was that my wife had been screwing around with some chap from the East

324

Coast. I had no idea who he was and quite frankly I didn't care."

MacLeod went on to tell Hatton about how SMB had funded his original genon research program, and during that time he found out by accident that it was someone from SMB who had had an affair with his wife. Naturally, MacLeod hated the man. He told Hatton the relevant history since that time, and how he had squeezed him and SMB out of the Genon deal. "He has been mad with me ever since."

MacLeod then explained how he found out about the extent of the man's obsession to get revenge.

"A couple of months ago, an American chap called Matt Price came to see me and told me he had been recruited by this man to come here last summer to dig up some dirt on me. Apparently, the chap fell in love with my assistant Brenda and they are planning to get married. I don't know whether it was her influence or not but he told me he really felt bad about what he had done."

MacLeod took another envelope from his folder. "I received this yesterday morning." He handed it over to Hatton, who opened it and removed a sheet of paper.

"This is a death threat," Hatton said. "Do you know who is responsible?"

"If it's genuine then I have to believe it must be him."

"What is his name?"

"It's not important, let's just say he works for SMB."

Hatton folded the sheet of paper, put it back in the envelope and slid it back across the desk to MacLeod. He nodded. "Have you told the police?"

"No, and I am not going to. I don't want the Cambridge plods all over the place at Wednesday's conference. End of discussion."

325

MacLeod put the death-threat letter in a larger brown envelope and addressed it to Detective Chief Superintendent Graham Duncan. He handed the brown envelope to Hatton.

"If the worst happens, please give this to Duncan."

"Heaven forbid," Hatton said as he put the envelope in a file with the others.

MacLeod then told Hatton that he and VJ had spent all night at the lab copying all of the perfect DNA data onto the micro storage devices. He pointed to the gold chain and locket around his neck.

"VJ and I have the only two copies."

Chapter 57

When VJ got back to the rented apartment, his wife and two children were sitting having breakfast. Their suitcases were all packed and ready to go. VJ kissed his wife and hugged his children, grabbed a cup of tea, then went for a shower and a change of clothes.

He had sold his house three months previously and moved the family to an apartment on the other side of the city. Two weeks later, all of their furniture was shipped to India.

The taxi arrived an hour later, and after loading the suitcases, he and his family got in for the ninety-minute journey to Heathrow Airport. A few minutes into the journey, Imelda started sobbing.

When the children saw how upset their mother was, they cried.

VJ shook his head. "It's all for the best," he said, trying to console her.

Imelda did not understand. "I would rather have you with us, regardless of your health situation. Ten years is such a long time," she sobbed loudly.

VJ put his arm around his wife's shoulder. "Imelda, you didn't see my grandmother suffer like I did. She was only in her early fifties and had such a painful and horrible death. I don't want you to have to witness that. At least this way we will have the rest of our lives to look forward to."

She pummeled her clenched fists into his chest. "I am not going to let you do it," she screamed.

The children cowered in the corner of the cab.

VJ grabbed her by the wrists. He had never seen her behave like this before. "Please, Imelda, get a hold of yourself."

Four hours later, with tears streaming down his cheeks, VJ waved to his family as they disappeared through the gate for the Air India flight to New Delhi.

He called Peter Fischer to finalize the arrangements and then boarded a shuttle bus to an airport hotel. Once in his room, he went straight to the bathroom and laid out a hand-towel next to the sink, then he opened up his overnight bag, took out a small plastic case, removed a syringe, scalpel and tweezers and placed them neatly on the towel. He took off his shirt, and then carefully removed the sterile wrapping from the syringe. He primed it so that the first few drops of liquid would push the air out of the needle. He didn't flinch as he stabbed the needle into his left shoulder and quickly pushed the plunger to deliver the full dose of anesthetic. As he stood there waiting for it to work, he wondered what the future, if he had one, would hold for him and his family. Only time could answer that.

Ten minutes later, when the top of his shoulder was numb, he grabbed the scalpel and made a swift cut into the flesh. He used the reflection in the bathroom mirror to guide the tweezers into the wound. After several tries, he hooked the biochip and pulled it out. He was faint, not from the pain but the image in the mirror. He thanked *Vishnu* - his god - that the chip in his thigh no longer functioned. He squirted a globule of heal-quick gel onto the wound.

He snatched a few sheets of tissue from the toilet roll and wrapped them around the bloody biochip. He flushed the toilet, then pushed the bundle of tissue into the bowl and up behind the bend. He flushed the toilet a second time and washed his hands.

He then put the syringe, scalpel and tweezers back into the case and wrapped it in a hotel laundry bag.

After an uncomfortable night, he got up early to go to the airport where he dumped the laundry bag in a restroom trash can.

He took the first flight to Basel.

Fischer met VJ at the airport and drove him to the MacLeod Clinic, where Meier was waiting.

After they greeted each other, VJ thanked Meier for coming out on a Saturday.

Meier said, "No problem. I did try to reach Francis to get his permission to proceed, but so far I have not been able to get a hold of him."

VJ handed Meier an authorization letter. Meier read it and looked at the signature. He gave it to Fischer. "Check it out."

Fischer returned ten minutes later. "It's definitely MacLeod's signature." He handed the print-out to Meier.

"Okay, then let's go over the preparations."

The three of them went across to Building 2 and took the elevator down to the ground floor. It was a lot colder than the last time VJ had been there. Meier had him sign a number of papers then went over the prep with him.

VJ said, "My biggest concern is that I suffer from claustrophobia. Is that a problem?"

Meier reassured him. "We will give you the cryoprotectant cocktail first, and then sedate you so you will not be aware of anything. You did bring loose-fitting clothes with you, didn't you?"

"A light weight track-suit," VJ answered.

"Perfect. If you would like to change into it we will get started."

As VJ changed into the track-suit, Meier noticed the gold locket around his neck.

"Do you want us to put that in the safe for you? Is it a family picture?"

"No, it's just a copy of research data from Genon, and I would like to keep it for safety, thanks," VJ replied.

Less than two hours later VJ entered suspended animation at -170°C.

Chapter 58

Saturday, April 22, 2028

"Code Blue! Code Blue!" the duty nurse shouted into the intercom system. Twelve seconds later, the medical team had the defibrillator pads on MacLeod's chest, desperately trying to shock him back to life. After one minute and thirty-two seconds, the heart monitor started beeping loudly as MacLeod's heart rate bounced erratically between seventy and eighty beats per minute.

Richard Simpson had just sat down to dinner with a group of friends in one of the city's newest restaurants when his pager went off. He knew there was only one reason why he would be paged on a Saturday evening. He jumped up from the table, apologizing as he hurriedly made his way to the exit.

When Simpson arrived at Addenbrooke's hospital, the duty intern briefed him on MacLeod's condition as they made their way to MacLeod's room. He told Simpson that MacLeod had been dead for ninety seconds. Once they had revived him, his heart beat at close to eighty per minute and was oscillating rapidly. After a few minutes, the heart rate gradually fell and it was now between ten and twelve beats per minute, the same rate it had been before MacLeod had arrested.

"What in the heck is going on, Francis?" Simpson muttered when he looked at the still body of his friend and colleague. Realizing MacLeod had actually died, even if only for a minute or so, he took the envelope from his inside pocket given to him by MacLeod's solicitor Hatton. Written across the envelope were the words, 'In the event of my impending death – open immediately'.

Simpson ripped it open and removed a letter and an envelope. He quickly read the letter and then shouted to anyone who was listening, "Get the EMTs in here urgently."

MacLeod's heart rate dropped again alarmingly. Simpson waited until he had no other choice and then activated the defibrillator machine again, shouting, "Come on, come on."

The EMTs stood there watching and waiting. MacLeod's heart sprung to life again and started to beat rapidly at around seventy-five beats per minute. Simpson took a set of instructions and a set of keys out of the envelope and handed them to the EMTs. "Hurry, get over to MacLeod's lab right away, read these and get started."

He turned to the duty nurse. "Take the other side. Let's go."

Together they pushed MacLeod's bed into the corridor and moved as fast as they could toward MacLeod's lab. Simpson kept looking at the heart monitor. MacLeod's heart rate had dropped below seventy.

Simpson, too concerned with his patient's condition, didn't notice the gold locket swinging back and forth around MacLeod's neck as they rushed him out.

The EMTs were waiting. They had opened the large pouch and taken out a linen body-wrap, foam sleeves and a seven-foot-long freezer bag. They moved MacLeod into position and quickly clasped the foam sleeves around his arms and legs, then draped the linen body-wrap around, him making sure the heart-monitor wires were free to be re-connected. They eased the limp body into the freezer bag, connected the vacuum pump, sucked out the air, then carefully lifted MacLeod into the chamber and quickly connected the cables to the inbuilt heart monitor.

MacLeod's heart rate had dropped to below thirty beats per minute.

"Hurry," Simpson yelled as the technicians prepared to cryogenically freeze the famous scientist. MacLeod's heart rate dropped steadily as the technicians opened the valves to allow in the liquid nitrogen. As the temperature rapidly dropped toward the targeted -170°C, MacLeod's heart rate plummeted.

Simpson had followed MacLeod's instructions to the letter, and the only question remaining was whether they had done it in time.

Simpson sat back in a chair and read the second part of MacLeod's letter. It asked him to first make a telephone call and then open the envelope. It gave him instructions on another matter that Simpson found hard to believe. He would make the call but would have to think very seriously about MacLeod's other request. He called the number.

"Stephen Hatton."

"Mr. Hatton, I am sorry to inform you that MacLeod passed away this evening."

"That is sad news indeed. Can you tell me how he died?"

"I am sorry, but I don't have any answers yet."

"I see, well, thank you for calling me, Professor Simpson. Good-bye."

Hatton got up from his fireside chair, took MacLeod's envelope from his briefcase and opened it. It instructed him to make three phone calls. He called the first number.

"Hans Meier."

"Herr Meier, this is Stephen Hatton, Sir Francis MacLeod's solicitor. I need to inform you that Sir Francis passed away this evening and he left me instructions to call you immediately and give you a message."

"I see. I am very sorry to hear that. What is the message?"

"The message is 'CGAT'. I have no idea what that means, do you?"

"Thank you for the message, Mr. Hatton, good evening."

Strange, Hatton thought as he looked at the second name on the list. He knew Sir Charles Palmer. He called the number.

"Hello, Charles Palmer."

"Sir Charles, its Stephen Hatton, I'm afraid I have some sad news. Sir Francis passed away this evening."

Palmer punched the wall, bruising his knuckles in the process, "Damn no, damn! So unnecessary!"

"He left me some instructions to give to you. Do you have a pen and paper available?"

"Yes, go ahead," Palmer answered as his eyes welled up.

"It says: Tell Sir Charles that I have already made arrangements for Mrs. Palmer, so all he has to do is contact Hans Meier at the following number and he will take care of everything." Hatton read out Meier's telephone number.

Hatton then called Graham Duncan and told him the news of MacLeod's death and that MacLeod had left an envelope addressed to him. Duncan said he would send one of his men to the solicitor's office first thing on Monday morning to pick up the envelope.

Shortly before four o'clock on Sunday morning, a white pharmaceutical delivery van with Swiss license plates pulled up outside of Addenbrooke's hospital. Three men got out and ran through the corridors. They knew where they were going. Less than forty-five minutes later, they emerged from the back entrance pushing the strange looking metal chamber. Heavier than last time, it took all three of them to maneuver it up the ramp and into the back of the van. The driver jumped out and closed the doors behind him as the two technicians connected the chamber to the liquid nitrogen bottles and then drove off into the darkness.

Chapter 59

Simpson read MacLeod's bizarre request over and over again and decided to sleep on it, but got no sleep that night. What a dilemma, how could he carry out his friend's wishes when he had taken a *Hippocratic Oath* to preserve life? Would he be preserving a life or putting it in jeopardy?

He decided he could not do it for he had no right to play with life or death; that was God's job.

But he could not pass the buck on the unpleasant task of telling Kathleen Murphy that her fiancé had passed away. But not by phone, he would have to tell her in person.

* * * * *

"No, no, no," Kathleen shrieked. "It's not true; God, tell me it's not true."

She crumpled into a heap on the floor and sobbed uncontrollably. He did his best to console her, but it was to no avail. He picked up her iPhone and scrolled through the contact list. He saw the name, Mary O'Sullivan, a fellow Irishwoman. He hit send, but after five rings he got voicemail, she was probably at Sunday Mass. He left a message. He scrolled further down and recognized a name, it was Brenda Thompson, MacLeod's assistant. He thought for a few seconds before he decided what to say to her.

This time, after three rings, there was an answer. "Hi, Kathleen," Brenda answered.

"Good morning, Ms. Thompson, this is Professor Simpson and I am at Ms. Murphy's home and she needs your help. Would it be possible for you get over here fairly quickly?"

Brenda went weak at the knees. Simpson at Kathleen's house, on her iPhone on a Sunday morning could only mean one thing: Francis.

"How is Sir Francis?" she stuttered.

"Not good, I'm afraid. Can you come over?"

"I'll be there in fifteen minutes." As she hung up, she burst into tears.

Kathleen was hysterical by the time Brenda got there. Brenda knelt down, put her arms around her and they cried together. Simpson took out a prescription pad and scribbled two medications for Kathleen; he handed it to Brenda.

"This is a prescription for some tranquilizers for now and some sleeping pills for tonight. There's a 24-hour chemist not far from here. If you could pop out and get this filled, I will stay with her until you get back."

Brenda returned within thirty minutes.

"I need to go but I will come by this afternoon to check on her," Simpson said as he let himself out.

Kathleen had calmed down a little, got up and sat on the sofa, wiping her eyes with the silk handkerchief Francis had given her. After Simpson had left she said, "I don't need bloody pills, what I need is a bloody drink. I just can't believe it, Brenda."

"I know, it's like a bad dream, only worse. What can I get you?"

"Bushmills, it's in the cabinet. I'll have it with a small drop of water."

Brenda stayed with her for several hours. Kathleen drank more than one third of the bottle. They had talked about Francis and how deeply Kathleen was in love with him, how they planned to marry.

"Please wake me up and tell me it is a bad dream," she said as she hugged Brenda closely.

"I should probably go and let you get some rest," Brenda said, "so let me help you into bed before I leave." She tucked Kathleen in and gave her a long, close embrace.

"Before you leave, could you pass me the bottle of Bushmills and put it by my bedside. Thanks."

"I am not sure that's a good idea."

"Jesus, Mary and Joseph, for heaven's sake, wull yuh just do it," she cried, her former Dundalk accent coming through.

Simpson stopped by around three o'clock and banged on Kathleen's door. After ten minutes, he called the police and told them he was concerned about her. They were there within minutes and smashed down the door. Simpson ran through the house and into the bedroom. Kathleen lay across the bed with her head hanging over the side, her eyes glazed. He checked her pulse; it was weak. He saw the three-quarter empty Bushmills bottle by the side of her bed and the open pill bottles on the floor.

"Damn!" He called for an ambulance and had her taken to Addenbrooke's. They immediately pumped her stomach and made her comfortable.

Simpson sat by her bedside and re-read MacLeod's letter. He made his decision.

"Nurse," he called out and then together they wheeled Kathleen's bed to MacLeod's lab.

"Thank you, nurse, that'll be all for now."

After the nurse had left, he took a syringe and a small vial out of a cupboard and injected Kathleen. He locked up the lab, then returned to his office to call Hans Meier.

Over the next few hours, he contacted the hospital morgues within a fifty-mile radius of Addenbrooke's until he found what

337

he was looking for. The deceased female was roughly the same age, height and weight as Kathleen, although she had blonde hair and blue eyes, a minor problem. Simpson went back to MacLeod's lab, removed Kathleen's outer layer of clothes and wrapped her in a hospital gown, putting the clothes in a laundry bag. Then he cut off two locks of Kathleen's hair, put them into two small plastic bags and labeled them: *Kathleen Murphy, DOD 23/4/28.* He shook his head at the irony. It was Francis' fifty-ninth birthday.

The mortician laid the bodies side by side and studied them from different angles then went to work. After taking a dozen photos of Kathleen's head, he placed a gel template over her face and gently pressed it around her features. He removed the mold and laid it on the bench to harden, then cleaned Kathleen's face with a damp cloth. Next, he dyed the woman's hair red and cut and styled it like Kathleen's. When the mold was ready, he placed a three-millimeter layer of theatrical putty on the inside and gently positioned the mold over the woman's face. Two hours later he added the final touch – green contact lenses. The two dead women looked like twins.

Simpson returned after dinner that same evening and examined the facial artistry.

"Nice job," he said. "Not even Kathleen's parents would believe it was anyone other than their daughter."

The mortician took a photograph of the woman while Simpson filled out a death certificate, on which he wrote, 'Accidental death'.

In the middle of the night, a white pharmaceutical delivery van pulled up at the back entrance of Addenbrooke's Hospital for the second night in a row and drove off into the darkness.

Chapter 60

Monday, April 24, 2028

Detective Chief Inspector Butterfield stopped by Stephen Hatton's office and picked up a brown envelope addressed to the Detective Chief Superintendent.

Graham Duncan opened the envelope, removing a smaller white envelope and a note from MacLeod explaining to Duncan that he had received the enclosed in the mail on the thirteenth of April. Duncan took a sheet of paper out of the white envelope and stared at it for several seconds before passing it over to Butterfield.

Butterfield looked up. "Shit, it's a bloody death threat. Why in hell did MacLeod not bring this to our attention when he was still alive?"

"Because his type think that stuff will never happen to them."

There was a knock on Duncan's door. "Who is it?" the Chief Superintendent roared.

The door opened and Detective Sergeant Mills, a stocky man with a cheery smile, popped his head around the door.

"Sorry to interrupt, Super, but could I have a quick word with Inspector Butterfield?"

"Aye, go on."

Mills held a sheet of paper in his hand. "I was just going through the 'stiff's list', and when I read it I thought you would be interested to know that one of MacLeod's staff died of an overdose on Sunday afternoon."

Butterfield looked at the list and the name of Kathleen Murphy. "You better come and tell the super."

"A heck of a coincidence," Duncan said. "Let me get the paperwork started and I will see both of you in the conference room in fifteen minutes. In the meantime, Mills, get a copy of her death certificate."

Mills showed the copy to Duncan. "It says 'accidental death' and it's signed by Richard Simpson," Mills said.

Duncan stood. "Mills, have someone round up MacLeod's key staff members and bring them in for questioning. Tom and I will pay a visit to Richard Simpson."

As soon as Mills left, Duncan called Simpson and told him they were on their way over to his office.

"So, Richard, what's the cause of death?"

"Well, to be honest with you, I don't know," Simpson said.

Duncan frowned. "He is dead, isn't he?"

"I don't know the answer to that question either because---"

Duncan interrupted. "You don't know if MacLeod is dead or alive? You are a medical doctor, aren't you?"

"Yes, MD, PhD," Simpson replied.

"Let me try a different approach. Assuming for the moment that MacLeod is dead, when will you know the cause of death?"

Simpson knew that what he was going to answer next would not go down well with the Detective Chief Superintendent. "Within the next ten years."

Duncan and Butterfield looked at each other.

"You mean, you don't know if MacLeod is alive or dead, and if he is dead you don't know the cause of death and it might take up to ten years for you to figure it out? What kind of medical gobbledygook is that? Listen, Richard, treat me as if I am just a simple plod, which I am sure will not be too difficult for you, and speak in plain old-fashioned English, will yer?"

"Well, it is a little complicated." Simpson started. "As you know, MacLeod was in a coma with a very slow heart rate and we had not determined the cause of either. Then, on Saturday evening, his heart stopped beating for about a minute and a half, but they were able to resuscitate him and his heart started to beat more rapidly and then deteriorated again. However, MacLeod had left me instructions that in the event of impending death we were to immediately have him cryogenically frozen. And, on Saturday evening, we carried out his wishes."

"So, he is dead, then?" Butterfield asked.

"That's it, you see, when we put him in the chamber his heart was still beating, so from a medical perspective I don't know which happened first, whether his heart stopped beating naturally or because he was frozen alive."

"Technically, either way the chap's dead, isn't he?" Duncan said.

"Unless he comes back to life."

"Uh?"

"MacLeod believed that with some concoction or other he could be frozen alive and then at some point in the next ten years come back to life."

"Why in hell would anyone want to do that?" Duncan asked.

"He was ill---"

Butterfield interrupted. "Bloody ill, was he? So, where is his body now? We'll need to have an autopsy done on him."

"That's not going to be possible," Simpson replied.

"Why not?" Butterfield asked.

"Because he chose to be frozen. Let me take you to him." With that Simpson took a set of keys out of his desk drawer and said, "Follow me." He unlocked the door to MacLeod's lab, walked over to the cold room and turned the key. He pulled the heavy door open and stood back. "He's in there."

341

Duncan and Butterfield looked inside. "Where?" Duncan asked.

Simpson peeked over their shoulders. "Oh shit, how is that possible? He was there on Saturday night when I left and I have the only set of keys."

"Okay, Richard, it's time for you to come clean. You know more than you have admitted so far and you are trying my patience."

"Graham, I have told you everything. Come on back to my office and I will give you Francis' letter of instruction to me and you can see for yourself."

Duncan and Butterfield studied the set of instructions and the letter from MacLeod.

"It says here that he had Parkinson's disease," Butterfield observed. "Did you know that?"

"No, not until I read his letter. I know he was working on a Parkinson's genon therapy together with Tronavis, so I can only put two and two together."

"Richard, you told me last week that you thought MacLeod's coma may have been induced and the implication to me was that someone might have tried to kill him. Is that still a possibility or not? Because if it's not, I don't need to waste any more time on this," Duncan said.

"Graham, all I can tell you is that these last five days have been a complete mystery to me and in the end all I did was carry out Francis' wishes. I don't have any answers for you. Someone else may have caused the coma, he may have done it himself or he may have had an accomplice. As I see it there are several possibilities. Remember this is not my field of expertise."

Duncan sighed. "Okay, tell us about Kathleen Murphy."

Simpson recounted everything that had taken place on Sunday morning and that afternoon when he went back to check on her he found her near to death in her bed from a combination of alcohol and medications that he had prescribed. There was no suicide note and he assumed that she was so distraught that she accidentally overdosed. He had her rushed to Addenbrooke's, but it was too late; she died a few hours later.

"Okay, I think we're done here for now, but we will be in touch again, I'm sure." Duncan said.

On the way back to the station, they stopped at the University Arms for lunch and discussed the increasingly bizarre circumstances of what they were dealing with. They confessed they didn't know whether they had a case or not.

Chapter 61

When they returned to the police station, Mills had five Genon employees in the conference room: Alan Coleman, Brenda, Darren, Ian and Rob.

The detective chief superintendent asked everyone to take a seat, then looked at his watch and turned to Mills.

"Is this everybody?"

"I believe there is one more senior employee, sir, a Dr Vinjay Gupta, whom we have not been able to contact. Is that right, Ms Thompson?"

Brenda answered directly to the detective chief superintendent. "That's correct, sir. We haven't seen him for over a week and he's not answering his iPhone."

"Okay, we can talk to him later. As you all know, Sir Francis collapsed and went into a coma last Wednesday and died on Saturday evening. The next day, Kathleen Murphy died of an overdose. We have since learned that Sir Francis and Ms Murphy were engaged to be married. In view of the circumstances and the two deaths, we are conducting an investigation into his business and private affairs. There is no need for alarm."

Tears filled Brenda's eyes as she thought about Francis and Kathleen.

Duncan asked Coleman to accompany him to his office and told Butterfield and Mills to take statements from the others. When he returned with Coleman, he addressed the group again.

"We believe it is necessary to close Genon until further notice, so Detective Sergeant Mills' men are over there right now doing just that. If any of you have personal belongings there, they will arrange an escort to let you inside to collect them. Also, I have just spoken with Mr. Coleman and he has agreed that you will all receive your full salaries until further notice, so try to look upon this as paid leave of absence. One last thing, I want to emphasize again that this is not, and I repeat, not a criminal investigation. It is simply a fact-finding exercise because of the unusual circumstances."

Duncan studied the expressions on their faces before continuing. "We appreciate your cooperation. Any questions?"

Rob looked at Darren, and then put his hand in the air.

"Yes, sir."

"Detective chief superintendent, it seems to me that there is more to this than meets the eye. I am sure you don't normally go around closing businesses just because the managing director passes away. Is there something you're not telling us?"

Duncan smiled. "Well, let me put it bluntly. From what I understand, this company was planning a multi-billion-pound public offering and MacLeod and the rest of you were going to make a lot of money. Then, for reasons unknown, the public offering was cancelled and not long after that MacLeod, who apparently was in excellent health, ends up in a coma and dies. Then Ms Murphy dies. I'd say there are some loose ends that need to be checked out, wouldn't you?" He paused, then, "It is true, isn't it, that all of you would have become multi-millionaires overnight if the IPO had gone through?"

No one answered. But Darren's face was bright red.

Duncan signaled to Butterfield to take over and asked Coleman to come back to his office.

"I understand that MacLeod owned fifty-five percent of Genon stock, is that correct?" Duncan asked.

"That's correct."

"In the event of his demise, who are the beneficiaries?"

"Upon his death, his shares are split so that the five pharmaceutical companies will get fifteen percent between them, giving them a holding of eight percent each. The five staff members will share twenty percent, giving them a holding of six percent each. The university will get the remaining twenty percent and become trustees of the business as the largest single shareholder, with a holding of thirty percent. He set this up about a year ago when he found out how much the company might be worth at the time of an IPO. He wanted to make sure there would be a good balance of the equity positions."

Duncan totaled up the list of shareholders he had scribbled on a pad.

"That's eleven reasons why someone might want him dead. Thank you, Mr Coleman."

Meanwhile, Butterfield explained to the others how they would be conducting the investigation.

"Before you leave, we will need to take a set of fingerprints from you and we will also be reviewing your statements and then talking to you individually, thank you."

After the Genon employees left, Duncan sat with Butterfield and Mills.

"Tom, have forensics check the death threat note for fingerprints, sweep the scene where MacLeod collapsed at the podium and talk to anyone you can find who was in that lecture hall, near the front."

"I sent it to them already, but if you want my opinion I think one of his staff, Darren Richards, is involved in this," Butterfield offered.

"Okay, tell me."

"During the interview it was very clear that he's hiding something. Besides, the death threat note points to him."

"In what way?"

346

"The date."

"It's the date of the bloody lecture, so what? Get to the point."

Butterfield smirked. "It's not the date itself. It's the order. The month is before the day, the way Americans write it; that suggests that the sender is American."

"Aye, I see yer point. You took his prints, didn't yer?" Butterfield nodded. "Okay then, that's a good start, you better have someone keep an eye on him. What else do you have?"

"Not much yet."

"Mills, what about this Gupta? Anything on him?"

It hadn't taken Mills long to discover that Gupta no longer lived at the address they had been given by Genon's financial director. Neighbors told him that Gupta's wife Imelda, and their two children had moved back to India more than three months ago. Imelda had told the neighbors that her mother was seriously ill and she was going back to take care of her. Gupta had sold his house at fifteen percent below market price for a quick sale; the neighbors weren't too happy about that.

Duncan fiddled with his moustache. "And they have no idea where he is?"

"No, and there was no forwarding address at the post office but he did have a PO Box at Sydney Street Branch. We got a warrant and checked it out but there was nothing but a week's stack of unopened junk mail. There was not one piece of regular mail. The postmistress checked her records. Gupta paid for a three-month rental, which is about to expire next week. He is definitely AWOL."

"Keep working it and locate the little bugger. I am going to meet with Stephen Hatton. See you both first thing."

"Have a seat, chief superintendent."

"Thank you. So, when did you last see MacLeod?"

Hatton admitted that MacLeod had been to see him a few days before his Watson and Crick lecture.

"Did he say anything that may be relevant to our investigation?" Duncan asked.

"Actually, he did."

"And, what would that be?"

"As you now know, a week before the conference, MacLeod received a death threat, which is why he came to see me and he left me instructions what to do if the worst happened, and sadly it did, and I passed on the threat to you immediately."

"And the reason you didn't come forward earlier?"

"Come on, detective chief superintendent, you know the answer – attorney/client privilege, but I can tell you he was definitely uptight," the solicitor said.

"What else did you discuss?"

Hatton also explained that MacLeod had told him that on the Thursday night before the conference he and the Indian chap, Gupta, had worked throughout the night and downloaded all of the company's research files onto two storage devices. Then they deleted all of the files from the central computers. MacLeod kept one copy and said that Gupta had the other.

"Gupta," Duncan said, "hasn't been seen since that Friday, and he has the only other copy of MacLeod's work. Anything else?"

"Not really, he just told me that he had received the threat and asked me to put it in his file. He was hoping it was a hoax. But when I asked him if he could think of anyone who might have done this, he said the only person he knew who might have a grudge against him was an old business acquaintance, but he couldn't believe he would want him dead."

"What's the name of this business acquaintance?"

"He didn't mention a name, but said he worked for SMB in the US. I did suggest that he contact you chaps, but he said he didn't want to do that. He was concerned about the effect it might have on the conference."

Duncan shook his head. "Now, why on earth would he take that chance?"

"I really don't know, but he was a very proud man, and the other thing he did say was that if it wasn't a hoax, he was prepared."

"What did he mean by that?"

"I don't know we didn't discuss that, but I can tell you this. Underneath all of his bravado I'm pretty sure that he was stressed about it. It was the first time that I had ever seen his hands shake the way they did."

"Do you know if he talked to anyone else about this?"

Hatton shook his head. "Not that I know of, although he did say when he left here he was going to Addenbrooke's to talk to his cardiologist, Richard Simpson."

"Did he now? Huh. This case is getting more interesting by the minute."

"What do you mean?" Hatton asked.

"Oh, never mind. A policeman's intuition, shall we say, and leave it at that."

Chapter 62

First thing on Tuesday morning, Duncan, Butterfield and Mills sat in the conference room at Parkside police station reviewing what they had so far. Butterfield's men had worked into the early hours going back and forth with US authorities looking into Darren's affairs.

"My chaps have learned that about a year ago Richards bought a seventy-foot yacht and a big house in the San Diego area. It appears he suddenly got rich to the tune of twenty million dollars. They traced the money to a local branch of Bank of America, but the trail went cold, so we have asked the FBI to help."

"Nice work, Tom." Duncan nodded.

Other detectives had focused on the Watson and Crick Conference and learned from those sitting close to the front that just before MacLeod collapsed, some of them heard what they described as a kind of low pitch 'phssh' sound.

"A dart, maybe?" Duncan said.

"I don't know for sure, but some described it like turning a tap on and off or the sound when you open a can of soda."

"What the hell sounds like a can of soda, apart from a can of soda?"

"Search me, boss."

"By the way, wasn't Richards sitting close to the front?"

"Second row, to be exact."

They had also learned from those sitting close to the rear of the room that a blind man and his guide had been standing against the back wall, near the door. After MacLeod collapsed, they had left immediately.

Duncan stood up and poured a cup of coffee. He shook his head.

"Okay, what are we missing here? A famous Nobel laureate in a coma, supposedly frozen alive, then his body disappears. The day after, his fiancée ODs, a key scientist gone AWOL, a 'phssh' sound like a bloody can of soda and a blind man at the back of the room. Somebody give me a crumb."

The phone rang, Butterfield answered. It was forensics; he listened intently.

"Well done," he said as he put the phone down.

"What?" Duncan asked.

"Forensics have a lead on the death threat. It's made up of letters, the font and font size match sub-headings from the *New York Times*."

"God bless those lab nerds. Doesn't Richards go back and forth across the pond?"

"Uh, huh," Butterfield nodded

Duncan turned to Mills. "Bring him in."

"Consider it done, sir," Mills answered.

Later, as Duncan entered the conference room, he heard Darren complaining to Mills.

"How much longer do I have to sit around here just twiddling my thumbs?"

Duncan immediately set the tone. "Let me reassure you, Dr Richards, that this is England and we are in the middle of an investigation and sarcastic comments like that are not appreciated. Unless, of course, you would like to do some research in one of our cells. Do I make myself clear?"

Darren sat up straight. "Yes, sir, I'm sorry. I was joking around."

"Well, this is not a joke. Did you murder Sir Francis MacLeod?"

"Of course not," Darren answered emphatically. "Why would I want to do that?"

"We know all about your house and yacht and the twenty million dollars that miraculously appeared in your bank account. So why don't you start at the beginning and explain that to us?"

Darren shuffled uncomfortably in his seat. "About one year ago I became acquainted with a guy from Harvard, Matt Price, and he arranged for an investment group to advance me a loan in exchange for Genon stock at the time of the IPO. It was all above board."

"Above board? It's illegal in this country to do that. And the name of this investment group?"

"I don't know, he never told me and I didn't ask, but I can assure you I did nothing wrong. I did it by the book. You see, I signed a promissory note to sell some of my stock to them after the IPO – three months after, to be precise – after the lock-down period. As soon as the shares have a marketable value, I can sell them to whomever I wish."

"Well, that's the thing, yer see, they're not going to have a marketable value, because there's not going to be an IPO, at least not for a long time. Do you know what I think? I think you got so pissed off at MacLeod for canceling the IPO that you took the matter into your own hands."

"That's ridiculous, I owe everything to him."

"So, you have no idea who put up the funds for you?"

"No, as I said, I didn't ask questions."

"Well, I guess we naïve British coppers are just going to have to take your word for that." Duncan banged his fist on the table. Darren jumped backward in his chair. "Like shit we are! Now why don't we try again, Dr Richards? Who gave you the money? Maybe it was Mexican drug lords? I hear it is pretty rife in your neck of the woods."

Visibly shaken, Darren sat up straight. "What I told you is the truth. I had no idea who put up the money, at least not until six months later when Matt Price 'fessed-up. It's a guy called Henry Anderson, the president of SMB Pharmaceuticals in New Jersey."

"And why in the world would he do that?"

"He wanted a stake in Genon, but he and MacLeod were rivals. They hated each other."

"Did they now? Well, that doesn't change the fact that what you did is illegal in this country. Book him."

The color drained from Darren's cheeks. "You can't do that, I'm an 'American citizen."

"Really. Red, white and blue to you, too."

"Wait, I didn't harm MacLeod in any way. Its Anderson and Price you should be talking to."

Butterfield's phone rang. "Forensics," he mouthed to Duncan. He tore a piece of paper in two and scribbled on one piece and pushed it toward Duncan.

Duncan looked down. It read, 'Forensics, 3 x fingerprints on note. MacLeod and Hatton. Negative match on other. Not Richards'.

The superintendent put a clenched fist to his mouth and coughed. He slowly raised his eyes toward Darren.

"And you could be fingering Anderson and Price, whoever they are, to cover your own arse. So maybe, the three of you are in this together."

Butterfield handed Mills the other piece of paper with the names of Anderson and Price scribbled on it. Mills nodded, got up and left the room.

Darren tried to stand up but Butterfield pushed him back down in the chair, keeping his hands on the back of Darren's shoulders and said, "Look at it from the chief superintendent's point of view. You and two other Americans, who obviously all know each other and have a connection to MacLeod, are all mixed up in this. It can't be just coincidence, can it?"

Duncan stood up. "Read him his rights."

Chapter 63

After lunch, Mills reported to Duncan and Butterfield what he had learned over the past two to three hours.

"Matt Price is definitely from Harvard but he has been spending quite a bit of time over here in the past eight to nine months, apparently spying on MacLeod. And, coincidently, he's is engaged to MacLeod's assistant Brenda Thompson."

"Is he now?" Duncan said.

Butterfield's phone rang, it was forensics again.

"Outstanding," he answered as he heard the news. "You know the letters on the death threat note that were pasted from the *New York Times*? They were from the eleventh of April, East Coast edition."

Duncan smiled. "You've got to love those lab nerds. I know I make fun of them all the time but sometimes they are geniuses."

Mills shook his head. He had just been beaten to the punch. "I was about to tell you that we were able to confirm that Anderson was here during MacLeod's lecture. He arrived at Heathrow on the morning of April the twelfth and rented a Mercedes from Hertz. He drove to Cambridge and stayed at the Cambridgeshire Moat House Hotel for five nights. On Monday April the seventeenth, he flew to Basel and returned the following day with two other men. He flew back to Basel on April the twentieth. He returned yesterday and is scheduled to fly back to New York tomorrow."

"Okay, that's sufficient evidence for me, Tom. Bring him in," Duncan said.

Butterfield got up and left the room. "My men will have him here by this evening."

The officers escorted Anderson back to Cambridge and settled him in a comfortable cell. Anderson had not slept during the night. The next morning they took him straight to an interview room. The duty officer filled out the paperwork, then took his fingerprints. He told him that Detective Chief Superintendent Duncan would be along shortly.

Anderson was dozing when Duncan and Butterfield arrived. He awakened quickly and stood up.

"Please take a seat, Mr Anderson." Butterfield gestured for Anderson to sit back down.

"Let me take this," Duncan said to Butterfield. "Now, Mr Anderson, we have every reason to believe that you are in some way responsible for the death of Sir Francis MacLeod."

"What? You can't be serious," Anderson stammered, his face reddening.

"Do you read the newspapers?"

"Er, yes, occasionally. Why?"

"Which one?" Duncan pressed.

"The *New York Times*. Why?"

"Just curious. Let me tell you what we know so far," Duncan sat down in a chair on the opposite side of the table. "It seems that you and MacLeod were not exactly close. In fact we have it on good authority that you hated each other."

"So what?" Anderson said.

"Some say you were out to get MacLeod and that you hired Matt Price to dig up some dirt on him. And in addition to that, you have one of MacLeod's staff members, Darren Richards, in your back pocket."

"That's absurd," Anderson said.

"Oh, I assure you Mr Anderson that we don't consider it to be absurd, we consider it to be criminal."

Anderson laughed nervously. "I haven't committed a crime." Beads of sweat began to appear on his forehead.

There was a knock on the door, it was Mills. He handed Butterfield a copy of a report, he read it and then handed it to Duncan. "Anderson fingerprint – positive."

Duncan took the death-threat note out of his pocket and slowly unfolded it in front of Anderson.

"Recognize this?"

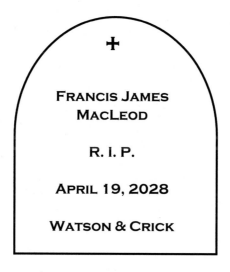

FRANCIS JAMES MACLEOD

R. I. P.

APRIL 19, 2028

WATSON & CRICK

"No. What is it supposed to be?"

Duncan smiled. "Let me refresh your memory, Mr Anderson. A few weeks ago, you cut and pasted these letters onto this sheet of paper. You then sealed the note in an envelope and posted it in Cambridge the week before MacLeod's lecture."

"That's not true. I had nothing to do with MacLeod's death and as much as I despised the man, it doesn't make sense that I would want him dead."

"Really?" Duncan shook his head. "So how do you explain that the note is made from sub-headings from the *New York Times* – the April eleventh edition to be exact – the very day you left New York to come to England? And more to the point, how do you explain that apart from MacLeod and his solicitor, yours are the only fingerprints on the note?"

Anderson slumped back in the chair, "Okay, chief superintendent. I sent MacLeod that note, but not as a death threat. It was just meant to scare him and let him know that I knew about his dirty little secret."

Butterfield jumped in. "A tombstone, RIP and the date of the lecture, and you say that does not constitute a death threat?"

"It doesn't mean Rest in Peace, it stands for Reputation in Pieces," Anderson said.

Duncan looked at Butterfield and nodded toward the door. Once in the corridor, he said, "A few more minutes. He's sweating in there and as I've always said, someone who feels the heat responds a lot faster than someone who has seen the light."

When they returned to the interrogation room, Butterfield closed the door and leaned up against the doorframe, while Duncan continued. "I'll grant you this. That's original," he said. "Reputation in pieces. Bloody good one!"

Anderson admitted that he had sent the note as a warning to MacLeod and that he turned up at MacLeod's lecture with the blind man to let MacLeod know that he knew about the failed clinical trial. His objective was to force MacLeod to include SMB in the genon technology opportunity or run the risk of having his reputation blemished. It was his best bargaining chip.

"Besides, what good would it be if MacLeod were dead? You can't negotiate with a dead man. So you see, I have no reason to kill MacLeod."

"I don't see it that way, Mr Anderson," Duncan countered. "I think that you thought if MacLeod was out of the way and you had someone publicly expose the failed clinical trial, the value of Genon would plummet and you would step in as a white knight and buy up all of the shares. You already knew that Darren Richards would be an easy sell and that the other employees would probably follow him. That would give you forty percent right there, and with MacLeod and his key employees gone, I am sure you were confident that the university would sell their twenty percent stake. SMB would then become the largest shareholder with a sixty percent holding, I'll bet you just couldn't wait to stick it to the other pharmaceutical companies."

Anderson stood up. "Can I go now? I don't need to sit here and listen to your ridiculous fairy tales."

"Fairy tales, eh? That's what you Americans think of our dedicated police work. No, I don't think so. Sir, as you Americans say, you are just going to have to 'sit tight' for a while."

"This is complete bullshit," Anderson shouted.

"I don't think you understand the severity of your situation, Mr Anderson," Duncan responded. "As I told your partner Dr Richards yesterday, there is something you should be aware of and that is that under Section 81 of the Companies Act 1985, you are prohibited from selling or buying unlisted shares here or anywhere else for that matter. It is a violation of UK Security and Exchange Commission regulations and it can carry a sentence of up to ten years in jail."

Anderson's face drained of all color.

Forty-eight hours later, Anderson and Darren were seated in the Cambridge courthouse. Neither of them had seen the inside of a British courtroom before and now they were sitting side by side in the dock appearing before Mr Justice Treadwell.

All of the seats in the public gallery were taken. The previous night, the late edition of the *Cambridge Evening News Online,* had announced, *MacLeod: Suspects in Court.*

Arraignment was set for ten o'clock Friday morning. Since MacLeod had collapsed the previous week, the story was front page news. When the papers reported that MacLeod's fiancée had died of an overdose on Sunday morning, the story became headline news. Amy Harper, the *Evening News'* top reporter, sat on the end of the crowded press bench.

The clerk of the court announced, "All rise," as Mr Justice Treadwell entered the courtroom.

The prosecutor, Mr David Johnson, addressed the judge. "Your Honor, the court requests that the defendants be remanded in custody for violation of the UK Security and Exchange Commission and regulations, under Section 81 of the Companies Act 1985."

Johnson paused as he looked up at Mr Justice Treadwell.

"Continue," the judge said.

"Your Honor, the prosecution will show that the defendants willfully collaborated in the selling and buying of unmarketable securities to the value of ten million pounds. Further, the court will produce in evidence copies of agreements and contracts confirming that these transactions took place." The prosecutor sat down.

Mr Justice Treadwell nodded to the defense counsel.

Mr Anthony Kim had been hurriedly appointed for the defense and his only task was to keep the amount of bail to a minimum.

"Your Honor, the defense requests that bail be set at half a million pounds for each defendant."

Johnson stood. "Your Honor, in addition to securities fraud the defendants are suspects in the death of Sir Francis MacLeod."

There were gasps all around the courtroom. Reporters were scribbling in their notepads.

Johnson paused for effect after he mentioned MacLeod's name, then continued.

"Your Honor, as both defendants are American citizens, the prosecution believes that they are a flight risk, and therefore requests that bail be denied."

Defense counsel jumped to his feet. "Your Honor, there is no evidence tying my clients to the death of Sir Francis MacLeod. It is true that my clients are American citizens; however, may I remind the court that Mr Anderson is a respected president of one of the world's largest pharmaceutical companies and Dr Richards resides here in Cambridge."

Johnson took his time as he stood. "Your Honor, not only do we have the documents confirming securities fraud, we have copies of contracts showing that Dr Richards used illegal funds to purchase a seven-million-dollar yacht and a ten-million-dollar home in the San Diego area in California. We also have a copy of a death threat sent by Mr Anderson to Sir Francis MacLeod."

"Bail denied," Justice Treadwell said. "The defendants will be remanded in custody and the court will set a date for the securities fraud trial."

The clerk of the court said, "All rise," then Justice Treadwell pushed back his chair and left the courtroom.

Several reporters rushed out of the courtroom and immediately dialed their office numbers.

As the two police officers led Anderson and Darren out of the courtroom and past Duncan and Butterfield, Anderson noticed their smug smiles and yelled, "What kind of damned justice is this?"

Butterfield turned to Duncan. "You do know that there is about a six-month backlog in securities fraud cases?"

"Aye, I thought as much. That'll give us plenty of time to find out what really went down here, and then we'll give those two buggers a real taste of British justice."

He grinned as they left the courtroom and walked to their cars.

"See you back at the station," Butterfield said as he opened his car door and climbed in.

Duncan was about to do the same, but stopped in his tracks and called out, "Hey, Tom, hang on a minute, I've just thought of something that Simpson told me last week. MacLeod and his team all had fancy biochip implants. If Simpson hadn't removed the chips from MacLeod, we could have traced him. But Gupta can be traced."

"I'm on it, Super." Butterfield took a call as he closed the car door. He jumped out quickly and shouted after Duncan.

"I just heard from the lab. Apparently, the remote control that they found at the podium had been tampered with. When you touch the forward and back buttons at the same time it sends out two additional frequencies. One of them deleted forever MacLeod's Power Point presentation, causing the 'phssh' sound. The other, they think, might have triggered the biochips in MacLeod's body, sending an electrical charge across his heart. That's what knocked him out. MacLeod did it to himself."

Chapter 64

On hearing the news of Kathleen's death, Pope John Paul III locked himself in his private chapel where he wept and prayed over the loss of his only cousin.

He summoned his private secretary. "Make arrangements for me to attend Kathleen's funeral on Friday."

"Papa, I don't think that will be possible."

"Do it."

An hour later, the secretary was back in the pope's office with the Cardinal Secretary of State.

"It's too dangerous, Papa," the cardinal said. "Especially at such short notice. How do we know that it's not a plot to lure you to Ireland? There are still a lot of Protestant extremists who are not too happy about the idea of an Irish pope."

"She was my only cousin, more like a sister, I have to go. Make sure that Alitalia has a plane ready to leave Rome first thing Friday morning and return later that day."

"Papa, at least give us twenty-four hours to verify that it is your cousin who died," the cardinal pleaded.

"Do it then. Twenty-four hours."

The cardinal went to see Bishop Keegan. "Find out who wrote the death certificate and tell them that you will need to travel to Cambridge immediately to identify the body on behalf of Ms. Murphy's cousin, the pope."

The Prefect of the Pontifical Household had met Kathleen on several occasions during her visits to the Vatican. He recognized the redheaded Irishwoman and nodded at Professor Simpson, "That's her." He bowed his head and prayed.

Simpson slowly pushed the morgue drawer closed.

"Oh, one other thing, we'll need a sample to do a DNA test, can't be too careful these days."

Simpson went over to a drawer and took out a pair of surgical scissors. "Be my guest, and while you do that I will go and get a plastic bag to put it in."

Simpson hurried to MacLeod's lab and took one of the plastic bags of Kathleen's hair out of the desk drawer and put in his pocket. He then took a spare bag from a cupboard.

The bishop pulled the morgue drawer open so that only the head and shoulders of the body were accessible. He snipped a lock of hair.

Simpson returned with the empty plastic bag. "Let me put that into this plastic bag and label it for you, bishop."

Bishop Keegan handed the hair to Simpson who went over to a bench. He pretended to write as he deftly took Kathleen's hair sample out of his pocket and switched it with the other.

At that moment, the bishop found himself saying, 'Chain of Custody.' He leaned over the body with his back facing Simpson, as if in prayer. He gently raised Kathleen's head, then quickly twisted the scissors into the back of the neck just above the hairline, pulled them out and carefully wiped the blood and tissue onto the center of his handkerchief. He folded it and slipped it into his pocket as Simpson was approaching him with the hair sample. He turned, smiled, handed the scissors back to Simpson and took the plastic bag.

"You have been most cooperative, professor."

"Not at all," Simpson responded as he led the bishop toward the door. The bishop noticed a box of latex gloves on a bench and as he passed by he grabbed a glove and stuffed it in his pocket.

Simpson was glad to see the back of the bishop, he could now relax. He had taken the two samples of Kathleen's hair for future reference, never thinking he would have to use one of them so soon. He went back to his office and flopped into his chair and thought, "Will I ever see Francis again? I am getting too old for this kind of thing, so late in my career. I don't know why I would risk my reputation this way, maybe it's time to retire. The medical profession is not what it used to be. Francis, on the other hand is worth an enormous amount of money, at least on paper, that's if the poor sod survives to enjoy it."

Once in his awaiting car, the bishop pushed the folded handkerchief into the latex glove. He knotted the glove and placed it in his briefcase along with the hair sample.

Back at the Vatican later that evening, he took the two samples to the PAS Laboratory and instructed the staff to have DNA results available first thing the next morning.

When he studied the report, Bishop Keegan called the Cardinal Secretary. "We have a problem and we need to talk to Papa as soon as possible."

On the way to the pontiff's office, the bishop showed the cardinal the results of the DNA testing.

"What does it mean?" The cardinal asked.

"You'll see. Papa understands these things."

John Paul III studied the DNA report with a perplexed expression on his face.

"You are sure about this?" he asked the bishop.

"I took the tissue sample myself," the bishop said.

"Can one of you explain to me, please?" the cardinal asked.

"According to the DNA tests, the hair sample and the tissue sample don't match, they are from two different people. The hair is a match with Kathleen's recorded profile but the tissue is definitely not a match; in other words. It's her hair – but it is not her body."

"How can that be?" the cardinal asked.

"That's what we need to find out. It raises the question, is Kathleen dead? Or is she still alive?" the pope said.

"If I may, Papa?"

"Go ahead, Bishop."

"It's possible that after I contacted Simpson and told him I needed to identify the body on your behalf he deliberately switched bodies at the morgue."

The pope raised his eyebrows. "Why would he do that?"

"To protect you and your family."

"From what? What are you getting at?"

"Well, according to Simpson, the cause of death was an accidental overdose of drugs and alcohol, but what if she had committed suicide?"

"Kathleen would never do that."

"Maybe not, but it wouldn't take much to start a rumor that she did, you know how the media and your detractors would feed about a scandal like that. Maybe Simpson thought you or her parents might request a post-mortem and he panicked and switched bodies just in case."

The pope nodded. "I suppose that is a possibility."

"Well, at least it solves one problem; you will not be going to a funeral." The cardinal sounded relieved.

"On the contrary, I most definitely will be. I must see for myself. Tell no one, not even Cardinal O'Leary, that I will be coming until you have made all of the arrangements."

"But, Papa, I beg you not to do this, it's far too risky, especially at such short notice. We could never deal with all of the security issues in three days, and especially without O'Leary's help. It goes against all protocol not to inform the cardinal," the Cardinal Secretary said.

John Paul III dismissed him. "Go. The sooner you start planning the better."

Bishop Keegan remained silent as the pope sat down at his desk and put the report in a drawer.

"I know you just got back from Cambridge last night but I want you to pack a bag for three to four days and go back there as soon as you can, there is something very wrong about this. I read in the Sunday paper that Sir Francis MacLeod passed away over the weekend and the police are treating his death as a homicide. You know Kathleen was engaged to him."

"Good heavens," the bishop said.

"Find out what you can, starting with Professor Simpson and the people closest to MacLeod and Kathleen. You can accompany the body to Dundalk on Thursday afternoon."

"I'll do my best, Papa."

Chapter 65

On Wednesday evening, Mrs. Murphy contacted Ian and asked him if he would be kind enough to represent Kathleen's colleagues and give one of the eulogies. Ian found himself hesitating but she was persistent and he gave in.

"If it is that important to you, Mrs. Murphy, and you want me to do it, I will gladly accept. Your daughter was a wonderful friend and colleague, so full of life."

Ian struggled all Thursday evening with what he was going to say. He sat in the back garden for hours thinking about it. At least a dozen crumpled-up notepad pages were strewn on the shaggy lawn beside him. He hadn't cut the grass this week, it would have to wait.

Ian's longtime girlfriend Angela yelled from the kitchen. "Would you like a cup of tea?"

"No, thanks. I need a beer." He went inside and grabbed a beer from the fridge.

"Making progress?" She asked.

"Not really. At least not yet."

As he sipped the beer, he looked up at the clouds and the bluish grey sky beyond. He could feel Kathleen's presence. Despite their constant hassling, they laughed a lot. They were a great team. The experiments proved that. Even though in the end she was right and he was wrong.

In a few short months, he had gone from an atheist to agnostic and then to a true believer.

The light experiment had started it all. There was no doubt that there was a high energy output at the time of death, at least in their experiments. And the speed was certainly faster than the speed of light. They proved that. Speed of Universal Light, Kathleen called it. He smiled at the acronym – SOUL.

Then the Western Blot experiments, they were fun. He had thought of that when he was at Alpha Genetics, but hadn't followed through. The Shroud of Turin was one of the most controversial artifacts in the world; not one of the famous scientists who had studied the Shroud before him had figured out its mysteries. Yet he had. It was gratifying to know his experiments had worked and then to be confirmed by seeing the original Shroud at the Vatican.

Testing blood samples from the Shroud, matching the old with the new and then the DNA sequence of the blood – the shivers he got when he looked at the symphony-like DNA pattern of the Shroud blood – what alignment of the stars brought it altogether? What were the chances of him working with Kathleen in the first place? Then Kathleen's cousin becoming the first Irish pope and his curiosity with science.

Because of Kathleen, he had got answers to some of life's most age-old questions - life after death, the mysteries of the Holy Shroud, divine DNA - the Holy Grail.

He finished off his beer and thought of the one mystery he had yet to solve; the purpose or meaning of life.

He went inside to ask Angela. "What is your view on the purpose of life?"

"Not again. I have told you many times before, I believe our purpose is two-fold; procreation and to be the best we can be. As the Bible says, we should love one another, help our neighbors, feed the poor and those less fortunate than ourselves."

Ian grabbed another cold beer from the fridge and walked back outside muttering to himself. "A typical touchy-feely

369

Venus-like response, that's not what I am looking for. I need facts, bloody real hard facts!"

"I take it that was not the answer you wanted?" she shouted from the kitchen window.

Ian launched his foot into the ever-growing mound of crumpled pages as if he were attempting to convert a try. He watched the papers scatter all over the lawn, sat down in his garden chair and took a large swig of beer.

What is it with women and feelings? Don't get into that. Concentrate. You're supposed to be writing a eulogy about Kathleen. Now, there was a man's-man kind of women, she had balls, that woman. A fiery temper, attractive with a great figure, and a brilliant scientist. What a mix.

He wished he had been there to see the pope's expression when Kathleen presented him with the sequence of the Shroud blood.

What was it she said when she came back from the Vatican? Something about the pope not being happy about the sequencing of the blood. What the hell was it? Oh, yes, she said for the first time in her life she had felt a little uneasy – or words to that effect – in the presence of her cousin. Why, he wondered? What had he said to her?

How did I respond at the time? I think I said, 'Oh, really'. Ugh, just like a Venetian. Ian shook his head and cringed. Why didn't I ask her what had made her feel uneasy or what the pope had said?

Why would Kathleen feel uncomfortable in front of her cousin, someone she adored and admired so much, and then tell me? If it were trivial she would not have said anything. The fact that she did must mean that it had a significant impact on her.

"Hey, Angela, could you bring me another beer? Thanks."

"Get it yourself, macho man from Mars."

"Women." He got up to go inside. She met him half-way with a cold one in her hand.

370

He kissed her. "Lot on my mind. Thanks."

He started at the beginning: the light experiments; scientifically sound. Yes, it happened. But spectral DNA? Come on, Kathleen, no proof – pure speculation. The Western Blot; it worked as he thought it would, but what did it prove? You can transfer proteins from one membrane to another through a liquid medium – proven science. Is that what really happened in the case of the Shroud? It's a possibility. He had to admit he got carried away by his need for it to be the answer. It did, after all, answer questions like the photographic negative and the right to left reversal of the image. No one else had figured that out in the past.

But what about the blood? Matching the old and the new blood as the same type. Pretty compelling. And the DNA sequence, God-like for sure, no doubt about that. Ian got up and strolled around the garden, reminding himself he needed to cut the lawn this weekend. He would do it on Sunday when he got back from Ireland.

Why am I having doubts? And now of all times, I have a speech to write about Kathleen. Is it the new pope? He *is* different from any image of a pope that he had in the past, but that's good isn't it? Kathleen, I miss you. He started to well up, then hurled his half-full beer at the fence.

What if this was a set-up? Not the light experiments or the Western Blot experiments but the Vatican connection? Did the pope use us for some greater purpose? Surely not, he and Kathleen were so close. She would never be underhanded, not even for God Himself. And the pope would never do that to her either.

He sat back down, took a fresh piece of paper and wrote 'The purpose of life' across the top. He jotted down his thoughts. Several pieces of paper later, he read the latest draft a couple times then crumpled it up into a ball and tossed it across the lawn. Who was he trying to fool? Explain the meaning of life. Like all the others, before him he had no bloody idea. He took another piece of paper and wrote, 'Kathleen was my friend and colleague for over twelve years'. He crumpled that up too, threw it in the air and headed it across the lawn. He leaned back and stared into space. Clarity slowly but consciously began to emerge.

Kathleen came out of the house and walked toward him with something in her hand.

Ian smiled at her. "Hi, this *is* a pleasant surprise I was just reminiscing about all of the scientific experiments we did together and in particular the ones involving the pope."

"Well, remember I told you that JP was a member of the PAS for several years before he became pope? He had access to the greatest scientific minds on the planet. But he chose us to analyze the blood on the Shroud? It was a great honor."

"Yes, it was an incredible experience. It seems like yesterday when we visited the Vatican together and on that Sunday morning we took blood samples from the Shroud. Afterward, the pope showed us the Shroud parchment handed down from Pope Clement VI and the letter from Pope John Paul II. I remember struggling with my Latin because it was so rusty but there was no question about it, we saw the signatures of Pope Clement VI, Paulo Aquinas and Geoffrey de Charny. And the letter left by Pope John Paul II about the visitation of Christ. That letter was also in Latin, wasn't it?"

"Ian, we never saw the actual letter. JP told us about it and showed it to us, but he didn't give it to us to read."

"That's right. We took his word, and why wouldn't we? We were in such holy surroundings."

"You know, I never thanked you properly for all the wonderful testing you did, especially on the Shroud blood, and what an incredible revelation that there were three Y chromosomes, and then to sequence the blood. You never did

372

show me the results, but I remember you describing it like some classical symphony – clearly Divine DNA."

"Yes, its unique and I doubt even these days you could create something as elegant as that. It certainly would take greater scientific minds than ours, like those at the PAS for example. Wait a minute; no, it wouldn't. Cloning. DNA replication. Genetic replacement. Start with a Y chromosome, clone it into three, substitute into a poly X or poly Y chromosome, replicate it about fifty times or so, then insert it into empty cells. Perform DNA sequencing and what will you get? Perfect symmetry. Do you think the pope could have done it? And why? Kathleen, do you follow me? Are you even listening? Kathleen, where are you? Kathleen? Kathleen?"

"Ian, are you okay?" Angela asked. "I think you were having a bad dream."

"Sorry, more like a bloody nightmare. Shit! I hope it was just a bad dream."

"Here, I saw you spill the last one." She handed him a fresh beer.

"Thanks."

Tomorrow he had to say farewell to Kathleen and do her proud. Why not just go with the flow and give her a nice thoughtful send-off? Is that what Kathleen would do if things were reversed? Hell, no, she would tell it the way it was and expect everyone else to do the same.

Ian stood, put the beer down on the table, and went into his study. He began typing. After an hour, he leaned back in the chair for the umpteenth time and read his final draft. He was satisfied.

"It's the best lecture I have ever written," he said aloud.

"You're not giving a lecture. It's a eulogy, for heaven's sake," Angela shouted back from the living room.

"Okay, so I'll make it more touchy-feely in the morning."

Satisfied, he switched off the computer and went to bed. The purpose of life that had eluded him and so many others before him was finally solved. He fell asleep within minutes. He was at peace with himself once more.

The next morning, he got up early and caught the first flight to Dublin.

Chapter 66

It was one of the best kept secrets of modern times. Neither Ian, Kathleen's family nor the Irish clergy were aware of the pope's intentions to attend his cousin's funeral.

When observers in the airport lounges at Dublin airport saw the extra security detail march across the tarmac, they assumed it must be a terror alert, or maybe an incoming plane was about to make an emergency landing.

As the Alitalia flight touched down and taxied from the runway several plane spotters noticed the Papal Coat of Arms decal on the L1 door, and all pandemonium let loose. Word spread as fast as a tsunami as social media took to the airwaves and local TV and radio interrupted their broadcasts to announce this breaking news of the pope arriving on Irish soil. The catholic clergy were in a panic mode.

Ian had landed earlier and picked up his rental car, which was just as well, as most of the roads exiting Dublin airport were cordoned off and there were detours everywhere. He got on the road to Dundalk in the nick of time. On the drive to Kathleen's funeral service he rehearsed his eulogy over and over again. The local radio he was tuned in to was interrupted by breaking news that 'in the last hour the pope had arrived at Dublin airport'. No wonder there was such tight security there. That changes everything. He wondered whether he should change his eulogy now that the pope was going to be attending. What would Kathleen say about that? He decided she would

375

agree with him to tell it how it is; from his heart. As Ian entered Dundalk, thousands of people were starting to line the streets on the way to the church. He drove around the church looking for a nearby parking spot but after the third time around gave up; it was useless, given the crowds already there. He drove a few streets further away and saw a van pulling out of a spot and lined up to take its place, horns honked, but he ignored them and slowly parked into the vacant spot. He unhooked his black jacket and put it on, it was a tight fit. He had packed on a few pounds since the last time he had worn it for an uncle's funeral. He removed his wallet and took the €350 he had left-over from his last vacation in Spain and put it in his back pocket. He put the eulogy in his inside jacket pocket. He stuffed his wallet, cell phone, pen and notepad into the small backpack that he had brought with him from England and put it on the floor behind the driver's seat.

Kathleen's funeral at St. Patrick's Catholic Church was an extraordinary event, the most attended service that any of the older members of the congregation could recall. In recent years, attendance at the church had dwindled, leaving it usually only half-full.

Modeled on King's College Chapel in Cambridge and Bath Abbey in Somerset, St. Patrick's Roman Catholic Church is known by locals simply as 'the cathedral'. It opened for worship in 1842, built under the supervision of Dundalk's leading merchants and traders who decided that a majestic, Gothic Perpendicular style church that could hold up to fifteen hundred people would be a fitting expression of their faith. Despite the building's size, the church did not feel austere or cold.

Simply but elegantly designed, it had been one of Kathleen's favorite buildings in her home town. She had long admired the clock tower that had been erected in 1903 in the same style and had, as a child, lit many candles to the Virgin Mary in the side chapels.

Pope John Paul III had ignored his advisors' advice that it would be both risky and inappropriate for him to attend his cousin's funeral. For his first visit to Ireland as pope – and the first Irish one at that – the hurriedly planned and unofficial visit did not sit well with the Irish hierarchy.

That was the last consideration on the new pope's mind. His private staff and Vatican security operations were not accustomed to such forceful orders coming straight from the pontiff himself. The Archbishop of Dublin, Cardinal O'Leary, only given twenty-four hours' notice, was beside himself. Despite the wall of silence, a few hours before the service the media had broken the news out about the pope's visit and the church was at full capacity. The congregants, particularly the older ones, believed that there were extra blessings to be granted in such circumstances.

Thousands of people lined the streets to get a glimpse of the first Irish pope.

Cardinal O'Leary said Mass. Pope John Paul III gave the first of two eulogies.

Much to the surprise of the congregation, the pope gave only a short but elegant tribute to Kathleen. He had been very fond of her and they had shared a common interest in science. But it was clear that he was holding back something. He had something on his mind. The congregation interpreted it as grief.

When the pope was finished, he stepped down from the pulpit and made his way to the coffin. With his back to the parishioners, he blessed the coffin and then bent forward over the body in prayer. He raised Kathleen's left hand and looked at the index finger. *There was no scar*. When Kathleen was five-years old and he was fifteen, he taught her how to ride her first bicycle. She had a nasty accident. He had pushed her down the street and as she set off she turned around to wave at him and the front wheel hit the curb. She fell and grabbed the wheel, the spinning spokes almost severing her finger. The surgery had saved her finger but left a permanent scar that looked similar to a red ring mark. *This is not Kathleen.*

The pope returned to his seat deep in thought as the choir blasted out *Danny Boy*, - Kathleen's father's favorite song.

Ian got up from his second-row seat, walked across to the altar and knelt in front of the pope, who put his hands on Ian's head and blessed him. The pope whispered in Ian's ear and thanked him for the book.

Ian climbed the steps of the pulpit, ready to honor the life and death of his friend. On the flight over from Stansted to Dublin, he had written and re-written his tribute to her. Kathleen was unquestionably a very talented scientist and they had become a lot closer since working on the congruence of science and religion. Would she be pleased with what I am about to say? Damn right! She would revel in it. 'This is for you, you fiery-tempered redhead.'

"Kathleen was a very close friend and colleague of mine for over twelve years and there is no doubt she deserves a lot of credit for the success of Sir Francis MacLeod's genon research and the company he founded. Sadly, Sir Francis is no longer with us and most of you will not know this, but Sir Francis and Kathleen had planned to get married."

Ian nodded to Kathleen's mother and father, who were sitting in the front row with other close family members.

"I am sure most of you felt the same as me when you heard the choir give such a beautiful rendition of *Danny Boy*. It gave me goose bumps. I could not help but think that Kathleen, lying there, had the same experience, especially echoing the last line,

. . . *I'll simply sleep in peace until you come to me.*"

There was hardly a dry eye in the church.

Ian continued. "As you know, Kathleen was a scientist, a geneticist to be exact, and a good one, I may add. We scientists have to find facts to support our opinions. We like to prove things. In the past year, Kathleen and I did a number of experiments to prove the connection between science and God. We did tests to prove that there *is* life after death and that Jesus Christ came from God. And we solved the mysteries of the Shroud of Turin and concluded that God exists, just like you and I exist. And just like Kathleen existed and still exists now. In fact there is no such thing as death, only transformation or change. Yes, the human form dies, but its energy and DNA live on. If it had not been for Kathleen's scientific and religious curiosity none of these scientific experiments would have taken place. But now, thanks to her, we have the answers to questions that have frustrated scientific minds for thousands of years. As her legacy, I want to share with you what I believe is the true purpose of life. But before I do that, I need to give you a little background."

He went on to tell the congregation that it was a well-established scientific fact that the universe started from a huge explosion of a tiny mass of highly dense energy some fourteen billion years ago and the Earth formed just over four billion years ago. Everything on Earth and in the universe comes from the same source, whether it is rocks, soil, trees, water, animals or man. They are all connected in that they are made up of the same chemical elements, even though they are configured in different ways. An orchid, for example, cannot be compared to man but it has fifty times more DNA than the human genome. Many refer to it as the perfect flower. And what determines the specific configuration of every living species? Its genome or DNA recipe.

"We are related to every living creature on this Earth and every living creature is a sub-set of God," Ian said. "If we hold this common belief, then we must accept that we are all equal members of the House of God and there is no one true religion. It is arrogant for any religion, whether it is the Catholic Church

379

or the Jews or Muslims to claim that they are the one true faith. It is time for all religions to unite in a universal belief in God, and I challenge the Catholic Church to take the lead."

Ian noticed some members of the congregation were shuffling uncomfortably in their pews, some even whispering to each other.

He ignored them. "You have all heard the old saying, that you 'cannot get blood out of a stone'. Well that is not necessarily true. There are rocks and stones that contain DNA, proving what was once flesh and blood had turned into stone. So what about the purpose of life? Why are we here? Well, our human form is all part of the great scheme of perpetuation or eternity. You see, every living thing and every piece of matter is part of God and when our human body dies our existing energy turns into a new form of energy. Infinity exists because of the law of conservation of energy and as a result the universe is in an eternal state of expansion and contraction from one big bang to the next one."

He paused for a moment. "Let me put this into layman's terms. *God made us in His own Image and Likeness,* which means we are all a sub-set of God. *We are all in fact god,* with a small 'g'."

The whispers grew louder. Two elderly ladies sitting a few rows from the front got up from their seats and started walking out of the church. As they did so, they stopped at several other pews and whispered to other older members of the congregation, many of whom joined them. Ian watched patiently as the movement grew to about twenty, then he heard one old lady, who was obviously deaf, whisper rather loudly, "This is heresy. He's a heretic, an' in the presence of the pope, an' all."

Once the old ladies had left the church, the rest of the congregation sat patiently waiting to hear what else Ian would

380

say. Most kept glancing toward the pope wondering what he must be thinking.

Ian paused and looked at the pope, who appeared deep in thought, staring into space.

"Jesus Christ did not preach Christianity – that was His followers. No, he preached divine revelation, an awareness of God through parables."

Cardinal O'Leary sat with a grim expression on his face. He dared not look toward the pope. The Catholic Church had enough controversy to deal with in recent years, it certainly didn't need a new movement to rise up and challenge its two thousand-year history.

Ian continued. "As a sub-set of God we are all going to be around for eternity, maybe in a different form and quite possibly in many different forms – after all, eternity is forever. The bad news or sad news, depending on your perspective, is that your physical form no longer exists. But the good news is that your 'inner being' or 'spirit' or 'soul' or whatever you wish to call it moves to another dimension, to a place of enlightenment. Kathleen's experiments proved that."

Ian nodded again toward Kathleen's parents.

"Kathleen's insight into the connection between science and religion led me to a hypothesis on the subject. It is now my belief that our purpose on this earth is to acquire *wisdom* and in time the *collective wisdom* of mankind will elevate man's consciousness and understanding to a level of enlightenment equal to that of the afterlife."

Ian looked toward the coffin.

"Kathleen, on behalf of your colleagues, I want to thank you for the great scientific contribution you made at Genon and on behalf of believers everywhere, I thank you for giving us all a better understanding of science and religion. It was an honor to know you in this life and as Vera Lynne once sang,

We'll meet again, don't know where, don't know when . . .

381

". . . but I know we'll meet again some sunny day."

Ian went back to his seat without looking at the pope or Cardinal O'Leary, who returned to the altar and continued with the Mass. After the final blessing, the cardinal nodded to the pope who led the procession toward the back of the church. John Paul III lingered in the vestibule, while family members and friends surrounded him to say their goodbyes and wave him off when his motorcade sped away. The pope had to return to Rome immediately, so he designated Bishop Keegan and two aides to attend the reception at the Murphy's home on his behalf, and asked Cardinal O'Leary to join him in his limousine on the way to the airport. They discussed Ian's eulogy. The pope told O'Leary that he agreed with some of Ian's remarks and it was time for the Church to be part of the twenty-first century and accept modern attitudes toward religion and embrace mankind as a whole. It was his intention to modernize the Church in the next few years and take it in that direction. However, it was important for the Church to take the lead and not let the tail wag the dog.

Cardinal O'Leary said, "I agree."

After the pope had left, Ian stood outside of the church with Kathleen's parents. Many of the parishioners who stopped to pay their respects to Mr. and Mrs. Murphy shook his hand and said, "Fascinating eulogy." Others ignored him.

Ian joined the back of the procession to the cemetery in his rental car and then went with the family members and friends back to the Murphy's house, where he had his first real experience of an Irish wake. He drank too much. As the afternoon progressed he couldn't help but notice that his movements were being closely watched. He slipped out of the Murphy's home to get his cell phone from the car to call Angela.

On the Sunday following Kathleen's funeral, the pope ate lunch alone in his private quarters. The server cleared the dishes

382

away and left him with coffee and dessert. John Paul III reached across the table and pulled the *Irish Times* from the stack of newspapers. He thumbed toward the back and opened it at the obituary page. He saw Kathleen's picture and a half-page obituary. He read it slowly. About one-third of the way down, he shook his head and muttered to himself. "How inappropriate". The latter two-thirds of Kathleen's obituary was about him, the writer over-emphasizing the fact that Kathleen was cousin to the pope. The commentary made the point that, as tragic as Dr Murphy's death was, it had brought other blessings to the community in that the first Irish pope in history had made his inaugural visit to Ireland. The country, abuzz with what the pope had accomplished since taking office, was excited about what he would do in the future. 'If only they knew,' he thought. He was about to close the paper when he noticed another obituary at the bottom of the page. It simply stated that Dr Ian Walton, a close colleague of Dr Murphy's, who gave a controversial eulogy at her funeral, was critically injured in a head-on collision on the way to Dublin Airport, and later died in hospital.

John Paul III put down the newspaper and quietly recited the *Requiem Aeternam*.

"Eternal rest grant unto them, O Lord: and let perpetual light shine upon them. May their souls and all the souls of the faithful departed, through the mercy of God, rest in peace. Amen."

The seven hundred-year-old secret of the Shroud was once again known to only one living person.

Chapter 67

Monday, April 15, 2030

Rob was in Basel for his annual review with Meier.

Several weeks after MacLeod's death, Stephen Hatton had studied his client's will. He had faced a real dilemma. Was MacLeod dead or alive? If he was dead, then he could carry out his wishes. The fact that he was missing and there was no body for the police to examine meant that, according to the law, he would have to wait five years until he could be declared 'missing – presumed dead'. Unless there was proof positive that he was dead, his assets would be frozen.

All Hatton could do at the time was to ensure that the shares were in the hands of the right people. Kathleen's parents and Ian's girlfriend Angela received their shares. Since VJ had disappeared and Darren was remanded in custody, their shares were held in trust. Cambridge University and the five pharmaceutical companies retained their shares. MacLeod's fifty-five percent was frozen with his other assets. Hatton had contacted everyone and informed them of the new share distribution.

A week later, Hatton was contacted by university officials who wanted to know when they would receive the additional twenty percent of shares left in MacLeod's will and what their holding was worth. He agreed to get back to them. Hatton, who was not particularly knowledgeable in the area of high finance, contacted KPMG. Ten days later, he received their preliminary valuation. Without MacLeod and his key staff members, the company was worth no more than twenty pence on the pound from the original IPO valuation and the value would continue to drop the longer the company was in limbo. They estimated that the current valuation was somewhere between one and one point one billion pounds based on its current and future income from royalties.

Hatton called the chairman of the trustees.

"I am afraid you are going to have to wait five years because MacLeod's assets are frozen. As far as your current holding is concerned, it is valued between a hundred and a hundred and ten million. I will mail you KPMG's report."

The trustees decided to act before it was too late. They instructed Hatton to contact the other shareholders and suggest that they sell off their shares. All were in agreement.

The pharmaceutical companies said they would only accept an offer that gave them at least a thirty-two percent return on their eight-year forty-million-pound investment; meager by any investment standard.

Meanwhile, the Tronavis attorneys contacted Jürgen Roeck's attorney and told him they were withdrawing their previous offer because Genon was on the verge of collapse.

The blind man's attorney panicked and countered that he would accept the last offer. Meier told his attorneys to stand firm. They settled on one third.

The following week, the shareholders voted to accept an offer of one point one billion pounds from an overseas investment bank acting on behalf of an unknown client. This was the high end of the latest KPMG valuation. The transaction was completed in less than nine weeks. Tronavis acquired the thirty-six percent of the available shares. With their existing five percent ownership, it gave them forty-one percent of the company's total equity.

The other fifty-nine percent of the shares were held in trust in the names of MacLeod, Gupta and Richards.

Meier had the voting rights locked up. For most, it would have been a huge gamble. Not for Meier. He had always been a risk-taker, but in this case he had insurance to back his decision. He was the only one who had the access code to the cryogenic chambers and the lockets containing perfect DNA.

Meier had appointed Rob to the position of managing director of Genon and had given him a package that included Tronavis restricted stock. This together with the money that he had received from the sale of his Genon shares made him a rich man. Not the hundred million he once thought, but plenty.

"Have a seat, Rob. I am pleased with what you have accomplished in the past two years and I think you are ready to take on more responsibility. I have recommended to my board of directors that you are the best candidate to succeed me when I retire in the next two to three years."

"Well, thanks, Hans. I appreciate your confidence in me."

"You deserve it. Besides, if you hadn't stepped in and filled MacLeod's shoes, we would not be enjoying the success we have today. Of course, we'll make sure we broaden your experience so you are ready when the time comes."

"Sure, and I will need to groom a successor at Genon."

"Exactly. Now, we need to talk about where we go from here. We are close to implementing all of the therapies that we have put into clinical trials in the past couple of years, but after that, we have nothing new. If all of the other genons were available to us, in three to five years we could be the world's largest healthcare company by a factor of two."

"I agree, and I still haven't figured out why MacLeod took all that information to the grave with him."

"Actually, he didn't take it to the grave."

"You mean you have it?"

"Sort of. I couldn't tell you this before, but now that you're officially my successor, I can tell you." Meier took a deep breath. "Francis, Kathleen and VJ are not dead."

Rob turned white. "What?"

"They are in the clinic."

Rob stood up and leaned across Meier's desk. "You're bullshitting me. All three are alive?"

"Well, frozen alive."

"Hans, enough of the surprises. What the hell are you talking about?"

"VJ was our first cryogenic human guinea pig, then Francis and Kathleen."

"Okay, start at the beginning."

Meier explained what had happened.

"Why would VJ volunteer to be a guinea pig? For bollock's sake, he's married with two kids."

"He said he had Parkinson's and wanted to wait for the therapy to be developed."

"And Francis and Kathleen?"

"Francis had Parkinson's." Meier said.

"They both had Parkinson's – there's no bloody way – what are the odds of that?"

"It's true, we tested Francis here. In fact, he came here every two weeks for conventional therapy to slow down the progression while we developed the genon therapy."

"Bloody hell! And none of us had a clue about that. That's unbelievable. Though, when I think back, I had noticed at several meetings before the lecture that his hands were shaking, I put it down to nerves and exhaustion. And Kathleen?"

"Francis made provisions for her too, just in case. And when she tried to end it, Dr Simpson acted on Francis' wishes to preserve her until he comes back."

"This is incredible, and when will that be?"

"Well, we're in phase III clinical trials for Parkinson's now, maybe a year or so."

"This changes everything. They were my colleagues for eight years, like family to me. I cannot possibly think about the other stuff we talked about now. We need to take care of them first."

"Fair enough, but getting back to the original discussion about growing the business, there is a way."

"And what's that?"

"Francis and VJ have the only two copies of perfect DNA in lockets hanging around their neck. If we de-freeze them we could have all the data we need."

"Without a therapy for Parkinson's, I don't think so. And besides, what is your chimpanzee re-animation success rate so far?"

"It's two out of three, which is great progress and we've learned a lot in the process."

Rob was uneasy at the thought of having to make a decision on the life or death of his colleagues, he had made such decisions many times in the past, but there was a big difference, because in every case they had been lab animals.

"Hans, this is a huge responsibility, I would never be able to forgive myself if I made a mistake and one or all of them end up DOA."

"I understand Rob, but don't you think Francis would want his work to progress regardless of the outcome to him personally?"

"Maybe, but unfortunately we cannot ask him. Anyway, before I make a decision I would like to see all of your records on your animal cryogenic program."

"Okay, I'll have Peter bring them to the conference room while we get a cup of coffee."

When Rob and Meier arrived at the conference room Peter had three sets of spreadsheets covering the whole conference table, he pointed to each of them, "The sheets on the left are nine years of data from the mice trials, in the middle seven years of data from the small dog trials and on the right five years of data from the chimpanzee trial."

Rob studied the data from left to right. "The mouse survival rate is phenomenal, you only lost one mouse in the first year and everyone since has been revived?"

"Yes, it is a great success and we will be reviving the last ten mice this summer and if it all goes to plan as we expect, then the success rate of the program will be ninety-nine percent." Peter said confidently.

Rob moved over to the middle spreadsheets and studied them, recalling that two dogs had died in the first year. However, each year after that all four dogs had survived until he got to the previous year when one dog out of the four had died. "So, what happened here?"

"We are not absolutely sure but we think the dog may have died from hypothermia, at least according to the autopsy report and as for an explanation we believe the dog may have received a lower dose of cryoprotectant cocktail."

"How could that happen with all of the stringent controls you have in place?" Rob asked.

Peter's look of confidence slowly dissipated. "Well, remember there were forty dogs in the program all cryogenically frozen at the same time eight years ago and we think that maybe this was the last dog in line to receive the cocktail. But on the positive side we have only lost three dogs out of twenty-eight to be revived so far, that is a success rate of eighty-nine percent, good by any standards."

Rob moved over to the spreadsheets on the right, he looked at the 'survived' and 'died' columns, it read ten and five. "Five chimps have died so far?"

Peter responded. "Yes, for the first two years all three chimps survived, then in the third year we lost all three, then we

389

have lost one out of three in the last two years, we think because the technicians tried to speed up the revival process."

Rob was clearly struggling. "It seems the bigger the animal the worse the odds are for survival, which does not bode well for humans."

Meier interjected. "Rob, I perfectly understand your dilemma but if you look at it this way, we have learned from our mistakes and we are improving our process constantly, so we minimize the risks."

"What is the schedule for reviving the next batch of animals?"

"May, June and July." Peter answered.

"Before we do anything I want you to revive a batch of each set of animals as soon as possible, how long will it take?"

Meier seemed a little annoyed. "That will take several weeks and be premature."

Rob became angry as he addressed Meier. "Listen Hans, if it was you in there or a member of your family wouldn't you want those in charge to take every precaution?"

"Peter do what Rob says and start the revival process on this year's batch of animals."

"Okay, I am going back to the UK so call me when you have the results and we will discuss what and if we do anything."

Chapter 68

"Bloody typical English weather, peeing all over you when you least expect it," Rob thought as he left the airport building. The sun had been shining earlier in the day and the forecast hadn't mentioned rain, let alone a full-blown thunderstorm. Lightning darted in huge bolts across the night sky. Rob hurried to the short-term parking lot, striding over puddles with his briefcase over his head to shield him from the pounding rain. He was like a drowning sewer rat by the time he got in the car and turned the ignition key. He wanted to go straight home but he knew he couldn't. There was something bothering him and he had to go to the lab.

Rob took the stored test tubes of blood out of the freezer and lined them up on the bench. He studied each number on the labels - AB 111, CD 222, EF 333, GH 444, IJ 555 and KL 666. He had no idea which samples came from which scientist, not even his own, although he could easily find out by calling the blood service company and giving them his original appointment time. He continued to study the tubes as he tried to figure out how to match them to himself and his colleagues. He smiled. He could sequence chromosomes 4 and 13 on all blood samples.

The following morning, Rob stared at the results of his overnight sequencing efforts, there was only one blood sample that had two mutated copies of the Parkinson's gene, KL 666. Just as he had expected, the odds of two people in the blood pool having Parkinson's was one in fifty thousand. 'So who is KL 666?' He arranged for a local blood typing company to test each sample.

Twenty-four hours later, he had the results, AB 111 - 0^+. CD 222 - AB. EF 333 - B^+. GH 444 - A^+. IJ 555 - 0^+. KL 666 - AB.

The one B^+ was his. His sample was EF 333.

Rob suddenly remembered overhearing a conversation between Kathleen and Ian, when she said, "Oh, you are blood type 0 too! We're just a couple of commoners."

That meant that KL 666 belonged to Francis, Darren or VJ.

Rob shook his head when he realized that Meier had already given him the answer when he told him that Francis had tested positive for Parkinson's at the clinic.

He called Meier. "Hans, when you took blood from Francis to test for Parkinson's did you check his blood type?"

"I believe so, why?"

"What is it?"

"Hang on a minute," Meier took a file from his desk drawer and thumbed through it, "Ah, here it is, type AB, why?"

"There is only one person who has Parkinson's and that's Francis."

* * * * *

A month later Rob received a call from Peter who had the results of the trials. "All ten mice have survived, all four dogs have survived, but one of the three chimps didn't make it."

"Okay, thanks Peter, could you transfer me to Meier?"

"Hans, one of the chimps died, which means one out of three do not make it."

"Yes, but two out of three do."

"It's risky, Hans. I need time to think about this."

"Okay, take a couple of days and we'll talk again."

Two days later Rob called Meier. "Hans, I am on the verge of a decision."

"So what are you thinking?"

"It depends on how long it will take you to prepare?"

"A few days."

"In that case, I will come over to the clinic on Friday lunchtime."

It was a very bumpy descent into Basel airport as the seasonal thunderstorms boomed through the ominous dark clouds. Rob was glad to get off the plane.

Meier was waiting in his office with Peter Fischer, who explained to Rob what had become normal procedure for re-animating chimpanzees from their cryogenic resting place.

"We are pretty confident from our recent successes that everything will be okay."

Meier looked straight at Rob. "Have you made a decision?"

"Yes. Here is my thinking, if we choose one of the three there is a two-to-one chance of success, however, if the first one survives the odds are going to be fifty-fifty that only one of the other two will survive. If the first one doesn't survive then the odds are that the other two will. So under the circumstances I think it is worth the risk," Rob answered.

Meier stood up. "Very well, then, let's go."

Peter opened the interlocking entry doors leading into the marble vault on the ground floor of the clinic and led Rob and Meier into Room One. The door had a plaque on it that simply stated, MacLeod Suite.

"Geez, it's bloody cold in here," Rob stammered, as he looked at the names on the chambers. 1- V. Gupta 16/4/28. 2 - F. MacLeod 23/4/28. 3 - K. Murphy 24/4/28. 4 - G. Palmer 17/5/28. The other two had no nameplates.

"So they're in there," Rob shook his head. "It's surreal. Who is G Palmer?"

"Sir Charles Palmer's wife, she has Alzheimer's," Meier replied.

"Oh, of course, Gillian. By the way I couldn't help noticing the plaque on the door, why is it called the MacLeod Suite?"

"Because Francis requested that we keep this room reserved for Genon staff, you included."

"Thanks, but no thanks," Rob replied as he stood in front of his choice. "What now?"

Peter noted the time – 3.10pm, then began turning off the liquid nitrogen supply.

"It will take thirty-six hours for the chamber's temperature to slowly rise to the vault temperature of -10°C. After that the chamber will be transferred to the revival room where the temperature will rise to 0°C. That will take five hours. At that point we have to monitor things very closely because it is the most critical time."

"So, approximately what time will that be?" Rob asked.

Peter did a quick calculation. "The body temperature should pass through freezing point around eight on Sunday morning."

"And until then?" Rob asked Meier.

"Nothing, it's now a waiting game, but if you want to be here, arrive before eight."

Rob walked into the revival room at seven thirty. Peter, Meier, two technicians and several nurses were already there watching as the chamber temperature climbed toward zero.

"Shouldn't be long now," Peter said, as Rob sat in a chair at the bottom of the bed.

A small temperature monitor indicated the body temperature was passing through freezing point. Like the crowd at a tennis match, pairs of eyes were darting back and forth from the temperature monitor to the heart monitor. Rob sat perfectly still, spellbound by it all.

As the temperature reached 15°C, the heart monitor started to beep, slowly at first, but gradually getting faster as the temperature rose. When it hit sixty-five beats per minute VJ's eyes blinked, then opened and closed a few times. Suddenly, there was a choking sound. His heart rate rapidly dropped toward zero. Peter calmly grabbed the defibrillator pads off the wall and placed them onto VJ's chest and side, then he activated the machine.

VJ's body convulsed forward, spewing out watery vomit onto his chest. The heart monitor sprang into life again.

"Quickly, increase the blanket temperature to 40°C, prop him up and put a tube in his throat," Peter shouted to the technicians.

"What's happening?" Rob asked nervously.

"It's not unusual," Peter responded, keeping a constant eye on the heart monitor. "Sometimes little frozen blood clots block the arteries and cause the heart to fail."

VJ coughed and spluttered and opened his eyes. "Where am I? What day is it?"

Rob leaned closer and whispered in his ear. "Back in the land of the living, mate. It's Easter Sunday 2030."

Tears formed in the corners of VJ's eyes as he slowly moved his right hand across his chest and out of the blanket. He put a tight grip on the gold locket and whispered weakly into Rob's ear.

Rob turned to Meier. "I think he said that he is very thirsty and could do with a large glass of water, followed by a nice cup of tea."

Meier nodded to Fischer, who quickly disappeared and returned about ten minutes later with a large tray, with a teapot, four cups and saucers and a bottle of mountain spring water. Rob grabbed the water, unscrewed the cap and handed the bottle to VJ, who gulped too fast and spluttered a mouthful of water all over Rob.

"Steady on, mate, your body needs to get used to ingestion again."

395

"What's happening, Rob?"

"Listen, mate, you need to take it easy for a while. You have done something that no other human being has done. You were dead for the last three years and you came back to life. You are going to be a hero, maybe even a saint in some countries."

Epilogue

Easter Sunday, April 17, 2033, Rome

A few minutes before midnight on Easter Saturday, John Paul III and his five regional popes sequestered themselves in the pope's private chapel to prepare for a twenty-four-hour vigil. Earlier in the evening, the pope had officiated at the Easter Vigil Mass in case he was not available to perform the traditional Easter Sunday Mass.

Two years earlier, John Paul III had shared the secret with his popes that Jesus Christ had visited John Paul II on Easter Sunday in 1983 and told him that he would return in fifty years. John Paul III and the popes had many long discussions about whether they should publicize the second coming of Christ and prepare the flock. After several meetings, they took a vote. The five popes were split three to two in favor of keeping the secret to themselves. They were more skeptical than John Paul III that the visitation had actually taken place. He accepted their decision; after all, he had not shared with them that the blood drops had been analyzed and that he was now in possession of the DNA sequence of Christ's blood.

As midnight approached, the pope took out the casket and carefully laid the Shroud on the altar. The pope kissed the cloth and made the sign of the cross just as the clock struck midnight. He kneeled in his usual spot with the five popes kneeling behind him and led them in prayer. As the hours ticked by, they took turns kneeling and praying before the Shroud.

At midnight, after an uneventful twenty-four hours, the pope said a final prayer. They all went to bed consumed by feelings of disappointment and emptiness.

As the popes prepared for sleep, they were unaware that a much happier scene had played out two thousand miles away in a remote tribal village in Tanzania, Africa. The twenty-seven residents of Betharam, just south of Lake Victoria, were celebrating their best harvest in more than twenty years. While the male elders sat around the fire happily smoking their pipes, the women were busily putting the finishing touches to their yearly community feast. The men were discussing the success of the past twelve months. It had been a wonderful harvest, hard work but rewarding. There had been no deaths, one marriage and two births, although they were concerned that none of the women had become pregnant in the past year.

The women and children laid out the food in a wide circle and signaled to the men that the feast was ready. The senior elder of the tribe rose and headed to the storage barn. It was a clear and starry night and as he entered the barn, the light from the moon and stars shone through the open window directly on his face. He grabbed four bottles of Betharam berry wine.

As he turned around to leave, he was stopped in his tracks. He dropped two of the bottles.

There, in the corner of the barn, highlighted by the night stars and nestled in the straw on the floor, was a newborn baby wrapped in swaddling clothes.